MERLIN'S ADVENTURE UPON THE LAKE.—P. 26.

LIFE AND EXPLOITS

OF

KINGARTHUR,

AND HIS

KNIGHTS OF THE ROUND TABLE.

A LEGENDARY ROMANCE.

LONDON:

MILNER AND COMPANY,

PATERNOSTER ROW.

LIFE AND EXPLOITS OF KING ARTHUR, &c.

INTRODUCTORY CHAPTER.

THE wonderful achievements attributed to this prince are supposed by many to be the offspring of the fertile imaginations of the ancient romance writers. Be that as it may, the history of the exploits of King Arthur and his Knights of the Round Table has in all ages been a favourite one.

Caxton (1485) took it as one of his first printed books. Again, in A.D. 1553, the history appeared to be in great request, for Roger Ascham, the tutor of the amiable Lady Jane Grey, says— "I know the time when God's Bible was banished the Court, and *Morte d'Arthur* received into the prince's chamber." Since this period various have been the versions afloat of the life and heroic deeds of King Arthur and his companions and several individuals, including the famous Jack the Giant Killer, have been set down as the veritable King Arthur.

For some time the "Romance of the Round Table" had been laid on the shelf by the poets and romancers; but Lord Lytton revived its theme, and later still, the Poet Laureate, Tennyson, enchanted his admirers by his exquisite "Idyls of the King."

To the school-boy the tale is one of infinite delight and wonder, and to those of mature age the exploits of Arthur have something akin to the interest created by the inimitable " Punch" among the modern exhibitions.

Amongst other instances, we find one which appears to be an authentic account of the descent of the warlike prince, which is as follows :—At the time of the departure of the Romans from Britain, Edric became King of Glamorgan and Gwent (Monmouth.) He was succeeded by Meyrick, Urban, Kynaw, and Theodrick, or Fewdrick. The latter flourished towards the end of the fifth century. He defeated a party of Saxon invaders at Pontsaison, near Tintern, and was buried at Matherne, near Chepstow. He was succeeded by his son Meyrick, whose son was Athewys, supposed to be King Arthur of Cambrian romance. The court of this King Arthur, or Arthrwys, was held at Caer Leon, but after his death the Saxons made such frequent incursions into the district that his son Morgan, the twenty-third king of Gwent, removed his court further westward, and resided sometimes at Cardiff and sometimes at Margam, Glamorganshire, which gave rise to the name of the county to which he removed, and it was called after him " Gwlad Morganwg," or the " Land of Morgan;" whilst Monmouthshire, the land he quitted, retained the name of Gwent. One of the legends, however, traces the descent of Arthur from Uther Pendragon, King of Britain, and brought up by a knight named Sir Ector as his son until after the death of his father, when he was produced by the prophet Merlin, who had a hand in his removal when an infant, and through whose agency he was in a romantic manner proved as the rightful successor to Uther Pendragon, King of Britain, and was crowned by Dubricius, Bishop of Caer Leon, at Cirencester, A.D. 506.

The scenes of King Arthur's exploits, as well as the place of his birth, have been fixed in Cornwall, and in North Wales, as well as in South Wales.

William of Malmesbury says, "Arthur was a man worthy to be celebrated by authentic history," and Lord Bacon says, "There is enough to make Arthur famous besides that which is fabulous."

This hero of battle and romance is extolled equally in the south of France and in the north of England, and he must unquestionably have been a prince of the true heroic standard; for it is absurd to imagine that a mere petty ruler could have won so much celebrity.

So great was the renown of this British prince throughout Europe, that even after the overthrow of the Saxon kingdom by William of Normandy, upwards of four centuries after Arthur's death, a hope was raised in the British mind of Arthur's re-appearance to fight their battles, and greater might was ascribed to the hero of the Kymric race than to any other that ever lived. As chivalry was then growing to be an institution, and the crusades causing much excitement, Arthur was taken as the central figure in all the fables of knightly romance, which were framed by the French as

well as the Germans, and round him was woven
every deed by which the sacred profession of
arms could be illustrated, and imaginary perfection of chivalrous excellence displayed.   In
Normandy an attempt was made to raise up
Raoul, the founder of the duchy, to a similar
pitch of renown, but it utterly failed, although
the "Lay of Roland," as he was called, was
chaunted at the battle of Hastings; but in
Germany the glory of Charlemagne and his
Paladins, and especially of Roland, whom the
Danish poets celebrated as Orlando, long dis-
puted the palm with Arthur and the Round
Table. Italy recounted the praise of the Frankish heroes, but they borrowed their incidents
from what had been narrated of the British
knights.   Spain affords an illustration of the
firm hold the class of stories of this kind had
upon the cultivated mind of Europe. The first
chivalric romance of Vasco Lobeira, *Amadis de
Gaula*, not only has its scene in Wales, but
most of the characters are derived from that
country also, as if Britain was the cradle of
true knighthood and of the glorious profession
of war.

Respecting the life and exploits of King Arthur fiction has said so much that history is
almost ashamed of the little she has to tell.

The hero was one of the chieftains of the
south-western part of Britain, and it appears
certain that he acted as supreme leader in the
contest maintained against the West Saxons.
Whether he fought in any other part of the
island we cannot tell, for the tale of Nennius
has so much fiction interwoven with what ap-

pears facts, that any attempt to fix the locality of the twelve battles he ascribes to Arthur is quite out of the question. His presence at the battle of Llongworth, by the river Llanèn, is spoken of by Slywarch Hen. His last battle was at Camlen against his nephew Medrawd, whose treachery to his uncle and Britain in joining the Saxons is condemned in the Triads with as much bitterness as the conduct of Vortigern is.

The account given in Nennius exhibits to us a full-grown legendary character. It runs as follows, altered to make it suit modern readers:—"In those days, Arthur, with the other British kings, fought against the Saxons, he being commander in the wars, and in every battle he was the conqueror." *Arthur* means "Dreadful Bear," or "Iron Mace," wherewith the teeth of the lions are dashed to pieces; and *Mab Uther* signifies "Dreadful Son," for from his very boyhood he was very cruel. His first fight was at the mouth of the river Glem, which some suppose to be the Glen, in Northumberland; others the Glem, in Lincolnshire; and others, again, the Glevi, in Devonshire. "The second, third, fourth, and fifth happened at another river, called the Duglas, in the region named Linuis. The sixth battle was on the river Bassas, and the seventh in the forest of Calidon, that is, *Cat coit Calidon*. His eighth victory was gained at Gunnion Castle, where Arthur bore the image of the Cross of Christ, and of the Blessed Mary, ever virgin; and the Pagans fled on that day, and many fell, through the power of our Lord Jesus

Christ and His Blessed Mother. The ninth was fought at Caer Legion; the tenth on the banks of the river Ribroit; the eleventh on a mountain called Agned Cathregonnon, Somersetshire; and the twelfth was at Mount Badon, in which 840 men fell by the sole attack of Arthur; none but he laid them low."

Whatever different ideas there may be as to the identity of King Arthur, all accounts point to Caer Leon on Usk, as the spot where King Arthur held his court, and as the scene of many of the exploits and incidents connected with his history. Caer Leon in those days was the capital of fifteen important stations in Siluria, and the suburbs on both sides of the river were supposed to have covered a tract of country nine miles in circumference. In 521 it was one of the three great cities of Britain.

Vestiges of its ancient grandeur are still to be found, the result of excavations being that statues, altars, columns, sarcophagi, fibulae, rings, seals, vases, brass and silver coins, and fragments of lamps and crosses have been discovered from time to time, and carried off by collectors of antiquities. At a short distance from the town the most perfect part of the original wall is to be seen. The wall is about thirteen feet in height, and ten or twelve in breadth, inclosing a great portion of two fields. Inclosed within the wall is the campestrian am·· phitheatre, an oval concavity in the ground, with sloping banks, seventy-five yards by sixty-four, called "King Arthur's Round Table." Around this hollow stone seats and many interesting relics have been dug up.

CHAPTER I.

Vortigern the Cruel—Arrival of Hengist and Horsa in Britain—Rowena's beauty captivates Vortigern—Vortimer chosen king—Vortimer poisoned by Rowena—Vortigern restored to the throne—The massacre of four hundred and sixty knights at Stonehenge—Building of the castle for Vortigern—Merlin discovered in the streets of Carmarthen—Merlin's prophecies—The battle of the dragons—The birth of Arthur foretold by Merlin—Death of Vortigern.

BRITAIN in the fifth century had several kings, and from the Tweed to the English Channel was occupied by three chief tribes—the Kymri—the Britons—and the Lloegrians—of which the last named was the most powerful.

Now among these kings was one Vortigern, or Gwortigern, who, by murder and perfidy, became king over the Britons. The whole of his reign was stained by cruelty and to him may be ascribed all the disasters which led to the dismemberment of the kingdom, and for giving the Saxons a footing in Britain.

The Britons had over them thirty flamens, or bishops, and three archflamens or archbishops. The archbishops were stationed in London, York, and Caerleon-on-Usk.

In the fourth year after Vortigern had become ruler of Britain, there appeared on the coast of Kent three war vessels commanded by Hengist and Horsa, two Jutish Ealdormen, who had been invited over to the island by this cruel monarch to assist him in expelling the Picts and Scots.

The three barques with their stalwart crews floated beneath the tall cliffs of Albion, and the hardly-pressed king engaged the eager warriors against his foes, and for their services he agreed to bestow upon them the island of Thanet. To the men of Jutland, Britain seemed fair indeed, and tidings soon reached the Fatherland of the favoured isle their swords may win. It induced fresh hordes in the following year to cross the sea to share the good fortune of their countrymen, and with the forces came the fair Rowena, daughter of Hengist, who was introduced by her father to the infatuated monarch, and her fatal " *Waes hael hlaford Cyning*" caused Vortigern to repudiate his faithful spouse to win the Saxon beauty.

Hengist now joined the Caledonian savages to ravage Britain, and Hengist obtained the earldom of Kent as his daughter's bridal portion.

As soon as Hengist obtained the principality of Kent, he hankered for more, and invited over others of his countrymen, so that the British people, seeing that they should be utterly consumed by the Saxons, at length revolted, and with one voice chose Vortimer, his son, as king, who sallied forth to drive the Saxons from the land. Four times he defeated them, but in one of the engagements Catigern, his brother, and Horsa, brother to Hengist, slew each other.

The Saxons now sent Vortigern to his son to obtain permission to depart for Germany.

Vortimer, however, had a worse enemy than the Saxons in his stepmother Rowena, who poisoned him, and Vortigern was restored to the throne of Britain. As soon as Hengist heard of Vortimer's death he raised an army of 300,000 men, and bent his course to Britain.

Vortigern resolved to encounter this host in

battle, but by Rowena's craft it was arranged that there should be a meeting between the British king and the Saxon chief, both parties to assemble unarmed lest contention should arise. They met on Salisbury Plain, now known as Stonehenge, and Hengist having armed his retinue with long knives, concealed under their cloaks, massacred 460 of his knights, and made Vortigern prisoner, and one British knight named Eldol, Count of Gloucester, alone escaped by slaying seventy of the enemy.

Vortigern, however, ransomed himself by giving up to Hengist the whole of Lloegria, and as he was supposed to be privy to the plot, he was never afterwards looked upon with favour by the Britons.

Lloegria having been thus ceded to the Saxons, Vortigern betook himself to Cambria, and at length had recourse to magicians, for there came messengers unto him who cried, "Arise, Lord King, for the enemy is come, even Ambrosius and Uther, upon whose throne thou sittest, and multitudes have joined them, and they have sworn a great oath to slay thee ere the year be out, and even now they march towards thee as the north wind of winter for bitterness and haste."

At these words Vortigern arose and sent for the best artificers and builders, and commanded them to build a strong castle to which he might fly for refuge, and cried he, "Let the work be done within one hundred days, or I will spare no life amongst you all."

Then the craftsmen in haste fixed on a piece of land whereon to build the tower, but no sooner were the walls raised above the ground than their work was destroyed by night, and no man perceived by whom it was done. The same thing happened night after night. At length all the workmen sought out the king, and beseeched him to interfere and help them by the aid of his wise men.

The king called his astrologers and sooth-sayers and took counsel with them as to the meaning of these strange things, and how to overcome them. The wizards worked their incantations, and declared that nothing but the blood of a youth, born without mortal father, sprinkled on the foundation of the castle could make it stand.

Vortigern sent messengers throughout the land to discover if any such miraculous child could be found, and as some of them were pass-ing down the streets of Caervyrddin (Carmar-then,) in Wales, they saw a band of lads quarrel-ling, and heard one of them shout to another, "Avaunt, thou Imp! thou art not fit to be amongst us, son of no mortal man; go, find thy father."

The messengers on hearing these words look-ed earnestly at the lad and inquired his name. One said that no one knew his parentage, another cried out his name is Merlin, and a third that the foul fiend was his father. Where-upon the officers seized the lad, and carried him before the king.

No sooner was he brought before the king than he said, "For what cause am I dragged here?"

"My magicians," replied Vortigern, "told me to seek out a child that had no mortal father, and to sprinkle my castle walls with his blood that they may stand."

"Order those magicians to come before me," said Merlin ; and the king ordered them to stand in the presence of Merlin, who cried to them,

"Because you know not what it is that hinders the foundation of the castle to stand, ye have advised my blood as a cement : but tell me what there is below the ground that will not suffer the tower to stand."

The magicians at these words were dumb with fear.

Then said Merlin to Vortigern, "I pray thee, king, that workmen may be ordered to dig deep into the ground until they find a pool of water."

When the workmen had dug a great depth they came to a pool, then turning to the magicians Merlin said,

"Tell me now, ye false sycophants, what there is beneath the pool ?" but they could not answer him the question.

Then said Merlin to the king, "Command that this pool be drained, and at the bottom two huge dragons will be found asleep, but when the night comes they will awake and fight. In their struggle the ground will shake and tremble, so that the foundation of the tower cannot stand."

The king ordered the pool to be drained forthwith, and when the pool was dried up the two dragons were found asleep as Merlin had said.

To see what would happen, Vortigern kept watch during the night, and he saw the dragons, one of which was white and the other red, come near to each other, and begin a sore fight, and cast forth fire with their breath.   In this terrific encounter the White Dragon gained the mastery, and drove the Red Dragon to the further end of the lake.   The Red Dragon turned on his pursuer, and renewing the combat, forced his enemy to retire in his turn, but in the end the Red Dragon was worsted and the White Dragon disappeared and was no more seen.

When the conflict was over, the King called Merlin, and demanded what these things meant.

Then was Merlin full of grief, and he cried out his prophecy wherein was first told the coming of King Arthur.

" Woe to the Red Dragon which figureth the British nation, for his banishment cometh quickly, and his lurking holes shall be seized by the White Dragon who represents the Saxons, whom thou hast called to this land.   The mountains shall be levelled with the valleys, and the rivers of the valleys shall run blood ; cities shall be burned, and churches laid in ruins, till at length the oppressed shall turn for a time and prevail against the stranger.   For a Bear shall arise in Cornwall, and trample their necks beneath his feet.   The island shall be subject to his power, and he shall take the forests of Gaul. The house of Romulus shall dread him—all the world shall fear him—and his end shall no man know.   He shall be immortal in the eyes of his people, and his words shall be food to those that tell them.   But as for thee, Vortigern, flee thou the sons of Constantine, for they shall burn thee in thy tower.   For thy own ruin wast thou traitor to thy father, and didst bring the Saxon heathen to the land.   Ambrosius and

Uther are now on their way from Brittany to revenge their father's murder, and the blood of the White Dragon shall waste thy country and shall lick thy blood.

The king, when he heard this, trembled greatly, but said nothing in reply, for his conscience smote him. He hasted the builders of his tower by night and day, and rested not until he had taken refuge within its walls.

The Britons now hailed Ambrosius, the rightful king, with joy, and flocked to his standard; but he, before leading them to expel the Saxon invaders, determined to first deal a death-blow to Vortigern. With this intent he marched to Cambria, and came before the tower which the usurper had set up. He then harangued his men-at-arms, and cried out, "Be revenged on him that hath ruined Britain and murdered my father and your king."

Then he rushed with many thousands at the fortress, but was driven back. He then caused burning brands to be cast into the building from all sides. A mighty conflagration ensued, and Vortigern perished in the flames.

CHAPTER II.

Ambrosius Aurelius succeeds Vortigern in the government of Britain—He leads his army against the Saxons —Gallimori, King of Ireland, defeated—Merlin removes the Giant's Dance from Ireland to Salisbury Plain— Ambrosius dies by poison—The bright comet and fiery dragon—Second prophecy of Merlin concerning Arthur.

AMBROSIUS now led his army against Hengist and the Saxons, Hengist being master of Kent, Essex, and Middlesex; Ella, another Saxon general, claimed dominion over Surrey and

527 B

Hampshire; while Cerdic, a third, governed Wilts, Somerset, Devon, and other parts. He defeated them in many places, and so weakened their power that the land had peace for a time.

The king, in his progress through the country, restored ruined churches and created order, and on a certain day he arrived at a monastery near Salisbury, where the four hundred and sixty British knights were slain by Hengist, who had made a solemn truce with Vortigern to meet in peace and settle terms, whereby himself and all his Saxons should depart from Britain.

The sight of the place where the dead were laid moved Ambrosius to great sorrow, and his thoughts were bent in devising how to build a tomb worthy the noble martyrs who had died for their country.

After consulting many artificers and craftsmen, he sent for Merlin, by the advice of Tramor, the Archbishop of Caer Leon, to ask him what to do.

"If you wish," said Merlin, "to honour the burial place of these men with an everlasting monument, send for the Giant's Dance, a huge structure of stones, which stands on Mount Killara, in Ireland, and if they can be placed here as they are there, they will be a memorial for ever."

Ambrosius, when he heard this, laughed, and exclaimed, "How is it possible that such vast stones can be moved from such a distance?"

"I pray thee, king," said Merlin, "to forbear vain laughter; what I have said is true, for these stones have healing virtues, and those who have a knowledge of the art could transplant them from that island to this. The giants of old brought them from the farthest coast of Africa and placed them in Ireland while they lived in that country to heal them of sickness, for if they washed the stones and put the sick into the water it healed them of their infirmities, as it did them who were wounded in battle."

Ambrosius resolved to send for these stones, and he sent his troops to Ireland to make war upon the people in case they refused to let the stones be removed. So the Britons chose Uther, the king's brother, for their chief, and he led 15,000 men into Ireland, accompanied by Merlin.

Here Gillamori, the king, withstood them fiercely, and not until after a great battle could they approach the Giant's Dance, the sight of which filled them with joy and admiration.

"Now," said Merlin, "remove those stones and carry them to the ships;" but the strength of the whole army was in vain.

Then Merlin contrived machines of wondrous cunning workmanship that took down the stones with ease, drew them to the ships, and they were transported to a plain in Britain, near Salisbury.

Then Ambrosius made the setting-up of the Giant's Dance a great holiday, and causing himself to be crowned anew, kept for four days the feast of Pentecost with royal pomp, and distributed honourable offices which were vacant to those who were most worthy of them, appointing Samson to the archbishopric of York, and Dubricius to that of Caer Leon, and thus showed honour to Merlin, who raised up the stones and set them round the sepulchre of the knights, and by whose skill the wonderful superiority of art to mere strength had been so wonderfully shown.

Afterwards Ambrosius died by poison, at Winchester, and was buried within the Giant's Dance.

At this time came forth a comet of amazing brightness, and at the end thereof was a cloud of fire in the form of a dragon, from whose mouth went forth two rays, one stretching over Gaul, the other ending in seven lesser rays over the Irish Sea.

At the appearance of this star, great dread fell upon the people, but Merlin, on being called before Uther, cried with a loud voice, "Oh, mighty loss! Oh, stricken Britain! Alas, the great prince is gone from us; Aurelius Ambrosius is dead. Haste, therefore, noble Uther, to destroy the enemy; the victory shall be thine, and thou shalt be king of all Britain. For the star with the fiery dragon signifies thyself, and the ray over Gaul portends that thou shalt have a son, whom all those kingdoms shall obey that the rays cover." Thus, a second time, was the coming of King Arthur foretold by Merlin.

CHAPTER III.

Uther Pendragon governs Britain—Octa, the Saxon, invades the country, and is defeated by Uther—The great feast to the nobles—Uther's love for Igerna, the wife of Gorlais, Duke of Cornwall—Igerna placed by her husband in Tintagel Castle—Death of Gorlais—Marriage of Uther with Igerna—The birth of Arthur—Arthur delivered into the hands of Merlin—Sir Ector becomes the foster father of Arthur—Death of Uther Pendragon—Arthur decreed to reign.

UTHER then waged war with Pasgen, the son of Vortigern, and Gallimori, King of Ireland, and having defeated them, returned to Winchester and received the kingdom, and then Ambrosius was interred.

Uther, when he was made king, remembered the words of Merlin, and ordered two dragons to be made of gold in the likeness of the dragon he had seen in the star. One of these he gave to Winchester Cathedral, and had the other carried into all his wars before him; and from that time he was called Uther Pendragon, or Uther of the Dragon's Head.

As soon as the death of Ambrosius became known, Octa and his followers invaded Britain, and reached York, when Uther completely routed them, and took Octa and his brother prisoners. He thus extended his kingdom as far as Alcluyd, and reduced that part of the kingdom; he passed through all the land into the country of the Scots, and tamed the fierceness of that rebel people, and then he came to London and there dispensed justice.

At Eastertide a great feast was ordered by the king, and there came among many other nobles with their wives and daughters, Gorlais, Duke

of Tintagel, in Cornwall, and his wife, Igerna,
who was the most famous beauty in Britain.

As soon as Uther saw her, he fell in love with
her, and bestowed so much attention on her
that her husband in a rage, quitted the court,
and took his wife with him.   When Uther was
made aware of it, in opposition to the remon-
strances of Merlin that evil would come of it,
he sent messengers to the duke, commanding
him to return; but Gorlais not only refused,
but hasted to his possessions in Cornwall, where
he placed the fair Igerna in the castle of Tintagel, an inaccessible fortress in a secure spot, on
the summit of a stupendous rock, separated by
the sea from the mainland, which was so strong
that half a dozen knights could hold it against
any numbers.

As he expected, the king marched into Cornwall, and invested the castle in which Gorlais
was on every side, and in a sally Gorlais was
killed by Sir Ulfius, one of the king's leaders.

The king's passion for the lady burnt too
fiercely to find any alleviation in this revenge,
and he confided the state of his mind to one of
his knights, Ulphin, of Caer Caradoc, who advised him to consult Merlin as to the way in
which he could obtain his heart's desire.

Merlin promised his aid on one condition,
namely, that the king should give him up the
first son born unto him, for Merlin, by his arts,
foreknew that this first-born should be the
long-wished-for King Arthur.

Then Merlin, by his art, put upon Uther the
likeness of Gorlais, transformed Ulphin into the
likeness of Jordan, of Tintagel, and took upon

himself the appearance of Brithael, two trusty servants of Gorlais, and thus obtained entrance into the fortress where Igerna was.

Uther confessed his wickedness to Igerna, and Merlin, by enchantment, wrought it so that she fell in love with the king, and they were married and lived together in great affection, and there was born unto them, besides Arthur, a daughter.

On a certain day Merlin came to the castle and said to the king, " Sir, thou must now provide for thy child," and the king said, " Be it as thou wilt."

Then Merlin replied, " I know a lord of thine in this land who is a man both true and faithful, let him have care of the child. His name is Sir Ector, and he hath fair possessions both in England and Wales. Let therefore, the child be delivered to me, unchristened, and I will give him into this good knight's charge."

So the king commanded two knights and two ladies to take the child, and they bound it in rich cloth of gold and delivered it into the hands of Merlin, who took it to a priest and had it baptized in the name of Arthur. Merlin then took the child to Sir Ector's house, and he was nourished by Sir Ector's own wife's breasts, and remained in Sir Ector's care for many years.

After this, Uther had a lingering distemper, and those who had charge of Octa and his brother suffered them to escape ; so they went to Germany, and raising an army, returned to Britain, and began to ravage the country, and laid it waste with fire and sword. Leo, son of Cynvarch, and Lot, who had married Uther's daughter, could not overcome the Saxon heathens because the British nobles were mutinous, therefore Uther commanded his nobles to come before him that he might upbraid them for their conduct. When he had rebuked them, he swore that he, himself, although nigh unto death, would lead them against the enemy, and causing a litter to be made in which he might be carried, he went up with his army against the Saxons.

When the enemy heard that Uther was coming in a horse litter, they disdained to fight with him, saying it would be a shame to fight with one that was half dead. So they returned into their city, and left the gates open.

Then Uther commanded his army to assault the town, and had reached the gates, when the Saxons rushed forth to the defence.

The battle raged till night, and begun again at daybreak. At last the Saxon leaders, Octa and Eosa, were slain, and their men fled, leaving the Britons victorious.

At this the king said, "They called me a half-dead king, and so I was; but victory to me half dead is better than defeat and the best of health. For to die with honour is far better than to live disgraced."

The Saxons soon renewed the war, and left nothing undone to destroy the land, and at last descended to the vile treachery of poisoning the water of a well near Verulem, of which the king always drank, and so he died and many others with him. His knights and barons, now took counsel together, and came to Merlin to know from him the king's will.

"Sirs," said Merlin, " there is no remedy,

and God's will must be done; but come ye all to-morrow, and God will make the king speak."

So on the morrow the knights assembled around the king, and Merlin said aloud, "Uther Pendragon, King of Britain, shall thy son Arthur be the king of all this realm?" Then Uther said in the hearing of them all, "I give him God's blessing and my own, and I bid him pray for my soul, and I desire that he claims my crown, or forfeit all my blessings."

Then the bishops and clergy and great multitudes of people bewailed their loss. They then carried him to the Giant's Dance, and buried him within the circle of heroes by the side of his brother.

CHAPTER IV.

Merlin's adventure upon the Lake—His plan for placing Arthur upon the throne—The storm and fiery clouds—The enchanted island—Merlin summonses the Nymphs of the Lake—His power over Morgan la Fay, the Queen of the Lake—Her vow of vengeance—Merlin descends to the cave beneath the Lake—Meeting of Merlin and Viviane—Forging of the magic glaive.

In the age of which the story treats, there were giants and dragons in the land; and noble knights in these chivalrous days traversed from place to place in quest of adventure, and dared every danger to gain the approval and win the smiles of "lady fayre;" then fairies and spirits, walked abroad, and wizards and necromancers worked their spells upon mankind. At this period, the great enchanter Merlin, walked the earth, and worked his powerful spells.

As he was gliding smoothly along in his barge over the dark waters of the mountain lake near

Caer Leon, strange sounds and fantastic forms hovered in the air around him.

" The ministers of my arch foe, Morgan la Fay, are moving around me, and the spirits of the lake are disturbed," mused Merlin ; " my enemy with her cruel crew in middle air have no power over me, for I partake of their nature —being half elf, and half mortal—and the water wraiths that dwell beneath the lake are subject to my gentle and obedient Viviane."

As he ceased speaking, he stood in his barge, and raising his arms towards the clouds, uttered some cabalistic sounds, when a thick mist descended and a number of flaming tongues settled down upon the lake ; they glimmered for a moment, and then vanished, while the air was filled with unearthly shrieks. Anon all was silent.

"They are gone," muttered the seer ; and then he added, " would I had no foes more powerful to contend against."

Again seating himself in his barge, the prophet gazed towards the sky. The sun set like a fiery furnace, and the sky was mantled in dark, clouds, but between the gloomy vapours a white star shone brightly from a heaven of azure blue.

Resting his head upon his hands, the seer sat engrossed in deep and anxious thought.

" I must to my task," he cried. " Since Uther's death no king reigns over the land, and the nobles contend among themselves, the common sort grow turbulent, and the realm is in jeopardy. Woe for the crime I sanctioned in obedience to the king. The heir is lost and they look to me to find him. Will they believe that Arthur, the foster child of Sir Ector, is the son of Uther Pendragon, the mighty King of Britain ? Will they consent to be ruled by the beardless boy, whose hand never held a sword ?"

In the distance loomed a lofty mountain, on whose summit wreathed mingled clouds and fire in the shape of a dragon, and the atmosphere was dark and dense. In an instant a blaze of lightning illuminated the sky, and there came bursts of thunder, crash upon crash. The sky again cleared—the mountain top was void— the form of the dragon had vanished!

His barge, made its way to a small island, and soon floated beneath its banks. The seer disembarked, and mounting some rugged steps, reached the level of the islet ; he soon reached the centre of the island, where there was a cairn, which marked the sepulchre of a chief of a remote age. Glancing around him, his eyes rested upon a number of scattered stones and bursting into a laugh of scorn, he cried, " Does the mighty spirit of Morgan la Fay stoop to such shallow artifice to deceive me ?"

" Comest thou here to pry into my secrets, and to baffle my purpose ?" replied a voice.

" Ill-minded Lady of the Lake, be as thou art wont to be ;" and, approaching, Merlin gathered up a handful of water, and sprinkled it upon the stones.

A shriek of terror then arose, and a group of nymphs of dazzling beauty appeared ; their arms entwined each other as though for mutual protection, whilst one more lovely than the rest advanced towards the wizard. Her voice had a commanding expression, her dark eyes glowed with revengeful fire, and her ravishing form quivered through the robe of spotless white in which she was apparelled; a golden coronet encircled her fair brow, and her raven locks floated wildly upon the evening breeze.

"Avaunt, juggler!" she exclaimed; "how darest thou pollute my dominions."

"I came on an errand of peace," replied the seer; "I seek Viviane, the damsel of the lake."

"And can thy blasted form still smoulder in love's fire; runs yet so warm the life-blood through thy veins; and is the arch magician, and the inspired prophet, so infatuated by the charms of my revolted vassal, Viviane? Oh, fool! Knowest thou not that she is fore-doomed to work thy ruin?" retorted the elfin queen.

"What will be, must be; I am willing to fall a sacrifice to the common weal of Britain and of Arthur," replied the seer.

"Arthur!" exclaimed Morgan la Fay, "Breathe not his name to me!—the offspring of my mother's rival, the perfidious Igerna, who took Uther Pendragon, the murderer of her husband, with hands covered with his blood! Who renounced my mother, the king's first love severed me from my kinsfolk of the lake, and yielded up her infant, this very Arthur, to you—a sorceror, a demon born—that you may work your vile arts upon him!"

"What avails all this, fair Queen of the Lake? Why visit the father's crimes and the mother's frailties on the head of the noble Arthur? Why visit on him the chastisement of other's deeds?" asked the magician.

"Revenge!" answered the queen. "My outraged mother, left to me a legacy of hate and vengeance, and I have sworn that I will take no rest until I have wrought the ruin of King Arthur and all his knights."

"Prythee cease thy idle words," said Merlin; "I have grave business on hand that will not brook delay. The fated hour has arrived—and all obstacles betwixt me and my purpose must be swept away; therefore, let me pass."

"Fiend-born usurper—no!" retorted Morgan la Fay. "You seek the rebel Viviane, to plot with her the restoration of my enemy; but rather than you should accomplish your purpose, I will unlock the fountains of the lake and deluge the whole country! Thou knowest my power!"

"And you mine," said the magician, raising his staff and waving it in the air. In an instant the lady of the lake was struck motionless and speechless."

"Are you convinced of my power?" cried Merlin. "But why do you go to extremes? Let me reverse the charm."

Merlin then struck his staff on the ground, and the spell was broken. The elfin queen, drawing a deep breath, gasped out, "Inexorable man, your power is resistless!"

She then fell upon her knees, and, entwining her delicate fingers in her coal black hair, exclaimed, "I must have patience to abide the hour," and starting to her feet, she darted from her black eyes a withering look, as she exclaimed, vehemently, "And the hour *will* come, and though tardy the retribution, it will be ample. Thinkest thou my mother's tears are swept from my memory—the scorn of her hated rival Igerna, is forgotten—the leaden hours I spent immured within the dull walls of yon dungeon-nunnery are ceased to be remembered? No! I am ever brooding over these wrongs! Woe to King Arthur! His consort shall prove faithless —his cherished friend turn traitor—his foeman shall prevail—and he, the great Pendragon, shall perish by the sword; and the mighty Merlin shall fall in his own snare. Go, then, fly to your false Viviane! Forge your magic glaive! Muster your gallant knights; and win your glowing honours! Farewell! I leave my curse with you." With these words, she clapped her hands, at the signal, her attendant nymphs along with her vanished into air.

The wizard for a time bent his eyes to the ground. He then muttered, " In my time I have seen sights and heard sounds that would have unnerved a weaker man, pass away like a shadow. Even so! What else are the pomps and glories of the world? A passing shadow—the pageant of a dream—the baseless fabric of a vision. Come then, the worst; but while we live, let us live; when we die, let us leave an example to those that follow us."

At length Merlin mounted the rock, and, raising his hands, chaunted some sentences, when the isle on which he stood sunk beneath the lake, and he found himself standing in a vast cavern. Arch after arch he passed, and from the roofs crystal spars dazzled the eye with brilliance. The floor was covered with silvery sand, whilst from the crevices of the rocks graceful ferns threw out their fan-like fronds. He paced the fairy halls, which were familiar to him, and presently a merry laugh greeted his ear, as a young and beautiful nymph greeted him, and with bewitching sweetness of tone exclaimed, "Welcome, master dear," laying her little hands upon his bosom with childlike simplicity; "I have counted the sands in the hour-glass for your return. Is all going on well?"

"Bravely, my peerless Viviane," replied the magician, smiling on her, and caressing her.

"I dreaded some mishap," cried she, "for I knew Morgan la Fay would bring her most powerful spells to work against our enterprise. To-night the spirits of the mountains were in arms, and on the summit of Mynydd Mawr I saw a dragon form writhing in clouds of smoke and fire. Met you the queen?"

"Yea, by the stones of the mystic circle," laughed the magician; "rather would I have encountered all the dragons and serpents that sprang from the blood of Medusa than have been confronted with Morgan la Fay; her envenomed tongue has the sting of a scorpion. But tell me, fair Viviane, is the great task accomplished?"

"Most satisfactorily," answered Viviane. "Welland and his goblin armourers have finished their task; Excalibur is forged. The noble sword lies in yon grot, which it illuminates with its brilliancy. Come and see."

The wizard was conducted into the recesses of the cavern by his companion, and there, on a block of black marble, stood an iron anvil, whereon lay a mighty sword that shone with dazzling lustre, and beside it lay its richly-jewelled scabbard.

Viviane attempted to raise the sword, but the weight was too much for her strength. "It is no woman's arm that can wield that mighty falchion," said she; "raise it for me, my master."

Merlin took up the sword, flourished it in the air, pressed its point on the earth to test its flexibility, examined its edge, and then rattled it into its sheath, exclaiming, "It is a faultless weapon, sure talisman of victory."

"The sword is your gift to Arthur," said Viviane; "but to me he owes the virtues of the scabbard. I have laid a spell upon it, and it is ten times more precious than the sword, for while Arthur keeps the scabbard at his side he shall lose no blood."

"A charm!" said the wizard, and muttering some words, he drew the sword, and striking a downward blow, stuck its point into the anvil, where it remained embedded.

"The spell is perfected!" exclaimed Merlin. "No hand but that of Arthur, the great Pendragon of Britain, shall draw the sword from out the iron.

CHAPTER V.

Dissatisfaction of the nobles—The struggles for the Pendragonship—The edict of the archbishop for the knights to assemble in London—The miracle of the sword—Joy of the populace at the prospect of the election of the Pendragonship of England—Sir Kaye and Arthur journey towards the tournament.

FOR a long season the land had been in disquietude, for every lord and baron sought possession by might, and the Saxons wasted and overran every town and village. The chief lords and princes, straightway set about raising armed men and multitudes of followers, each one determined to gain the crown for himself.

When Merlin found so much discontent and rivalry prevail, he went to the Archbishop of Canterbury, and advised him to send an edict to all the lords of the realm, knights, and gentlemen-at-arms, to assemble in London, under pain of cursing, that they might learn the will of heaven as to who should be king.

This the archbishop did, and upon Christmas-eve the greatest princes, lords, barons, and knights met in London, and they prayed in St. Paul's Church, and besought heaven for a sign who should be lawful king of all the realm.

And when matins and the first mass were done, there was seen in the churchyard, before the doorway of the church, a huge square stone, whereon was an anvil with a sword stuck in the midst of it, and on the stone was written in letters of gold, " *Whoso pulleth out the sword from this stone is born the rightful King of England.*"

Then the people marvelled, and told it to the archbishop; and when mass was over, the princes, nobles, and knights ran out eagerly from the church to see the stone and sword, and it was forthwith decreed that whoso should pull out the sword should be acknowledged straightway King of England.

The bells from every steeple in London clanged merrily, banners floated in the air, and the trumpets sounded loudly. The multitude assembled, and with shouts rent the air, whilst the neighing of steeds, the measured tramp of the men-at-arms, and the songs of bards and minstrels, produced sounds of excitement and joy.

Then many nobles and knights strove to re-move the sword, and some of them tried many times, but not one of them could stir it.

When all had tried in vain, the archbishop said, "He is not yet here that shall achieve the sword, but God will doubtless make him known ere many days. Therefore let ten knights be chosen, to watch and guard the sword." The knights were then selected, and there was a proclamation made that whosoever would try to remove the sword should have liberty to do so. Great multitudes came day after day to make the attempt, but no man could remove the sword a hair's breadth from its place.

At length, New Year's Day arrived, when a great tournament was fixed to be held in London. Pleasure beamed in every eye as the cavalcade of knights and ladies wended their way to the tilting-ground.

Among those who came to the tournament, and among the knights, was Sir Ector, Arthur's foster-father, who had some possessions near London, accompanied by his son, Sir Kaye, who had been recently made knight, and Arthur.

Sir Kaye, was a stripling, with merry black eyes, and nut-brown hair. He was dressed in a habergeon of glittering link armour, and rode a powerful black horse.

Young Arthur rode beside him on a milk-white jennet. He was a noble-looking youth, with piercing blue eyes, and long yellow hair. His eyes beamed with truth and his lip smi'ed with tenderness and good nature. His deter-mined look betokened him a lion in war, and he seemed to eclipse the many handsome youths around him.

As Sir Kaye gazed upon the dense throng of the soldiery and knights, he turned to his companion, and said, "You have your wish at last, Arthur. What say you to this gay scene, after our old grey towers. This beauty, and chivalry is a change for you, and a pleasure to myself, although I have seen it all before."

"It joys me well," said Arthur. "I love to hear the people so joyous, and watch the anxious faces of the brave knights, the blythe yeomen, and the beauteous damosels; yet I love my native tower also, and to me, the whistle of the husbandman, the lilting of the milk-maid, and the sound of the hunter's horn are sweeter than the continued cry of 'Largesse!' as though half the people were beggars."

For some time they rode on in silence. At length Sir Kaye exclaimed, "To-day I couch a spear for the first time, and I mean to earn my spurs."

" St. Mary be you fair speed, fair brother !" replied Arthur.

" I am older than you by two years," said Sir Kaye, " but your time will come, and I have no doubt that you will gain much honour."

"Your thoughts are ever kind, dear brother," replied Arthur, " yet I would rather win my spurs in the field than on the tilting ground."

" I am of the like mind," said Sir Kaye ; " and when the king is found, there will be brave wars forward. How I long to break a spear against a Paynim shield. I wonder on whom the election will fall : for my part, I would rather be a leader of a band of knights than the monarch; the burden on a king's shoulders is too heavy.   What say you ; would you wish to be Pendragon ?"

" Yes, were I worthy. By St. George, methinks it were a noble thing to be ruler of a mighty people—in war to shed one's life-blood for the flock, in peace to walk through golden harvest fields and pleasant villages, and note the contented husbandman pursuing his labour, or returned to his village home ; to know that honour and security reigns throughout the land ; and to feel glory swelling in the heart, the consciousness of being the chosen instrument for the spread of Heaven's blessings 'mongst a grateful nation, and be the king of men in heart and mind and might," cried Arthur.

Sir Kaye was surprised and exclaimed, " Why, Arthur, you talk so strangely   ! This is mere prompting of boyish glory."

" Have I not said," replied Arthur, " I am not worthy ? Were it otherwise, I would be, crowned or uncrowned, ever a king of men !"

They now halted at an encampment of rich pavilions near the list where the tournament was to be held, and Sir Kaye and Arthur dismounted and entered a tent—the former to array himself for the mimic battle, and the latter to assist his brother in putting on his armour.

CHAPTER VI.

Sir Kaye misses his sword—Arthur goes in quest of one —Merlin desires him to go to the church and pull the sword out of the stone—The sword is brought to Sir Kaye—Sir Ector pronounces it to be Excalibur—Sir Ector, Sir Kaye and Arthur go to the stone—Arthur replaces the sword in the stone, and no one can draw it out besides himself—Arthur declared king—The trial of the drawing of the sword put off to Easter, and then from thence to Pentecost—Sir Ector disclaims Arthur as his son.

SIR Kaye and Arthur having looked round on the knights and ladies, the former lifted his baldric, and his surprise was great to find it supported no weapon.

"A malison upon my thoughtlessness," exclaimed Sir Kaye, "I have left my sword at my father's house. I pray you ride back and fetch it for me.

"That will I with right good will," said Arthur, and was proceeding on his way, when an armourer, who was fastening on his master's leg armour, looked up, and cried out to Arthur as he passed, "You will find a good sword in the next tent."

"Thanks, Owen," returned Sir Kaye; and turning to his brother he added, "Go, Arthur, and loose no time in fetching it, for the trumpet calls."

Arthur hurried towards the tent, but ere he reached it, an old man, with a long white beard, touched him on the arm as he passed.

"Seek it not there," said the stranger.

"Father, where else?" cried Arthur.

"Go to the church, and draw forth the sword you will find stuck in the stone."

Arthur was about to question the old man, but he strode away and mixed with the crowd.

"What can this mean?" thought Arthur. "However, come weal, come woe, I will ride to the churchyard and bring away the sword, if I can;" so, setting spurs to his horse, he galloped towards the church.

Upon reaching the spot, he alighted. As he approached the stone, he gazed upon the sword that stood shining in the sunlight, and read the inscription.

Then, finding he was alone, he went into the adjoining tent, and found it empty, for the ten knights who had been placed to watch the sword had gone to the jousts. Arthur returned to the church-door, and after a moment's hesitation, he approached the stone, and seizing the sword by the hilt, drew it from the stone. Then he remounted his steed, and rode back to the field of the tournament.

As he entered his brother's tent, Sir Kaye turned to him, and rebuked him for the delay, saying, "Why hast thou lingered? Thrice the trumpets have sounded, and I am unprepared."

"Pardon, dear brother," replied Arthur, "for the prize I have brought you is worth the delay." Arthur then recounted all that had occurred since he left the tent, and presented the sword. Sir Kaye listened with feelings of awe.

"This is a miracle," said he; "yet can it be that I am the elect Pendragon of England?"

"It must be so," replied Arthur, "for you are my elder brother."

"And the less worthy," said Sir Kaye. "We must to our father, and tell him."

At this moment, Sir Ector entered to reprove his son for delaying. "At your age," said he, "I was ever the first in the field, and the last to leave it."

"Sir," said Sir Kaye, "I had left my sword at home, and sent Arthur to find one."

Sir Ector glanced at the weapon with amazement and excitedly exclaimed, "It is Excalibur! How came it here?"

"My brother Arthur," said Sir Kaye, "brought it to me. It is the sword of the stone, and therefore I am king of this land!"

The old knight heeded not the last remark, but turning to Arthur said, "How gottest thou the sword?"

"Sir, I will tell you," replied Arthur. "When I went to seek a sword for my brother, I met an old man—"

"Merlin, I doubt not; but go on," said Sir Ector.

"He bade me go to the cathedral, and there I should find what I was seeking. I should have asked him wherefore this command, but when I looked where he had been standing, he had vanished as if by magic. So, thinking my brother should not be swordless, I went thither and drew the sword out of the stone without effort.

"Found you not the knights about the sword guarding it?" asked Sir Ector.

"No, sir," answered Arthur, "they had all gone to the tourney."

"Then," said Sir Ector, looking steadfastly at Arthur, "if it indeed be thus, 'tis thou shalt be king of all this land, and God will have it so, for none but he who is rightwise Lord of Britain might draw this sword forth from the stone; but let me now with mine own eyes see thee put back the sword into its place, and draw it forth again."

Sir Ector grasped the hand of Arthur, and looked admiringly into his face, saying, "It needed not Merlin's wonderous art to approve the birthright of him upon whose brow is set the impress of sovereignty; but come, let us return to the cathedral and see if you can put the sword where it was and draw it forth again."

"That is no mastery," said Arthur.

As they spoke, the trumpets rang out their stirring blast, and the shouting of the people resounded from the tilting ground; but they thought no more of the jousting, and hurried to the churchyard, where they found the stone and anvil, but the knights were still absent.

"Now, assay," said Sir Ector, taking the sword from Arthur, and handing it to his son.

Sir Kaye took the weapon, and, poising it for a moment, struck it upon the anvil, but the steel rang upon the iron, and then glanced off without making the slightest impression. He again attempted to achieve the feat, but all his efforts proved of no avail.

"Now, Arthur, take the sword," said Sir Ector.

The youth seized the sword, which he flourished aloft, and with one swift downward blow, struck the point into the iron, and left the falchion quivering there.

Sir Ector tried to draw out the sword, but could not.

Then Sir Kaye, setting his foot against the

stone, tugged so violently that his limbs trembled from the strain; but he was forced at last to reel backwards, out of breath.

Arthur now approached, and, with a light fillip, pulled the weapon from the anvil.

"It is a marvel," said Arthur, tossing the shining brand high in the air, "but it seems amiss that I should be preferred to my elder brother."

Then Sir Ector and Sir Kaye owned him as their sovereign lord.

"Alas, my dear father and brother," cried Arthur, "why kneel to me ? It is your loving counsel I need, and not your homage."

"Nay, my Lord Arthur," exclaimed Sir Ector, "we are of no blood kinship to thee." And then he told him all he knew about his infancy, and how a stranger had delivered him with a sum of gold into his hands to be brought up as his own born child, and then disappeared, and added, "I wot well that you are of nobler blood than I thought you were, though no longer a son to me, you will become my good lord when you are king."

When Arthur heard these things, he fell upon Sir Ector's neck and wept, crying, "Else were I to blame, for are you not in all the world the man to whom I am most beholden, and to my good lady and mother, your wife, who has so well cherished me ; and if it be heaven's will that I be the king, you shall desire of me what I may do, and I shall not fail you."

"I will but pray," replied Sir Ector, "that you will make my son, Sir Kaye, seneschal of all your lands."

"That shall be so," said Arthur, "and more,

by the faith of my body ! never man shall have the office but he, while he and I do live."

"Come, then," said the old knight, "let us to the archbishop, and tell him how the sword was achieved, and by whom." When the archbishop saw the sword in Arthur's hand he set a day apart, and summoned all the princes, knights, and barons to meet at St. Paul's Church and see the will of heaven signified.

The news of Arthur's achievement spread throughout the land, and many of the lords were enraged, thinking it a shame to be governed by a mere boy. On the day appointed, the sword was put back in the anvil by Arthur, and all tried to move it, but not one could move it save Arthur alone.

At this a great confusion arose, for some cried out it was the will of heaven, and "Long live King Arthur," but many were full of wrath, and said, "What! would ye give the sceptre of this land unto a boy born none know how ?"

And the contention growing greatly until nothing could be done to pacify their rage, the meeting was broken up, and the trial put off till Candlemas. When Candlemas was come, there was a vast gathering, and many great lords attempted to draw the sword from the stone, but none could prevail but Arthur.

Then were the barons sorely vexed, and the party opposed to his accession had grown so strong that it was resolved to defer the decision until Easter. At Easter another trial was made, and Arthur being again the one that could draw out the sword, it was arranged that a further delay should take place until the Feast of Pen-

tecost, at which season it was agreed that the
verdict should be considered final and decisive.
But now the achbishop called together, by
Merlin's counsel, a band of knights and men-
at-arms, and set them about Arthur to keep him
safely till the Feast of Pentecost. The powerful knights set to guard Arthur were those
whom Uther Pendragon had placed most confidence in in his days, amongst whom were Sir
Dawdewine, Sir Ulfius, and Sir Brastius, and
the whole realm of Britain waited in suspense
for the great that day should settle Arthur's
claim to the crown of Britain.

CHAPTER VII.

Arthur's visit to Merlin's tower at Caer Leon—Merlin discloses to Arthur the secret of his birth—Arthur's sorrow at the recital—Arthur foretold of his long and
glorious career, and is warned of the enmity of Morgan la Fay.

MERLIN sat in the turret-chamber in the citadel
of Caer Leon, and thither he sent for Arthur.
The future Pendragon had returned to the castle of his foster-father, which had been strongly
garrisoned with a body of knights and men-at-
arms. This castle lay near the city of Caer Leon.
Arriving at the citadel, Arthur ascended by the
turret-stair to Merlin's chamber. It was not
without some feelings of awe that Arthur approached the enchanter's cell. As he drew near,
the door slid mutely back into the stone of the
wall, and, when Arthur had passed closed of its
own accord. It had eight small loopholes, which
commanded a view of the whole surrounding
country. He gazed with wonder on the varied

contents of the wizard's studio. The walls were hung with maps, and charts, diagrams, horoscopes, and scrolls of cabalistic figures. Testtubes, retorts, cylinders, and vessels of all shapes and dimensions were scattered everywhere about the floor. On one side of the room was a huge open volume, supported on a brazen stand; opposite to this a large mirror hung against the wall. In one corner of the room, a great furnace was constantly burning.

Merlin was seated upon a raised seat, constructed of carved oak. His dress was similar to that of the Arch-Druid—a stole of white—a girdle on which many cabalistic characters were traced, and a tiara of plain gold surmounted his brow, and on his finger the ring of divination. His head was bent on his breast as if he were buried in deep thought. Casting one hurried glance of interest around the place, Arthur approached the wizard, and bent his knee in veneration of a power superior to his own.

"Hail! great Merlin!" he said.

The wizard drew the young prince to his bosom; then he said, "I have sent for you, partly because I knew your wish to learn the secret of your parentage, and partly because, here we may confer in security, which cannot be elsewhere, as all your actions are closely watched."

"Father, you read my heart," returned Arthur. "I burn to know by what Providence one so humble as myself should be singled out for such high honour as is promised me."

"Listen, my son," replied the wizard. "It befel, in the days of Uther Pendragon, when, he reigned King of all England, that there was a mighty duke in Cornwall that had long held war against him. This was the Duke of Tintagel. At length peace was made between the king and this vassal. Then the king sent for the duke to come to court, and to bring with him his fair young wife, Igerna. They came, and smitten by her beauty, King Uther loved her, and conspired against her husband's life, thinking, by removing him, he might gain possession of the hand of fair Igerna.

"I blush at such dishonour, unworthy of a churl—much more unworthy of a king!" said Arthur.

"You speak the truth, and the crime that followed brought its own punishment," answered Merlin. "The duke fled the court, and retired to his Cornish fastness. The war was renewed, and siege was laid to the Castle of Terrabil, whither the duke retired, while the fair Igerna had been left by her husband in the Castle of Tintagel, another of his fortresses. A sally was made by the duke from Castle Terrabil, in which he was slain by Sir Ulfius. Then the king sought the fair Igerna, and, by my enchantment, wrought it so that she, though a virtuous lady, at first sight loved the king."

"It cannot be!" cried Arthur, his lip quivered with indignation. "Would the great Merlin lend himself to arts so base?"

"My son, thou knowest not to what lengths worldly ambition will lead men onwards," returned Merlin. "But to my story. The king married Igerna, and she bore a son—yourself, my noble Arthur. As soon as you were born, you were delivered by me into the hands of Sir

Ector.   I told him that it was by order of the king, who put command upon him that he should ask no questions.   Sir Ector, knowing I was in the king's counsel, seeing the infant wrapped in cloth of gold, and being, moreover, a man of a large warm heart, accepted the charge, and thus were you nourished by the knight and his wife."

"And dearer far are they to me than those unnatural parents who so deserted me," answered Arthur.   "Rather would I be the poor knight's son than what I am, since dishonour taints high blood like poison; and better foul water than poisoned wine!"

Merlin smiled on him with a look of sadness mingled with self-reproach; but he continued, "Within two years after your birth, the barons of Cornwall—eager to avenge the death of the Duke of Tintagel, revolted, and waged fierce war against the king. He at the time was sick, even unto death ; but I foresaw that unless he went to the field, the battle would go against him, and thither he was carried in a litter. The conflict raged from sunrise until night fell ; and on that day Sir Ulfius and Sir Brastius won for King Uther a signal victory. The barons came to me and asked for counsel ; but Heaven will have its will; his time was come, and death is inexorable. Yet my power extended thus far : I roused him from his swoon and made him speak, and he left his blessing upon his son Arthur, and bade the barons keep their allegiance to him, for that he was his true begotten son, and rightwise Pendragon of England."

Young Arthur listened with a troubled brow.

"Would I had never heard this sad story," he said—"that I had been what I have so long seemed to be! But who can control his fate? Oh, much I fear my father's crime will bring its fatal consequences! Come what may, I will, by the saints' blessing, do my *devoir* as a true king and honourable knight, and meet the worst that may befall with Christian patience!"

"You will do well, fair son," returned the enchanter. "And though the end of all is buried in dark clouds of threatening aspect, yet your career shall be long and glorious, and you shall leave behind a name of such high renown that when in after times, men talk of noble deeds wrought in a golden age, they will say, 'It was in Arthur's days.' But heed me well, for I have words to speak that touch you near!"

"Say on," returned young Arthur—"your counsel is a light to the thorny path that lies before me; you are the pilot that must guide the Ship of State through every storm."

"The opening of your reign will be stormy and troublous," returned the enchanter; " your youth will repel many of the proud barons, yet fear not, for, by my aid you will prevail against your most powerful enemies. Guard well the magic sword, which shall be thine, and wield it as becomes your kingly dignity, and the high courage of a dauntless champion. There is rebellion in the north which must be quelled; while at home the most powerful of your vassals will conspire against you: but most you have to fear are the wiles of Morgan la Fay. Leave me to deal with her. This very night I hold a tryst with Viviane, the bright damosel of the lake, and we shall devise such spells as shall baffle all her malignant practices. Therefore, go in peace, my son. We meet again on the great day when you shall stand before all England, approved, and acknowledged England's king!''

CHAPTER VIII.

Final test for the sovereignty—Merlin calls Arthur, who again draws the sword from the stone and thrusts it back into the anvil—King Clarience disputes Arthur's right to be king—The stone and anvil shivered to atoms, and the sword disappears—The revolt of the barons—Clarience's feigned homage—Merlin cautions Arthur against Clarience.

THE feast of Pentecost arrived, and a goodly number of lords, knights, and common people assembled in the churchyard of the cathedral to witness the final test for the sovereignty of Britain. In front of the door, stood the anvil, and in it was the magic sword. The nobles and knights, stepped up to the stone, and assayed to draw out the sword. All failed of the prize they had to win. So great was the excitement of the mob to know the result of the ordeal, that the men-at-arms had much ado to keep back the rush that was made to see what was going on. Many even ran upon the points of the soldiers' spears and halberts, and received serious wounds.

Last of all appeared young Arthur. He stood forth in the sight of the vast multitude, who, as they beheld the gallant form, the frank, noble face, and long golden locks of the royal youth, set up such a shout of joyous recognition, as almost to shake the firm foundation of the mighty pile that loomed above him. Upon his head blazed a helmet with a long drooping white plume; his jupon was of dazzling white, void of the coat-of-arms generally emblazoned upon that garment, but richly and fancifully embroidered; a girdle, set with gems, encircled his waist; below this covering his body and limbs were encased in a suit of complete steel (of Merlin's providing, and the work of no human hand,) that flashed in the sunshine. He bore no weapons, except a little miserecorde, or poniard, on his left hip.

As Arthur descended the stairs of the cathedral, Merlin raised his wand, and cried, "Advance, son of Uther Pendragon, approve thyself rightwise king of this fair realm of England."

Arthur smiled, but there was more of sorrow than of triumph in his look, as, seizing the handle of the sword, he drew it "lightly and fiercely" from the anvil. He grasped it with a warrior's grasp; hurled it high in the air, and caught it by the hilt, holding it aloft, and shaking it till it flashed like a streak of lightning.

"Hail! Arthur Pendragon!" cried Merlin and Viviane, sinking upon their knees. "All hail! true born King of England!" The common people took up the cry, and rent the welkin with their deep-mouthed shout of "Arthur is son of Uther! Long live our king!" Then followed such a tumult as no words can express.

Arthur, to give a convincing proof of his right, thrust the sword back into the anvil, and a throng of the infuriated knights rushed upon it, and tried to drag it from the stone; but Viviane threw up her snowy arms, and, in a moment the sky was overcast with black clouds, and the air was darkened as though the sun had suddenly vanished from the heavens. A loud roar of thunder burst on the ear, and then a red bolt crashed down from the sky, and shivered stone and anvil to atoms. The sword was gone!

The astounded nobles fell back; while the mob, with quarter-staves, broke through the line of men-at-arms, shouting wildly, "The sword—the token—the Excalibur!"

Then Clarience, King of Northumberland, who thought to have been king, held up his warder, and shouted, in a stern voice, "Stand back, ye churls! This youth is not your king! The sword has disappeared—snatched by some higher power from the grasp of yon juggling wizard, Merlin Wylt, who deserves no other grace than a short shrift and the stake and tar-barrel!" "A witch!—to the flames with him!" roared the nobles. "Where is the Excalibur?"

Merlin laughed, Viviane waved her hand, the nobles murmured, and the mob shouted again.

"It is sorcery!" cried King Clarience of Northumberland. "Down with the warlock Merlin!"

While the common people clamoured for the king's rescue, the disaffected barons would have charged upon them with drawn swords, had not Merlin, raising his wand, stayed their advance. Each man seemed turned to marble; yet the poorer sort heeded naught of the wonder! they only watched Arthur.

Then the king's friends interposed, and the refractory barons were glad enough to yield when they found how strongly the tide was turned against them; for still the populace, fascinated by the regal Arthur, rent the air with shouts of "Mercy, Arthur! Our king! Our king!"

Then Clarience walked up to the hero of the hour, and said, with a covert sneer, "My young, but noble liege, accept my homage. If I dare speak bluntly, that could I have my will, I would that the great Pendragon of England had been approved by other and higher tests than this; but as it is, I yield you my allegiance." Arthur stretched out his hand, but Merlin, with a dark frown, stepped between them.

"Touch him not," he whispered. "Better an open foe than a pretended friend."

With this he drew Arthur away.

Most of the hostile nobility, seeing that the people were determined to elect the youth for their sovereign, offered no further resistance to the popular will; but a few retired from the scene vowing that Merlin was a wizard, and deserved to be sent to the stake, and that Arthur was an impostor.

CHAPTER IX.

Coronation feast at Caer-Leon—Arthur's presents to the nobles—The refusal of the presents by some—Six kings concert to destroy Arthur—Sir Launcelot of the Lake and the disaffected nobles—Merlin warns the nobles of their overthrow—Arthur meets the nobles.

KING ARTHUR determined, in thankfulness, to hold a grand festival at Caer Leon-on-Usk. Ambassadors were sent into all the subject lands, and the kings and chief persons, both clerical and lay, were invited; and so great was the concourse that it was impossible to ascertain the

numbers.   Here Arthur was again crowned by
the three archbishops, and St. Dubricius sang
the service.   Then were great banquets given,
and processions of bards, and games for the
display of knightly skill, throwing the pike, and
casting of heavy stones; and hounds, and hawk-
ing, and dice; and these amusements were carried on for three days.

And at the coronation at Caer Leon the lords
and commons swore allegiance to King Arthur;
and many complaints were made unto him of
great wrongs that had been done since the
death of Uther, and of many estates that had
been wrested from many lords and knights.

Arthur then installed Sir Kaye seneschal of
England; Sir Bawdewine, constable; Sir Ulfius,
chamberlain; and Sir Brastius, warder of the
marches.

Those knights and barons who had so long
delayed him from the crown met together, and
also came up to the coronation feast at Caer
Leon, as if to do homage to the sovereign; and
there they drank and ate such thnigs as were
set before them at the royal banquet.

Arthur was   glad of so   many kings and
knights coming, supposing they had come with
 friendly intentions.   He therefore sent them
messages of welcome;   but his heralds were
roughly received by the conferated princes
and nobles, amongst whom were six kings of
great renown and might, who raged against
King Arthur and determined to destroy him,
and these were King Lot of Lothian and the
Orkneys with five hundred knights;   King
Urience of Gore, with four hundred knights;

King Nentres of Garlock, with seven hundred knights; King Caradoc, with five hundred knights; King Owin, with six hundred knights; and King Aguisant, with five hundred knights. Their leader was King Urience of Gore, the husband of Morgan la Fay, a chieftain of stalwart form, and savage demeanour.

The knight whom King Arthur had selected as his ambassador was the noble and courteous Sir Launcelot of the lake. Upon his repeating the king's message, and offering the presents, Urience turned upon him with a scowl.

"What carpet knight is this," he growled, " that thinks it no scorn to bring men to worship the paltry gifts of a beardless boy of low blood? Back, sir, and tell your puppet king and master that we spurn him and his gifts; and, by the rood! you can tell him also that we are come to give him gifts in the shape of blows with hard swords, betwixt the head and shoulders. What say you, my lords?" he added, as he turned to the assembled barons as if for confirmation.

"It is well said," rejoined Lot of Lothian and the Orkneys. "For it is foul shame to us that such a boy should rule so noble a realm."

"Sir king, you know not Arthur," replied Launcelot. "For his youth, that is a fault which time will amend; but for his blood, it is royal, he being descended from the Pen-dragons of England!"

"Are you advised of that?" sneered Nentres of Garlock, another of the chiefs. "Upon whose warrant can you vouch for the truth of what we are unable as well as unwilling to believe?"

"Upon mine!" cried a loud voice, and a venerable man suddenly appeared in the midst of them.

"It is Merlin!" shouted the astonished nobles.

"Whence comest thou, wizard?" asked Urience.

"From the king?" returned the enchanter.

What king, may't please ye? We know of none since Uther's death!" retorted Urience.

"From Arthur, the Pendragon," answered Merlin, "son of Uther, and your rightful sovereign."

"What proof can you give of that?" asked Urience. "If more be needed, I have proof enough," replied the enchanter. But methinks the miracle of the sword and stone is sufficient."

"We hold that lightly," rejoined Nentres of Garlock. "It may be some trick of witchcraft."

"Yes," returned the others; "we must have better testimony. Tell us of what cause this boy is chosen king?"

"Sirs, hear me patiently, and I will tell you," replied Merlin. "He is King Uther Pendragon's son, born in wedlock of Igerna, the wife of the Duke of Tintagel. The duke was slain in battle, and thirteen days after his death, King Uther wedded Igerna; and king shall young Arthur be, and vanquish all his rebel peers at home and his foreign enemies."

"Can this be true?" asked Lot. "What think you of it, Lords?"

"It is a lie, as false as he who speaks it!" returned Urience. "By my halidame! it moves me to wrath that any here should be so weak as for one moment to be cheated by a falsehood so palpable. What, then! must we put our necks under the heel of an urchin unknown to us? Enough! I know your minds, and, as your chosen leader, I speak for one and all. Go, Sir Launcelot ; return to him that sent you— we send him scornful defiance! Bid him man his walls in Caer Leon, for we intend to lay siege upon the place, to whip your schoolboy-king, and lay his town in ashes !"

"A knightly message, worthy of the sender," replied Sir Launcelot. "Break we off the parley, and Heaven defend the right !"

"Tarry a moment, herald !" said Nentres of Garlock. "Let us see this king, whether he resemble Uther Pendragon or no. Let us have speech of him."

"It shall not be !" cried Urience. "This wizard may throw some spell upon the youth that may beguile us to our ruin !"

But this objection was overruled by the majority, who shouted, "Let us behold your mighty Pendragon !"

"You shall have your will," said Merlin, "if you will swear that he shall be safe to come and go."

"It is agreed," returned Lot of Lothian. "He shall have no hurt."

And so they parted, Launcelot, Merlin, and their retinue turning their horses to the city, the revolted nobles retiring to their camp.

Merlin went to King Arthur, and told him all that had passed, and bade him ride out boldly and speak in such a manner as became their king.

"You shall overthrow their forces," he added, "and bend the proudest to your will."

Then King Arthur rode forth attended by

his knights, squires, yeomen, archers, and men-at-arms; behind the king was borne the mighty gonfalon, on which was depicted the standard of Great Britain.

The king wore his dragon helmet, encircled with the ancient Cymric crown, and under his emblazoned tabard a jesseraunt of double mail; and there went with him the archbishop of Canterbury, and Sir Bawdewine of Britain, and Sir Kaye, and Sir Launcelot, with other chieftains.

"And when they were met," says the ancient chronicle, "there was no meekness, but stout words on both sides; but Arthur said he would make them bow if he lived, wherefore they departed in wrath." So the king returned to the city, and prepared himself for battle. Merlin, however, made one last attempt to bring the rebellious lords to reason, but without avail.

"What will ye do?" he said to the kings. "You were better to submit, for ye shall not here prevail were ye ten times so many!"

"Begone!" cried Urience, "we are not to be defied by a milk-faced boy!"

With that Merlin vanished.

CHAPTER X.

King Arthur goes with Merlin to seek the sword—The Lady of the Lake appears and gives him the sword—The virtues of the sword and scabbard—Arthur's first battle against the six kings—The valour of Arthur—His horse killed under him, and himself struck down—Arthur is rescued by Sir Launcelot of the Lake—Arthur's victory—Rejoicing at Caer Leon.

WHEN Merlin again came into the presence of King Arthur, the king said, "I have now need of a sword that will chastise these rebels terribly."

"Come with me," said Merlin, "for hard by there is a sword that I can gain for thee."

So they rode out till they came to a broad lake, and in the midst of it King Arthur saw an arm thrust up, holding a sword in the hand.

"Lo! yonder is the sword I spoke of," said Merlin.

Then saw they a damsel floating on the lake, in the moonlight.

"What damsel is that?" asked the king.

"The Lady of the Lake," said Merlin; "for upon this lake there is a rock, and on the rock a palace where she abideth, and she will come towards thee presently, and then speak fair to her that she will give thee that sword."

"Sir king," said the damsel of the Lake, "that sword is mine, and if you will give me a gift when I ask it of you, ye shall have it."

"By my faith," said Arthur, " I will give you any gift that you shall ask or desire."

"Well, go into yonder barge," said the damsel, "and row yourself unto the sword, and take it, together with the scabbard, and I will ask my gift of thee when I see my time."

So King Arthur and Merlin went into the barge, and rowed to the sword. And King Arthur took it and bore it away, and the hand went down under the water. Then Arthur and Merlin returned to Caer Leon. As King Arthur journeyed, he looked upon the sword and liked it passing well.

" Which liketh you best," said Merlin, " the sword or the scabbard ?"

" Me liketh best the sword," said Arthur.

"Ye are unwise," said Merlin, "for the

scabbard is worth more than the sword, for while ye have the scabbard upon you, ye shall lose no blood, be ye ever so sore wounded; therefore keep the scabbard always with you."

When they arrived at Caer Leon, the knights were glad to see Arthur return all safe. On the morrow Merlin bade Arthur set fiercely on the enemy. And in the mean time three hundred knights and fighting men went over to King Arthur from the rebels' side.

"To arms, my liege!" cried Merlin. "Ride forth and conquer! but fight not with the sword that ye had by miracle until you find yourself sore beset, then draw it and do your best!"

Arthur girded on the wondrous falchion and mounting a milk-white charger, sallied forth and promised to obey Merlin's injunction.

When the king's army was drawn out in array against the mighty forces of the rebels, many a knight looked anxious; but Merlin, seizing his harp, chaunted a martial lay that breathed into their breasts hope and confidence by its high promises of victory, while the fearless demeanour of their boy-king aroused the most experienced warriors to enthusiasm. Silence pervaded the field for a moment, and then King Arthur rode along the line, his beaver up displaying his heroic countenance to his troops, followed by Sir Ector, Sir Kaye, Sir Launcelot, and the flower of his nobility. As he rode, he addressed the men with eloquence, and was greeted with shouts of acclaim.

Anon he galloped to the front, and shouted, " Banners, advance! St. George for England!"

To this King Urience retorted with a cry of "Strike now! Forward—forward!"

Then the two hostscharged furiously, while
the archers and cross-bowmen darkened the air
with their flights of arrows.

Sir Bawdewine, Sir Kaye, and Sir Launcelot
struck down all opponents right and left; while
King Arthur, in the very centre of the van
performed such prodigies of valour, as to raise
the admiration of the opposing kings.

It was a desperate struggle, but Arthur,
throwing himself into the hottest vortex of the
fight unhorsed many a gallant rider and drove
back whole companies of knights He was nobly
supported by the brave knights. King Lot
charged in the rear of King Arthur's army, and
King Caradoc set fiercely on Arthur in front:
but the gallant prince hewed down all who
opposed him on either hand, until his horse was
slain, and he was thrown to the ground, where
he lay half-stunned by the fall, while King
Urience, striding over him, pressed the point of
his sword to his throat, and called upon him
to yield or die.

Then Sir Launcelot, with three other knights,
rushed to the king's rescue, and beat off his
assailant.

King Arthur now mounted another horse, and
drew his good sword, Excalibur. Then putting
himself at the head of a gallant company of
knights who had rallied round him, he made a
furious onset, and drove the foe back with great
slaughter; and the common people of Caer-
leon at the same time joined in the fray, and
with their clubs and staves slew many knights.
Then Merlin came to Arthur, and counselled
him to stay the pursuit. The victorious young

king took this advice, and commanded that the trumpets should sound the retreat. After the victory there was great rejoicing in Caer-Leon, where the king held high feast and festival, and where his faithful knights exhibited their skill and prowess in a splendid tournament.

CHAPTER XI.

Merlin informs King Arthur that the defeated kings were joined by five other kings, and the war would be renewed—Merlin counsels Arthur to send across the sea for King Ban and King Bors to come to aid him—Sir Ulfius and Sir Brastius embark at Dover for Calais—They reconnoitre a band of Frankish warriors in a forest—They follow the troop which joins King Claudas of Germany and his knights—The Envoy escapes to a wood unobserved.

SHORTLY afterwards the King repaired to London, and called his barons to council. Merlin told the King that the six princes were by no means conquered, and would soon be prepared to renew the war. Arthur consulted the peers in council, who could not but admit that the situation was perilous; for the six allied kings could bring a large army into the field; but the valiant knights swore to stand by their King, and declared themselves hopeful of success.

"Ye say well, my lords," said Arthur. "From my heart I thank you for your good courage, but let us speak with Merlin. You know well he hath done much for me, and knoweth many things; and when he is before us I would that you pray him heartily for his advice."

Merlin was at once sent for, and "fair desired" of the whole conclave for his counsel.

"My lords," said Merlin, "I warn you all

that your enemies are passing strong for you; and there are no better men-at-arms. By this time they have joined unto themselves five other great kings. You are staunch, fearless, and resolute; but it is useless to strive against a multitude, and unless our king had with him more chivalry than he can muster within the loyal provinces of this distracted realm, he would be overcome and slain."

"What is it the best now to be done?" inquired the barons.

"I will tell you," said Merlin, "and you will do well to take my advice. There are two brethren beyond the sea, valiant warriors—the one is King Ban of Benwicke, and the other King Bors of Gaul. Against these two kings warreth Claudas of Germany, who putteth these two kings to the worst. Let our sovereign liege, and you my lords, the peers of England, send trusty messengers to the two kings, with letters well advised, and if they will come to King Arthur and so help him in his wars, we, on our part, will be sworn to help them in their war against Claudas."

"It is well counselled," said the king, and so said the barons.

Now the six kings began to prepare for a new war, and joined to themselves five other powerful kings, who swore together, that, whether for weal or woe, they would keep steadfast alliance till they had destroyed King Arthur.

Then King Arthur sent over the sea Ulfius and Brastius, and with them rode a young knight named Sir Lionel, and they were attended by a large company of men-at-arms.

These warriors went to ask aid of King Ban of Benwicke and King Bors of Gaul in the wars, on a promise to help them in return against Claudas, their foe.   They reached Dover without adventure, and there embarked in the ship that was to convey them to France.

They, landing at Calais, were received with enthusiasm by the populace, and after remaining for a day's rest and refreshment, rode on towards the city of Benwicke.

As they passed over a wood-clad mound they distinguished the distant clatter and jingle of horsemen on the march.   They knew that if they were soldiers, they must conceal themselves.   They were not long hidden, before the deep voices of men blended in a monotonous chorus. The tune beingplaintive, and mellowed by the distance, was not a little solemn.

" Tis the chaunt of the Frankish warriors," said Sir Ulfius.

" Certes," replied Sir Brastius, " their voices sweep through the wood like the chaunt of heroes of ancient days.   There is grandeur in this harmony. Go, Sir Lionel, and reconnoitre."

Sir Lionel instantly sprang from his saddle, and creeping to the verge of the little island, looked across the twinkling waters. A splendid body of stalwart knights and soldiers passed, chaunting a triumphal hymn, while among them rode the bards and troubadours, leading off the concert with their high-sounding harps.

When the sound of their voices was fast dying away, Lionel, clambering the bank, looked after them for a moment, and then rejoined his companions on the island.

"What tidings, Sir Lionel?" asked Sir Brastius. "Who and what are those knights?"

"Franks, if I mistake not," replied Sir Lionel, "and partisans of King Bors of Gaul; but they rode with banners furled."

"Ride we on," said Sir Ulfius, "but let us proceed with caution. If they prove enemies they are too many for us."

Leaping their horses on to the opposite bank, they took a route through the forest with which Sir Ulfius was acquainted—he having resided for some time in that part of the country—and spurred on to have a further view of the stranger knights and their followers. To this end they hurried on at a rapid trot. At last they reached the highway. It curved in the direction of a straggling hamlet. The village presented a stirring spectacle, being thronged by soldiers, with their standards and baggage-wains. The troop which the English knights had seen in the forest had joined their comrades, who received them with a cheer.

Conspicuous amongst them was a stern-faced warrior of haughty bearing. He wore upon his head a helmet, encircled by a royal crown, blazing with jewels. His gorget, arm-pieces, and gauntlets, were of the finest steel, curiously inlaid with gold, and his hauberk, or shirt of mail, sparkled with dazzling radiance. He wore a loose surcoat, or cassock, of cloth of gold. Upon the breast was emblazoned an imperial eagle sable, on a field, or, membered and beaked gules, holding a naked sword and sceptre in his left. His knees and legs were protected by hose of mail, and his shoes were of steel; a strong poniard hung by his right side; a splendid baldric hung upon his left shoulder, supporting his huge double-handed sword; and in his right hand he swayed a ponderous battle-axe, as though it was a hazel switch.

With a slight inclination of his head, the monarch—for such his dress and bearing proclaimed him, acknowledged the salute, and entered the house, followed by his retinue of knights, squires, and pages.

"By the Cross of St. George!" whispered Sir Ulfius to his companions, "we have happened upon a den of lions. See, yonder flaunts the gonfanon of Germany, and the leader we have just seen is King Claudas himself."

"Let us retire with speed," returned Sir Brastius, "ere our dress and the crests we bear provoke remark. If we are taken we shall not be liberated without paying heavy ransom."

With this he rode back into the forest, the rest followed his sensible example.

They spurred fast through the wood, and did not draw rein till they had placed a full league between themselves and danger, about noon halted on the banks of a broad, fair river.

CHAPTER XII.

Sir Ulfius and Sir Brastius encounter German knights, and defeat them—They afterwards fall in with Sir Pharience and Sir Lionese, partizans of King Claudas—Their courteous greeting—The English knights' interview with King Ban and King Bors—Their promise of assistance to Arthur—Sir Ulfius and Sir Brastius recross the sea to Britain—Festivals at Caer-Leon-on-Usk.

THE three knights and their followers dismounted, and seated themselves in a meadow by the water side. Their attendants spread a repast for their masters, who regaled themselves with the zest of a keen appetite after their long ride.

The meal concluded, they listened with enjoyment to the carol of the larks. But they were not permitted long to remain undisturbed, for two of their men who had been picketed in the wood came galloping up in hot haste.

"To horse!" they shouted. "A company of men-at-arms are approaching; but whether friends or foes we know not."

In an instant, Sir Ulfius and Sir Brastius, with young Sir Lionel, sprang to their arms.

"Whoever they be," said Sir Ulfius, "we will ride boldly forward and meet them."

They remounted their horses, and grasping their lances, rode on. They shortly encountered a retinue of troopers finely mounted. Their leader was a fierce-looking chieftain, riding a black charger. As he advanced, he shouted, "Stand ho! and declare yourselves who you are, and whence you come!"

"Sir knight, we are strangers in this land, having crossed the seas on an envoy from King Arthur, whose liegemen we be," answered Sir Ulfius, with stately courtesy.

"And your errand one of peace or war?" asked the chief.

"Our mission is one of peace," replied Sir Ulfius. "We bring letters of greeting and presents to King Ban of Benwicke and King Bors of Gaul, with whom King Arthur desires to form an alliance. We therefore pray you, suffer us to proceed."

"It may not be, sir knight," returned the

527 E

chief. "We are the liegeman of King Claudas of Germany, with whom the kings you name are at war, and those who avow themselves the friends of these two kings are, by consequence, the enemies of our royal master. Sirs, ye are my prisoners, and must yield up your arms."

"By St. George! we shall do no such thing!" replied Sir Ulfius. "We are ready to break a lance with you in this cause."

"Be it so," returned the hostile knight "Take your ground, and do your best."

The Englishmen answered with a cheer, and riding back to a distance sufficiently great to give impetus to the charge, couched their spears and prepared for the onset.

Sir Ulfius selected the commander of the German knights for his antagonist, while Sir Brastius and Sir Lionel picked out two others whose bearing betokened them as being second in rank to the leader. Then the trumpeters blew a blast as a signal for the assault, and the two lines started at full gallop, and dashed furiously against each other. The lance-point of Sir Ulfius struck against the shield of his adversary, while that of the German knight swerved aside, and, coming in contact with the other's breast-plate, shivered it to pieces. The German knight was borne from the saddle, and rolled on the ground. Sir Brastius and Sir Lionel were both successful, for each unhorsed his man; the rest of the English party were not so fortunate, three or four of them being borne down to five or six of the Germans. Wheeling round their horses, and measuring their distance, the three principal knights of the English party dashed on to the charge, and met with signal success; only Sir Lionel brought off his lance undamaged, the weapons of his two companions being shattered. Then followed a furious hand to hand conflict, with swords and battle-axes. The English had a hard fight of it, for the Germans outnumbered them two to one, and contended with bravery; but were at length repulsed, and fled the field. The loss on the English part was very sericus, for more than a third of their number were slain, while of the remaining scarce one escaped unwounded. The three knights had each received hurts, and Sir Brastius had two horses killed under him before the enemy give way. Sir Lionel would have pursued the foe, but Sir Brastius objected.

"Enough has been done, Sir Lionel," he said; "we are few in numbers; and, until we have performed the king's errand there is neither wisdom nor honour in risking life or liberty."

Sir Ulfius consented to forego further fighting, and Sir Lionel, out of respect to his elders, gave up the point. The adventure was scarcely when over, the sound of trumpets greeted their ears, a group of spears were seen in the valley.

"By my halidame! the tide of fortune has set against us," said Sir Ulfius. "Whom have we here? We are scarce breathed from one passage of arms when we are called upon to engage in another battle, and that with a force too strong for us."

"Better fortune, Sir Ulfius," returned Sir Brastius. "See, they march under the golden lilies of France, and I make no doubt are liegemen of the two kings whom we are seeking."

The advance-guard approached, and at its head rode two knights in resplendent armour.

These were Sir Pharience and Sir Lionese, and proved to be partizans of King Ban of Benwicke. They halted, and saluted the English cavalry, who, when told how they had been sent by King Arthur, and on what business, were welcomed by the Franks. They were invited to accompany their new acquaintances to the Court of Benwicke. Sir Ulfius and the other knights consented to the arrangement. The wounded having been cared for, Sir Brastius was provided with another horse, and the cavalcade started on the march, with banners flying.

"You come at a happy time," said Pharience. "King Claudas hath just fought a stubborn battle with King Ban."

"To whom has the victory fallen?" asked Ulfius.

"It was claimed by both sides, and the advantage was small for us or the enemy. King Claudas has raised the siege of Benwicke, and is retreating to his own frontier, where he will be joined by reinforcements. The kings will send to your king what powers they can spare, and when he has crushed his rebel barons, he will not fail to return our service. With the chivalry of England at our side we shall have no fear of the tyrant Claudas."

And so they rode on to Benwicke.

Here they found kings Ban and Bors, and when they told the kings they were messengers from King Arthur of England, the kings took Sir Ulfius and Sir Brastius in their arms, and made great joy each of the other; and they welcomed them cordially, and said they were more welcome to them than any knights living; and therewith they kissed the letters, and delivered them into the hands of King Ban. And when King Ban and King Bors understood the letters they said they would fulfil the desire of King Arthur. And Ulfius and Brastius tarried as long as they would, and had as good cheer as might be bade them in those long marches, and had their answer by mouth and by writing, "that those two kings would come to King Arthur in all the haste that they might."

So the English knights crossed the sea, and came to their lord, and told him how they had sped, whereof King Arthur was glad.

"At what time think ye the knights will be here?" asked Arthur.

"Sir," said they, "before Allhallowmas."

Then the king prepared for a feast and grand joust, as peace prevailed for a time, for the rebel barons were preparing to carry on the war with redoubled vigour; while the king was obliged to await the arrival of the kings from France before he recommenced hostilities.

During the interval, King Arthur and his knights passed their time merrily.

CHAPTER XIII.

Arrival of King Ban and King Bors with three hundred knights—Merlin goes across the sea to fetch ten thousand horsemen—The tournament at Caer Leon between the English and the French knights—The return of Merlin—Merlin's counsel as to the disposal of the army—King Arthur's first great conquest—King Ban and King Bors return to their own country—Merlin goes to Bishop Blaise to recount the battle, and returns disguised to King Arthur—News of war between the King of North Wales and King Leodegrance.

Now when Allhallowmas had come, the two kings

with three hundred knights had crossed the sea, leaving behind them a great army on the other side of the sea to follow as arrangements might be made. King Arthur met them ten miles from London, and there was joy at the meeting. He then called Merlin to ask his advice as to the disposal of the troops; and Merlin agreed to go across the sea to fetch the army. He departed, and next day brought over ten thousand horsemen and led them to the forest of Bedgraine, and there he lodged them. In the meantime the three kings journeyed to Caer-Leon-on-Usk, and there at the feast the three kings sat in the hall, and Sir Kaye the seneschal, and Sir Lucas the butler, son of Duke Corneus, and Sir Griflet, son of Cordol, had the rule of all the services that served the king. King Arthur and the two kings let depart seven hundred knights. Those of Benwicke and Gaul on one side, and those of Britain on the other.

Then these seven hundred knights prepared for the joust; King Arthur, King Ban, and King Bors, with the Archbishop of Canterbury and Sir Ector, were in a tent carpeted with cloth of gold, and there was present a vast concourse of ladies to behold who did best, and give judgment.

Sir Griflet was the first that met with a knight called Ladinas, and they met so desperately that their shields went to pieces, and horses and men fell to the earth, and they lay so long that all men weened they were dead. Then Lucas went to Griflet, and horsed him again, and his opponent being remounted, they did marvellous deeds of arms. Then Sir Kaye came out with five knights, and met Sir Grastian and five other knights of France. And Sir Kaye and his knights did many valiant deeds on that day, and overthrew the French knights.

Then came there Sir Placidas, and attacked Sir Kaye, and smote him down, wherewith Sir Griflet was wroth, and met Sir Placidas with such a shock that horse and man fell to the earth.

When the five knights saw that Sir Kaye had a fall, they were wroth, and each bore down a knight.

When King Arthur and the two kings saw them wroth and furious, the trumpet was sounded to stay the jousting, and the knights departed unarmed, and all went into the feast. The three kings afterwards went into the garden, and gave the prizes to Sir Kaye, Sir Lucas, and to Sir Griflet, and then they went to counsel, and thither went Sir Ulfius and Sir Brastius.

Then came Merlin unto King Arthur, and told how he had sped, and the king marvelled that any man could go and come so soon. So Merlin told him that ten thousand men were in the forest of Bedgraine, well armed.

King Arthur ordered his knights to prepare for the battle, and with twenty thousand men he passed through the country. Then the three kings came to the forest of Bedgraine and found there good fellowship.

Then, by the counsel of Merlin, who knew which way the eleven kings would ride and sleep, King Arthur and his two allies made ready with their army for the fight, having of thirty thousand men.

"Now shall ye do by my advice!" cried Merlin. "King Ban and King Bors, with ten thousand men, shall lie in ambush in this wood, and shall not stir until this battle has waged long; and thou, King Arthur, at daybreak, shall lead forth the army before the enemy, and so array thy warriors that they may be seen all at once by the enemy, who, when they view the smallness of the number, will be rash."

To this the three kings assented, and in the morning when the army of the north saw so few against them they were cheered. Then King Arthur commanded Sir Ulfius and Sir Brastius to take three thousand men to open the battle. The command was obeyed, and they set furiously on the enemy with great slaughter. When the eleven kings saw the mighty deeds performed by so small a band, they were ashamed and charged fiercely in return. Then was Sir Ulfius's horse slain under him, but he fought valiantly on foot against Duke Eustace and King Clarience, who both set on him with vengeance, till Sir Brastius rode towards them, and so smote the duke through with his spear that horse and rider fell together, whereat King Clarience attacked Sir Brastius, and rushing together each unhorsed the other.

Then came Sir Kaye with six knights and did wondrous execution until the other ten knights went against them and overthrew Sir Griflet and Sir Lucas. And when Sir Kaye saw Sir Griflet fighting on foot, he charged King Nanters and smote him down, and with the same spear did Sir Kaye so smite down King Lot, and wound him. On seeing this, the King of the Hundred Knights rushed at Sir Kaye, and overthrew him

in return, and helped King Lot to a horse.
when Sir Griflet saw Sir Kaye's mishap, riding
at a mighty warrior, he cast him to the earth,
and catching his horse, led it to Sir Kaye.

The battle now raged furiously on both sides,
and Sir Ulfius and Sir Brastius, being on foot,
were in danger of their lives.

Then King Arthur rushed into the midst of
the fight, and singling out King Cradlemont of
North Wales, smote him through the body and
overthrew him, and taking his horse brought it
to Sir Ulfius, and said, " Take this horse, and
charge beside of me." And as he was speaking
he saw Sir Ector smitten to the ground by the
King of the Hundred Knights, and his horse
was taken to King Cradlemont.

When King Arthur saw the fury of the enemy, he drove his horse here and there, and staid
not until he had slain twenty knights, and
wounded King Lot so sore that he retired, and
cried out to the other kings, " do as-I advise,
or we shall be all destroyed. Let me, with the
King of the Hundred Knights, King Anguis-
sant, King Owen, and King Caradoc, and the
Duke of Cambinet, take fifteen thousand men,
and make a circuit, while ye kings hold the battle with twelve thousand ; then will we come
behind and come upon King Arthur and his
knights and put them to the rout, or else shall
we never stand against them."

Then King Lot and the four other kings departed with their troops, and the six other kings
dressed their ranks against King Arthur, and
fought long and stoutly. Now, with their army
fresh, King Ban and King Bors broke from

ambush, and met the five kings and their host as they came behind, and then began a dreadful conflict.

At length King Lot espied King Bors, and cried, "Our Lady now defend us; our perils grow great, for yonder cometh one of the worshipfullest knights in all the world."

"Who is he?" said the King of the Hundred Knights.

"It is King Bors of Gaul," replied King Lot; "and I marvel how he may have come with his host into this land without our knowledge."

"Ah!" cried Caradoc, "I will encounter this king if ye will rescue me when there is need."

"Ride on," said King Lot.

So King Caradoc and his host rode within bow-shot of King Bors, and then both hosts rushed at each other. On the onset King Bors encountered a knight, and struck him through with a spear; drawing his sword, he did such mighty work, that all who saw gazed with wonder. Then came King Ban upon the field with his knights, and did great havoc on the enemy, till both hosts of the eleven kings began to quake, King Urience and his confederates prepared to meet the worst, while a multitude fled the field. King Lot said, "Lords, we must take other means. See ye not what people we have lost in waiting on the footmen, it has cost ten horsemen to save one of them? Let us put away our foot-soldiers for it is almost night, and King Arthur will not stay to slaughter them, and they can save their lives in the wood. Then let us gather into one band all the horsemen that remain and swear we will not fail each other."

"It is well advised," said they all.

They took possession of new spears, setting them against their thighs, stood so compact that no assault could shake them.

When King Arthur saw them he marvelled and was wroth. "Yet," he exclaimed, "I may not blame them, for they act as brave men ought to act, and are the best fighting men, that I ever saw or heard tell of:" and King Ban and King Bors likewise praised them for their noble chivalry.

Anon came forty knights out of King Arthur's host and prayed they might be suffered to break the enemy, and their wish being granted, they rode forth with their spears on their thighs.

Then the eleven kings, with their knights, rushed to meet them, and when they met, all the crash of their spears and armour rang with a mighty din, and so fierce was the encounter that nearly every knight bled. At this moment King Arthur rode into the thickest of the struggle with King Ban and King Bors, and did such slaughter on both hands, until the horses went to their fetlocks in blood.

When the contest was at its greatest, Merlin came through the battle on a black horse, and riding to King Arthur, he cried, "Alas, my lord! will ye have never done? Of sixty thousand have ye left but fifteen thousand men alive. Is it not time to stay this slaying?—for God is ill pleased with ye that ye have never ended, and yonder kings shall not be overthrown this time. Withdraw, and take thy rest, for to-day thou hast gained a great victory, and now for many years those kings shall not disturb thee. Therefore, I fear them no more, for they are beaten, and have nothing left them but their honour, and thou shouldst not stay them to take that."

Then said King Arthur, "Thou sayest well, and I will take thy counsel." And gathering all the spoil, he gave it not among his hosts, but to King Ban and King Bors and all their knights, that he might treat them with courtesy as strangers. Then Merlin took his leave of King Arthur and of the two kings to go and see his master, Bishop Blaise, who dwelt in Northumberland; and when he arrived there, the Bishop was glad to see him. Merlin then told him how King Arthur and the two kings had sped at the great battle, and how it was ended. Bishop Blaise wrote an account of the battle, and Merlin told him how it began and ended. After that Merlin departed and came to King Arthur, who was in the castle of Bedgraine, in the forest of Sherwood. And Merlin was so disguised that King Arthur knew him not, for he was all furred in sheepskins and a great pair of boots, with a bow and arrows, and brought with him wild geese, and it was the morrow after Candlemas.

"Sir," said Merlin, "give me a gift?"

"Wherefore," said King Arthur, "should I give thee a gift, thou churl?"

"Sir," replied Merlin, "ye had better give me a gift than to lose riches; for here, where was the great battle, is great treasure hid in the earth."

"Who told thee so, churl?" said King Arthur.

" Merlin told me so," said he.

Then Sir Ulfius and Sir Brastius, who were there, knew Merlin, and said to King Arthur, " Sir, it is Merlin that speaketh so unto you."

Then King Arthur was abashed that he knew not Merlin, and they had sport at him. Then there came word that Rience, King of North Wales, made war against King Leodegrance of Camelford, for which King Arthur was wroth, for he loved King Leodegrance and hated Rience.

CHAPTER XIV.

King Arthur, with King Ban and King Bors, defeat King Rience of North Wales—King Ban and King Bors return to their own land—The trouble that befel the eleven kings—King Lot's wife and her four sons visit King Arthur at Caer Leon—King Arthur's dream—His pursuit of the white beast—Merlin appears to King Arthur in the shape of a child, and afterwards as an old man, and foretells many things—King Arthur returns to Caer Leon, and sends for queen Igerna—Sir Ulfius impeaches the Queen—Sir Griflet jousts with the Knight of the Fountain.

So King Arthur, with Kings Ban and Bors with their troops, twenty thousand, journeyed to Camelford to the assistance of King Leodegrance, and encountered King Rience's men, of whom ten thousand were slain, and the remainder took to flight.

Then King Leodegrance and the three kings had great cheer, and King Leodegrance thanked them for their help in revenging him on his enemy. It was at that time that King Arthur first saw Guenevere, the daughter of King Leodegrance, and from thence loved her, and afterwards was wedded to her.

Then King Ban and King Bors took their

leave of King Arthur to depart into their own country, where King Claudas worked great mischief and destruction on their lands. King Arthur would have gone with them, but they refused his offer, saying, "Nay, ye shall not at this time, for ye have much to do in these lands of your own, therefore we will depart, and with the riches we have gotten in these lands we shall withstand the malice of King Claudas; but if we have need, we will send to you for succour; and if ye have need, send for us, and we will hasten to you."

"It shall not need," said Merlin, "that these two kings come again in the way of war, but I know well that King Arthur may not be long from you, for ere twelve months be passed ye shall have need of him, and then he shall revenge you on your enemies as ye have revenged him on his, for these eleven kings shall all die in one day by the great prowess of two valiant knights, Ben Balin la Savage and Balan his brother."

We now return to the eleven kings. After their defeat, they went to Sorhante, which city was within King Urience's land. And there came a messenger and told them there were coming into their lands hordes of lawless people as well as Saracens, who had burnt their towns and slain their people.

"Alas!" cried the eleven kings, "here is sorrow on sorrow, and if we had not warred against King Arthur, he would have revenged us; and as for King Leodegrance, he loveth King Arthur more than us."

So they laid their plans for keeping the marches of Cornwall, Wales, and the North, and placed many thousand men in fortresses in those parts to guard the land; and they allied unto them many mighty kings, among whom were the renowned King Rience, of North Wales, and also Nero, a mighty man of war; and for three years they furnished all the men-at-arms with food and all manner of ordnance, to avenge the battle of Bedgraine.

After King Ban and King Bors had departed, King Arthur rode to Caer-Leon-on-Usk, and thither came to him his half-sister, Belisant, wife of King Lot of Orkney, who was sent by her husband to espy the manner of the court, under the appearance of a messenger, and with her came a noble retinue, her four sons—Gawaine, Gaharis, Agravaine, and Gareth.

But when she saw King Arthur and his nobleness, she forbore to spy on him as a foe, and told him of her husband's plots against him and his throne. And as she was a passing fair lady, King Arthur admired her for her beauty, and loved her, not knowing that she was the daughter of his mother, Igerna, and his half-sister; and he entreated her to stay at the court at Caer Leon a long season, and had born unto him a son, who was named Mordred; wherefore her husband, King Lot, was more than ever King Arthur's enemy, and hated him until death with ceaseless hatred.

At that time King Arthur had a marvellous dream which gave him great and severe pain. He dreamed that the whole land was full of fiery griffins and serpents, which slew the people everywhere, and then he thought that he fought with them, and that they did him great damage, and wounded him; but at last he slew them all. When he awoke, he sat in heaviness of spirit on account of the dream, and could not imagine what it meant; and since he could not satisfy himself as to the elucidation, a forester came to tell him of a white hart that had been seen ; and so to rid himself of his thoughts of the dream, he made ready to ride out hunting.

As soon as he was in the forest, the king saw a hart before him. "That hart will I chase," said King Arthur; and he rode after it, and continued the chase until his horse fell. Seeing the hart escape him, he fell into deep thought. After a while, he heard the noise of sixty hounds baying, and on looking up he saw coming to him the strangest beast he ever beheld, which ran towards the fountain to drink of the water. Its head was pointed, with a leopard's body, and a lion's tail, and it was footed like a stag, and the noise it made was like the baying of dogs. Having finished drinking it departed with a greater sound than ever.

The king was amazed, but being weary he fell asleep. He had not slumbered long before he was awakened by a knight, who said, "Knight, tell me if thou sawest a strange beast pass this way."

"Such a one I saw," said King Arthur, "but it is two miles distant at the least. What would you have with the beast?"

"Sir," replied the knight, "I have followed it a long time, and have killed my horse, and would to heaven I had another to follow it."

At that moment there came one with a horse belonging to the king, and as soon as the knight saw it he earnestly desired to have the horse, saying, "I have followed this quest for twelve-months, and I shall either slay the beast or bleed of the best blood of my body."

"Sir knight," said King Arthur, "leave the quest and suffer me to have it, and I will follow it other twelve months."

"Ah, fool," said the knight, "thy desire is vain, it shall never be taken but by me or by my next akin."

Therewith he started to the king's horse, and mounting cried, "Gramercy, this horse is mine."

"Well," said the king, "thou mayest take my horse by force, and I will not say nay until we prove whether thou wert better nor I."

"Then," said the knight, "seek me here when thou wilt, and here, nigh unto this well, shalt thou find me." With these words he galloped off. Then sat King Arthur in study, and bade his servant fetch him another horse.

And whilst King Arthur sat alone, Merlin came unto him disguised as a child, and asked him why he was so pensive.

"I may well be so," replied the king, "for here I saw the strangest sight I ever saw."

"That I well know," said Merlin, "but thou art foolish to take thought, for that will not amend it. I also know who thou art, and know thy father and thy mother."

"It is false," said King Arthur. "How shouldst thou know? Thy years are too few."

"Yea," said the child, "I know it better than you or any man living."

"I will not believe thee," said the king.

So Merlin departed, but came again in the likeness of a man of four score; whereof the

527　　　F

king was glad, for he seemed a righteous man. Then said the old man, "Why art thou sad?"

"I may well be sad," said the king, "I have seen strange things this day, a few moments since there came a child who told me things beyond his years to know."

"Yes," said the old man, "but he told you the truth, and more he would have told you hadst thou allowed him; but I will tell you wherefore you are sad, for thou hast done a thing of late for which God is displeased with you, and what it is thou knowest in thy heart."

"Who art thou," said King Arthur, starting up all pale, "that tellest me these things?"

"I am Merlin, and I was in the child's likeness also."

"Ah!" said the king, "thou art a right fearful man, and I would ask thee whether I may die in battle."

"Marvel not," said Merlin, "for it is God's will, but thou hast done a thing that is displeasing to God in respect to thy half-sister, and her son Mordred shall destroy you and all the knights of your realm; but I shall be put into the earth alive, and thou shalt die a worshipful death, and I will tell thee other marvellous things; and after thy death vessels shall float upon the waters of thy realm drawn by horses; and carriages shall run through its valleys, driven by fire and smoke, and the horses shall be of iron, and their snorting as that of a giant, they shall rush through the bowels of the earth with a great shriek.

And as they thus talked there came one with the king's horses, and the king mounted one and Merlin another, and they rode to Caer-Leon.

Then King Arthur said unto Merlin, "I will that my mother be sent for, that she may tell me of my birth."

The queen was sent for and she came anon, and brought with her Morgan la Fay, her daughter, who was a fair lady, and the king welcomed Igerna in the best manner.

Then came Ulfius and said to Igerna that all might hear, "Ye are the falsest lady of the world, and most traitorous to the king's person."

"Beware, Ulfius," said King Arthur, "what thou sayest, for thou speakest a great word."

"I am aware," said Sir Ulfius, "what I speak, and here is my glove to prove it on any man that sayeth to the contrary that this Queen Igerna is the cause of all your troubles, and of the war that ye have had."

Then Igerna said, "I am a woman and may not fight; but is there not some good man that will take up my quarrel. Merlin knoweth well, and you, Sir Ulfius, how King Uther came to me in the castle of Tintagel in the likeness of my lord that had been dead for three hours, and how King Uther wedded me, and how, by his command, when the child was born it was delivered to Merlin, and so I saw the child never after, and never knew his name."

Then Sir Ulfius said unto the queen, "Merlin is more to blame than you."

Then Merlin took the king by the hand, saying, "This is your mother."

Then King Arthur took his mother in his arms and kissed her ; and the king made a feast which lasted eight days. On a certain day whilst the feast lasted there came to the court a squire on horseback, leading a knight who had been wounded, and told how there was a knight in the forest who had reared a pavilion by a well side, and had slain his master; and he beseeched that his master might be buried, and that some good knight should avenge his master's death.

Then came Griflet, who was but a squire, and young in years, and besought the king to give him the order of knighthood.

"Thou art full young," said King Arthur, "to take so high an order upon thee."

"Sir," said Griflet, "make me a knight."

"My lord," said Merlin, "it were a pity to lose Griflet, for he will be a good man when he cometh of age; if he venture his life with yonder knight of the fountain he shall be in peril, for he is one of the best knights in the world."

"Notwithstanding," said King Arthur, "as Griflet desires it I will knight him."

"Vow," said the king, "since I have knighted thee, thou must promise me that when thou hast jousted thou shalt come again to me."

"I promise as you desire," replied Griflet.

Then Sir Griflet dressed his shield, and taking a spear, rode off till he came to the fountain. In the front of the pavilion stood a war horse saddled, and on a tree hung a shield of divers colours, and a great spear. Sir Griflet rode up to the shield and smote it with his spear, and the shield fell to the ground. With that came the knight out of the pavilion, and said, "Fair knight, why smote ye my shield?"

"I would joust with thee," said Sir Griflet

"It were better that ye did not," said the knight, "for ye are but young, and your might is nothing to mine; but I will dress my shield."

So they ran together, and Sir Griflet's spear was shivered, and the knight smote Sir Griflet through the shield and the left side, and the horse and rider fell. When the knight saw him on the ground, he unlaced his helmet to give him air, and having replaced him on his horse, he bade him God speed. And so Sir Griflet rode to the court, and through good leeches was healed of his wound.

CHAPTER XV.

Messengers from Lucius Tiberius come to demand from King Arthur tribute to Cæsar—Merlin pursued by three churls—The battle between the Knight of the Fountain and King Arthur—King Arthur rescued by Merlin—Spell cast over King Pellinore by Merlin—King Rience of North Wales sends and demands King Arthur's beard to complete the fringe of his mantle—A damsel girded with a sword appears in Arthur's court—Sir Balin obtains the sword—The damsel asks for the sword to be returned to her—The Lady of the Lake calls on Arthur to fulfil his promise, and demands Sir Balin's head—Sir Balin cuts off the lady's head—King Arthur displeased with Sir Balin, sends him from the court.

THEN came to King Arthur twenty knights from Rome, and demanded tribute for his realm, or the Emperor would destroy him.

"Well," said King Arthur, "I owe the Emperor no tribute, nor none will I send him; but on a fair field I will give him tribute with a sword or spear, and that within a short time, by my father's God." The messengers departed, and were wroth; and King Arthur was as wroth as they, for the King was passing angry for the hurt Sir Griflet had sustained. As the king rode forth he saw three churls chasing Merlin to slay him, so he rode after them. When the churls saw a knight riding after them, they fled.

"Oh, Merlin," said King Arthur, "here wouldst thou have been slain had I not come."

"Nay," said Merlin, "not so, for I could have saved myself ; but thou art nearer thy death than I am, for now thou goest to thy death."

And as they thus talked, they arrived at the fountain and the pavilion, and King Arthur saw sat within the pavilion a knight full armed.

"Sir knight," said King Arthur, "for what reason abideth thou here ? I prythee leave off thy custom."

"This custom," said the knight, "have I need of, and whoever is grieved with the custom let him amend it if he will."

"I will amend it," said King Arthur.

"And I will defend it," said the knight.

He took his spear, and King Arthur prepared himself for the attack. They rode toward each other, and met so hard that they shivered their spears. Therewith King Arthur drew his sword.

"Nay, not so," said the knight; "it is fairer that we again meet with sharp spears."

Then a squire brought other spears, and King Arthur took one and the knight another. So they came together and each brake his spear as before. Again King Arthur clasped his sword.

"Nay," said the knight, "ye are a passing good jouster as ever I met , and for the love of knighthood, let us joust once more."

"I agree," said King Arthur.

And two other spears were brought and they ran furiously together, and King Arthur's spear was shivered, but the knight struck him so hard in the centre of the shield that horse and man were felled to the earth. King Arthur jumped

up and said, " I will assail thee, sir knight, on
foot, for I have lost the honour on horseback."

"I will remain on horseback," said the knight.

Then was King Arthur wroth, and dressed
his shield towards him with his sword drawn.
Then the knight thought it cowardly to have
his opponent at so much advantage, so he alighted, and there began a strong battle, and they
so hewed with their swords that their helmets
and armour were cut through, and much blood
was shed, so that all the place where they fought
was bloody.   And after the battle had lasted a
long time, they rested, and renewed the combat, and hurled together until they fell to the
earth.   At length their swords met with such
force that King Arthur's flew in two pieces.
Then said the knight to King Arthur, " Thou
art in my power, and I can either save thee or
slay thee, and unless thou yield as overcome
thou shalt die."

" As for death," said the king—" to yield to
thee as a recreant knight I would rather die
than be ashamed ;" and the king leapt upon
the knight, and threw him down, and raised
his helm.   When the knight felt this, he rolled
round on King Arthur, and raising his helm,
would have smitten off his head had not Merlin
come up.

" Knight, hold thy hand," said Merlin, " for
if thou slayest that knight thou puttest the
realm into greater danger than ever realm was
in, for this knight is more worshipful than thou
thinkest."

" Why, who is he ?" said the knight.

" It is King Arthur," said Merlin.

Then would the knight have slain him and raised his sword to do so, but Merlin cast an enchantment on the knight, and he fell to the earth in a sound sleep. Then took Merlin the knight's horse, and rode toward King Arthur.

"Alas, Merlin," said King Arthur, "what hast thou done?—hast thou slain this good knight by thy craft? There lived not so worshipful a knight as he was."

"Care ye not," said Merlin, "for he is not so near dead as you are, for he is but asleep. I told you what a knight he was, and ye would have been slain had I not been there. There is not a better knight living than he is, and he shall hereafter do you good service. He is King Pellinore, and shall have sons that shall be passing good men, and, save one, they shall have no fellow of prowess and good living. The one shall be named Percival of Wales, and the other Lamorack of Wales.

Then came a messenger from Rience, saying that King Rience had overcome eleven kings, each of whom did him homage and sent him their beards clean slain, and he came to demand King Arthur's beard; for King Rience had trimmed a mantle with the king's beards, and there was one part of the mantle unfinished, and he therefore sent for his beard to complete it; and if he failed to send his beard, he would enter into his lands and slay all before him; and would not leave until he had his head as well as his beard.

"Well," said King Arthur, "thou hast said thy message, which is the most villainous and impudent that ever man heard, but thou canst tell thy master my beard is too young to trim his mantle ; that I owe him no homage, neither do mine elders, but he shall do me the homage before the year be passed, or else shall lose his head, by the faith of my body."

Then the messenger departed.

" Now is there any here," said King Arthur, " that knoweth King Rience ?"

" Yes," answered Sir Noran, "I know him well, and there are few better knights upon a field than he, and he is a proud man, and I doubt not, he will war with thee with mighty power."

" Well," said King Arthur, " I shall be ready for him, as he shall surely find."

As he thus spoke, there came into the hall a damsel with a richly-furred mantle, which she let fall and showed she was girded with a noble sword, which caused the king to marvel, and he said, " Damsel, wherefore hast thou that sword girded to thee, for it be-seemeth thee not."

" Sir," said she, " I will tell thee. This sword gives me great sorrow, for I may not be delivered from it until I have found a knight who is faithful, and pure, and true ; he must be strong of body, and without treachery ; such a man only shall be able to draw it from the scabbard. I have been at King Rience's, for it was told me there were good knights there, and he and all his knights have tried to draw it forth in vain."

" This is a great marvel," said the king. " I will try to draw the sword, not thinking that I am the best knight, but rather to encourage my barons to try after me."

Then King Arthur took the sword pulled it with all his might, but he could not move it.

"Thou needest not pull so hard, my lord, for he that shall pull it out shall do it with little might."

"Thou sayest well," said the king.

"Now try ye all my barons, but beware ye be not stained with shame, treachery, or falseness," and King Arthur mused on the sins that he had been guilty of, and which his failure brought to his mind. Then all the barons present made the attempt, but failed; and the damsel cried with sorrow,

"Alas, alas, I thought to have found in this court a knight pure and free from treachery."

"By my faith," said King Arthur, "here are as good knights as any in the land, but their grace is not to help you."

Now there was at the court a poor knight who had been prisoner on a charge of accidentally slaying a knight. He was named Balin la Savage, and had, by the intercession of the barons, been delivered from prison, for he was of gentle blood. He longed to try to draw the sword, but being shabbily dressed, he was ashamed to make the trial; so, as the damsel left the king, he said, "Damsel, I pray thee of thy courtesy to suffer me to try the sword, for though I am but poorly clad I feel assurance in my heart."

The damsel, seeing his poor garments, said, "Sir, there is no need to put me to any more labour, and it is not likely thou wilt succeed where so many worthy ones have failed."

"Ah, fair lady," answered Balin, "excellence, and brave deeds are not shown by fair raiment, but manhood and truth lie hid in the heart. There may be many worshipful knights unknown to the people."

"By my faith, thou speakest right," replied the damsel; "try, if thou wilt, what thou canst do."

So Balin grasped the handle and drew it out.

The king and the barons were surprised at Balin's success, and many envied him his fortune

"Truly," said the damsel, "this is the best man I have ever found, being free from treachery, and villany, and many wonders shall he achieve. Now, gallant knight," continued she, "give me the sword again."

"Nay," said Sir Balin, "save it be taken from me by force I shall keep this sword evermore."

"Thou art unwise," said the damsel, "to keep it from me; for if thou persisteth in doing so, thou shalt slay thy best friend with it, and it shall be thy own destruction."

"Nevertheless," said Sir Balin, "the sword I will keep, by the faith of my body."

"Thou wilt repent it," said the damsel. "I would take the sword for thy sake rather than my own, for I am grieved for thy sake, and that thou wilt not believe the peril I foretell thee."

With that she departed with much sorrow.

Then Balin sent for his horse and armour.

Meanwhile there came to the court a lady; she was the Lady of the Lake, who had given King Arthur the sword Excalibur, having saluted the king, she asked him the gift he promised her when she gave him the sword.

" In sooth," said King Arthur, " I promised thee a gift when thou shouldst desire it; ask what thou wilt, and ye shall have it, if it lie in my power to give it."

" Well," said the Lady of the Lake, " I ask the head of the knight that hath won the sword, or else the head of the damsel that brought it ; and though I may have both their heads, I should not be recompensed, for he slew my brother, and the damsel who brought the sword was the cause of my father's death."

" Verily," said King Arthur, " I may not grant you either of their heads ; therefore ask what else ye will, and I will fulfil your desire."

"I will ask none other thing of you," said the lady, and as she spake Balin came on his way to leave the court, and saw her where she stood, and knew her straightway as the murderess of his mother, whom he had sought for three years.

And when it was told him that she had asked King Arthur for his head, he went up to her and said, "May evil betide thee ! thou asked for my head, therefore shalt thou lose thine own," and he drew his sword and smote off her head.

"Alas, for shame !" cried King Arthur, "Why hast thou done this, shaming me and all my court so greatly ? I am beholden to this lady. Thy deed is passing forgiveness."

"Lord," said Sir Balin, "hear me : this lady was the falsest living, and, by her witchcraft, hath destroyed many, and caused my mother to be burnt to death by her and treachery."

"What cause soever thou mightest have had," said the king, "thou shouldst not have revenged it in our presence. Thou shalt repent this sin, for such disgrace was never yet brought upon my court. Depart now with all the haste thou mayest."

Then Balin took up the head of the lady and carried it to his lodgings, and rode from the town. Then said he to his squire, "Now must we part : take ye this head and bear it to my friends in Northumberland, and tell them how I speed, and that our worst foe is dead; also tell them I am free from prison, and of the adventure of my sword."

"Alas," said the squire, "ye are greatly to blame to have so displeased King Arthur."

"As for that," said Sir Balin, "I go to find King Rience, and destroy him or lose my life; for should I take him prisoner and lead him to the court, perchance King Arthur would forgive me."

"Where shall I meet thee again?" asked the squire.

"In King Arthur's court," replied Sir Balin.

CHAPTER XVI.

Sir Lancear seeks to kill Balin—They fight, and Sir Lancear is slain—Sir Balin meets his brother, Sir Balan, and they overcome King Rience, and take him prisoner to King Arthur—Sir Balin seeks the sorrowful knight —Sir Herleus slain by Gorlan—Adventures of Balin and the Damsel—Sir Balin searches after Gorlon, and kills him at the feast—Sir Balin wounds King Pelles with the spear of Longius—Sir Balin fights with Sir Balan, his brother, and they slay each other.

AT that time there was in King Arthur's court a knight named Lancear, who was a son of a king of Ireland, and was counted one of the best knights within the court: he was envious of Sir Balin on account of his achievement of the sword, and he begged leave of the king to follow after Balin, and avenge the insult he had given to the court.

"Do your best," said King Arthur, "for I am very wroth with Balin."

And whilst Lancear was making ready, Merlin came to King Arthur, and was told of the adventure of the sword and the lady of the lake.

"Now hear me," said Merlin, "the same lady who brought the sword is the falsest damsel living."

"Say not so," replied the king, "for she hath a brother a good knight, who slew another knight that this damsel loved; so she went to the Lady Lile of Avilion, and besought her help : and she gave her the sword, and told her that the man who should draw it from the scabbard should avenge her on her brother."

"I know it well," answered Merlin, "and would to God she had never come hither—for never came she on good intent, and that good knight, Balin, shall himself be slain with that sword, which will be a great loss, for better knight there liveth not; and he shall be of great service to you."

Sir Lancear rode after Balin and in a short time had a sight of Balin, in a loud voice he called to him, "Abide, sir knight, wait yet awhile: or I will make ye do so!"

Balin turned his horse, and said, fiercely, "What will you with me; will ye joust with me ?"

"Yea," said the Irish knight, "therefore am I come after you."

"Peradventure," said Sir Balin, "it had been better for you to have stayed at home; for many a man who thinketh himself victorious hastens his own downfall. Of what court art thou?"

"I am come from the court of King Arthur," said the knight of Ireland, "and am come to revenge the insult thou hast put on it this day."

"Well," said Balin, "I see I must fight thee; and am sorry I am to be obliged to grieve King Arthur or his knights; thy quarrel seemeth foolish to me, for the damsel I slew did great damage through the land, or I would have been as loath as any knight living to have killed her."

"Make thee ready," said Sir Lancear, "for one of us shall rest for ever on this field."

They came together with a great shock, and the King of Ireland's son smote Balin upon his shield, and his spear went into splinters; and Sir Balin's lance pierced with such force through Sir Lancear's shield that it rove the hauberk also, and passed through the knight's body and the horse's croup. And Balin, turning fiercely round again, drew his sword, but Sir Lancear was already a corpse.

At that moment a damsel came galloping towards him, and when she saw Sir Lancear dead she cried, "Oh! Sir Balin, two bodies hast thou slain, and one heart; and two hearts in one body; and two souls hast thou lost!"

Therewith she took the sword from her lover's side (for she was Sir Lancear's lady-love,) and, setting the pommel of it in the ground, ran and threw herself on the blade, which pierced her through the body.

And when Sir Balin saw that she was dead he was grieved and repented the death of her knight. He then turned his horse's head towards a forest, and he perceived the arms of his brother Balan. And when they met, they embraced each other. Then Sir Balin told Sir Balan all his late adventures, and that he was on his way to King Rience, who was besieging Castle Terrabel.

"I will go with thee," said Sir Balan, "and we will help one another as brothers ought to do."

As they thus talked, King Marke of Cornwall came up, and when he saw the two dead bodies, and heard of the manner in which they met with their deaths, he sorrowed greatly, and vowed to erect a tomb over them before he left the place. So he sought through all the country round to find a monument; and at last he found a rich one in a church. And he buried the knight and his lady, and put the tomb on their grave, and wrote on the tomb, "Here lyeth Lancear, son of the king of Ireland, who was slain in fair fight by Sir Balin; and here beside him lyeth his lady, Colombe, who slew herself with her lover's sword for grief."

As this was being done, Merlin came unto King Marke, and said, "In this place shall a battle be fought between the two greatest knights and truest lovers that ever was or ever shall be: but they shall not slay each other:

and their names are Sir Launcelot of the Lake and Sir Tristam the Lion."

Then Merlin turned to Sir Balin, and said, "Thou hast done thyself great harm in not saving the lady's life who slew herself."

"By the faith of my body," replied Sir Balin, "I could not save her, for she slew herself suddenly."

"Because of it," said Merlin, "thou shalt strike the most dolorous stroke that ever man struck, save he that smote our Lord; for thou shalt smite the most worshipful of living knights, who shall not be recovered from the wound for many years, and through that stroke three kingdoms shall be overwhelmed in poverty and misery."

"If I believed what thou sayest," said Sir Balin, "I would slay myself to make thee a liar."

At that Merlin vanished away; but met Sir Balin in disguise, and told him he could lead them to King Rience whom they sought; and, said he, "this night he will ride with sixty lances only through the wood hard by."

At that Sir Balin and Sir Balan laid themselves in ambush, and about midnight they heard the king approach. They then sprang from their hiding-places, and smote the king fiercely, and grievously wounded him, and, turning on his knights, wounded and slew forty of them, and put the rest to flight. Then returning to King Rience they would have slain him, but he yielded to their grace, crying, "knights, slay me not; for by my life ye may win, but by my death shall ye win nothing."

"Ye say truth," said the knights; and so

they put him on a litter, and went in the night, till they arrived at King Arthur's palace. There they delivered King Rience into the hands of the guards to be taken to King Arthur, with this message, "That he was sent to King Arthur by the knight of the two swords (for so was Balin known,) and by his brother," and they rode away before sunrise.

A few weeks afterwards, as King Arthur lay in his pavillion, he heard the sound of a horse, and he looked out, and saw a knight riding by, making great lamentation.

"Abide, sir knight," said the king, "and tell me wherefore thou makest this sorrow."

"Ye can little amend it," said the knight.

Presently Sir Balin came before the pavillion, and when he saw King Arthur, he alighted, and knelt before the king.

"Ye are welcome, Sir Balin," said King Arthur; and then he thanked him for avenging him on King Rience. And then the king told him how Nero, who was brother to King Rience, had attacked him to deliver Rience from prison, and also how King Lot of Orkney had joined King Nero, and how he had defeated them both—and of the deaths of Nero and Lot. After they had talked for a time, King Arthur told Sir Balin of the sorrowing knight that had just passed the tent, and desired him to pursue and bring him back. So Sir Balin rode and overtook the knight in a forest with a damsel, and said, "Sir knight, thou must come back with me to my lord, and tell him the cause of thy sorrow."

"That will I not," replied the knight: "for it will harm me much, and do him no good."

"Sir," said Sir Balin, "I pray you make yourself ready, for you must go with me, or I must fight with you, and bring you by force."

"Wilt thou be my warrant for safety if I go?" inquired the knight.

"Yea, surely, or I will die for it," said Balin.

And so the knight made ready to go with Sir Balin, and left the damsel in the wood. But as they went towards King Arthur's pavillion, there came one unseen, and smote the knight through the body with a spear.

"Alas," said Herleus (for such was the name of the knight), "I am slain under thy guard by that traitor knight, Garlon, who through witchcraft, rideth invisibly; take, therefore, my horse, and ride to the damsel whom we left, and follow the quest I had in hand as she will lead thee, and revenge my death when ye may best."

"That will I do," said Sir Balin, " and therefore I make a vow to you of my knighthood." Then Balin went to the damsel, and rode forth with her, taking with him the truncheon of the spear wherewith Sir Herleus had been slain.

And as they went, a good knight joined them, and his name was Perin de Mountbelgard, and he vowed to take adventure with them wheresoever they should go, and so rode forward with Sir Balin and the damsel; but as they passed by a hermitage, there came the knight Garlon, and smote Perin de Mountbelgard with a spear, and slew him as he had slain Sir Herleus. At this foul act Sir Balin raged greatly, and swore to have Sir Garlon's life whenever he might behold him. Then he buried the good knight, Sir Perin, and Balin rode on with the damsel till they came to a great castle, and there Sir Balin alighted, and he and the damsel thought to have gone into the castle, but as Balin passed through the gateway, the portcullis fell behind him leaving the damsel on the other side with men around her drawing their swords as if to slay her.

When Sir Balin saw that, he jumped into the moat, and rushed towards the damsel with his sword drawn. But the men who surrounded the damsel refused to fight with him, for they said they did nothing but the old custom of the castle. Then they told him that the lady of the castle had been grievously ill for many years, and might never be cured unless she had a silver dish full of the blood of a pure maid and a king's daughter; therefore the custom of the castle was, that no damsel pass that way but she must give a dish full of her blood. Then Sir Balin said, "Well, she shall bleed if it be of her own free will, but I will not that she lose her life while mine lasteth."

But her blood helped not the lady of the castle. So Sir Balin and the damsel rested there all night, and had right good cheer; and in the morning they departed.

After riding four days they came to the abode of a rich man, who lodged and fed them. And as they sat at supper, Sir Balin heard some one groaning. "What noise is that?" asked Balin.

"I will tell thee," said his host. "I was lately at a tournament, and there I jousted with a knight who is brother to King Pelles, twice I smote him down, for which he swore to be revenged on me through my best friend, and he wounded my son, who cannot be restored until I have that knight's blood; but he rideth through witchcraft, invisibly, and I know not his name."

"Ah!" said Sir Balin, "his name is Garlon, and he hath slain two knight companions of mine in the same manner; therefore would I rather meet with that knight face to face, than have all the gold in the realm."

"Well," returned the host, "let me tell thee that King Pelles has proclaimed a great festival at Listeniss within twenty days, and no knight may come there unless he bring his wife or lady-love with him. At that feast we may find out this Sir Garlon, for many will be there, and if it please thee we will set forth together."

In a few days they rode forth towards Listeniss, and reached it on the day the feast had begun. They alighted, and went to the castle; but Balin's host was refused admittance because he had no lady with him, but Sir Balin was heartily received, and taken to a chamber, where they dressed him in rich robes, and told him he must lay aside his sword.

"Nay," said Sir Balin, "that I will not do, for it is the custom of my country for a knight always to keep his weapon with him, and that custom will I keep, or else I will depart as I came." Then they gave him leave to wear his sword. Then he went and sat among knights of worship, and his lady sat beside him. Balin turning to a knight, said, "Is there not a knight in this court whose name is Garlon?"

"Yes," answered the knight, "yonder he goeth—he with the black face; he is the most

marvellous knight now living, for he destroy-
eth many knights, and goeth about invisible."

"Ah, well," said Balin, "is that the man?
I have often heard of him." Then Balin mused
within himself. "If I slay him here, I should
not escape; if I suffer him to go, peradventure
I shall never meet with him again, and much
harm will he do if he live."

While he thus thought, and cast his eyes
on Garlon, that false knight saw that he was
watched, and so he came up to Balin, and with
his hand smote him on the face, saying, "Knight,
why watchest thou me? Eat thy meat, and
then do that thou camest for."

"Thou sayest well," said Sir Balin, rising
fiercely. "Now will I do that which I came to
do." With these words, he whirled his sword
aloft, and clove the knight's skull to his shoulders; then turning to the lady, he said, "Now
give me the truncheon wherewith he slew your
knight," and she gave it him; and therewith
Balin smote him through the body, and said,
"With that truncheon thou hast slain a good
knight, and now it sticketh in thy body."

Then Balin called for his host, and when he
came he said to him, "Now may ye fetch blood
enough to heal your son with."

Then all the knights leaped from their seats
to slay Balin, King Pelles being the foremost,
who cried out, "Knight, thou hast slain my
brother at my board; die, therefore, for thou
shalt never leave this castle."

"Slay me thyself, then," shouted Sir Balin.

Then King Pelles seized a murderous weapon, and smote at Balin, but Balin put up his

sword to save his head, and the sword was shivered to pieces, but his head was saved. So he ran to to find a sword, from room to room, with King Pelles in pursuit. At last he came to a chamber richly ornamented, where there was a bed whereon was laid a cloth of gold, and some one quite still lay within the bed; and by the bedside there stood a table of gold, and on the table stood a spear, of curious workmanship.

When Sir Balin saw the spear, he seized it, and turned upon King Pelles, and smote him so that he felled him to the ground. At that awful stroke, the castle was riven throughout, and the walls fell, and Sir Balin himself fell in the midst, and he lay for three days in the ruins.

At length Merlin came and raised him up from under the stones, and set him upon a good horse, and bade him ride out of the land.

"I would have my damsel with me," said Sir Balin.

"Look where she lies dead," said Merlin. "Ah, little knowest thou, Sir Balin, what thou hast done: for in that chamber which thou so savagely defiled was the blood of our Lord Jesus Christ, and also that most holy cup—the Sangreal— wherefrom the wine was drunk at the Last Supper of our Lord. Joseph of Arimathea brought it to this land when first he came here to convert it; and on that bed of gold it was himself that lay embalmed: and the strange spear beside it was the spear wherewith the soldier Longuis smote our Lord, which evermore hath dripped with blood. King Pelles is the nearest kin to Joseph in direct descent, wherefore he held all these things in trust, but now have they all gone at thy dolorous stroke no man knoweth whither; and great is the damage to this land by the dolorous stroke thou gavest to King Pelles, for three countries are destroyed, and doubt not but vengence will fall on thee at the last." Then departed Merlin from Sir Balin, and said, " In this world we shall never meet more."

.Sir Balin then passed the boundaries of the country, and rode eight days without adventure. At length he came to a cross, on which was written, "It is not for a knight alone to ride to this castle." Looking up, he saw an aged man, who said, " Balin la Savage, thou passest thy bounds this way; therefore turn back;" and with these words he vanished. Then he heard a horn blow as it were the death-blow of some hunted beast. "That blast," said Balin, "is blown for me, for I am the prey, though yet I am not dead." As he spoke he saw a hundred ladies with a great troop of knights coming to meet him, who led him to the castle. Then the lady of the castle said, " Knight of the two swords, thou must fight with a knight hard by, who dwelleth on an island; for no man may pass this way without encountering him."

" It is a grievous custom," said Sir Balin.

" There is but one knight to defeat," replied the lady. "Be it as thou wilt," said Sir Balin. "I am ready and quite willing, though my body and horse be full weary, yet is my heart not weary save of life; and truly I should be glad if I met my death."

" Sir knight," said one standing by, "methinks your shield is not good; I will lend you a better."

"I thank thee," said Sir Balin, and took the unknown shield and left his own, and so rode to the island where he saw a knight dressed all in red, with a horse trapped in the same colour, coming towards him.

When the red knight saw Sir Balin, he thought it must be his brother; but when he saw the strange arms on his shield, he came fiercely against him. At the first course they overthrew each other, and both lay on the ground, but Sir Balin was the most hurt. So Sir Balan first rose to his feet and drew his sword, and Sir Balin arose, and raised his shield. Then Sir Balan smote him through the shield, and broke his helmet; and Balin smote him with the fated sword, and well nigh slew his brother.

Then Sir Balin looked up and saw the castle full of ladies. So they went again to battle, and wounded each other until the ground was covered with blood; but still they rose against each other, although their hauberks were all unnailed. At last Sir Balan, withdrew a little, and laid down. Then Sir Balin la Savage asked, "What knight art thou?—for never before have I found a knight to match me thus."

"My name," said the other, "is Balan, brother to the good knight Balin.'

"Oh, God!" cried Balin, "that ever I should see this day," and fell down in a swoon.

Then Sir Balin put his brother's helmet off his head, and when he came to himself he said, "Oh, Balan, my brother, thou hast slain me, and I thee!"

"Alas," said Sir Balan, "that I ever saw this day; and through mishap alone I knew thee not; if it had not been for the strange shield, I should have known thee."

"All this sorrow lieth at the door of one un-happy knight who made me change my shield. If I live I will destroy that castle and its evil customs," replied Sir Balin.

"It would be well to do so," said Balan, "for since I came hither, I have not been able to depart; for here they made me fight with one who kept this island, whom I slew, and, by enchantment, I might never quit it more; nor could thou, brother, hadst thou slain me, have escaped with thine own life."

Thereupon came the lady of the castle, and Sir Balan prayed her that for his service she would bury them both together in that place, which she promised to do. Then a priest was sent for, and they received the holy sacrament.

On the morrow of their death came Merlin, who took Sir Balin's sword and fixed it in a new pommel, and set it in a huge stone, and, then, by magic, he made it float upon the waters; and so for many years it floated around the island.

CHAPTER XVII.

King Arthur drives the Saxons out of Britain and de-feats the Picts and Scots—King Arthur's conquests in Norway, Denmark, Sweden, and Gaul—His fight with Flollo, the Roman tribune—Death of Flollo—Arthur returns to Cornwall, and with Cradoc Vreich-vras and Geraint ab Erbin goes to attack the giant on Saint Michael's Mount—Arthur fights and slays the giant—King Arthur returns to Caer-Leon-on-Usk.

ABOUT this time, the Britons were in great dan-ger from a foreign foe: for a new force of Saxons, with Colgrin at their head, entered the kingdom with the intention of exterminating all its inhabitants. Arthur had little difficulty in raising an army to march against the invaders. As soon as Colgrin heard of the movements of the Britons, he advanced to the river Duglas and was defeated and driven to York, where he was besieged. His brother, Baldolf, who was waiting on the coast for the arrival of Cheldric and his followers from Germany, hearing of it, hastened with six thousand men to his relief; but being met by Cador, Duke of Cornwall, at the head of three thousand foot and three hundred horses was routed.

Just at the same time, Cheldric, with a fleet of six hundred sail, descended upon Albania; so King Arthur broke up the seige, and marched his army to London; and it was resolved to ask for succour from Hoel, King of Brittany, who was the son of a sister of King Arthur, and he put himself at the head of fifteen thousand men, and crossed the sea to assist his uncle.

The Pagans were now besieging Caerllwyd-y-coid, in the province of Lindisia, and at the first encounter were defeated, and they who escaped made for the wood of Celidon, where for a time they defended themselves against King Arthur; but the British king soon brought them to a capitulation, and they agreed to return to Germany, leaving hostages for the fulfilment of the promise. As soon as they weighed anchor, they tacked about, landed at Totnes, and ravaged the country as far as the Severn. King Arthur had just entered on a campaign against the Picts and Scots, and was further harassed by the sickness of Hoel at Alclwyd;

but he, without loss of time directed his arms against the heathens, and coming up with them as they were besieging Bath he addressed some words to his army ; and the address of the Archbishop Dubricius filled the Britons with enthusiasm. The king then put on a coat of mail and a golden helmet, which had the figure of a dragon upon it; took his shield called Prydwen, upon which was delineated the likeness of the Virgin Mary ; his sword Excalibur, which had been forged in the island of Avallon; and his spear called Ron-cymminiad ; and having marshalled his men, he led them against the enemy. The fight lasted all day, and as night drew on the Saxons retreated to a hill named Caer Vaddon. On the following day, the Saxons resisted the attacks of the king's troops. At length, King Arthur drew his sword, and calling upon the name of the Virgin Mary, rushed upon the Pagans.

The assault was a dreadful one. At length his soldiers, inspired by the heroic deeds of their king, redoubled their efforts. Not one of all that Arthur smote escaped alive, and four hundred and seventy men were slain by his arm alone. Colgrin and Baldolf were among the number, and Cheldric, who made a stand in the Isle of Thanet, was killed by Cador, Duke of Cornwall. Arthur now hastened to the relief of Hoel, and drove the Caledonians to Loch Lomond, and in fifteen days the Picts and the Scots yielded to his arms.

Britain being now freed from internal strife, King Arthur resolved to follow his enemies into their own lands. He fitted out a fleet, sailed first to Ireland, where he took the king prisoner, and obliged the other princes to pay homage to him. From hence he sailed to Iceland, and thoroughly subdued that island; and as winter approached he returned to England.

Next year he sailed for the Norwegian coast, and there gave so terrible a lesson to the heathens as made his name fearful to them; and after a mighty slaughter of the people, Riculf, their king was killed, and their cities set on fire. From thence he went to Dacia (Denmark) and subdued it, and added all Sweden to his sway.

Having thus chastised these Pagans, he voyaged to Gaul to defeat the Roman governor, and carry out the threats which he had pronounced to the twelve ambassadors who came to demand Roman tribute from him. King Arthur and his host moved into Champagne, and Flollo, the Roman tribune, retired into Paris. While he was preparing to levy forces from other countries, King Arthur came suddenly upon him, and besieged him in the town.

After a week had passed, Flollo, finding his people dying of starvation, was sorely perplexed, and sent a letter to King Arthur, desiring that they might fight together, for he was a man of great power and and thought to gain the victory. King Arthur accepted the challenge, for he was weary of the siege. On the following day they met on an island near the city. As the king and Flollo approached the other, each sat so firmly in the saddle, that no man could say which way the battle would terminate. After they had saluted each other, they encountered fiercely. King Arthur struck his spear on

Flollo's breast and hurled him to the ground, then drew his sword and called on him to rise. Flollo started up, and with couched spear pierced the breast of King Arthur's horse, and overthrew the animal and the rider.

The Britons, when they saw their king upon the ground, could scarcely restrain themselves from breaking the truce and falling upon the Gauls; but instantly King Arthur recovered his feet, and guarding himself with his shield, rushed on Flollo, who as furiously met him, each bent upon destroying the other. At length Flollo gave Arthur a stroke upon the helm, which nigh overthrew him. King Arthur was as furious as a lion, and raising Excalibur, he struck a blow with all his might, which cut through the helmet and Flollo's head, dividing it into two halves, and he fell down and expired.

As soon as the news spread, the citizens surrendered the city to the conquerors.

After this acquisition, he spent nine years in consolidating his conquests, subduing with the aid of his nephew, Hoel, Aquitaine, Poictiers, and Gascony; and afterwards, at a court at Paris, he gave Normandy to Bawdewine, and Anjou to Sir Kaye; and other provinces he gave to other great men. And when King Arthur had overrun the whole province with his armies, and subjected it, he returned to Britain.

As soon as he landed, there came a messenger to tell him of a giant named Dyroybus, who had murdered and devoured many people and children, so that the children fled, and he had seized upon a duchess, and took her away to his cave on St. Michael's Mount, and though five hundred people followed her, yet they could not rescue her from his hands. King Arthur made inquiries of the messenger, and he learnt that the lady was his nephew Hoel's wife.

"Alas," said King Arthur, "this is a sad tale ye tell. I would rather lose the best realm that I have than not have rescued this lady ere the giant had her in his power; but tell me, good fellow, canst thou show me this giant's haunt?"

"Yes, my lord," replied the man; "lo, yonder, where thou seest the two great fires upon the rocks in the middle of the sea, there shalt thou find him. Then the king returned to his tent, and calling to him Sir Cradoc Vreichvras and Geraint ab Erbin, desired them to get his horses ready for himself and them, as they would that evening ride with him to Saint Michael's Mount.

So in the evening they departed, and rode as fast as they could along the coast until they came to a small town opposite to the mount, where they took a boat and sailed for the steep rocks in which was the giant's dwelling. When the three had landed, the king commanded the two knights to await him at the foot of the hill while he went up alone. Then he began to ascend the rocks until he came to a great fire, and there he found a lady sorrowing over a new-made grave. King Arthur approached her, and said, "Wherefore, fair lady, make ye such heavy lamentations?"

"Sir knight," said she, "speak softly, for yonder is a devil, who, if he hear thy voice, will come and slay thee. Alas! unhappy man, what dost thou here? Fifty such men as thou are powerless to resist him. Here lyeth my lady, the Duchess of Brittany, who was the fairest lady in the world, foully murdered by that fiend."

The king replied, "Nevertheless, in spite of what thou sayest, I will attack this monster, for I grieve sorely for thy lady."

"Beware, approach him not, for he hath vanquished and overcome fifteen kings; but if thou art so hardy, and will speak with him, at yonder great fire shalt thou find him at his supper."

"I will accomplish my errand," said the king, "notwithstanding thy fearful words," and he went to the crest of the hill, and saw the giant gnawing on the leg of a man for his supper, while three damsels turned three spits whereon were spitted twelve young children.

When King Arthur saw all that, he shook with rage; then he cried, "God that ruleth all the world give thee short life and shameful death. Why hast thou murdered these innocents? Now, arise and prepare for death, thou fiend, for this day shalt thou die by my hands."

Then the giant, seizing a large club, smote at the king, and struck the crown off his head.

But Arthur smote with his sword so mighty in return that the giant's blood gushed forth in streams. At that the giant, threw away the club of iron, and caught the king in his arms, and strove to break his ribs; but Arthur struggled and twisted so that the giant could not hold him tightly; and as they wrestled, both tumbled over each other from rock to rock till they came to the sea; and as they tumbled the king smote the giant with his dagger till his hold stiffened in death around King Arthur's body, and he died. Presently the two knights found the king locked fast in the giant's arms, and loosened him from the hold. Then the king commanded Sir Cradoc to smite off the giant's head, and set it on the truncheon of a spear, and bear it to Sir Hoel, and tell him that his enemy was slain; and afterwards to have it fastened on the castle gate, that all people might behold it; and said to the two knights, "Go ye up the mountain and fetch me my sword and shield, and also the large iron club that ye see there; and as for the treasure, ye shall find ye can divide among yourselves, for if I have his kirtle and club, I desire no more."

Then the knights did as he commanded; and when this deed was noised through the country, the people came in crowds to thank the king. And Arthur desired Sir Hoel to build a church upon the mount, and dedicate it to the Archangel Michael, who had visited the rock.

King Arthur then with all his knights returned to his court at Caer Leon, and invited all the kings, and dukes, and barons, that he might treat them royally. And never was a city more gay: festivals, and tournaments, and hunting, prevailed for many days.

CHAPTER XVIII.

Festivities at Caer Leon—The hunt in Wentwood—King Arthur loses his followers, and chases the White Fawn —The Lady of the Lake appears to King Arthur—Guinevere, his future bride, is shown to him—King Arthur returns to Caer Leon.

KING ARTHUR having now defeated most of his enemies, he and his knights spent their time right merrily at Caer Leon. On a certain day,

527   H

as King Arthur and his nobles were hunting in the Forest of Wentwood, the king became separated from his followers, and drew rein in a shady dell in the wood. The aspect of the place seemed strange to him, and he listened in vain for the cry of the hounds, and echo of the bugle; then, he became aware that he had lost his way. He was about to blow a loud recall, when a rustling among the bushes caused him hold his hand. Springing over a thicket, a beautiful white fawn stood gazing at him with timid curiosity. In this circumstance there was nothing remarkable; but what moved the king's wonder was that the hoofs of the graceful creature appeared to be of gold, while forming a collar for its neck was a sort of coronet, studded with gems. So astonished was the king that he stood rooted to the spot. The fawn fixed its beautiful dark eyes upon him, and stamped its golden hoof with impatience as though to challenge pursuit, and once more bounded into the thicket.

" This is some trick of enchantment," thought Arthur. "I will not follow it."

A feeling of curiosity, however, overcame his first-formed opinion that it was a trick of enchantment, and in a moment he plunged into the thicket. Emerging again in an open glade, he looked for the fawn : it flew along the ledge of a rocky tree-crowned bank, known as the Fairy Knoll, on Mynydd Llwyd.

The king whistled for his hounds, but they had disappeared, and he was forced to give chase alone. He scarcely hoped to run down the creature, but felt a desire to follow it. Away flew the deer, and Arthur in wild pursuit. Leaping through bush, and briar, the white fawn again rushed into the thicket. Arthur once more lost sight of the animal in the underwood. Presently, he saw her white sides gleam, and across a park-like glade she was seen speeding like the wind. Arthur followed excitedly. The fawn burst through the meshes of an ivy-clumbered thicket, and leaping over barriers of fallen timber, glided down into a deep and rocky valley, in the bottom of which was a dark pool, reached the verge of the water, sprang in, and disappeared. Lost in astonishment, the king rode his horse to the margin of the pool, and, dismounting, stood staring upon the water, which was of great depth. A laugh broke on his ear, and he turned round to see from whence it came. Leaning upon a rock beside him was a female of matchless beauty, half veiled in a robe of bright greenish hue.

"What seeks the great Pendragon in the haunt of the Fairy of the Well?" asked the maiden.

"Lady," said Arthur, "I scarce know whether I am dreaming or awake, but fear I am the victim of some lure of necromancy."

"And so you have seen the white fawn," she said. "But ere you leave this dell I will, if you be so minded, show you a greater wonder still. That pool possesses wondrous powers: he who drinks of its waters shall have that wish which he most cherishes at heart at the moment of drinking! and a spell has been cast on it by the great wizard, Merlin, and he who knows the charm may change its surface into a mirror, wherein scenes of the future reveal themselves."

"I would I knew this charm, and might behold the wonder," said Arthur.

"I have the spell, and in fair courtesy will grant your wish, for I am one of the damsels of the lake," she replied. "But what information do you ask?—a question of state, or war, or the love of lady fair?"

"It would ill become my knighthood," said young Arthur, "if aught but thoughts of love possessed my mind in such a presence."

"Ah! so soon a courtier," replied the maiden. "Come, then, I will show you the semblance of the most beauteous lady in all England—nay, more, in all Christendom—worthy to be the bride of the great Pendragon—worthy to be the mother of the Kings of Britain."

With that she, filling her hand with water, sprinkled some of it upon the king.

The benevolent smile passed from Arthur's face, and was succeeded by a look of suspicion, as something discordant in her laugh struck on his heart; but his doubts were forgotten in an instant when she pointed to the pool.

The surface of the pool shone with electric brightness, then the colour changed to a rich opal, then faded off into a rich azure, in the midst of which appeared the figure of a lady of surpassing beauty; her golden hair waved down from a regal coronet; her robes were those of a princess; her sweet smile, and large eyes, qualified the Juno-like majesty of her voluptuous form, and beamed with a light of passionate tenderness.

"What think you of your future bride—the king-born Lady of Camelot—the peerless Guinevere?" asked the damsel.

"By my faith," cried Arthur, half wild with

love, "I have smiled when I heard the bards vaunt her beauty beyond the loveliness of all other ladies, but I now see the beauty is beyond all praise."—The Lady of the Lake laughed.

"She is indeed a prize the veriest dastard would break a lance for," she said. "And daughter of the brave King Leodygrance, she is a fitting consort for the King of England. But see— now! the brilliant illusion vanishes, and so will vanish your inconstant passion."

"Believe it not!" returned Arthur." I will seek this beauteous Guinevere—will lay my crown and my heart at her feet. I will at once despatch Launcelot to her father's court, to bear my message of devotion."

"Launcelot, ay—send Launcelot," returned the fairy. "But now farewell—I dare not linger. A stronger power controls me—wrests me away. Farewell, forget me not."

"Stay!" cried the king, turning hastily.

Arthur gazed around him at the dark branches, the patch of vivid blue sky, the tarn, the Fairy Knoll, but he could see no trace of her. Then his heart seemed to swell within him, and his brain to whirl with a sense of glad exhilaration.

"Guinevere! the queenly!" he murmured, "She shall be my bride; and I, her own true knight, will have no thought but to render myself worthy of her priceless love and esteem."

So he reached Caer Leon, where he was joined by his knights, who had been much alarmed and distressed by his absence, but he told them nothing of what he had seen, stating only that he had lost himself in the forest, and had not, for a long while, been able to find his road.

CHAPTER XIX.

Merlin and Viviane at Caer Leon consult on the fate of King Arthur—King Arthur seeks Merlin in his turret-chamber at Caer Leon, and confesses his love for Guinevere—Merlin warns him of his fate—King Arthur's tribe thrones.

MERLIN, sat alone in his turret-chamber at Caer Leon; before him, upon its brazen stand, his book of magic lay open; his eyes were fixed upon its mystic page, and his brow lowered with deep thought and inward care.

"The hour is at hand, and the stars bode evil," he murmured. "Ah, Viviane, is there no counter-spell of loyalty that can disarm the power of my great enemy? Will my love, the virtues of the blameless Arthur, the youth and beauty of Guinevere, the valour of the matchless Launcelot avert the doom that lowers in the mists of the future? It may not be! The guilt of Uther has left its blight upon the land and Pendragonship, and there is no answer to be made to Morgan's taunt when she told me that she had but to wait for vengeance. Alas! it is vain for feeble man to contend against the decrees of Fate! But, hark! His trumpets blare upon the night! He comes! I know his errand!"

He, stalking across the 'lonely chamber, placed himself at the window, and looked anxiously forth.

The phantom 'moon was sailing amid bright fleecy clouds, bridging with her wake of living silver the dark bosom of the distant lake, flashing up the towers and battlements of the illuminated castle. The stars spangled the

clear blue ether, and the fresh breath of spring
wafting over the sleeping landscape, and silvery
stream and dusky far-off hills, cooled the
magician's heated brow, and stirred his long
gray elf-locks.

In the court-yard a troop of knights and men-
at-arms appeared, the moon beaming on their
bright armour. Conspicuous amongst them by
his crown-encircled helmet with its dragon
crest, by his wavy hair, and youthful form,
was King Arthur. He sprang to the ground,
and entered the castle, then, opening the door,
and flinging aside the tapestry that veiled it, he
entered the wizard's chamber.

"All hail, fair Arthur!" cried Merlin. "You
are most welcome, my thoughts were busy with
a thousand cares, and much I wished to see you."

"My best of councillors," returned Arthur,
"I seek you that you may advise me on a matter that touches me near."

"Even to the heart's core?" suggested Merlin.

Arthur drew off his gauntlet, and tapping
the ground with his foot cast down his eyes and
reddened to the temples.

"You say truly, my father," he answered.
"Love's shafts pierce the closest-fitting armour."

"I know it," returned Merlin, with a sigh.
"The spell begins to work."

"What spell, Sir Merlin?"

"The fatal spell cast upon you by Morgan
la Fay—your foe and mine," replied the enchanter. "But speak on."

"Merlin, my lords and barons have urged me
to take a wife, and I would consult thee in this
matter, for thou hast helped me since I first came
to the crown."

" It is well," said Merlin, " that thou shouldst take a wife : for no man of noble nature should be without one; but is there any lady whom thou lovest better than another ?"

"I love," said Arthur, "Guinevere, the daughter of King Leodygrance of Cameliard ; and I think her the fairest of any lady I ever saw ; and her father holdeth in his house the Round Table that thou told me he had from my father, Uther Pendragon."

" My lord," said Merlin, " she is the fairest lady in the land; but if ye had not loved her so much as ye do, I would fain have had ye choose some other, for Launcelot shall love her, and she shall return his love. But where a man's heart is fixed he will be loath to change."

" There is no other I could love so well," returned Arthur—" none other so worthy to share my throne."

A shrill burst of laughter rang through the room.

" None so worthy—none !" shrieked a voice.

" Saint Michael be my good speed !" exclaimed the king, pale and amazed.

"Heed it not," returned the enchanter; "within these walls such airy voices are often heard ; and through the evil ruling of the stars at this time, the power of Morgan la Fay hath increased, and she uses it to harass me."

" Can any good end be served by means that are evil ?" said Arthur. " Ah, my generous friend, I am often troubled by the doubt that you are imperiling your soul's weal by these dark practices."

" Enough of that, Sir Arthur ; fear not for

me; I am elfin-born, and do but hold communion with beings allied to myself in nature," replied Merlin. "But for the princess : let us speak of Guinevere : is your heart set upon the marriage with her ?"

"Unalterably," replied Arthur.

"The worse for you and for England," returned the enchanter.

' The worse—the worse for me ?" repeated Arthur, in angry surprise. "I understand you not."

"Nor will you believe when you do understand," returned the enchanter. "Yet it is written in hieroglyphs of fire upon yonder blue tablets that cannot lie, that Saxon, nor dragon, nor questing beast shall ever work such woe to England as the will of the false Guinevere."

Arthur started up in a passion, and instinctively clutched the handle of his sword.

"Base juggler !" he said, "thou sayest well that I cannot lend credence to slander prompted to thee by the Father of Lies. But for thy white beard I would teach thee to respect the name of the lady of my love—at least in the presence of her own true knight."

"So hot !" returned Merlin, with a smile of indulgence at Arthur's burst of anger. "I know that this must be, yet e'en before thou takest the first irretraceable step on the downward path, hear what the end will be."

The enchanter paced through the chamber, as though under a fit of despair too great for endurance. At length the old man started wrung his hands, and seizing Arthur in his arms,

"Oh, fair son—noble Pendragon—flower of knighthood, save thyself !" he exclaimed.

"My friend, do not so distress yourself for me," returned Arthur. "The worst that can befall me is death upon the battle field, or by the hand of treason—no uncommon fate of kings. Such an end has no terrors for one who is conscious of having adhered faithfully to his knightly vow."

"Thy doom will be less hard than mine," said Merlin, "and I may well be sorry, for I shall die a shameful death, and be entombed alive. Your sister shall bear a son that will destroy you and all the knights of your realm; but it will only be when treason shall break the bond of unity, and render you unable to resist your great foemen—the barbarous Saxons shall overwhelm this land like a flood."

"No more!" said the king. "For my enemies, I shall know how to meet them; for the treachery of my friends, I will do my endeavour to disarm that by gentleness and good government; for my priceless Guinevere, no truthless scandal shall shake my trust in her. Let the ravens croak! I put my trust in Heaven and Heaven's good providence."

With this Arthur returned to his knights. King Arthur then established three tribe thrones in his realm. First, Caer Leon or Wysg (Caer Leon), where Dewi Sant ab Cunnedda was installed chief bishop, and Maelgwn Gwynadd, chief elder; second, Celliwig, in Cernyw (Cornwall), where Bedwini (?) was chief bishop, and Caradawg Vreichvras chief elder; third, Penrhyn Rhionydd (Glasgow, or St. Andrews in the North), where Cyndeyrn Garthys was chief bishop, and Gurthmwl Wledig chief elder.

CHAPTER XX.

Arthur sends for Sir Launcelot, and commissions him
to go to King Leodygrance and ask his daughter in marriage—The Princess Guinevere and her maidens—Hilda
recounts her strange dream to the Princess—Arrival of
Sir Launcelot at the castle.

ON the next day, King Arthur sent for Sir
Launcelot of the Lake, and told him his wish
that he should go to King Leodygrance and ask
of him his daughter, Guinevere, and related to
Sir Launcelot the whole of his adventure with
the white deer.

"Beware, my lord," said Sir Launcelot, "lest
ye fall into some snare. I doubt not ye have
met with no other than Morgan la Fay, and she
would work your ruin."

"I cannot think so," said King Arthur.
"Never came evil councillor in so sweet a guise.
But hear me, Launcelot, to your friendship I will
commit this charge. Take this ring, and bear
it to Guinevere, and tell her that King Arthur
dedicates to her his homage, and beseeches her
that he may wear her glove or some other token
in his helmet at the forthcoming tournament,
and say that he will do his best to win for her
the prize awarded by the Queen of Beauty."

"At first Sir Launcelot was loth to undertake
this errand, and half determined to tell the king
so, and implore him to select some other messenger ; but then the thought of seeing, and
speaking with, the object of his passion, over-
balanced all other considerations, and he prepared for his departure, selecting for his companions young Sir Lionel and Sir Kaye, the
king's foster-brother, with a numerous retinue
of men-at-arms.

The king made Sir Launcelot take with him
many expressions of love ; and, amid the flourish
of martial music, the party set out for Camelot,
[now Winchester,] all in high spirits except their
leader, who looked passion-worn ; yet, judged
by appearances, Sir Launcelot was well adapted
for his delicate and courtly mission. In figure
stately, his features perfect, and his countenance
bold, and commanding ; his bearing knightly,
his manner graceful, and when it suited his purpose, irresistibly fascinating. As this gay cavalcade rode through the fertile land, the people
of the towns and villages received them with
joyous acclaim. The castle of King Leodygrance, of the land of Cameliard, a large fortress, was situated at the head of Rough Tor,
and overlooked a rich vale. On either hand the
valley was enclosed by lofty rugged mountains.
The king's daughter, the peerless Guinevere,
sat in her bower with her maidens working at a
large piece of tapestry, and the apartment was
furnished in every way comfortable with the
dignity of its fair occupant. The walls were
hung with tapestry and various coloured silks
interwoven with gold and silver thread. The
cushions were of the costliest velvets, and a fine
oriel window admitted light to the apartment. At
one end of the room stood a throne, overhung
with a cloth of gold, on which the princess was
seated. The group of maidens and their mistress made a beautiful picture, not one of the
bright bevy but was as fair as day. The commanding beauty of Guinevere impressed itself
upon an observer, though she was surrounded by
so much loveliness. Her stately figure moved

with dignity, her features cast in faultless mould, her complexion brilliant, her eyes sparkling and full of tender expression. Her dress was of pure white samite, fringed with gold, and over this hung a loose robe of crimson velvet, purflewed with ermine, and adorned with gold embroidery, interspersed with precious stones of great value. She wore bracelets on her fair arms, while her luxuriant tresses were confined by a golden frontlet, set with gems. She was sitting at the open window, her cheek resting on her hand, her eyes ranging over the landscape below, and was oppressed by a feeling of dislike of the monotonous life she led, cooped up within the grim walls of the old castle, for her father was absent at the head of his army, having been called upon to aid one of his allies in a war with a neighbour.

At length the princess rose, and, drawing a deep sigh, turned towards her maids.

" Ah, blessed Mary, what a life this is," she said. " I would this war were over, and that my father and his knights were returned. Tell me, girls, what shall we do to amuse ourselves ? Put by your work, and let me see if I can catch the sweet infection of your spirits."

The maidens clapped their hands with glee, and, deserting their frames, came grouping round the princess.

" Madam, shall we sing to you ?" said one of them. " Marcel, the troubadour, has taught us a new romaunt, "The Lay of the False Helene."

" I care not to listen to those idle tales of love and chivalry," replied Guinevere ; " they are so false to life. In a romance, though she

may be immured in a brazen castle, and guarded by giants, she is sure in the end to be rescued by some noble knight as brave as he is
beautiful. I grow so weary of these dull change-
ful days, and long for my father's return."

" So, madam, do we all," returned the
maidens.

" Yes; and then there will be brave doings,"
rejoined Elgiva. " The king has promised that
at Easter he will hold high festival ; and there
will be breaking of lances at the grand tournament, over which our Lady Guinevere is to
preside as the Queen of Love and Beauty."

" No," said a beautiful girl, " the king has
changed his intentions, and the feast and tourney will not take place—at least, not at the
time at first decided on."

" Who told you that, Ida ?" asked the
princess.

The girl blushed deeply, and cast down her
eyes, and as she answered, " Madam, it was
Morven told me so.   He had it from his father, Hugo, the seneschal."

" And why has the king, my father, changed
his purpose ?" asked Guinevere.

" Madam, it is reported that levies for a war
against your father, are being made," replied
the girl ; "and our liege, by ordinance in council
made has put off the feast and tourney."

The maidens gave a cry of disappointment.

" I like not this news," said Guinevere,
" We have seen no pomp or pleasure worth
mentioning since the jousting at London in
King Uther's days, when my father went thither to do homage to his great suzeraine, the

Pendragon; but that is long ago—I was a mere child then."

"True, madam; but I will be sworn no incident of that noble pageant has passed from your memory," said Elgiva.

"No," returned Guinevere, "I would such pleasant times might come again."

"Indeed, madam, the whole affair was delightful," said Elgiva. "You surely have not forgotten the victorious knight who jousted as your champion, and who bore down all before him, winning for my lady the coronet of sovereign beauty—I mean Sir Launcelot of the Lake?"

The blood stole from the fair cheeks of Guinevere, and then, mantled her face with a blush.

"You are too forward and malapert, Elgiva," she said. "For Sir Launcelot, I do not deny that he is a right valiant knight; but there are better men than he."

"Truly, madam; as for instance, that spotless knight, and noble Sir Gawaine."

"How dare you say so?" cried Guinevere. "What is Sir Gawaine compared to Sir Launcelot? He is as yonder sedgy pit in the river compared with the whole Island of Britain."

"I cry your mercy, my lady," returned Ida, smiling covertly; "but methought you said that there were better men than Sir Launcelot, and to whom else could be given the preference? In my humble thought, to none but Sir Gawaine."

"Enough of this foolish jargoning," said the princess; "it is unmaidenly."

For a while there was embarrassment, but at

length the princess smiled kindly, and beckon-
ed to her side a girl of fifteen summers, who
had remained apart, working at the tapestry.

"Come hither, Hilda," she said; "I have
something to ask of you."

The girl approached her mistress and sank
on her knees.

Guinevere took the child by the hand, and,
placed one arm round her waist, and smoothed
her flowing golden hair caressingly.

Hilda was the daughter of the chief of a
rebellious clan of mountaineers, who had given
King Leodygrance much trouble, but had been
finally subdued.   The child had fallen into the
hands of her father's enemies, and was detain-
ed at Cameliard as a sort of hostage for her
father's good behaviour; but she was a favourite with everybody, and especially petted
by Guinevere.

It was discovered as she grew older that she
was subject to fits; and for days she would
wander about the brinks of the tallest cliffs and
mountains, and when in such moods could not
be prevailed upon to eat or sleep, and was wont
to chant strange snatches of mystic rhyme.
The sages of Cameliard began to think that
Hilda was no mortal child, but a changeling
.of the water wraith; and superstitious people
encouraged the notion that Hilda was by an
unprotected seen spirit, and treated her with
kindness.

"Tell me, dear Hilda," said the princess,
" for they say that the spirits whisper many
secrets to you——"

"Nay, madam, the people laugh at me," said
Hilda, " and call me witch."

"Heed them not, child," returned the
princess, kindly. "You are too glad to be
possessed by a lying spirit, so answer me the
question I would ask. Last night, your sleep
was disturbed by some harassing dream, for
you cried out aloud, and made use of these
words: 'Woe—woe to England!' What did
this mean?"

The child slunk from her side, trembling.

"I dare not tell you, madam," she said.

"Dear child, speak roundly. I shall not be
angry with you," said the princess.

"I dreamed, madam, that King Arthur, with
all his brave knights, visited this castle, and
that their coming was celebrated with great
rejoicings. There were feasts, and tilting, and
high harping in bower and hall: for King Arthur came as a suitor for the hand of the peerless Guinevere."

"For my hand!" cried the princess, blushing
deeply. "I, to be consort of the great Pendragon! I, Queen of all England! 'Tis impossible"

"Madam, I am telling you a dream."

"A dream indeed!" returned Guinevere.

"The revels ended, the king and his be-
trothed rode forth from the castle on their
journey to London, amid the shouting of the
people, the sounding of trumpets, and the
clanging of bells, the maidens strewing the
path with flowers. Then I was left alone. In
my desolation I hurried away into the mountains, and wept in solitude till I was blinded
in my tears. Then I was awakened from my
despair, and, rising, I was about to bend my
steps homeward, when the plain suddenly ap-

peared covered with moke as with a mantle; and through the flashes of flame that mingled with it I beheld burning towns, towers, and villages, and mighty hosts meeting in the rush of battle; the field was heaped with the wounded and the slain, and the air rang with the voices of the hovering spirits: 'Woe for King Arthur! Woe for the false Guinevere!'"

"False!—the false Guinevere!"

"And 'Woe to England!' then I started from my sleep."

"A strange, dream!" said the princess, "without coherence. Wherefore should this ruin follow the marriage of King Arthur with the daughter of King Leodygrance? You have kept something back: I will know the worst."

"Madam, do not urge me further, I beseech you," returned the girl. "Something I dreamed of Sir Launcelot of the Lake."

"Of Launcelot?"

"Of stolen meetings with the knight, of revolt, of a sad cell at Almsbury, of tears and penitence. But under stress of your command, I had not told you this, my lady; and heed it not—it was an idle dream."

"Ay, but through that mystic halo you discern the shadows of coming events floating dimly," returned Guinevere. "But hark!" she added, "what means that blast? Run to the window, and tell me who comes."

The mellow note of a bugle rang in the air.

"A stranger, madam," cried Elgiva; "a gallant knight and his retinue. I see their plumes wave, and their helmets flash; and now the drawbridge is lowered, and the portcullis raised, and the chivalry are crossing the moat."

Guinevere rushed to the window, but recoiled, with a scream.

"It is his banner!" she exclaimed. "It is Sir Launcelot of the Lake!"

CHAPTER XXI.

Sir Launcelot's interview with the Princess Guinevere—He recounts King Arthur's praise—His message to King Leodegrance—His return with the answer to King Arthur—The Princess's journey to Camelot—Her marriage and coronation—Installing the Knights of the Round Table.

A PAGE announced the arrival of Sir Launcelot of the Lake with a message from King Arthur, and desired an audience with the lady Guinevere.

"Hilda, you have proved a true prophetess," said the princess. Then, addressing the page, she said, "Go, and at once conduct the noble SirLauncelot to our presence."

The page retired. Then there was a flutter of expectation among the damsels, and they busied themselves in a task of adjusting the hair and dress of their beautiful mistress.

The princess then dismissed all her maidens excepting Ida and Elgiva, who retired to a distance, while Guinevere, gracefully reclined upon her chair of state. Sir Launcelot entered the room. He was attended by a page, who carried his helmet and shield. For a few moments the pair regarded each other with a look of embarrassment, for this interview may be said to be the first meeting of Launcelot and Guinevere.

As a matter of fact, they had seen each other before, but that was in their early youth, and only for a few moments : Launcelot, at the age of eighteen, had won his spurs in the tilting-ground, and had selected Guinevere, then fourteen, as the lady whose favour he should wear, and whose beauty he should uphold against all comers. At the close of the tournament, he had received from her hand the chaplet that was assigned to the knight who had been the victorious hero of the day.

They now regarded each other with admiration. Launcelot and Guinevere gazed upon each other; and then the knight approached the throne of Guinevere. Bending upon one knee, he said, "Fair princess, on the part of my liege lord, Arthur Pendragon, I bring you greeting, and am commanded to speak the passion of my sovereign's heart. He bids me say that he declares himself your true knight, and prays that he may wear your favour in the lists, and, by his prowess, approve himself worthy of your esteem. Moreover he bade me place this ring upon your finger as a token of his love and homage."

"I know not how I have deserved so high an honour," returned the princess. "But I accept Lord Arthur's condescension as becomes my duty, and with more joy that he has conveyed it by so noble a messenger as Sir Launcelot."

Sir Launcelot placed the ring upon her finger; and then, he clutched her hand. She did not withdraw it from his clasp.

"Peerless Guinevere," sighed Sir Launcelot, "the king is happy. Would to Heaven that he had found one of stronger mind than I for this errand—one less selfish."

"What do you mean, my lord?" asked Guinevere.

"Madam, pardon me; I know not what I say," he answered. "Some joys there are that cost too much. A moment's borrowed bliss is dearly repaid by a life's unhappiness. Ah, traitor that I am! Madam, farewell; I humbly take my leave."

"Nay, but methinks this is scant courtesy, brave Sir Launcelot," she answered. "Tarry a little, for I have more to say in answer to the king's most gracious message."

She retired towards the window, her hand resting in his, and her eyes bent on the ground.

"Sir Launcelot," she said, "have you forgotten the day when you yourself were my champion in the lists?"

"No, madam, by this token," replied Sir Launcelot, drawing a little glove from his bosom.

Guinevere took it with a trembling hand.

"Is it possible that Sir Launcelot could preserve so trifling a memento?" she said.

"Yes, madam; and never since have I worn lady's favour in the lists," he answered, "and never will I!"

"Oh, this is folly!" returned Guinevere. "But since you prize it for my sake, take it back again. For my part, I should be ungrateful if I could forget the knight who upheld my cause so valiantly; and when, in my girlish innocence, I indulged in dreams, bright and illusive. But it is vain to sigh for childish visions, that flee the stern realities of maturer life."

"Oh, heavens!" muttered Launcelot, "she loves me!"

"Let us not speak of the past, but let us look to the future—its hopes and its duties," answered the princess. "What manner of man is my lord, King Arthur?—all men speak his praises."

"Arthur is the noblest knight in Christendom!" returned Sir Launcelot, "as gracious as he is valiant; as modest as he is wise. He is a king of men, the flower of knighthood, and a paragon of manly vigour."

"You speak with warmth," said Guinevere.

"Else were I most ungrateful," said Sir Launcelot. "King Arthur is my best friend. He has honoured me with implicit confidence. From me he withholds no secret; and to him I have devoted my sword, my allegiance, and my life!"

"And shall this blameless man give me his noble heart in exchange for my fickle one?" she said. "I fear he may regret his sacrifice. But now we must part, Sir Launcelot. Bear to my Lord Arthur this pledge of my esteem, and say he has my loving leave to wear it as his colours in the lists; and may Heaven send him victory." She took a gold-embroidered scarf from her waist, and handed it to Sir Launcelot, who took it reverently.

For a moment the pair stood gazing on each other in silence, each moved by sympathetic emotion; then Guinevere gave Launcelot her hand, and in a faltering tone, bade him farewell. The knight pressed the jewelled fingers to his lips, and then stalked out of the chamber. When he was gone, the princess stood lost in painful thought; the tears welled up her blue eyes, and her lip curled in sorrow.

"Ah, Launcelot!" she exclaimed, "would we had never met! I grieve for myself! Now do I know how it is to feel as you do—constant, but hopeless. They say love dies when hope perishes. They speak of women as fickle; but what libellous stuff is that! Every woman loves once, and only once. In an hour of madness she may sacrifice her lover to win ambition, but she cannot stifle the small voice within: it whispers the clearer in the hollow heart. And yet I think what might have been. Away with such gloomy suggestions! Is it not something to make the heart glow with pride to know that I am accounted worthy to be the wife of the valiant Pendragon—the queen of all broad England?"

The consent of King Leodygrance to an alliance between his daughter, and King Arthur was joyfully given; and King Leodygrance exclaimed, "Never yet did I hear more joyful tidings than those you bring, Sir Launcelot, that a king of such prowess as the great Pendragon seeks to wed my daughter. And as for my lands, I would share them with him freely, but as he needeth them not, I will send him a gift which shall please him more: I will give him the Round Table which his father gave to me, with a hundred knights towards the furnishing of it, and he will soon be able to find other fifty knights to make the table full."

When Sir Launcelot returned to King Arthur and told him what had been said, the king sent

a goodly retinue under Sir Launcelot to bring
the princess to his court.   Then king Leodygrance delivered his daughter, Guinevere, to the
messengers of King Arthur, and also the Round
Table with the hundred knights.   The royal retinue departed from the land of Cameliard, and
pursued their journey towards Camelot. In the
evening many minstrels sang before the knights
and ladies as they sat in the tent doors, and a
knight would tell adventures.   Among these
Sir Launcelot told the knightliest tales, and
sang the goodliest songs of all the company;
and Guinevere heard him with joy. When they
came near Camelot, King Arthur, riding forth
in splendid state, met Guinevere and her escort,
and he led her to the palace amidst the shoutings of the people and the pealing of bells. And
King Arthur said : " this fair lady is welcome
unto me, for I have loved her long, and therefore there is nothing so dear to me ; and these
knights of the Round Table please me more than
right great riches."

When the day of marriage arrived the archbishops led the king to the cathedral, clothed in
his royal robes, and having four kings bearing
golden swords before him, and a choir of passing sweet music going with them.

The princess, led by archbishops and bishops,
was taken to the Chapel of the Virgins, the
four queens of the kings walking before her,
bearing four white doves ; and after her there
followed many damsels, singing and making
every sign of joy.   When the two processions
were come into the chapel, so transporting was
the music and singing that all the knights and

nobles pressed on each other, as in the crowd of battle, to hear and see the most they could.

After the marriage ceremony was performed, King Arthur called together all the knights that came with the Round Table from Cameliard (?) great and valiant men, and desired Merlin to espy in all his land fifty knights which were of most prowess and worship. Then Merlin, out of all the realm, chose twenty-eight towards making up the full number of the table, but the other twelve he could not find.

Then the Archbishop of Canterbury blessed all the seats of the knights; and when they rose to pay their homage to King Arthur, there was found upon each knight's seat his name, written in letters of gold; but upon one seat was found written, "*This is the seat Perilous, wherein if any man shall sit save him whom Heaven hath chosen, he shall be devoured by fire.*"

CHAPTER XXII.

Sir Gawain and Sir Tor made knights—King Pellinore acknowledges Sir Tor to be his son—The ordinary of the knights of the Round Table—The adventure of the white hart—Merlin advises that Sir Gawain be sent in pursuit of the white hart, that Sir Tor be sent after the knight and the white hound, and that King Pellinore be sent to bring back the knight and the lady—The adventure of Sir Gawain—He jousts with a knight, and slays a fair lady—He is attacked by four knights, and is taken prisoner—His release and return to King Arthur.

THEN came young Gawain, the king's nephew to the court, and prayed to be made a knight. "I will do it with a good will," said King Arthur, " and do unto you all the worship that I may."

Then came a poor man into the court, who brought a young man eighteen years of age, and falling at the king's feet, he said, " Lord, it was told me that at this time of thy marriage thou wouldst give to any man the gift he asked for, so it was not unreasonable."

" That is truth," said the king, " such gifts will I give so it impair not my realm."

" Thou sayest graciously," said the old man. " Sir, I ask nothing more than that ye will make this young man, my son, a knight."

" It is a great thing that thou asketh of me," said the king.   " What is thy name, and cometh this request from thee or thy son ?"

" Sir," replied the man, " my name is Aries the cowherd, and the prayer cometh not from me, but from my son, for I shall tell you I have thirteen sons, and they all fall to what labour I put them, but this child will do no labour for anything I or my wife can say, but will always be shooting or casting darts, and delights in battles and to behold knights, and always desireth of me that he may be a knight."

" What is his name ?" asked the king.

" Sir, his name is Tor."

Then the king was well pleased with his figure, and said to the old man, " fetch all thy other sons before me ;" and when they were brought, none of them resembled Tor in size or power.

" Now," said King Arthur " where is the sword that he shall be knighted with ?"

Then Tor pulled out the sword, and kneeling before the king, requested to be knighted. The king thereupon smote him on the neck, saying, "Be a good knight and true, as I pray God thou mightest be, and if thou provest thyself worthy, one day thou shalt be counted in the Round Table." Then turning to Merlin, the king said, "Prophecy now, shall Sir Tor become a worthy knight or not?"

"Yea, lord," said Merlin, "so he ought to be, for he is no son of the cowherd, but the son of that King Pellinore whom thou hast proved to be one of the best knights living. Cowherd, fetch thy wife before me, and she shall tell thee so."

And when she was brought before the king, she told him that when she was a maid a stern knight came to her and had his desire of her, and she bare unto him her son Tor, and the knight took away the grey-hound she had with her, and said he would keep it for her love. On the next morn King Pellinore came to the court, and when he was told how Sir Tor was his son he had great joy. And King Pellinore did homage to King Arthur, and was graciously accepted, and was led by Merlin to a high seat at the Round Table, near to the "perilous seat;" and Sir Gawain was full of anger at the honour done to King Pellinore, and said to Gaheris, his brother, "He slew our father, therefore will I slay him."

"Do it not yet," said Gaheris; "wait till I also be a knight, and then will I help ye in it."

"As ye say, so shall it be,' said Sir Gawain.

Then the king spake to all his knights, and charged them to be true knights, to do neither outrage nor murder, nor any violence, and always to flee treason; to give mercy to him that asked for mercy, upon pain of forfeiting the liberty of his court. Moreover, at all times to give succour unto ladies and children, and never to take part in any vengeful quarrel;" and to all this he swore them, knight by knight. Then he ordained that every year at Pentecost they should all come before him, and give account of their doings and adventures during the past twelve months. And so he installed the most noble order of the Round Table, whereto the best knights sought to gain admission. Then was the feast made ready, and the king and Queen Guinevere sat before the assembly and great was the banquet. After the feast was over, Merlin rose and told them to sit awhile, for they should see a marvellous adventure. In a short time there rushed into the hall, a white hart, with a white hound after him, and thirty couples of black hounds followed in full cry; and the white hound sprang upon the hart, and tore a piece out of his haunch, whereat the hart with a great leap overthrew one of the knights at the table, who instantly got his horse, and took the white hound with him.

But no sooner had he left than there came in a lady mounted on a white palfrey, who cried to the king, " Lord, suffer me not to have this despite, for the white hound was mine that the knight led away;" and as she spoke there came in a knight, on a horse, and took the lady with him by force, she moaned sadly. Then the king ordered Sir Gawain, Sir Tor, and King Pellinore, to follow the adventure to the uttermost, " For ye may not," said Merlin, " leave this adventure so lightly, or it will be disworship to you and to your feast."

"I will do all," said the king, "by your advice."

Then Merlin said : " You, Sir Gawain, must bring back the white hart ; you, Sir Tor, must bring back the white hound and the knight, or slay him ; and you, King Pellinore, must bring back the lady and the knight, or slay him ; and you shall each do marvellous things before you return."

Then Sir Gawain rode at a swift pace, and his brother Gaheris rode with him to do him service. And as they went they saw two knights on horseback fighting, and when they reached them they asked them the cause of their quarrel.

" We fight for a foolish matter," said one of them, " for we are brothers ; but there came a white hart this way, and thinking it was an adventure for the high feast of King Arthur, I would have followed to have gained worship, but my brother declared that he was the better knight, and would go after it instead, and so we fight to prove which of us is the best."

" This is a foolish thing," said Sir Gawain ; " fight with all strangers if ye will, but not brother with brother. Take my advice : set on with me, and if ye yield to me, as I shall do my best to make ye, ye shall go to King Arthur and yield ye to his grace."

" Sir knight," replied the brothers, " we will do thy wish without encountering thee ; but by whom shall we tell the king we were sent ?"

" By the knight in pursuit of the white hart," said Sir Gawain ; " now tell me who ye are."

"Sorlous and Brian of the forest," they replied, and went their way towards the king's court.

Then Sir Gawain, came to a river, and saw the hart swimming to the bank. And as he was about to swim after it, he saw a knight upon the other side, who cried, "Come not over here, sir knight, after that useless hart, unless thou wilt joust with me."

"I will not fail to do that," said Sir Gawain, and he made his horse swim across the water; and they got their spears and ran together and Sir Gawain smote the knight from his horse and bade him yield him.

"Nay," said the knight, "though ye have had the better of me on horseback, I pray thee alight, and match we on foot with swords."

"What is your name?" asked Sir Gawain.

"Allardin of the Isles," replied the knight.

Then they fought, but Sir Gawain smote him through the helm, and the knight fell dead.

"Ah," said Gaheris, "that was a mighty stroke for a young knight."

Then Gawain and Gaheris followed the white hart, and let slip three couple of greyhounds, and chased him to a castle, and there slew him in the court-yard.

At that rushed forth a knight from a chamber with a sword, and slew the two greyhounds, and chased the others crying, "Oh my white hart, it repenteth me that ye are dead, for my sovereign lady gave thee to me, and thy death shall be dear bought if I live." And then he went into the chamber to arm himself, and came out fiercely and met Sir Gawain.

"Why have ye slain my hounds?" said Sir Gawain. "They did but after their nature, and I had rather you had wroken your anger on me than on my dogs."

"I will avenge me on thee also," said the knight, "ere ye depart this place."

Then the two knights struck each other mightily, and stoned their helmets, and brake their hawberks, that the blood ran down to their feet. At last Sir Gawaine smote the knight so hard that he felled him to the earth, and besought of him his life.

"Thou shalt die," said Sir Gawaine, "for slaying my hounds."

"I will make all the amends in my power," said the knight, "if you will grant me my life;" but Sir Gawaine unlaced his helmet to strike off his head, when there came a lady out of the chamber and fell over him, and so he smote off her head by misadventure.

"Alas," said Gaheris, "you have done a foul deed. You should have given mercy unto the knight when he asked it of you, for a knight without mercy is a knight without worship."

Sir Gawain said unto the knight, "Arise, I will give thee mercy."

"I care not for mercy now," cried the knight, "for thou hast slain my love that I prized most of all things."

"I repent me of the blow, for I thought to strike thee," said Sir Gawain, "but now thou shalt go to King Arthur and tell him of thy adventures. Now tell me thy name before we part."

"My name is Abiamor of the Marsh," said

the knight; and he departed towards Camelot. Then Sir Gawain went into the castle and prepared to rest himself there for the night.

"What will ye do?" said Gaheris. "Will ye unarm in an enemy's country?"

As soon as he had said this, there came four knights and assailed Sir Gawain, and said unto him, "Thou new-made knight, thou hast shamed thy knighthood, for a knight without mercy is dishonoured, and thou hast slain a fair lady, doubt not thou shalt have great need of mercy ere thou depart." And there-withal one of them smote Sir Gawain a stroke that nigh felled him to the ground, and Gaheris smote him in return, and Sir Gawain and Gaheris were in jeopardy of their lives. And one with a bow, an archer, smote Sir Gawain through the arm. And as they were in jeopardy of their lives, there came four ladies and besought the four knights to give mercy to Sir Gawain and Gaheris.

And Sir Gawain and Gaheris yielded.

Early on the morrow there came to Sir Gawain one of the four ladies that had heard his complaint, and said, "Ye have brought this evil upon you by slaying the lady. But be ye not of King Arthur's kin, and what is your name?"

"My name is Gawain, and I am King Lot of Orkney's son, and my mother is King Arthur's sister."

When he arrived at court, Merlin desired of King Arthur that Sir Gawain should be sworn to tell all his adventures. When the king and queen heard of his slaying the lady, they were displeased with Sir Gawain, and the queen ordained that a jury of ladies should judge him; and they judged him that while he lived he should fight for all ladies' quarrels, and that he should never refuse mercy to him that asks for it.

CHAPTER XXIII.

Sir Tor's adventure after the knight with the hound—His combat with two armed knights—Sir Tor, accompanied by a dwarf, discovers ladies sleeping in a tent—Sir Tor defeats the knight Abellins—A damsel demands the knight's head—Sir Tor goes with the lady to her castle, and on the morrow departs for Camelot.

SIR TOR set forward in pursuit of the knight who took with him the hound, and as he rode he met a dwarf, who smote his horse on the head with a staff so that he went backwards a spear's length.

"Why strikest thou my horse so, thou foul fiend?" said Sir Tor.

"Because thou shalt not pass this way," replied the dwarf, "unless thou fight with yonder two knights in those pavillions," pointing to two tents.

"I may not be hindered, for I am on a quest I needs must follow," said Sir Tor.

"Thou shalt not pass," replied the dwarf.

Then rode out an armed knight and attacked Sir Tor, who was as quick as he, and bore him from his horse and made him yield. Directly came another very wroth, but with a few buffets Sir Tor unhorsed him also, and sent them to Camelot to King Arthur.

Then came the dwarf and asked Sir Tor to take him into his service, "for I will serve no more recreant knights," said he.

527   K

"Then journey with me," said Sir Tor.

"Ride ye after the knight with the white hound?" asked the dwarf. "If so, I can soon bring you to where he is."

So they rode until they came to two more tents, and Sir Tor went into the first, and saw three damsels sleeping. Then he went into the other tent, and found a lady sleeping, and at her feet lay the white hound he sought, which began to bay so loudly that the lady awoke. But Sir Tor had seized the hound and given it into the dwarf's charge.

"What will ye do, sir knight?—will ye take my hound by force?" asked the lady.

"Yea, lady, for so I must," said Sir Tor, "having the king's command; and I have followed it from King Arthur's palace at Camelot unto this place."

"Well," said the lady, "ye will not go far from hence before ye will be ill-handled, and will repent ye of the pursuit."

"I shall cheerfully abide, come what may," said Sir Tor, and so he rode back the way he came; as night came on he turned to a hermitage in a wood, and there abode until the next day. In the morning, as he rode forth, he heard a voice calling after him, "Abide, sir knight, and yield me up the hound thou tookest from my lady." On hearing this, he turned, and saw a strong knight, armed in splendid mail, riding towards him.

Now Sir Tor was ill provided, for his courser was weak, but he waited for the strange knight to come, and after the first meeting, wherein each of them unhorsed the other, they fell to

with their swords like two mad lions. At length
Sir Tor, doubled his stroke until he bent him
to the ground, and then bid him beg for mercy.
But Abellins refused to yield, and said, "That
will I not while my life lasteth unless thou first
givest me the hound."

"I will not," said Sir Tor, "for it was my
quest to bring again that hound to King Arthur, or otherwise to slay thee."

At that instant came a damsel riding on a
palfrey as fast as she could drive, who cried out
to Sir Tor, "I beg of thee, for King Arthur's
love, a gift."

"Ask, and whatever it might be that will I
give to thee," said Sir Tor.

"Gramercy," said the damsel, "I ask the head
of the knight Abellins, for he is the most out-
rageous knight that liveth."

"I repent me of the gift I promised," said Sir
Tor, "let him make thee amends for his tres-
passes against thee."

"He can make no amends," replied the damsel, "for he slew my brother before mine eyes,
who was a far better knight than he, and for all
that I could do he struck off his head; wherefore I require of thee, as thou art a true knight,
to give me the gift I ask, or else I will shame
thee in all the court of King Arthur, for this
Abellins is the murderer of many."

When Abellins heard this he begged for mercy.

"I cannot now," said Sir Tor, "lest I be false
to my promise. Ye would not take my advice
when I offered it, and now it is too late;" and
therewith he took off his helmet, but Abellins,
struggled to his feet and fled, until Sir Tor overtook him and smote off his head.

"Now," said the damsel, " I pray you lodge with me in my castle which is hard by,"

" I will with right good will," said he; "for my horse and I have fared ill ever since I left Camelot." So he went to the lady's castle and she thanked him for his services. On the morrow he departed and reached Camelot, where the king and queen rejoiced to see him. Then the king made him swear to tell his adventures; and so he told, and made proof of his deeds, when they both were well pleased, and the king made him an earl. And Merlin prophesied that these adventures were but jests to what he should achieve hereafter, for he should prove a knight of great prowess, as good as any living. Thus ended the quest of Sir Tor, King Pellinore's son.

CHAPTER XXIV.

King Pellinore's adventure after the lady and the knight —He passes a lady attending upon a wounded knight— He meets with a poor man who gives him tidings of the knight and lady--He discovers the lady and two knights fighting for her—King Pellinore kills Sir Houslake, and proceeds towards Camelot with the lady— King Pellinore overhears the plans to poison King Arthur—King Pellinore finds the head of the lady of the wounded knight—His arrival at Camelot.

THEN King Pellinore rode after the lady the knight had taken away. And as he rode through a forest, he saw a damsel sitting by a well with a wounded knight in her arms. And Pellinore saluted her, and she entreated his help; but he would not tarry he was so eager in quest of the knight and the lady.

When the damsel saw he would not give her help she prayed that God may send him as much need of help as she had. And her knight died, and she out of sorrow, slew herself with his sword. As King Pellinore rode along the valley, he met with a poor man, and the king asked him if he had seen a knight riding away with a lady.

"Yea," said the man; "I saw that knight, and the lady was very sorrowful. And yonder in the valley ye shall see two pavillions, and one of the knights of the pavillions came out, and spoke to the lady with the knight and said she was his cousin, and therefore he should lead her no further. And the knights quarrelled for the lady, and I left them fighting, and if ye shall go apace ye shall find them fighting."

"I thank thee," said King Pellinore; and he rode onward until he saw the two knights fighting. And on entering the pavillion he found the lady, and said to her, "Fair lady, ye must go with me into the court of King Arthur." And King Pellinore went between the two knights who were fighting, and asked the cause of the quarrel.

"Sir knight," said the one; "this lady is my kinswoman, and when I heard her complain that she was taken with him against her will, I fought to release her."

"Sir knight," said the other, whose name was Houslake of Wentsland; "this lady I gained by my prowess of arms this day in King Arthur's court."

"That is untruly said," replied King Pellinore; "for ye seized the lady before any man might make ready to prevent it, and I am sent to bring her and you back or else one of us is to abide on the field, and fight ye no more, for neither of you shall have her."

"Well," said they both, "make you ready, and we will assail thee with all our power."

And as King Pellinore would have turned his horse, Sir Houslake ran the horse through, and said, "Now thou art on foot as well as we are."

When King Pellinore found his horse was slain, he drew his sword and put his shield before him, and with a fierce stroke he clave Sir Houslake's head and he fell dead. And then he turned upon the other and wounded him, who knelt down and said, "Take my cousin as ye require, and as ye be a true knight, put her to no shame or villany."

"Well," said King Pellinore, "ye say well. I promise you that she shall have no villany from me as I am a true knight; but I require a horse and will have Houslake's horse."

"Ye shall not need him," said the knight, "for I will give you such a horse as shall please ye better, if ye will lodge with me this night."

"I will abide with you for this night," said King Pellinore. And passing good cheer was given him, and he passed a merry night, and in the morning a fair bay courser was brought out with King Pellinore's saddle upon him.

"Now, what shall I call you?" said the knight.

"Sir, I will tell you: my name is King Pellinore of the Isles, and a knight of the Round Table."

"Now I am glad," said the knight, "that such a noble man shall have rule over my cousin. My name is Sir Meliot of Logers, and this lady's name is Nimue, and the knight that was in the other pavillion is my brother, a good knight, and his name is Brian of the Isles, and he wishes not to fight with any man except at his request.

"Bring him to the court," said King Pellinore, "one of these days."

"We will come together," said the knight.

Then King Pellinore took the lady towards Camelot. And as they rode in a valley full of stones the lady's horse threw her down, whereby her arm was bruised, and she nearly swooned with the pain.

"Alas!" she said, "my arm is out of joint, and I must needs rest me."

"Be it as you wish," said Pellinore.

And so he alighted, and laid himself under a tree, and slept until night. When he awoke he would have proceeded on his journey, but the lady desired to stay, as they might miss their way. So the king consented, and lay down to rest. About midnight the trotting of a horse was heard, and King Pellinore desired the lady to be still, and he put on his armour. Thereupon two knights rode up to near where they were; the one came from Camelot, the other from the north, and they saluted each other.

"What tidings from Camelot," said the one.

"By my head," said the other, "there have I been and espied the court of King Arthur and there is such a fellowship they may never be broken, and well nigh all the world holdeth with Arthur."

"As for that," said the other knight, "I have brought greatest poison ye ever heard speak of, and to Camelot will I with it; for we have a friend nigh King Arthur, and well cherished, that shall poison him; for so he hath promised our chieftains, and received great gifts for to do it."

"Beware," said the second knight, "of Merlin. For he knoweth all things by the devil's craft."

With these words they parted; and King Pellinore and the lady rode towards Camelot. As he came by the well where the wounded knight was with the lady, he found the knight dead, and the lady had been eaten by wild beasts. At the sight, King Pellinore made great sorrow, and said, "Alas! had I not been so inveterate in my quest, her life might have been saved."

"Now I beg of you to do by my advice," said the lady; "let this knight be buried in a hermitage, and then take the lady's head and bear it to King Arthur."

So King Pellinore delivered the corpse to the hermit in order that service should be rendered for his soul.

"It shall be done," said the hermit.

Therewith King Pellinore and the lady departed, and reached Camelot about noon.

And the king and the queen were glad at his coming to the court, and there he swore to tell the truth of his quest.

"Ah! Sir Pellinore," said Queen Guinevere, "ye were greatly to blame that ye saved not the lady's life."

"It repenteth me, and shall all the days of my life," said King Pellinore.

"Truly," said Merlin, "ye ought to repent it: for the lady was your own daughter, and that knight that is slain was her lover, and would have wedded her; and he was a good knight and would have proved a right good man. To this court was he coming: his name was Sir Miles of the Lands; and a knight came behind him and slew him with a spear, whose name was Loraine le Savage, a false knight and a coward. And the lady, in her sorrow, slew herself with his sword, and her name was Eleine. And because ye would not help her, ye shall see your best friend fail you when you are in distress, and that penance God hath ordained you for that deed, that he that ye shall most put confidence in any man alive shall leave you to die."

Thus when the quest of the white hart, and the hound, and the lady that the knight took away, was accomplished, the king established all his knights. And to those who had no lands he gave some. And he charged them never to do murder, and always to flee treason; also by no means to be cruel, but to show mercy unto him that pleadeth for it, upon pain of forfeiture and worship of King Arthur for evermore.

CHAPTER XXV.

Merlin in his dotage becomes enamoured of Viviane—He confesses to her the secret of a charm—She puts forth the charm and encloses Merlin within the rock on a mount at Carmarthen.

AFTER these things Merlin in his dotage sought to be continually with Viviane, and would let her have no rest. And she endeavoured to draw from him all things that she desired to know of his art. She played about him, and with sprightly talk endeavoured to gain her end; and the loving seer would gaze upon her with devotion. He felt her flattery, and half believed her intended love was true. On a certain day Merlin stepped into a boat, while Viviane unperceived followed close behind, and he observed her not. She took the helm and the boat sailed for the land of Merlin's birth; and as they glided on she sought to gain from Merlin the charm he had told her of, by which the man so wrought upon should be closed within a tower, from which escape would be hopeless, and his prison should be unknown to any except the one that worked the charm upon him.

And Viviane lay by the great enchanter's side, and fondled in love upon his bosom, and crying, said, "Oh, Merlin, if you love me tell me your charm. Dear master, whom I will follow through the world to pay you worship, impart to me the secret and by that means grant me some power upon your fate, and the charm so taught will give rest and happiness to both; for I, feeling that you deem me worthy of trust, will make me think doubly mine. But if you believe me so wicked that I should practise it on you unawares, then our intercourse had best be loosed for ever,—think me not so base."

Merlin took his companion by the hand, saying, "Oh, Viviane, you talk of trust; too much I trusted when I told of the charm and stirred within curious thoughts. I will not yield to give you power over my life. Ask me some other boon."

"Nay, Merlin," cried the wily Viviane, "I ever feared you were not wholly mine, and now your words confirm my doubt, but hear my words: if ever I have harboured treachery towards you, may the earth swallow me up. You know me not if you think me such a traitress."

"Oh, Viviane," said the seer, "when I spell the lines upon your face, I find it practised to some vice, and I will not give you power over me." Then Viviane said, "Oh, Merlin, be not so harsh upon the one that loves you, let her fond heart feel that she is forgiven, for having no other boon to ask."

So sweetly her timorous voice responded to his refusal, so fair her face, that Merlin half believed her true, and said, "Oh, Viviane, you think you love me well; love should have some pleasure in itself, and not be too curious for a boon. And blame me not if I fear giving you power by the charm, that you might use it to my ruin."

Viviane replied, "Have I not sworn not to use it against thy life and fame? Well, keep it from me, but I shall find it out, and being a woman and not trusted, I may, in anger that some fair captive is enclosed within the hollow tower, practise the charm you would conceal from me."

To this Merlin replied, "In youth I needed no charm to keep them true."

At this Viviane encircled the prophet's neck with her arms, until Merlin, overcome by her smile, yielded, and told her the charm, and slept.

Then Viviane instantly put forth the charm of waving hands, and in the cave on Carmarthen's mount he lay as dead. And she exclaimed, "I have made thy glory mine."

CHAPTER XXVI.

King Arthur and his knights slay the five kings who invaded the land—King Arthur returns to Camelot and selects eight knights of the Round Table to fill the places of those slain in battle—Sir Bagdemagus is displeased at not being chosen one of the knights—He goes to Merlin's cave and attempts to remove the stone.

AND as King Arthur held a great feast with mirth at Caer Leon, there came tidings that the King of Denmark, the King of Ireland, the King of the Vale, the King of Sweden, and the King of the Isle of Longtainse, had entered his land, and had burnt and destroyed many of his cities and his castles, and had slain many of his people.

"Alas!" said King Arthur, "I have not had peace for one month since I was crowned king, and I shall have no peace until I meet these five kings in a fair field, and this I will do, therefore those who fear, let them abide at home."

King Arthur sent a messenger unto King Pellinore, and prayed him to haste and make ready with as many of his people as he may, and join him against the five kings. Then came King Arthur to Guinevere, and said, "Lady, make you ready, for I cannot abide your absence, and your presence will make me more valiant in whatever adventure may be undertaken, and I will not see my lady in jeopardy."

"Sir," replied the queen, "I am at your command, and am ready when ye list."

In the morning the king and queen wended their way towards the north, and lodged in a forest beside the Humber.

When tidings reached the five kings that King Arthur was beside the Humber, one of the knight said unto the kings, "Know ye not that King Arthur hath the flower of chivalry of the world with him, as was shown in the battle with the eleven kings? Therefore march night and day until you come nigh unto him, for the longer he tarrieth the bigger will his army be, whilst yours will become weaker."

Unto this counsel the five kings gave hear, and so they with their host came upon Arthur by night, and set upon him and his knights as they were in their pavillions. King Arthur at the time was unarmed, and had laid himself to rest by the side of Queen Guinevere. Anon, a great noise was heard and many cries of "Treason, Treason!"

King Arthur girding on his armour, called on his knights to arm themselves for they were betrayed. Then Sir Kaye, Sir Gawain, and Sir Griflet, armed themselves at all points.

Then there came a wounded knight unto the king, and said, "Sir, save yourself and the queen, for our host are dispersed. So the king and the queen and the three knights rode towards the Humber but the water was so rough that they were afraid to pass on. "Now may we choose," said King Arthur, "whether we will abide and be taken and slain, or perish in the water."

"I had rather," said the queen, "die in the water than fall into your enemies' hands and there be slain."

And as they stood talking, Sir Kaye saw the five kings coming towards them without any followers, with spears in their hands.

"See," said Sir Kaye, "yonder come the five kings, let us go to them and match them."

" That were folly," said Sir Gawain, " for we are but four, and they are five."

" Nevertheless," said Sir Kaye, " I will undertake two of them, and then may ye three encounter the other three." With these words Sir Kaye galloped his horse towards the kings, and struck one through the shield, and the spear passed through his body, and he fell dead. Then Sir Gawain rushed at another of the kings so hard that he smote him through the body. Therewithal King Arthur encountered another of the kings, and smote him through the body with his spear so that he fell dead to the earth. Then Sir Griflet ran at the fourth king and gave him such a buffet that he fell and broke his neck ; whereupon Sir. Kaye charged the remaining king, and smote him so that he fell mortally wounded.

" That was well stricken," said King Arthur, "and right worshipfully hast thou kept thy promise ; therefore I shall honour thee as long as I live."

And Queen Guinevere likewise praised Sir Kaye and said, " What lady that ye love, and she not love you again, she were to blame, and among ladies I shall speak of your fame, for ye spoke a word, and fulfilled it worshipfully."

Then the king and his knights rode into the forest, where King Arthur found most part of his people, and said, " Let us keep together until day, and when our enemies have espied that their chieftains are slain, they will be very sorrowful in heart, and they shall not help themselves.

And it was as the king had said, for when they

found the five kings dead, they made lamentation, and King Arthur led his men against them,
and slew full thirty thousand. And when the
battle was ended, the king thanked God for the
victory. And then he sent for the queen, and
she made great joy of the overcoming of the
battle.

Then came there one to King Arthur, and
told him that King Pellinore was within a mile
with a great host. And the king said unto the
messenger, "Go and tell him how we have sped."

Then King Arthur found his loss to be eight
knights and two hundred men slain. Then the
king reared on the spot a fair abbey, and en-
dowed it, and named the structure the Abbey
of La Belle Adventure. And when all King
Arthur's enemies, such as the King of North
Wales and the King of the North, heard of the
battle, they were grieved. And King Arthur
returned to Camelot, and when he arrived there
he called King Pellinore and said, " We have
lost eight good knights of the Round Table, and
by your advice we will choose other eight of the
best we may find in this court."

" Sir," replied King Pellinore, " I shall counsel to the best of my knowledge that ye choose
half of the old and half of the young ; of the
old I would name King Urience, who hath wedded your sister Morgan la Fay ; and the King
of the Lake, and Sir Hervise de Revel, and Sir
Galagars."

" This is well devised," said King Arthur,
" and so shall it be. Which are to be the four
young knights ?"

" Sir," said King Pellinore, " the first is Sir

Gawain your nephew; the second is Sir Griflet, who shall prove a good knight ; and the third it seemeth to me should be Sir Kaye, the seneschal, for many times he hath done full worshipfully, and now at your last battle he did honourably to undertake to slay two kings."

" By my head," said King Arthur, " he is best worthy to be a knight of the Round Table of any that ye have rehearsed."

" Now as for the fourth," said King Pellinore, " I shall put to ye two knights, and ye shall choose which is the most worthy : they are Sir Bagdemagus and Sir Tor, my son, but because Sir Tor is my son I may not praise him; but if he were not my son, I durst say that of his age there is not one in the land a better knight than he is."

" By my word," said King Arthur, " he is as good knight as any ye have named this day, for I have seen him proved, and he sayeth little and doeth much. I will therefore have him this time, and leave Sir Bagdemagus until another time."

So when they were thus chosen by the assent of all the barons, so were they set in their seats. When Sir Bagdemagus heard that Sir Tor had been preferred before him, he was wroth, and suddenly departed from the court and took his squire with him, and rode into a forest until they came to a cross, at which he alighted and said his prayers.

And meanwhile his squire found written on the cross that Bagdemagus should never return unto the court again until he had won a knight's body of the Round Table. And as Sir Bagdemagus rode he came to the rock where the Lady of the Lake had put Merlin under the stone, and he heard him making lamentation ; and he would have helped Merlin, and went to lift the stone, but it was so heavy that one hundred men could not lift it up.

When Merlin saw that he was trying to release him, he told him all was in vain, for he might never be helped out but by her who put him there. And so Sir Bagdemagus departed and proved a good knight, and came again to the court, and was made Knight of the Round Table.

CHAPTER XXVII.

Lucius Tiberius a second time demands tribute from King Arthur—King Arthur asks counsel of his lords and knights—His message to Lucius—Great promises of aid —His expedition to Rome—Lucius, with the aid of sixteen kings, threatens to destroy him and his hosts—Sir Gawain and Sir Bors go to the Emperor's tent—Sir Gawain slays the knight Ganius, and Sir Bors kills the Pavian knight—The great battle between the armies of Lucius and King Arthur—The defeat of the Romans— Lucius and the sixteen kings slain—King Arthur's message to the Romans.

AFTER King Arthur had rested from his wars, he held a feast among his knights of the Round Table. And there came twelve ancient men, each of whom bore a branch of olive, as ambassadors from Lucius Tiberius, Emperor of Rome, who had sent them a second time demanding, under pain of grievous war, tribute and homage from King Arthur, and the restoration of all Gaul which he had conquered from the tribune Flollo.

When they had delivered their message the king commanded them to withdraw for a time,

527   L

while he consulted with his knights and barons. Then some of the younger knights would have slain the ambassadors, saying that their message was a rebuke unto all the knights present to suffer such a message to be delivered unto their king.

But when King Arthur heard their speeches, ne desired none to touch the ambassadors on pain of death, and ordered them to be entertained with the best cheer, and, said he, "Let no dainty be spared, for the Romans are great lords, and though their message pleaseth me not, yet must I remember mine honour." Then the king called his knights and lords to council.

Sir Cador, of Cornwall, speaking first, said, "Sir, this message pleaseth me, for we have been many days idle, and now I hope we shall make sharp war upon the Romans and gain honour."

"That may be," said King Arthur, "but we must send an answer to the Emperor of Rome, and his demand doth grieve me sorely, for I will never pay truage to Rome; wherefore, lords, give me your counsel. I have understood that Belinus and Brennius, kings of Britain, held the Roman empire in their hands, and also that Constantine, son of Queen Heleine, possessed it. Therefore I, who am descended from them, not only owe the Emperor no tribute, but of right, claim the empire."

Then said King Anguish of Scotland, "Sir, thou oughtest to be above all other kings, for in all Christendom there is not thine equal, and I counsel thee never to obey the Romans; for when they reigned here they grievously oppressed us, and put the land to heavy burdens;

for my part I swear to avenge myself on them, and will furnish twenty thousand good men-at-arms, whom I will keep, and who shall wait upon thee with me when it shall please thee."

Then the king of Little Britain promised thirty thousand men; the king of West Wales promised twenty thousand, and Sir Ewaine and his cousin thirty thousand. Many other kings, and dukes, and barons promised a great host; and Sir Launcelot of the Lake and every knight of the Round Table promised aid. The king being joyful at their courage thanked them all, and sent his answer, "Now go back unto the Emperor your master, and tell him I give no heed to his words, for I have conquered all my kingdoms by the will of God, I am strong enough to keep them without paying tribute to any earthly creature. But, on the other hand, I claim both tribute and submission from himself, and the sovereignty of all his empire, whereto I am entitled by the right of my ancestors; say to him that I will shortly come to Rome, and take possession of my empire, and subdue them which are rebellious; and, lastly, I command him and all the lords of Rome that they forthwith pay me homage under pain of chastisement."

Then he commanded his treasurer to give the ambassadors great gifts, and pay their expenses, and appointed Sir Cador to convey them out of the land. When they arrived at Rome and came before Lucius they delivered the message. He was sorely enraged at the reply they brought, and said, " I had supposed that this Arthur would have submitted to me as other kings, but because of his fortune in Gaul he hath grown insolent."

"Refrain from such vain words, my lord," replied one of the ambassadors, "for truly, I and my companions were full sore afraid to behold his royal majesty and his fearful countenance; I fear ye have made a rod for yourself, for he meaneth to be master of this empire. He is a different kind of man to what thou supposest him to be, and holdeth the most noble court of all the world. We saw him on New Year's Day served at his table by nine kings and the noblest company of princes, lords, and knights that ever was in all the world, and in his person he is the most manly-seeming man we ever beheld, and looketh likely to conquer all the earth."

"Well," said Lucius, "before Easter I will pass the mountains into France, and, with the Genoese and other mighty warriors of Tuscany and Lombardy, bereave him of his lands, and will send for all my allies of Rome to come to mine aid."

Lucius straightway sent many old knights with messages to his allies; to Ambage and Arrage, to Alexandria, to Inde, to Hermonie, to Affrike, to Asia, to Ertaine and Elamie, to Arabia, Egypt and Damascus, to Capadocia, to Tarce, Turkey and Galacia, to Greece, Cyprus, Macedonia, Calabre, Cateland, Portugal, and Spain, and many other provinces. Then all these kings, and many princes, dukes and lords with a multitude of people, assembled at Rome. And with fifty giants as a body guard, Lucius passed over the mountains into Gaul; there he ravaged all the country in rage for their submission to King Arthur, and afterwards moved on to Little Britain.

Meanwhile, King Arthur left the realm in

charge of Sir Bawdewine and Sir Constantine, and crossed the sea to meet Lucius. And as soon as he was landed he sent Sir Gawain, Sir Bors, Sir Lionel, and Sir Bedevere to the Emperor, commanding him to move out of the land. Anon these knights rode forth to where they saw many tents of divers colours, and the Emperor's pavillion in the midst, with the golden eagle set above it. Then Sir Gawain and Sir Bors gave King Arthur's message to Lucius, who said, " Return and tell your lord that I am come to conquer him and all his land."

At this Sir Gawain cried out, " I had rather than have all France that I might fight with thee alone !" At this a knight named Ganius, laughed aloud, and said, " Lo ! how these Britons boast as though they bare up all the world."

As the knight uttered these words Sir Gawain could restrain his anger no longer, but drew his sword, and smote off Ganius's head, and then, with Sir Bors, rode to the wood where Sir Lionel and Sir Bedevere lay in ambush. The Romans followed fast behind them until the knights turned and stood, when Sir Bors smote the foremost of them through the body with his spear. Then came on Sir Calibere, a huge Pavin, but Sir Bors slew him also. And then the company of Sir Lionel and Sir Bedevere brake from their ambush, and fell on the Romans, hewing them down, and forced them to return to their tents. But as they neared the camp a great host rushed forth and turned the battle backwards, and Sir Bors and Sir Berel fell into the hands of the enemy. When Sir Gawain beheld this he drew forth his sword, and swore to see King

Arthur's face no more if those two knights were not delivered, and with Sir Idrus made such an onslaught that the Romans fled and left Sir Bors and Sir Berel to their friends.

When Lucius saw the discomfiture of his knights, he marched forth with his vast army to crush King Arthur, and met him in the vale of Soissons. Then, addressing all his hosts, he said, "Warriors, I admonish you that this day ye acquit yourselves as men, remember how Rome is mistress of the world, and suffer not these barbarous Britons to abide our onset." Then at the sound of the trumpets did the rival hosts draw near with great shoutings, and when they closed no tongue can tell the fury and fearfulness of the struggle.

Then King Arthur with his most approved knights rode into the thickest of the fight, and slew as lightning slays for swiftness and for force. And in the midst King Arthur met a giant, Galapas by name, and struck off both his legs at the knee joint, then saying, "Now thou art a better size to fight with," smote off his head. Then King Arthur spied where Lucius fought, and he rode at him and each attacked the other fiercely till at last Lucius struck Arthur a blow across the face, and Arthur, lifting up Excalibur on high, smote Lucius on the head, shivering his helmet, splitting his head and body to the breast. When the Romans saw their Emperor fall, they fled, and King Arthur and his army slew one hundred thousand men.

Then King Arthur rode to the spot where Lucius lay, and found dead around him sixteen other kings and sixty Roman senators, all noble men. Then calling for three senators, who were taken prisoners, he said to them, "As the ransom of your lives I will that ye take these dead bodies to Rome, and present them for me with these letters, saying I will myself be shortly there, and tell the Romans to beware how they again ask tribute of me, and say that these dead bodies I send them are for the tribute they dared to ask of me, and if they wish for more, when I come I will pay them the rest."

So with that charge the senators departed, the body of the Emperor being borne on a chariot blazoned with the arms of the Empire, and the bodies of the kings two and two in chariots following.

CHAPTER XXVIII.

Feast of the Round Table at Caer Leon—Queen Guinevere invites Sir Launcelot of the Lake to tell of his birth—Sir Launcelot and Sir Lionel seek adventures —Sir Lionel is taken prisoner by Tarquin—Sir Launcelot and the four queens—His imprisonment and release by a damsel, the daughter of King Bagdemagus—Sir Launcelot takes the side of King Bagdemagus against the side of the King of Northgales, and defeats many knights.

ON the day of Pentecost following King Arthur's return from Rome, there was held a feast of the Round Table at Caer Leon, with great splendour.

Mounted upon a platform of marble pavement, stood the Round Table, which, according to Merlin, was in shape of the rounded plane of the earth. The table was instituted by Uther Pendragon, Arthur's father, to assemble the best knights of Christendom and to number those which 'achieve the Holy Graal.' When it came

into Arthur's possession it was blessed by the
Archbishop of Canterbury. It had seats for a
hundred and fifty knights, a number always to
be made up at the feast of Pentecost, when they
were sworn to do no outrage, to be loyal and
merciful, to succour all women in distress, and
to fight in no unjust quarrel, 'upon pain of forfeiture of their worship and lordship of Arthur
for evermore.'

The great Pendragon stood on the dais in his
robes, his handsome face radiant with pleasure,
upon his head was the golden crown of state;
Sir Gawain standing on the steps of the dais,
modestly inclined towards the king. Around
the memorable emblem of the knightly brother-
hood, to which it gave the name, were grouped
the principal officers of King Arthur's court
and household: Sir Kaye, the king's foster
brother, and steward or seneschal, with old Sir
Ulfius, the chamberlain; Sir Lucas, the butler;
and Sir Bawdewine of Britain, constable.

The ladies of the court, knights, and civilian
spectators, filled the body of the hall. Conspicuous among them was the fair Guinevere, in
flowing robes and glistening diadem. She was
surrounded by a lovely bevy of her attendant
damsels. Of all the knights who resorted to
the court to take part in the jousts and tournaments, Sir Launcelot of the Lake excelled in
fame all others, for he overthrew all comers,
and was never unhorsed. When Queen Guinevere witnessed his wondrous feats, she looked
upon him with favour, and smiled upon him more
than on any other knight. And ever since he
had gone to the land of Cameliard to bring her

to the king, he had looked upon Queen Guinevere as fairest of all ladies, and had done his best to win her grace. And the queen sent for him, and bade him tell his birth, lineage, and adventures, from which she found he was the only son of King Ban of Brittany, and how one night his father, with his mother, Helen, and himself, fled from his burning castle, and how his father fell to the ground and died with grief, and how his mother left her son to run to her husband, and how as the son lay wailing, there came the Lady of the Lake and took him in her arms and went with him into the midst of the waters, where with his cousins, Lionel and Bors, he had been cherished and nursed until he came to King Arthur's court, and how this was the reason he was called Launcelot of the Lake.

And when Sir Launcelot saw that Queen Guinevere rejoiced to hear of his adventures, he resolved to set forth again, and win more worship still, that he might increase in her favour. So he desired his cousin Lionel to make ready to go with him to seek adventures. They mounted their horses and came to a great plain. About noon-tide Sir Launcelot wished to rest himself; so they tied their horses, and Sir Launcelot lay down under a tree and slept, whilst Sir Lionel kept watch. Whilst he watched he saw three knights riding at a fast pace before a single knight, and when Sir Lionel looked at him he thought he never saw a man so great and strong. And he saw him overtake the last of those who fled, and smite him to the ground. Then he overtook the second and smote him so that both man and horse went to the earth. Then he rode after the third and struck him off his horse. With that he alighted, and bound the three knights fast with their own bridle reins. When Sir Lionel saw this, he rode after them, and on overtaking the victor he cried out to him to turn, which he did, and smote Sir Lionel so that horse and man went down. Then he bound Sir Lionel on his own horse's back as he had served the other three knights, and rode with them to his own castle, where they were thrust into a prison with many more knights; and they all cried, "Alas, there is no man now can help us against Tarquin, our conqueror, save Sir Launcelot of the Lake."

All this while Sir Launcelot lay sleeping under the tree, and at length four ladies, riding on four mules, saw him lying, asleep, and knew him to be Sir Launcelot of the Lake. Then each began to claim him as their charge. But Queen Morgan la Fay, said, "We need not quarrel which shall have him, for I have enchanted him for six hours; so let us take him to my castle, and when he wakes, himself shall choose which of us he would rather serve." So Sir Launcelot was borne on horseback to Queen Morgan la Fay's castle, and there laid till the spell should pass. When he awoke they sent to him a damsel bearing his meal, who asked him how he was. "I cannot tell, fair damsel," said he, "for I know not how I came to this place, save by enchantment."

"Sir," said the damsel, "be of good cheer, and to-morrow at dawn of day ye shall know more." And so she left him, and he lay all night. In the morning came the four queens unto him, and said, "Sir knight, thou art our prisoner, and we know thee well to be Sir Launcelot of the Lake, son to King Ban; and also that there is one lady only in this world may have thy love, the beauteous Guinevere; nevertheless, we are resolved to have thee serve one of us; choose, therefore, which of us thou wilt serve: I am Morgan la Fay, queen of the land of Gore; and here is the Queen of Northgales, and the Queen of Eastland, and the Queen of the Out Isles. Choose then at once which thou wilt serve, or else thou shalt abide in prison till thy death."

"Ladies," replied Sir Launcelot, "it is a hard case that either I must die or choose one of you for my mistress! Yet I had rather die than serve any living creature against my will; and I will serve neither of you. And as for my lady Guinevere, were I at liberty I would prove that she is the truest lady living to her lord the king."

"Is that your answer, that ye refuse us all," said Queen Morgan la Fay.

"Yea," replied Sir Launcelot, "refused ye be of me."

Then the four ladies turned in great wrath, and left Sir Launcelot grieving in the dungeon. At noon his dinner was brought by the damsel, who inquired of him how he fared.

"Truly, in all my life never so ill," replied Sir Launcelot.

"Sir," said the damsel, "I grieve to see ye so, but if ye do as I advise, I can help ye out of this distress, and will do so if ye will promise me a boon."

"Right willingly will I grant it thee, fair damsel, for I dread the threats of those four queens, who have destroyed many good knights with their enchantments."

"Then promise me to help my father on Tuesday next, for he hath a tournament with the King of Northgales, and last Tuesday he lost the field through three knights of King Arthur's court who came against him. And if thou wilt aid him, to-morrow I will deliver thee."

"Tell me thy father's name, fair maiden, and I will answer thee."

"My father is King Bagdemagus."

"I know him well for a good knight, and I will do him all the service I can on that day," replied Sir Launcelot.

"Thanks, sir knight," said the damsel. "To-morrow, when thou art delivered, ride ten miles hence to an abbey of white monks, and there abide until I bring my father to thee."

"Be it as thou desirest," said Sir Launcelot.

The damsel then departed, and on the morrow came again, and taking him through twelve gates, brought him his horse and armour; and taking a great spear in his hand he rode forth saying, "By the grace of God, fair maiden, I shall not fail thee."

All that day he rode in a forest, and as he could find no highway he spent the night in the forest; but the next morning he came to the abbey of white monks. And there he found King Bagdemagus and his daughter waiting for him. As they sat together in a chamber, Sir Launcelot told the king how he had been imprisoned in Queen Morgan la Fay's castle, how his brother Lionel was missing, and how he had been delivered by the king's daughter. "Therefore if I live," said he, " I will do service for her and all her kindred, and will not fail thee on Tuesday next; but tell me what knights were they who last week defeated thee and took part with the King of Northgales."

" Sir Mador, Sir Mordred, and Gahalatine, and against them I and my knights had no power," replied the king.

" As I understand," said Sir Launcelot, " the tournament shall take place but three miles from this abbey; send to me three of thy best knights, and let each of them have a plain white shield, and such a one will I also have. Then will we four come suddenly into the midst between both parties, and fall upon thy enemies, and none will know who we are."

And so it was arranged that on the Tuesday, Sir Launcelot and the three knights concealed themselves in a grove hard by the lists. Then came into the field the King of Northgales with one hundred and sixty helms, and the three knights of King Arthur's court, who stood apart by themselves.

As soon as King Bagdemagus had come into the field with eighty helms, both companies rushed at each other with a fearful clash. And in the shock, twelve of the knights of King Bagdemagus and six of the knights of the King of Northgales were slain, and the party of King Bagdemagus was driven back.

At that instant Sir Launcelot and the three knights thrust themselves into the thickest of the press, and Sir Launcelot with one spear smote down five knights, and brake the backs of four others, and cast down the King of North-gales and brake his thigh by the fall.

When the three knights of Arthur's court saw this they rode at Sir Launcelot, and each after the other attacked him, but he overthrew them all.

Then taking a new spear he bore to the ground sixteen more knights, so that they could not carry arms again that day; and when his spear was broken, he took another and smote down twelve knights more and wounded them mortally; in the end the party of the King of North-gales would joust no more, and the victory was cried to King Bagdemagus.

Then Sir Launcelot rode forth with the king to his castle and there he had hearty welcome, and received large gifts. And on the morrow he took leave to go in search of his brother Lionel.

CHAPTER XXIX.

Sir Launcelot seeketh Sir Lionel—His hard fight with Sir Tarquin—Sir Tarquin slain—Sir Launcelot sends to release sixty-four knights, and accompanies a damsel to guard her from a foul knight—He goes to a castle and slays two giants and releases sixty ladies.

SIR LAUNCELOT in his quest for his brother Lionel, came to the same forest where the four queens had found him sleeping, and there met a damsel riding upon a white palfrey, whom he saluted thus: "Fair damsel, knowest thou where any adventures may be had in these parts?"

"Sir knight," she replied, "there are adventures close by if thou darest prove them, for hard by this place there dwelleth a knight who cannot be defeated by any man, so strong he is. His name is Sir Tarquin ; and in his castle are confined three-score knights, most of whom belonged to King Arthur's court, and whom he has taken with his own hands. But promise me ere thou undertakest to deliver them to free me and other ladies from the power of a false knight."

Then said Sir Launcelot, " Bring me to Tarquin, and I will afterwards fulfil all your desires."

So the damsel led the way to a tree, whereon a brass basin hung. And Sir Launcelot struck the basin long and hard, and then rode before the castle gates for half an hour, when he observed a powerful knight coming towards the castle, driving before him a horse, across which hung an armed man, bound. And when they came near, Sir Launcelot knew the prisoner for a knight of the Round Table.

As soon as the knight saw Sir Launcelot, he set his spear in the rest, and Sir Launcelot made himself ready to resist his attack, and call out, "Put off that wounded man, I pray thee, from his horse, and let him rest while thou and I shall prove our strength upon each other; for thou doest and hast done great injury to knights of the Round Table."

"If thou be one of the Round Table," answered Tarquin, "I do defy thee and all thy fellows."

Then they spurred their horses towards each other, and smote so fearlessly on each other's shields that both their horses' backs broke under them. As soon as they could free themselves from their saddles they placed their shields before them, and fell to with fearful strokes, until they had many fearful wounds and bled in streams. Thus they fought for two hours, until they were both out of breath, and stood leaning on their swords.

"Let us wait awhile, and answer me what I ask thee," said Tarquin.

"Say on," said Sir Launcelot.

"Thou art the best man I ever met, and seemest like unto one that I hate above all other knights," said Sir Tarquin; "but if thou be not he, I will make peace with thee, and for the sake of thy great valour will deliver all the three-score knights and four who lie in my dungeon, and thou and I will be companions for evermore. Therefore tell me thy name."

"And who is he thou hatest above all others?" asked Sir Launcelot.

"His name," said Sir Tarquin, "is Sir Launcelot of the Lake, and he slew my brother, Sir Carados, ; wherefore if ever I meet him, I will slay him or he shall slay me, for so I have sworn. And to destroy him I have slain a hundred knights, and crippled as many more, and many have perished in my prisons, and I have now many more therein, who shall be delivered, as I told thee, if thou tell me thy name, and thou be not Launcelot."

"I am the knight, and son of King Ban of Benwicke, and knight of the Round Table; so now I defy thee to do thy worst!" cried Sir Launcelot.

"It is then so at last," cried Sir Tarquin. "Thou art more welcome to my sword than was ever lady to a feast, for never shall we part till one of us be dead."

Then did they hurtle together like wild bulls, slashing with their swords. For two more hours they fought, until at last Sir Tarquin grew faint, and bare his shield full low for weariness. When Sir Launcelot saw this, he leaped upon him, and took him by the crest of his helmet, and dragged him to his knees, and smote off his head. Then went Sir Launcelot to the damsel who had brought him to Sir Tarquin, and said, " I am ready, to go upon thy service, but I have no horse."

" Take ye the horse of the wounded knight whom Tarquin was taking to prison, and send that knight on to deliver all the prisoners," replied the damsel.

So Sir Launcelot went to the knight, and prayed him for the loan of his horse.

" Fair sir, ye are welcome to it, for to-day ye have saved both me and my horse, and I see that ye are the best knight in the world, for in my sight have ye slain the mightiest man that I ever saw," replied the wounded knight.

" I give thee thanks," said Sir Launcelot ; " and now go unto yonder castle, where thou shalt find many noble knights of the Round Table, for I have seen their shields hung upon the trees around. On yonder tree alone there are Sir Kaye's, Sir Brandle's, Sir Galind's, and Sir Aliduke's, and many more ; and also my two kinsmen's shields, Sir Ector de Maris and Sir Lionel. I pray thee greet them all from me, Sir Launcelot of the Lake, and tell them that I bid them help themselves to any treasures they can find within the castle; and that I pray Lionel and Ector to go to King Arthur's court, and

527 M

stay there till I come, by the feast of Pentecost I must be there ; now I must ride forth with this damsel to fulfil my promise unto her."

Then said the damsel, " Sir, we are near the place where the foul knight haunteth, against whom I have sought thy aid."

It was arranged that the damsel should ride on alone and Sir Launcelot should follow under cover of the trees, and if he saw her come to any mishap he should ride to her succour. As she rode on at ambling pace, a knight and page burst from the road-side, and forced the damsel from her horse, till she cried out for help. Then Sir Launcelot rushed to her assistance, and cried out, " Thou traitor to all knighthood, why dost thou distress the fair damsels thus ?"

Then the foul knight rode at Sir Launcelot, who drew his sword, and struck the knight such a blow as clove his head asunder. Then Sir Launcelot rode in a great forest, and had but scanty food, and on the third day he rode over a bridge, when there started up a foul churl, who smote his horse across the nose, and the churl cried out, " Why ridest thou over here without my leave ?"

" Why should I not ?" said Sir Launcelot; "there is no other way to ride."

" Thou shalt not pass here," said the churl, and dashed at Sir Launcelot with a club, so that Sir Launcelot was fain to draw his sword and smite him to the earth. Then Sir Launcelot rode to a castle, where he tied his horse to a ring in the wall ; and on going inside the castle, he saw a wide green court ; and as he looked about he saw people watching him from the windows, and making signs of warning. In the next instant came upon him two giants, with two clubs in their hands. Then he warded off one giant's stroke, and clove the head of the other giant with his sword. Then was the first giant in great terror for his life, and ran away; but Sir Launcelot followed him, and smote him through the shoulder till he fell dead.

Sir Launcelot then walked to the castle hall, there he was met by sixty ladies, who thanked him for their release from the giants. And when Sir Launcelot told them his name, they cried aloud, "Well may it be so, for we know no knight save thee who could have vanquished these giants, and many a day have we sighed for thee, for the giants feared no other name among all knights but thine."

Then he desired them to take of the treasures of the castle as much as they desired, as a recompense for their grievances, and to return to their houses.

CHAPTER XXX.

Sir Launcelot rescues Sir Kaye from three knights—He sleeps with Sir Kaye, and in the morning takes Sir Kaye's armour—Sir Launcelot overthrows three knights and sends them to King Arthur's court—Sir Launcelot overthrows four other knights of the Round Table—Sir Launcelot discovers a dead knight with a lady weeping by his side—He meets with a damsel who asks him to save her brother's life—His adventures in Chapel Perilous.

SIR LAUNCELOT after a days' travelling came by chance to a fair mansion, wherein he found an old gentlewoman who gave him and his horse good cheer, and a bedchamber was over the gate, where he went to bed.   After he had slept for some time, he was awoke by a knocking at the gate below, so he arose, and by the moonlight he saw three knights riding after one man and lashing on him with their swords.

Then Sir Launcelot getting through the window, let himself down by a sheet, and going to the knights cried out, "Turn on me, ye cowards, and leave fighting with that knight."

Then they left Sir Kaye, for the knight pursued was he, and began to fall upon Sir Launcelot, who with six strokes of his sword, felled the three knights, who cried out, "Sir knight, we yield to thee as a man of might."

"I will not take your yielding," said Sir Launcelot, "yield ye to Sir Kaye, the seneschal, or I will take your lives."

"Excuse us in that, fair knight," said they, "for we have chased this knight so far, and should have overcome him but for thee."

"Well, do as ye list, but if ye live, ye shall holden to Sir Kaye."

Then they yielded to him, and Sir Launcelot commanped them to go unto King Arthur's court at the next Pentecost, and say Sir Kaye had sent them prisoners to Queen Guinevere; and this they swore to do upon their swords.

Then Sir Launcelot knocked at the gate, and both Sir Kaye and himself were admitted. And when a light was brought Sir Kaye knew Sir Launcelot, and thanked him for his courtesy.

"Sir," said Sir Launcelot, "I have done no more than I ought to do, and ye are welcome; therefore, let us take some rest."

On the morrow Sir Launcelot took Sir

Kaye's shield and armour, and set forth on his journey.

And when Sir Kaye found Sir Launcelot's armour by his bedside, and his own arms gone, and he thought, "Now will he grieve some knights at our king's court, for those who meet him will be bold to joust with him, mistaking him for me; while I shall ride along in peace."

As Sir Launcelot rode through the great forest and came upon a plain, he saw a bridge whereupon were three silk tents of divers colours, and on each tent was hung a white shield and by each shield stood a knight. And Sir Launcelot passed on without speaking. But when the three knights saw him pass they said it was Sir Kaye, "who thinketh no knight equal to himself, although the contrary is often proved upon him."

"By my faith," said one of them, whose name was Gaultier, "I will and attack him for all his pride, and ye shall see how I fare." So he rode away towards Sir Launcelot and called to him, "Abide, proud knight, and turn, for ye shall not pass free."

Then Sir Launcelot put his spear in rest and rode against Sir Gaultier, whose spear broke short, and both horse and man rolled upon the earth.

When the other two knights saw this they said, "Yonder knight is not Sir Kaye, but a bigger man, and no doubt he hath slain Sir Kaye and taken his horse and armour."

"Be it so or not," said Sir Reynauld to Sir Gilmore, "let us go to our brother's rescue, and we shall have enough to do to match that knight, for I believe he is Sir Launcelot or Sir Tristram." So they rode towards Sir Launcelot, and Sir Gilmore first assailed him, but was stricken down, and lay stunned.

Then Sir Reynauld said, "Sir knight, thou art a strong man, and I doubt not ye have slain my two brothers, wherefore my heart is sore against thee; yet I would avoid thee; nevertheless, as that cannot be, keep thyself." So they hurtled together, and their spears were shivered to pieces. Then they drew their swords and slashed out furiously.

And as they fought Sir Gaultier and Sir Gilmore rose from the ground and mounted their horses, and came at full tilt upon Sir Launcelot. But he saw their approach, and putting forth all his strength struck Sir Reynauld off his horse; then with two other strokes served the others likewise. Then crept along the ground Sir Reynauld, with his head all bloody, toward Sir Launcelot.

"It is enough," said Sir Launcelot, "I know thee for a valiant knight, and was full loath to slay thee."

"Gramercy for thy goodness!" said Sir Reynauld, "and my brother will yield to thee when thou tellest unto us thy name; for we know that thou art not Sir Kaye."

"As for that," said Sir Launcelot, "be it as it may, but ye shall most assuredly yield yourselves unto Queen Guinevere at the next feast of Pentecost, and say that Sir Kaye sent ye."

Then they swore that they would do as he had commanded, and Sir Launcelot proceeded through a forest where he came upon four knights of King Arthur's court: Sir Sagramour, Sir Mabel, Sir Gawain, and Sir Ewaine. And when they saw him they thought it was Sir Kaye.

"By my faith," said Sir Sagramour, "I will prove Sir Kaye's might," and rode towards him, but Sir Launcelot smote him so that man and horse fell to the earth.

"Lo!" said Sir Mabel, "I see that the knight is stronger than Sir Kaye; now will I try what I can do against him." And he galloped toward Sir Launcelot, but that knight smote him so severely that his spear passed through his shield and shoulder. Then said Sir Ewaine, "By the strength of that blow I see it will be hard to match him, but I will try to do so." And he rode straight at Sir Launcelot, and was overthrown as the others had been. "Now I will encounter thee," said Sir Gawain; and he levelled his spear and guarded himself with his shield. And he and Sir Launcelot met at full speed, and furiously smote each other on the middle of each other's shield, but Sir Gawain's spear broke, and the blow of Sir Launcelot was so mighty that Sir Gawain and his horse rolled on the earth.

Then Sir Launcelot rode away smiling, and the four knights made their way to King Arthur's court.

After encountering many dangers on his way, Sir Launcelot saw a black bloodhound running with his head towards the ground as if he tracked a deer. But the hound ever and anon looked behind him and ran towards an old house. So Sir Launcelot followed and went into the hall, and there he saw a dead knight, whose wounds the hound licked, and a lady sat beside the body weeping, who cried, " Oh! Sir 'Knight, too great is the sorrow you have brought upon me!"

"Say not so, dear lady," said Sir Launcelot, "for I never injured this knight, and am sorely grieved to see thy sorrow."

"I see now," said the lady, "that it was not thee who slew my husband, for he that did it is wounded and shall never recover."

"God send thee comfort," said Sir Launcelot, and rode on his way. And he met with a damsel, who cried to him to help her brother who was sore wounded. "For," said she, "there is a sorceress who dwelleth in a castle hard by, and she hath told me that my brother's wounds shall never be healed until I find a knight to go to the Chapel Perilous, and bring from thence the sword and the bloody cloth in which a wounded knight is wrapped."

"This is a marvel," said Sir Launcelot, "but what is thy brother's name?"

"Sir Meliot de Logies," said the damsel.

"Then he is a fellow of the Round Table, and I will do my best to help him," said Launcelot.

"I will abide thy return at this place, for if ye speed not there is no hope of his being cured."

Then Sir Launcelot departed, and when he came to the Chapel Perilous, he tied his horse to a gate. And as soon as he was within the church-yard he saw on the front of the Chapel many fair shields turned upside down; and many of the shields Sir Launcelot had seen knights have before; and he saw standing by him thirty great knights, more by a yard than any man that he had ever seen, and all these gnashed at Sir Launcelot; and when he saw their countenances he dreaded them sore, and so put his shield afore him, and took his sword in his hand ready to do battle; and they were all armed in black harness, ready with their shields and swords drawn. And when Sir Launcelot would have gone through them they scattered on every side of him, and gave him the way to pass; and therewith he waxed bold, and entered the Chapel, and there he saw no light but a dim lamp burning, and then he was aware of a corse covered with a cloth of silk. And as Sir Launcelot stooped down and cut a piece of the cloth away, the earth quaked, and he was afraid. He then saw a sword lying by the side of the dead knight, and that he took in his hand, and hied him from the Chapel. As soon as he was in the chapel-yard, all the knights spoke to him in grim voices, and said, "Knight Sir Launcelot, lay that sword from thee or else thou shalt die."

"Whether I live or die," said Sir Launcelot, "with no great words get it ye again, therefore fight for it if ye list."

Therewith he passed through them, and beyond the chapel-yard there met him a fair damosel, who said "Sir Launcelot, leave that sword behind thee or thou wilt die for it."

"I will not leave it," said Sir Launcelot, "for no threats—"

"No," said she, "if ye did leave that sword, Queen Guinevere should ye never see."

"Then were I a fool, and I would not leave this sword," said Sir Launcelot.

"Now, gentle knight," said the damosel, "I require thee to kiss me once."

"Nay," said Sir Launcelot, "that God forbid."

"Well, sir," said she, "hadst thou kissed me thy life's days had been done; but now, alas! I have lost all my labour, for I ordained this chapel for thy sake, and for Sir Gawain; and once had I Sir Gawain within it; and at that time he fought with that knight which there lyeth dead, Sir Gilbert the bastard, and he smote off Sir Gilbert's left hand. And so, I now tell thee that I have loved thee these seven years; but there may no woman have thy love but Queen Guinevere. But since I may not rejoice to have thy body alive, I had no more joy in this world but to have thy dead body; and I would have balmed it, and so have kept it all my life's days; and daily I should have kissed thee, despite Queen Guinevere."

"Ye say well," said Sir Launcelot, "Jesus preserve me from your subtle craft," and he departed from her, and returned to the damsel.

When she saw him she wept for joy, and conducted him to the castle, where Sir Meliot lay. And when Sir Launcelot saw him, he knew him, although he was very pale from bleeding.

When Sir Meliot saw Sir Launcelot, he cried, "Oh! Sir Launcelot, help me." Then Sir Launcelot touched his wounds with Sir Gilbert's sword, and wiped them with a part of the bloody cloth, and he was restored to health. And they made Sir Launcelot all the cheer that they could, and on the morn Sir Launcelot bade Sir Meliot hie him to the court of King Arthur at Pentecost, and there he should find him.

Then Sir Launcelot returned home two days before the Pentecost, and the king and all the court were glad to see him.

CHAPTER XXXI.

The high feast of Pentecost—Sir Tristram is brought to the court at Caer Leon—He sits in the seat of Sir Marhaus—Sir Tristram's birth—His stepmother attempts to poison him—Sir Tristram rescues his stepmother from death—Tribute demanded from the King of Cornwall by King Anguish of Ireland—Sir Tristram fights with and defeats Sir Marhaus, the Irish champion.

At the high feast of Pentecost King Arthur sat on his throne at Caer Leon; and it was a custom on that feast, that he would not go on that day to meat until he had heard or seen a great marvel. So, he sat and waited until some adventure should arise, or some knight return to court whose deeds might be told. Whilst he sat, he saw Sir Launcelot and a crowd of knights approaching, and leading the mighty knight, Sir Tristram. As soon as King Arthur espied him, he went towards him, and took him by both his hands, saying, "Good Sir Tristram, right welcome art thou into this court; long have I wished for thee amongst my fellowship."

Then all the knights and barons approached Sir Tristram, and bid him welcome. Queen Guinevere came also with many ladies, and they said the same.

Then the king led Sir Tristram to the Round Table, and said, "Welcome here, as one of the best knights in the world, a chief in war—a chief in peace—a chief in the field—and a chief in the hall!" He then looked round at every empty seat until he came to the one that had been Sir Marhaus', and on that he found written in gold letters "This is the seat of the noble knight, Sir Tristram;" and in that seat did Sir Tristram sit.

And Sir Tristram's history was as follows:

There was a king of Lyonesse named Melio.
das, and he wedded a lady named Gwendoline,
who was sister of Mark, King of Cornwall.

As Meliodas was hunting in a wood, he was
taken by enchantment and made prisoner in a
castle. When his wife found he did not return
home, she was well-nigh mad with grief, and
ran to the forest in search of her lord, but after
many days wandering she could find no trace of
him, and, being worn out by fatigue, she lay
herself down in a valley, and prayed to meet her
death. And as she lay in the midst of sorrow,
she gave birth to a child, and before she died
she called him Tristram, for she said with her
last breath " his name shall show how sadly he
came into this world."

Then the gentlewoman who was with her took
the child, and lay with it in her arms, expect-
ing death to come to her in turn. But a company of lords and barons, seeking the queen,
came up to where she lay, and took her and the
child home with them; and some of them would
have slain the child, in order that they might
become lords of Lyonesse, but through the sup-
plicating speech of the gentlewoman the barons
would not assent thereto, and carried away the
dead body of the queen.

In the meantime King Meliodas contrived to
be released from his prison, and when he came
home the barons rejoiced greatly, but the king
was afflicted by the news of his wife's death,
and did her inter richly, and afterwards had
the child christened " Tristram," as his wife
had desired. Then King Meliodas lived seven
years without a wife, and had his son nourished

well, and at the end of that time wedded the daughter of King Howel, of Brittany, who had children by her husband, King Meliodas, which made her wroth against Tristram, as her own children should not enjoy the kingdom, and she cast about in her own mind how she might destroy him. So she put poison in a cup, where her children and Tristram were playing together, so that he might drink of it and die. But it so happened that her own son saw the cup, and thinking it contained good drink, drank deeply of it, and fell dead.

When the queen was aware of her child's death she was very heavy, but the king knew nothing of her treason; and the queen, because of her son's death, was more envious of Tristram, and put more poison in the cup for him to drink. And by chance her husband took up the cup and was about to drink of it, when she sprang up with a great cry and dashed it from his hands.

The king at this marvelled greatly, and called to mind the sudden death of his child, and taking her fiercely by the hand, exclaimed, "Traitress, tell me what drink is in this cup, or I will slay thee in a moment;" and pulling out his sword, he swore to slay her unless she told the truth.

"Ah! mercy, my lord," exclaimed she. And then she told of her plot to murder Tristram, that her own son might enjoy the kingdom.

"The law shall judge thee," said the king, and she was tried before the barons, and condemned to be burnt to death. And as she stood prepared before the fire young Tristram besought his father to grant him a boon.

"Whatsoever thou askest I will grant thee," replied the king.

" Give me then the life of the queen, my step-mother," said he.

" Thou doest wrong to ask it," said the king, "for she would have slain thee with her poisons if she could, and chiefly for thy sake she ought to die."

" Sir," said Tristram, " I beseech you to forgive her, and may God forgive her as I do."

" Since it is so," said the king, "take thou her life, for to thee I give it, and do with her as thou wilt."

Then went Tristram to the fire and loosed the queen from her bonds, and delivered her from death; but after that the king would never live with her as his wife, and would not suffer Tristram to abide any more in his court, but sent him to France in care of one named Gouvernrail, and there for seven years he abode, and learned all knightly exercises and gentle craft, and was foremost in music and hunting, and when he returned at the age of nineteen, he was strong of body, and noble of heart.

Soon after his return it happened that King Anguish, of Ireland, sent to King Mark, of Cornwall, for seven years' tribute of his land due to Ireland, and King Mark sent answer that if he would have it he must fight for it, and he would find a champion to defend him.

So King Anguish called for Sir Marhaus, his wife's brother, who then lived at his court, and sent him with a knightly retinue in six great ships to Cornwall, and casting anchor by the Castle of Tintagil, he sent up daily to King Mark for the tribute or the champion; but no knight would assail him, for he was famed throughout the land for his strength and valour.

Then King Mark issued a proclamation that if any knight would contend with Sir Marhaus he should stand at the king's right hand for evermore, and have honour and riches.

When Tristram heard this, he was ashamed to think that no knight of Cornwall durst assail the Irish champion, and cried, "Would that I were a knight, that I might match this Marhaus!" And he said to his father, "I pray you give me leave to depart to King Mark's court, and beg of his grace to make me a knight."

Then King Meliodas gave him leave, and Tristram rode to Tintagil to King Mark, and said to him, "Sir, give me the order of knighthood, and I will fight with Sir Marhaus of Ireland."

"Whence come ye?" said the king.

"My name is Tristram," said he; and I was born in the country of Lyonesse."

"But this knight will fight with none who is not of royal blood, and nearly related to kings and queens, as he himself is, being brother to the Queen of Ireland," said King Mark.

"Then let him know," said Tristram, "that I am come of both, for my father is King Meliodas, and my mother was thy sister, who died in the forest at my birth."

When King Mark heard this, he welcomed him, and knighted him, and armed him in armour covered with gold and silver. Then the king sent Sir Marhaus word that Sir Tristram of Lyonesse, son of King Meliodas and King Mark's sister, should fight with him.

So the battle was arranged to be fought on an island near Sir Marhaus' ship, and there Sir Tristram landed with Gouvernail for squire, whom he sent back as soon as he was armed for the combat.   When Sir Marhaus and Sir Tristram were left alone, Sir Marhaus said, "Sir Tristram, I am grieved for thy rashness, for I have been assailed in vain by the best knights in the world; be warned in time, and return to those who sent thee."

"Well-proved knight," said Sir Tristram, "be sure that I shall never quit this quarrel till one of us be overcome; for this cause I have been made knight, and thou shalt know before we part that though I am yet unproved, that I will deliver Cornwall from this burden or die; and thy valour, Sir Marhaus, is a reason why I should assail thee, for win or lose I shall gain honour to have met with so great a knight as thou art."

Then they began the battle, and tilted against each other, so that both knights and horses fell to the earth.   But Sir Marhaus' spear smote Sir Tristram a wound in the side.   Then springing up, they lashed together with their swords, and hurtled together to bear one another down.   Thus they fought for half the day, till blood covered the ground on every side; but Sir Tristram at length, with a mighty stroke, smote Sir Marhaus such a buffet as cut through his helmet to his brain-pan, and there his sword stuck so fast, that Sir Tristram could not get it away.   Then fell Sir Marhaus down, and the edge of Sir Tristram's sword broke off in his brain-pan.   Then suddenly, when he appeared to be dead, Sir Marhaus rose, and threw his sword and shield away, and ran to his ship.   And Sir Tristram cried out to him, " Ah ! sir knight of the Round Table, dost thou withdraw thee from so young a knight ? It is a shame to thee, and I would rather have been hewn into a hundred pieces than have fled from thee."

Then was Sir Marhaus taken to Ireland, where his wounds were dressed, and when the wound on his head was searched, the piece broken out of Sir Tristram's sword was found therein, and Sir Marhaus died.

The queen, his sister, then took the piece of the broken sword, and put it into safe keeping, for she thought that some day it might aid her to revenge her brother's death.

CHAPTER XXXII.

Sir Tristram is met by King Mark and his nobles, and taken to the Castle of Tintagil—He is to sent Ireland to be cured of his wounds—He is healed by the king of Ireland's daughter—His love for La Beale Isoud—Sir Pelamoides overthrows all comers at the tournament—Sir Tristram goes to the joust and overthrows him—The Queen discovers Sir Tristram by the piece of his sword—The king of Ireland allows him to depart—Sir Tristram arrives at Tintagil—King Mark's jealousy of Sir Tristram.

Now turn we again to Sir Tristram, who was sore wounded in the fight with Sir Marhaus the Irish champion, and who sat himself down on the hill side.

And anon came Gouvernail, his squire, with a vessel, and conveyed Sir Tristram from the Island, and when he was come to the land the King and his barons came to meet him, then King Mark took him in his arms, and when he and the barons saw Sir Tristram's wounds, they made great dole, and the king and Sir Dinas, his seneschal, led Sir Tristram into the castle of Tintagil, and had his wounds dressed. So Sir Tristram lay several weeks in pain from the stroke that Sir Marhaus smote him; for the spear had been envenomed with poison. And King Mark and all his barons were heavy, for they deemed none other but that Sir Tristram could not recover. Then the king sent after leeches and surgeons, both men and women, but none of them could cure the wound.

At length there came a wise lady, who plainly told the king that Sir Tristram should not be healed until he went into the country where the poison came from. Upon this King Mark fitted up a vessel, in which he put Sir Tristram and Gouvernail, to sail for Ireland : and when they reached that island they landed near to a castle, where King Anguish and his queen abode; and on his arrival Sir Tristram harped a merry lay, such as had never been heard before that time in Ireland. And when it was told the king and the queen that the harper was a wounded knight, they sent for him to the castle, and after having his wounds searched, asked him his country and name, to which he answered that he was from Lyonesse, and that his name was Tramtrist (for he durst not tell them his true name,) and had been wounded in fighting for a lady's right.

"Then," said King Anguish, "ye shall have all the help that may be; but be not surprised if I am sad, for but lately the best knight in the world was slain in fighting for my cause in Cornwall;" and then he told all the story of Sir

Marhaus' battle, to which Sir Tristram feigned surprise. Then the king, ordered Tramtrist to be put in his daughter's ward, and when she probed his wound she found therein poison, and she healed him after a while; and for her care Tramtrist had great love for La Beale Isoud, and he taught her to play on the harp, and she began to have a fancy unto him. At that time Sir Pelamoides, a Saracen, was in the country, and was favoured by the king and queen; and every day Sir Palamoides drew near unto La Beale Isoud and proffered her many gifts, for he loved her well, which caused Tramtrist to have despite towards him.

Then King Anguish proclaimed a great tournament to be held, and the prize was to be a fair damsel called the Lady of the Lanus, who was a cousin of the king, and whatever knight won her, was to wed her in three days, and have all her lands. This cry was made throughout England, Wales, Scotland, France, and Brittany.

When La Beale Isoud told Sir Tramtrist of this tournament, he said, " Fair lady, I am but a feeble knight, and but late I had been dead but for you. What would thou I should do ? Thou knowest well I may not joust."

" Ah, Sir Tramtrist," said she, " why wilt thou not fight in the tournament; well I wot Sir Pelamoides will be there, and do what he may; I therefore pray thee to be there."

"Madam," said Sir Tristram, " I will go, but ye shall be my better lady, and for thee will I do my best, but let it be unknown to all men, and I pray thee to keep my counsel and

help me to disguise, and I will jeopardise myself
for thy sake."

"I will provide horse and armour for you at
my devise," replied La Beale Isoud.

So on the day of the jousting came Sir Pelamoides, with a black shield and horse, and overthrew many of the knights. And all the people
wondered at his deeds, on the first day he
put to the worse Sir Gawain, Sir Gaheris, Sir
Agravine, Sir Kaye, and Sir Dodinas, Sir
Sagramour le Desirous, Sir Griflet, and many
more knights. On the morrow he was the conqueror again, and had overthrown the Kings of
Scotland and many others ; when Sir Tristram
rode up to the lists, dressed in white armour,
with a white plume and shield, and riding on a
white horse, all of which had been provided by
La Beale Isoud, and so he came in the list.

As soon as Sir Pelamoides saw him, he ran at
him full tilt, but Sir Tristram was prepared for
him, and at the first encounter hurled him to
the ground : and a cry arose that the knight
with the black shield was overthrown. And
Sir Pelamoides, sorely shamed, would have left
the ground, but Sir Tristram riding after him,
bade him stay.

Then did Sir Pelamoides turn with fury,
and lash most furiously at Sir Tristram with his
sword, but at the first stroke Sir Tristram
struck him to the earth, and cried "Do now
all my commands, or take thy death."

Then he yielded to Sir Tristram's mercy, and
promised to forsake La Beale Isoud, and for
twelve months to wear no arms or armour, and
rising up, he hacked his armour to pieces for

madness ; and Sir Tristram rode back to the castle through the postern gate.

Then was Sir Tristram well favoured by the king and queen, and ever after gained the love of La Beale Isoud. But on a certain day, while he was bathing, came the queen and La Beale Isoud into his chamber, and saw his sword lie naked on the bed, and the queen took it up, and saw that within a foot of the end there was a piece broken out, and while the queen was looking at the gap she remembered the piece of sword found in the brain of her brother, Sir Marhaus, and turning pale, she cried out, " By my faith, this is the felon knight that slew thy uncle." Then she ran to her chamber, and took from the casket the piece of iron taken from Sir Marhaus' head, and took it to the chamber and fitted it in Sir Tristram's sword.

Then the queen sped fiercely into the room where Sir Tristram was bathing, and would have pierced him through had not Sir Hebes, his attendant, pulled the sword from her, on which she ran to the king, and falling on her knees before him, cried out, " My lord and husband, thou hast here in thy house that felon knight that slew my brother Sir Marhaus."

"Who is he ?" said the king.

"It is Sir Tramtrist, whom Isoud hath healed," said the queen.

" Alas !" said the king, " I am full grieved, for he is a good knight as ever I have seen in any field, but leave thou him to me."

Then the king went to Sir Tristram's chamber, and found him ready to mount his horse, and said unto him, " Sir Tramtrist, it is not to prove myself against thee that I come, for it would not be knightly of thy host to seek thy life. Depart in peace, but tell me first thy name, and whether thou slewest my bro- ther, Sir Marhaus."

Then Sir Tristram told him the truth, and how he had had his name to be unknown in Ireland; and when he had ended, the king declared he held him in no blame, but for his honour's sake he could not retain him at his court, for by doing so he should displease his barons, his wife, and kin."

Then Sir Tristram thanked the king for his favour and for the goodness his daughter had shown him; he said he would be her servant and knight, and never fail to do as much as knight could. He then went to La Beale Isoud to take his leave, when she exclaimed : " I never yet saw man to love so well, and your departure sore grieveth me."

" Madam," replied Tristram, " faithfully do I promise, as long as I live to be your knight ;" and he took off a ring and gave it to the princess, and she gave him another in return, and they parted sorrowful.

Sir Trisrtam then went to the barons to take his leave of them, and said, " Fair lords, it so befalleth that I must depart; therefore, if there be any to whom I have given offence, let him now say it, and before I go I will amend it to my utmost power; and if there be but one who would speak shame of me behind my back, let him say it now or never ; and here is my body to prove it, against any body."

All were silent, although some amongst them

were of the queen's kindred, and would have assailed him if they dared. So Sir Tristram departed from Ireland, and in a short time arrived at the Castle of Tintagil. Now when the news came to King Mark that Sir Tristram had arrived in Cornwall, and had been cured of his wounds, he was glad. So Sir Tristram made all haste to see his uncle, and afterwards rode to his father, King Meliodas, and there he had the heartiest welcome, and the king and queen parted largely with their lands, and bestowed them on Sir Tristram.

Then again Sir Tristram went to King Mark's court, where he lived for a time, but at length King Mark became jealous of the love shown towards him by all his damsels, and although there was fair speech between them, King Mark liked him not.

Now it befell on a certain day that a knight named Sir Bleoberis de Ganis, a cousin to Sir Launcelot of the Lake came to ask a favour of King Mark, and the king marvelled, seeing he was a man of renown, and a knight of the Round Table, but promised to grant him whatever he desired.

Then Sir Bleoberis demanded to have the choice of the fairest lady in the court.

" I may not say thee nay ; choose therefore, but take all the issues of thy choice."

So when the knight had cast his eyes around the court his choice fell upon the wife of Earl Segwarides, and set her upon horseback behind his squire, and rode on his way. Presently the Earl came in and rode after him in a rage. But all the ladies of the court cried out shame upon

Sir Tristram that he should see a lady forced away from his uncle's court, and not prevent it; to which Sir Tristram answered, "Fair ladies, it is not my place to take part in this quarrel while her husband is present to do it. Had he not been at the court, I may have been her champion; and if it happen that he speed ill, then may I speak with this champion before he passes out of this realm. At this moment ran in a messenger and told that his master, Sir Segwarides, was sore wounded, and at the point of death. When Sir Tristram heard this, he mounted his charger, and Gouvernail, his squire, followed with shield and spear. And as Sir Tristram rode, he met his cousin, Sir Andret, whom King Mark had commanded to bring home, if it lay in his power, two knights of King Arthur, who roamed about seeking adventures.

"What tidings?" asked Sir Tristram.

"God help me, never worse, for those I went to seek have defeated me," replied his cousin.

"Ride ye on your way, and if I should meet them you may be revenged," said Sir Tristram.

And as Sir Andret rode towards the court Sir Tristram rode after the two knights; he soon saw them at a distance before him, and he knew them to be Sir Sagramour le Desirous and Sir Dodinas le Savage, and riding after them he called on them to stop. Sir Sagramour looked haughtily at Sir Tristram, and mocking his words, said, "Fair Knight, be ye a knight of Cornwall?"

"Wherefore asketh thou so," said Sir Tristram.

"Because it is seldom proved that Cornish

knights are as valiant with their arms as with their tongues," replied Sir Sagramour, "and but two hours since there met us such a Cornish knight, who spoke great words, but with little mastery he was laid upon the earth, as I trow thou wilt be also."

"It may chance that I be a better man than he; be that as it may, he was my cousin, and for his sake I will assail ye both,—one Cornish knight against ye two."

"When Sir Dodinas le Savage heard this speech, he seized his spear and said, "Sir knight, keep well thyself," and then they came together furiously, and the spear of Sir Dodinas was split asunder, but Sir Tristram smote him with so full a stroke as hurled him over his horse's crupper. Sir Sagramour, on seeing his companion fall, marvelled who this knight may be, and with all his might came against Sir Tristram. But him likewise Sir Tristram smote with such a buffet as rolled him with his horse on the ground, and in the fall his thigh was broken.

Sir Tristram, looking at them both as they lay on the grass, said, "Fair knights, will ye joust any more; are there no bigger knights than ye in King Arthur's court; will ye again speak shame of Cornish knights?"

"In truth thou hast defeated us," replied Sir Sagramour, "and on the faith of knighthood I require thee to tell us thy name?"

So Sir Tristram told them his name, and when they heard it they were right glad they had met Sir Tristram, for his deeds were well known through the land, and they prayed him to abide in their company.

"Nay," said Sir Tristram, "I must first find a fellow-knight of yours, Sir Bleoberis de Ganis."

"God speed you well," said the two knights, as Sir Tristram rode away.

CHAPTER XXXIII.

Sir Tristram encounters Sir Bleoberis—King Mark becomes envious of Sir Tristram, and sends him to Ireland—Sir Tristram brings La Beale Isoud to Cornwall—On his voyage he lands at Castle Pleure, and is taken prisoner—The beauty of La Beale Isoud and the Lady of the Castle compared—Sir Tristram cuts off the head of the Lady of the Castle, and slays Sir Brewnor—Sir Tristram yields to Sir Galahat and his hundred knights—La Beale is married to King Mark—La Beale Isoud is taken away by Sir Pelamoides—Sir Tristram goes after them, and rescues her, and restores her to King Mark.

AND Sir Tristram had not rode very far before he saw Sir Bleoberis in the valley, and he cried to him, "Abide, Sir Knight of King Arthur's court, and bring back that lady, or deliver her to me."

"I dread no Cornish knight, and will not do either," said Sir Bleoberis.

"Why may not a Cornish knight be as good as any?" said Sir Tristram; "this day two knights of thy own court met me, and they found one Cornish knight sufficient for both before we parted."

"Tell me their names," said Sir Bleoberis.

"Sir Sagramour and Sir Dodinas," replied Sir Tristram.

"Hast thou indeed met with them! By my faith they were two knights and men of worship, and if thou hast beaten both thou must needs be a good knight; but for all that thou shalt beat me ere thou hast this lady."

"Defend thyself, then," exclaimed Sir Tristram, and came upon him swiftly, but Sir Bleoberis was on the alert, and firm, and each bore down the other, horse and all to the earth. Then they sprang clear of their horses and lashed together furiously with their swords for two hours, and often struggling together on the ground.

At last Sir Bleoberis exclaimed, "Hold hard awhile, and let us speak together."

"Say on," said Sir Tristram.

"I would fain know thy name, thy court, and thy country," said Sir Bleoberis.

"I have no shame to tell thee," said Sir Tristram. "I am the son of King Meliodas, my mother was sister to King Mark, and my name is tram of Lyonesse."

"Truly, I am glad to hear it," returned Sir Bleoberis, "for thou art he who slew Sir Marhaus fighting for the Cornish tribute, and defeated Sir Pelamoides at the Irish Tournament, he who overcame Sir Gawain and his nine companions."

"I am that knight," said Sir Tristram; "and now pray tell me thy name."

"I am Sir Bleoberis de Ganis, cousin of Sir Launcelot of the Lake."

"Thou speakest truth," said Sir Tristram, "for of all men Sir Launcelot is peerless in knighthood, and for the love I bear to his name I will not fight more with thee."

"In good faith, I am as loath to fight thee more," said Sir Bleoberis, "but since thou hast followed me to win this lady, I proffer thee and courtesy, and this lady shall go with which of us she pleaseth best."

So the squire brought the lady forth, and sh
selected to abide with Sir Bleoberis.

When Sir Tristram heard her choice, he wa
in anger with her, and felt he could not return
to King Mark's court; but Sir Bleoberis said
" gentle knight; because King Mark gave me
choice of any gift, and because this lady chose
to go with me, I took her, but now I have fulfilled my adventure, and for thy sake she shall
be sent to her husband at the abbey where he
lyeth."

So Sir Tristram rode back to Tintagil, and Sir
Bleoberis to the abbey and delivered up the
lady and departed.

Sir Tristram abode for a time at his uncle's
court, till King Mark devised a plan to be rid
of him by sending him to Ireland to demand La
Beale Isoud to be his queen, for Sir Tristram
had so praised her beauty and goodness that
King Mark desired her for his wife, and thinking his nephew would be slain by the queen's
kindred if he returned to Ireland.

But Sir Tristram made ready to depart, and
took with him the noblest knights he could find.
When they arrived in Ireland, Sir Tristram
delivered his uncle's message, and King Anguish consented to his daughter's departure.
The queen gave Dame Bragwaine a flask of
wine, and charged her to cause La Beale Isoud
and King Mark to drink of it on their marriage
day, and then they should love each other all their
lives.   So Sir Tristram and Isoud departed for
Cornwall.

And it so chanced that one day as Sir Tristram and the lady were sitting in the cabin,

they saw the flask and being thirsty, Sir Tristram took it and offered it to La Beale Isoud, who tasted of the wine, and Sir Tristram afterwards drank some himself, and never before had they tasted any wine that seemed so good, and by the time they had finished drinking they loved each other so well that their love nevermore might leave them; and so it came to pass that though Sir Tristram might never wed La Beale Isoud, he did the mightiest deeds of arms for her love.

So they sailed on until they came in sight of Castle Pleure, landed, and went to the castle; and as soon as they approached the gates they were taken prisoners, for it was a custom that whoever rode towards it with a lady he must fight with its owner, Sir Brewnor, and if it proved that Sir Brewnor won, then the stranger knight and his lady were put to death, but if it were that the strange knight won, then should he be put to death, and his lady also.

As Sir Tristram and La Beale Isoud lay in the prison, there came a knight and lady to cheer them.

And Sir Tristram enquired of the knight concerning the custom of the castle, and the knight replied it was an old custom and he that was the castle, defeated must lose his head, and if his lady be not so fair as my lady of the castle, she should also lose her head.

"Now," said Sir Tristram, "this is a shameful custom, but I have one advantage, my lady is the fairest that ever eyes saw, and she shall lose her head, and I will fight for my own on a fair field. Therefore, tell thy lord that I will be ready in the morning to do battle with him."

Then said the knight, "take thy rest, and be up by times in the morning, and you shall want nothing that I can help thee to."

He departed, and in the morning the same knight came to Sir Tristram, and brought him his horse and armour, and bade him make speed, for all the estates and commons of that lordship were ready to behold the battle.

Then came the lord of the castle with his lady, and enquired of Sir Trisrtam for his lady.

" Sir," said Sir Tristram, "this is a foul custom, but before my lady shall lose her head I will lose mine own."

" Nay," said Sir Brewnor, "the ladies shall be shown together, and the one shall have her judgment."

"I doubt not," said Sir Tristram, " that mine is the fairest, and that I will prove, and whoever shall say to the contrary I will prove it on his head."

And Sir Tristram showed the countenance of La Beale Isoud. And all the people gave judgment that La Beale was the fairer of the two.

" Now, therefore," said Sir Tristram, " as my lady is deemed the fairest, it were a pity that she should lose her head, but because thee and thy lady have used this wicked custom, it were no loss to destroy you both."

" Truly," said Sir Brewnor, " thy lady is fairer than mine, and so I hear the people say therefore, if thou wilt slay my lady I doubt not I shall slay thee, and have thy lady."

"Thou shalt win her as dear as ever was lady won," said Sir Tristram ; and he strode to the lady, and smote off her head.

"Well, knight," said Sir Brewnor, "now hast thou done me sore despite, therefore since I am ladyless, I will win thy lady."

Then they came together and Sir Tristram smote Sir Brewnor off his horse. And Sir Brewnor arose and thrust Sir Tristram's horse in the shoulder, and it fell dead, and rushing at Sir Tristram would have slain him also, but Sir Tristram was light of foot, and they rushed and hustled for two hours, and wounded each other until Sir Tristram thrust Sir Brewnor down and struck off his head. Then all who belonged to the castle did homage to Sir Tristram, and prayed him to undo the foul custom of the castle, and he consented thereto.

And anon came Galahat, a noble knight, who was Sir Brewnor's son, with one hundred knights, and proffered to fight with Sir Tristram.

And Sir Galahat and Sir Tristram met so hard, that both horses and riders went to the ground. They dressed their swords, and with ire lashed and fought nearly the whole day. At length Sir Galahat was driven back, and was likely to have been slain, when the hundred knights fell upon Sir Tristram.

Then cried out Sir Tristram to the prince, "Sir, ye show to me no knighthood to suffer all your men to have to do with me at once."

"Truly," said Sir Galahat, "there is none other way that ye must yield to me, or else die."

"I will rather yield to ye than die,' said Sir Tristram,

And Sir Tristram took his sword and put the pommel into the hand of Sir Galahat,

"Now, fair knight," said Sir Galahat, "I r quire thee to tell me thy name."

"My name is Tristram of Lyonesse, ar from King Mark I was sent to King Angui of Ireland to fetch his daughter to be his wif and she is ready to go to Cornwall."

"Well, Sir Tristram," said Galahat, ", shall depart so ye go unto Sir Launcelot, and will promise you that no such custom be us in this castle as heretofore."

"Sir," said Sir Tristram, "I promise y as soon as I may I will see Sir Launcelot, ar have fellowship with him."

He departed, and landed in Cornwall, ar forthwith King Mark was wed to La Bea Isoud. And Sir Tristram had high honou at the king's court. And ever after S Tristram and La Beale Isoud loved each oth

Then was there great rejoicing and tourn ments, and Sir Tristram gained most prai After the feast was over, there were two ladi of Queen Isoud's court who hated Dame Bra waine. So they sent her into the forest ar had her tied to a tree, where she remained thr days. She was discovered by Sir Pelamoid and he took her to a nunnery close by. Wh Queen Isoud missed her maiden, she was sa and as she walked into the forest, suddenly S Pelamoides overheard her complaints, and said, "Madame Isoud, if you will grant me boon, I will restore Dame Bragwaine."

The queen was so glad to hear his offer th she agreed to grant all his bidding.

"Well, Madame," said Pelamoides, "I tru to your promise, and if ye will abide here ha an-hour, I will bring your maiden unto you

Then Sir Pelamoides came again, bringing with him Dame Bragwaine. And when the queen saw her she was glad.

"Now, Madame," said Sir Pelamoides, "I have fulfilled my promise, I pray you to fulfil yours."

"Sir Pelamoides," replied the queen, "I wot not what is your desire ; however, I promised you largely, but I thought no evil, and no ill will I do."

"Madame," said the knight, "at this time ye shall not know my desire, but I demand of your husband ;" and they rode to the court.

When they came before the king, Sir Pelamoides said, "My lord, I require you will judge me of my right. I promised your queen to bring Dame Bragwaine again unto her if she would only grant me that I should ask, which she promised."

"What say ye, my lady ?" said the king,

"To say truth," replied the queen, "I promised him his asking for joy that I had to see her."

"Then if ye were hasty to grant him what boon he did ask, I will that ye perform your promise," said the king.

"Then I would have your queen," said Sir Pelamoides, "to govern her as shall me list."

At these words the king was astounded ; but he deemed that he would rescue her, and said, "Take her, with the adventures that shall fall of it."

"As for that," said Pelamoides, "I dare abide the adventure ;" and so he took her and said, "fair lady, grudge not to go with me, seeing I desire nothing but the fulfilment of your promise."

"I fear not to go with thee," said the queen: "howbeit, thou hast me to advantage, but I shall be rescued from thee."

So Queen Isoud was set behind Sir Pelamoides, and they rode away. Then the king sent after Sir Tristram, and he could not be found, as he was hunting in the forest.

"Alas," said the king, "now I shall be shamed for ever, that my queen be taken away."

Then came to the king a knight named Lambegus, and said, "My lord, since ye have trust in my lord, Sir Tristram, for his sake I will ride after your queen and rescue her."

Sir Lambegus rode in pursuit, and overtook Sir Pelamoides, who turning to him said, "Art thou Sir Tristram?"

"Nay," said the knight, "I am his servant, and my name is Lambegus."

"I had rather thou hadst been Sir Tristram," said Sir Pelamoides.

"I believe you well," said the knight, "but when thou meetest Sir Tristram, thou shalt have thy hands full."

Then they hurtled together, and fought until Sir Lambegus was wounded, and fell to the ground. Whilst they were fighting the queen ran into the forest, and seeing a well she thought to have drowned herself, when there came to her a knight named Sir Adtherp, and took her to his castle. And when he found who she was, he rode to avenge her on Sir Pelamoides. And so he rode until he met him. They fought, and Sir Pelamoides wounded him and made him tell where the queen was.

"Now, bring me there," said Sir Pelamoides, "or thou shalt die by my hands."

"Sir," said Sir Adtherp, "I am so wounded that I may not follow, but ride thou this way, and it will take thee to my castle."

Now when Queen Isoud saw him coming to the castle, she had the gates fastened, and when Sir Pelamoides saw he might not come within the castle, he put the horse to pasture, and sat down at the gates. As soon as Sir Tristram returned and heard that Queen Isoud was gone with Sir Pelamoides, he cried out to Gouvernail, "Help me to arm, for well I wot Sir Lambegus hath not strength to withstand Sir Pelamoides."

Then rode they through the forest, and Sir Tristram found Sir Lambegus wounded. And as Sir Tristram rode forward he found Sir Adtherp wounded, who told him how the queen would have drowned herself, and how he had taken upon himself to do battle with Sir Pelamoides, and placed her in his castle, where she now was.

Then Sir Tristram rode to the castle, and there he saw Sir Pelamoides by the gate asleep, so he sent Gouvernail to awaken him, and bid him make ready to fight, and to tell him he was his mortal foe.

Sir Pelamoides arose and equipped himself, and took his spear in his hand. And they hurtled fast together, and Sir Tristram smote down Sir Pelamoides over his horse's tail. Then Sir Pelamoides drew his sword, and a fierce battle began between them.

Thus they fought for several hours, and

wounded each other passing sore; and Queen Isoud was sad to see the gashes they made, and said, "Alas, the one I loved, and the other I loved not, yet it were a pity to see Sir Pela. moides slain, and I would be loath to see him die a Saracen." And therewith she besought Sir Tristram to fight no more.

"Madame," said Sir Tristram, "will you have me shamed, yet will you know I will be ruled by you."

"I would not bring dishonour upon you," said the queen, "but I would that ye would spare this unhappy Saracen, Pelamoides."

Then said the queen to Pelamoides, "I charge you, that you shall go out of this country while I am therein."

"I will obey your commands, although against my will," replied Pelamoides.

"Then go to King Arthur's court, and com- mend me to Queen Guinevere, and tell her I send her word there be within the land but four lovers, and they are Sir Launcelot and Queen Guinevere, and Sir Tristram de Lyonesse and La Beale Isoud.

So Sir Pelamoides departed, and Sir Tristram took the queen and brought her unto King Mark, and there was joy of her return. Then Sir Tristram went to bring Sir Lambegus, and he was cured of his wounds. And there was great joy at the court, and none was cherished more than Sir Tristram.

CHAPTER XXXIV.

Sir Andred tells King Mark of the meeting of Sir Tristram and La Beale Isoud—King Mark seeks to destroy Sir Tristram—Sir Tristram jousts with Sir Lamorak de Gaul—Sir Tristram is made prisoner by forty knights—He kills ten of the knights—His escape into Brittany, where he marries King Howel's daughter—His return to England.

At length Sir Andred lay in wait to watch Sir Tristram and La Beale Isoud, for to slander them. And upon a certain day, Sir Tristram talked with La Beale Isoud in a window, and that espied Sir Andred, and he told it to the king.

Then King Mark would have slain Sir Tristram as a traitor, had not Sir Tristram wrested the sword from his hand. Then cried the king, "Where are my knights? I charge ye to slay the traitor!" But no one would obey his commands.

When Sir Tristram saw there was not one that would be against him, he shook the sword at the king; and King Mark fled, and Sir Tristram smote him five times with the flat of the sword on his neck, so that King Mark fell on his face.

Then Sir Tristram, mounting his horse, rode into the forest, and met two knights of King Mark, and he struck off the head of one, and made the other bear his head to King Mark.

Then the king called his barons to ask advice as to what they should do with Sir Tristrm.

And Sir Dinas said, "Sir Tristram is matchless of any Christian knight, and none is so good save Sir Launcelot; and if he depart go to King Arthur's court, he will get himself such friends that he will defy your malice, and therefore, I counsel you to take him to your grace."

"I will, then," said the king, "that he b sent for, that we may be friends."

Then the barons sent for Sir Tristram, and so he came to the king, and was made welcome

On a certain day the king and queen, with Tristram, went hunting, and they pitched their pavillions in the forest. By chance there came Sir Lamorak de Gaul and Sir Driant. And Sir Driant jousted well, but had a fall.

"I marvel," said the king, "what knight is he that doeth such deeds of arms."

"Sir," said Sir Tristram, "I know him, and there are few such living, and his name is Si Lamorak de Gaul."

"It were a great shame," said the king "that he should go thus away."

"Sir," said Sir Tristram, "it seemeth to me no worship for a knight now to have to do with him, because at this time he hath done over much; therefore, it were great shame to temp him any more at this time, for the deeds of arm he hath done this day were enough for Si Launcelot of the Lake."

"Nevertheless," said the king, "I require you as ye love me and my lady the Queen La Beal Isoud, to take your arms and joust with him."

"Sir," replied Sir Tristram, "ye bid me do thing that is against my knighthood; but I wil not displease you, as you require, so will I do.'

So Sir Tristram went forth to joust. An Sir Lamorak met him mightily, and what with the might of his own spear and Sir Tristram' strength, Sir Lamorak's horse fell to the earth He then arose lightly, and drawing his swor and placing his shield before him, he bade Si Tristram alight.

"Sir Lamorak," said Sir Tristram, "I understand your heart is great, but it would grieve me that I should strike down a weary knight, for that knight nor horse was never yet found that always might stand and endure."

"As for that," said Sir Lamorak, "I shall quit you when I see my time."

So he departed, and with him went Sir Driant.

Now Sir Tristram always used to go to Queen Isoud when he might, and ever Sir Andred watched him to take him with Queen Isoud. And on a certain day Sir Andred espied them together, and took twelve knights, who set upon Sir Tristram secretly and took him with the queen, and bound him and so kept him until the next day, when by command of King Mark Sir Tristram was led into a chapel which stood on the sea rocks, by forty knights. And when Sir Tristram found that he must die, he said, "Fair lords, remember what I have done for Cornwall, and in what jeopardy I have been in for the weal of you all; and when I fought for the truage of Cornwall with Sir Marhaus. I was promised better reward, when ye refused to take the battle upon you. Therefore, see me not thus shamefully die—for I dare say that I never met with a knight but I was as good or better."

"Fie upon thee," said Sir Andred, "traitor that thou art, for all thy boast thou shalt die this day."

"O Andred!" said Sir Tristram, "thou shouldst be my kinsman, but thou art most unfriendly; if there were no more than thou and I, thou wouldst not put me to death."

Therewith Sir Andred would have slain him.

Then Sir Tristram looked upon both his hands, which were fastened to two knights, and suddenly he pulled them both to him, and released his hands. He then leaped upon Sir Andred, and wrested his sword from his hand, and smote Sir Andred. And so Sir Tristram fought until he had killed ten knights.

Then Sir Tristram got into the chapel and kept the door, and much people gathered together, and when Sir Tristram saw them draw near to take him, he remembered that he was naked, so he shut the door and brake the bars of a window, and then leaped out, and fell upon the crags in the sea.

By the aid of Gouvernail, Sir Tristram was rescued, and went to Brittany to King Howel, and there the king's daughter, Isoud la Blanch Mains, cured him of his wounds, and great love grew between Sir Tristram and Isoud, and they were wedded.

CHAPTER XXXV.

Queen Isoud writes to Queen Guinevere of Sir Tristram —Sir Tristram sails from Brittany to England—King Arthur rides with a lady into the perilous forest—The nymph Nimue seeks Sir Tristram to go to the help of King Arthur—King Arthur is rescued from two knights and the false lady—Sir Tristram on his way with a false lady meets Sir Gawain—The lady's treachery exposed —Sir Bruise-without-pity chases a lady to kill her, and is made to flee by Sir Tristram—Sir Tristram jousts with Sir Pelamoides.

" It repenteth me," said Sir Tristram, while in Brittany, "for of all knights I loved to be in Sir Launcelot's fellowship."

And in the meanwhile, Queen Isoud sent a

letter unto Queen Guinevere, complaining how Sir Tristram wedded the King of Brittany's daughter, and Queen Guinevere bade her be of good cheer, for she should have joy after sorrow, and it shall be that he shall hate her and love you better than ever he did before.

Some time after, Sir Tristram sailed unto England with his wife and her brother, Sir Kehedius. And the wind drove their barge on the coast of Wales. Sir Tristram and Isoud la Blanch got into the forest and took up their abode in a fisher's hut. And as Sir Tristram walked forth, he met a lady, who told him the perils of that valley, and how there never came a knight there but he was taken prisoner or slain. And anon King Arthur came unto this perilous forest, having been led there by a lady named Annowris, who, by fair promises, made him ride with her into that forest. Now this lady was a sorceress, and had loved King Arthur for a long time, and therefore she came into that country.

After the king was gone, many knights went in search of him, but failed to find him. When she had brought the king to her tower, she sought his love; but he would not love her, notwithstanding her craft. Then would she make him ride into the forest, with the intent to have him slain. Then Nimue, the damsel of the lake, sought out Sir Tristram on that day, knowing the king would be slain unless he had help from Sir Tristram or Sir Launcelot. And so she rode until she met Sir Tristram, and cried out, " O, Sir Tristram, well be ye met, for within two hours shall be done the foulest deed that ever was done in this land."

"Fair damsel," replied Sir Tristram, "can I prevent it?"

"That can ye, for ye shall see the most worshipfullest knight in all the world hard beset," said the damsel.

"Then I am ready to help such a noble man," rejoined Sir Tristram.

"He is no other," said the lady, "than the noble King Arthur of Britain."

"God defend," said Sir Tristram, "that he should ever be so sorely pressed."

Then Sir Tristram rode with her until they came to a tower, and saw a knight on foot fighting with two knights, and at last the two knights smote the one knight down, and one of them unlaced his helm, whilst the lady Annowris got King Arthur's sword in her hand to have stricken off his head.

Therewithal Sir Tristram cried out, "Traitress, hold thy blow," and he smote one of the knights through the body, and the other's back asunder.

In the meantime the nymph Nimue cried to King Arthur, "Let not that lady escape."

Then King Arthur overtook her, and wresting the sword from her hand, smote off her head, and the lady of the lake picked up the head and hung it by the hair on her saddle-bow. Sir Tristram horsed King Arthur, and rode with him; but he charged the lady of the lake not to discover his name to the king.

Then the king thanked Sir Tristram, and desired to know his name, but he would not tell him, but said he was a poor adventurous knight; and so he bare King Arthur's fellowship until they met Sir Ector, when Sir Tristram took his departure, and the king and Sir Ector went on their way.

On the following day Sir Tristram met with a herald, who proclaimed a tournament between King Sawney of Scotland and King Caradoc of North Wales, and said how King Sawney sought Sir Launcelot to fight on his side, and how King Caradoc sought Sir Tristram to fight on his side.

And as he rode, a damsel told him of a knight who did great harm, and prayed him for his help. And as he rode with the damsel they met Sir Gawain, and Sir Gawain knew the damsel for a maiden of Queen Morgan la Fay. He then demanded of Sir Tristram whither he was going, and Sir Tristram told him that he was led by the damsel.

"Sir," said Sir Gawain, "ye shall not ride with her, for she and her lady never did other than ill," and he demanded for what cause she led the knight.

"Mercy, Sir Gawain," said the lady; "if ye will spare my life I will tell thee all."

"Say on," said Sir Gawain.

"Queen Morgan la Fay," replied the damsel, "hath appointed thirty ladies to seek after Sir Tristram and Sir Launcelot, and whichever found either of these knights should take them to Morgan la Fay's castle, telling them they should do deeds of worship; and if either of these knights came there, there be thirty knights lying and watching in a tower to make an attack upon Sir Launcelot or Sir Tristram, whichever should come."

"Fie, for shame," said Sir Gawain, "that ever such treason should be used by a king's sister."

Then turning to Sir Tristram he said, "Sir knight, if ye will stand by me we will together prove the malice of thirty knights."

"I will not fail thee," said Sir Tristram, "for but a few days since I had to do with thirty knights of that same queen, and I trust I may win honour now as I did then."

So Sir Gawain and Sir Tristram departed, and as they rode along a valley they saw a knight named Bruise-without-pity chasing a lady to slay her.

"Hold you still," said Sir Gawain, "and ye shall see me reward yonder false knight."

So he rode to Sir Bruise and the lady, and cried out, "False knight, leave her and have a do with me."

Then Sir Bruise rushing at Sir Gawain, overthrew him, and rode his horse on him as he lay on the ground.

When Sir Tristram saw this he cried, "Forbear that villany," and rode to him; but as Sir Bruise saw his shield he knew it was Sir Tristram, and he fled.

Then Sir Tristram and Sir Gawain came nigh the "Maiden's Castle," and there Sir Persides, the son of the owner of the castle, came out and gave them welcome.

And as they stood talking they saw a knight ride by on a black horse, and they knew it was Sir Pelamoides. Sir Pelamoides saw Sir Persides he sent his squire to him to ask him to joust. So they jousted, and Sir Persides was overthrown.

Then Sir Tristram prepared to joust, but before he had his spear in rest Sir Pelamoides, struck him from his horse. At this Sir Tristram was wroth, and he sent his squire to Sir Pelamoides to ask him to joust again, but he refused, saying " Tell thy master to revenge himself to-morrow at the Maiden's Castle, where he shall see me."

CHAPTER XXXVI.

The tournament at Maiden's Castle—Jousts between the Knights of King Caradoc and King Sawney—Sir Tristram gains the prize on the first day—On the second day Sir Tristram performs many marvellous feats, and again has the prize given to him—On the third day King Arthur overthrows King Sawney and his knights —The encounters of Sir Tristram and Sir Pelamoides— Sir Tristram and Sir Launcelot joust together—Sir Tristram is wounded, and leaves the field—The search for Sir Tristram—Sir Launcelot and Sir Tristram arrive at King Arthur's court.

KING ARTHUR sat in the gallery at Maiden's Castle to see the jousting, and to give judgment; Sir Launcelot sat on his right hand, for he did not intend to take part in the jousts that day. And Sir Tristram called unto him his servant, and commanded him to bring him a black shield with no device on it, and, after he had armed himself, he departed with Sir Persides, and rode towards the tournament, and joined King Caradoc's side.

Then the knights of King Sawney came forth, and there was great fighting and many knights and horses were overthrown.

And Sir Persides and Sir Tristram encountered Sir Bleoberis and Sir Gaheris; and Sir Persides was smitten down by Sir Bleoberis, and nigh slain, for four horsemen rode over him. But Sir Tristram jousted with Sir Gaheris, and smote him from his horse, on which Sir Bleoberis rode against Sir Tristram, and was overthrown also. Then they horsed themselves again, and with them came Sir Dinadan, whom Sir Tristram smote so that he fell to the ground. Then rising, he said, "Ah! sir knight, I know ye better than ye deem, and will joust with thee never more." Then Sir Bleoberis the second time rode against Sir Tristram, and received such a buffet that he was felled to the ground.

Thereupon the king commanded the jousting to cease, and all men marvelled who the knight with the black shield might be, and the prize of the day was awarded to him.

Now Sir Pelamoides, who was on King Sawney's side, and knew not Sir Tristram when he saw the great feats which he performed, sent to ask his name.

"As for that, I refuse to tell him," said Sir Tristram, "but when I have broken two spears upon him, he shall know."

On the second day of the tournament, Sir Pelamoides went on the side of the King of North Wales, and Sir Tristram hearing this, said, "Then will I be on the King of Scotland's side, because Sir Pelamoides will be on the other side." And he came in to joust, and he began so roughly that no knight could stand against him; but at last he came upon the followers of King Ban, and there fell upon him Sir Bors de Ganis and Sir Ector de Maris, and Sir Blamor, and many other knights. Then with fury smote Sir Tristram right and left,

and all were astonished at his deeds.   But Sir
Tristram would have been overcome, had not the
king with the hundred knights come to his help.
Then Sir Tristram saw forty knights, and Sir
Kaye, the Seneschal, was their leader.   And he
rode amongst them, and smote down Sir Kaye.

Now Sir Launcelot sought Sir Tristram, and
rode in search of him; and he espied him and
how he hurled down a knight at eve ry stroke.

"Oh! mercy," cried King Arthur, "since
the time I first bore arms, I have never seen a
knight do such marvellous deeds."

"If I should set upon that brave knight,"
said Sir Launcelot, "surely I should do shame
to myself," and therewithal he put up his sword.

Then the King of the Hundred Knights and
the knights of King Sawney set upon twenty
knights who were of Sir Launcelot's kin, who
fought well together to assist each other.

When Sir Tristram beheld the nobleness and
courage of these twenty knights, he exclaimed,
"Well may ye be full of prowess who have
such noble knights for kindred;" and he
thought it shame to see two hundred men as-
sailing twenty, and riding to the King of the
Hundred Knights, he said, "I pray thee, leave
off fighting with those twenty knights, for ye
shall gain no worship if ye win, and that I see
ye will not do unless ye slay them; but if ye
will not cease, I will help them."

"Nay, ye shall not do so," said the king, "for
gladly will I do your courtesy;" and he ordered his knights to withdraw.

Then King Arthur gave the prize to King Sawney, because Sir Tristram was on his side: and

then there arose a cry through the field that the knight with the black shield had won the day.

But when they sought for Sir Tristram he could nowhere be found, for he had ridden away. King Arthur then comforted his knights, and said, "Be of good cheer for to-morrow I, myself, will be in the field, and fare with you."

And on the morrow, King Sawney and the King of the Hundred Knights encountered with King Caradoc and the King of Ireland, and overthrew them. Then came King Arthur forth, and overthrew King Sawney, his fellows and twenty knights; and then came Sir Pelamoides into the field, and made great fight on King Arthur's side. But when Sir Tristram espied him, he rode towards him, and knocked him from his horse.

Then cried King Arthur, "Knight of the Black Shield, keep thyself," and he smote him to the ground, and passed on to attack other knights. Then Sir Pelamoides, rushed at Sir Tristram, who was on foot, with the intent of running over him, but Sir Tristram, grasping Sir Pelamoides in his arms, pulled him off his horse. Then drawing their swords, and rushing together, began a fierce combat. And Sir Tristram smote Sir Pelamoides three strokes on the helm, and at each stroke said, "Take this for Sir Tristram's sake;" and Sir Pelamoides lay upon the earth.

Fresh horses were brought to the combatants and having mounted, they again began to joust with fury. And Sir Pelamoides made a thrust at Sir Tristram, but he avoided his spear, and striking Sir Pelamoides on the neck, bore him off his horse, ten spears length. Then

King Arthur smote the spear in two, and gave Sir Tristram two or three strokes ere he could draw his sword. But as soon as Sir Tristram had his sword in hand, he assailed the king with furious blows. With that eleven knights of Sir Launcelot's went against Sir Tristram, but he smote them all, so that all who witnessed it marvelled at his courage.

Then Sir Launcelot came down upon Sir Tristram, saying, "Knight of the Black Shield, make ready." When Sir Tristram was aware of him, he levelled his spear, and both ran together with a terrific shock, and Sir Tristram's spear broke short, but Sir Launcelot struck a deep wound in his side, and brake his spear, but did not overthrow him. Then Sir Tristram rushed on Sir Launcelot, and struck upon his helm, and forced Sir Launcelot's head to his saddle bow, then he left the field, feeling pain from his wound.

Then Sir Launcelot held the field against all comers, and when King Arthur saw him do such feats of valour, he rode to help him, and King Sawney and his knights were put to the worse. And the prize on that day was given to Sir Launcelot, but Sir Launcelot said, "Sir Tristram is the victor for he endured each day." Then King Arthur and Sir Launcelot returned to the Castle of Maidens, making great dole for the hurt Sir Tristram had received.

And King Arthur departed for Caer Leon, as the feast of Pentecost was nigh at hand.

And many sought Sir Tristram, and Sir Launcelot found him, and brought him to King Arthur's court at Caer Leon.

CHAPTER XXXVII.

King Arthur ordains a great tournament at Winchester. Queen Guinevere refuses to go to the jousting—Dissatisfaction of her maidens.

KING ARTHUR gave a banquet to his guests, his peers, and chivalry, at Caer Leon; and he declared, that within fifteen days he would hold a great tournament at Camelot (Winchester.)

On the day before that appointed for the tournament, King Arthur sent to the queen to hold herself in readiness to go with him; but the messenger came back to say that the queen cared not to go. The king received this answer with regret, and hurried to her chamber. He found her sitting silent among her maidens.

When Arthur approached Guinevere, she held out her hands, and the king placed his arm round her and kissed her.

"My dearest wife and love," he said gently, "what is this I hear? You will not go with me to Camelot to the tournament? What ails you, Guinevere?"

"My lord, I know not," she replied, "but I am sick at heart. I do not wish to go."

"Sick at heart!" said the king. "Wherefore, lady mine? Have you one wish ungratified? Are you not the fairest lady in the land? What gift hath youth, or beauty, left to bestow on you? Am I the cause of your unhappiness? Tell me some proof that I may give you of my love for you, and prove me!"

"Trust me," replied Guinevere, "this fit of apathy is natural. Even the summer sun fatigues by its glowing odours, and lucious viands pall on the appetite after awhile. Who could for ever listen to the sweetest music? I am worn out with happiness—weary of pomp and pageantry! I need some rest and quiet, that is all. Go you, my lord, to this jousting, and leave me to the pleasant pain of longing for your return, and to its joyous recompense—once more to bid you welcome!"

"Fie, Guinevere! This gloomy mood indulged in, will grow upon you," said Arthur. "Come to the joust; for, our sport is marred if you withhold your presence. Come with me, Guinevere."

"My lord, if you command, I must obey."

"Command! out on the word!" said Arthur.

"Why then, my kind lord, hold me excused," said the queen. "I will not go."

"Adieu, dear love. The time flies with broken wing until we are re-united." With this, the king imprinted a lingering kiss, smoothed her golden tresses, and tearing himself away, rushed from the room. In the donjon of the castle at Caer Leon, three of the queen's maids were gathered, watching the departure of King Arthur, with his retinue, for the jousting at Camelot.

"Oh, I could weep my eyes out for vexation!" said Elgiva. "Is it not a shame that we should be made thus to suffer for the queen's caprices? I had set my heart upon being present at these jousts; and now we can but watch the other ladies of the court depart to enjoy pleasures we may not share in."

"Your disappointment is not so keen as mine," rejoined one of her companions. "For you, who have passed three summers at the court have seen many such grand sights, while I, alas! but just released from my father's dull towers, and newly come to the capital, have never seen a tournament."

"I pity you, Elfrida," rejoined the third. "The queen is much to blame."

"And why has she so strangely changed her purpose is more than I can tell," returned Elgiva. "For, dear Ida, Sir Launcelot will be there."

"Do you think so ?"

"Can you doubt it ?" rejoined Elgiva. "He is the greatest of all King Arthur's knights: the jousts were nought without Sir Launcelot."

"Besides," rejoined Ida, " this is the day on which the knights will tilt for the ninth diamond, the last and most precious of all."

"What diamonds are those ?" asked Elfrida,

"Do you not know ?" asked Ida. Then she added; "But I remember you are a stranger at the court. I will tell you the story : Arthur, long ere he was king, and the youngest son of Sir Ector, was one day roving through a glen, when he came to a sluggish tarn. The spot was held accursed, for it was said that two brothers, one a king, in ancient days had fought there, and each had slain the other, and there they lay till time had bleached their bones white; but he that was a king had on a crown of diamonds, one set in front, and on each side four. As King Arthur rode to the pool, his horse's hoof struck on the skull and crushed it, the crown rolling towards the lake. The king caught it up and placed it on his head. Then his heart whispered him : "Rejoice ! thou too shalt yet be king !" When he had approved himself the true-born son of Uther Pendragon, and rightwise king of England he had the jewels plucked from the crown, and ordained that once every year there should be a joust for one of them. Eight years have passed, and there have been eight jousts, and eight times has Sir Launcelot won the diamond. The present joust is for the central diamond, the largest and last. And I doubt not Sir Launcelot will win it."

"I would we might be there to see," returned Elfrida, pouting.

CHAPTER XXXVIII.

The sorrow of Queen Guinevere—Sir Launcelot intrudes into the royal chamber—The queen's anger—the departure of Sir Launcelot for Camelot.

"Look, girls?" cried Ida, "the kings and all the chivalry are moving forwards. See! they pass through the arch of the barbican."

"Who is that knight that rides to the avant guard?" asked Elfrida. "He with the demi-griffin on his shield. Is he not a proper man?"

"That is Sir Sagramore!" returned Ida. "But mark that knight with the black plume; that is Sir Griflet. With what grace he rides his huge charger—he, they say, has the mightiest arm of all the Round Table ; and yonder comes Sir Kaye, the seneschal."

"Now come Sir Lucas," rejoined her companion, " and Sir Meliot, and Sir Safire. And yonder, on that fiery steed, I see Sir Bevedere."

"But see the kings ! and in the centre rides the great Pendragon, as a sun among the stars!"

" He is indeed a matchless prince !" cried Elfrida. " See as he rides along, how the people press forward to catch a glimpse of his lion-like head : and now he lifts his visor. And how they shout, ' Arthur—Arthur ! long live our great Pendragon !' Look with what graciousness he smiles upon them !"

" But where is Sir Launcelot ?" asked Elfrida.

" I saw him not," said Ida.

"Nor I," rejoined Elgiva: " he was not there."

" But is not that a marvel ?" cried Elgiva.

" It is strange ; yet perhaps the hurts that he got at the tournament at Maiden's Castle, where he was sore pressed, prevents him."

" Yes, or perhaps he has gone on before the rest to Camelot," said Elgiva, " to complete the preparations for the jousting."

" One thing is very sure ; he was not among the chivalry that passed but now," said Elfrida.   " But hush !—hush !—the queen !"

Guinevere now swept into the room. She looked pensive.   "Leave me, my maidens," she said ; " I am weary and would be alone."   She threw herself upon a couch, and resting her head upon her white arms, closed her eyelids.

" Gracious madam, is there aught that we can do to give you solace ?" returned Ida.

" No ; only by leaving me," she said.   "Let no one approach ; anon I will call for you."

The girls retired from the room.   When they were gone the queen half rose from the couch, pressed one hand upon her brow, and the other against her heart, as if to still the throbbing.

" Memento mori !' she murmured, " While I am young, ere the evil days befall, would I might die, and bury my shame in the grave !"

Then she started with flushed cheek, at the sound of a familiar footstep.

" No; it cannot be," she murmured. " By this time he is on the road to Camelot !"

Then a deep stern voice exclaimed :

" My lord, you cannot pass !"

" It is the sentinel," gasped the queen. "He acts upon my orders; yet, had I known—hist !"

" What sayest thou ?" cried a voice, well known to Guinevere. "Knowst thou who I am ?"

" Your pardon, Sir Launcelot," returned the sentinel. "The queen has given command that none should be admitted to her presence."

" Sirrah, the prohibition extends not to me. I must see the queen : my business is urgent," returned Launcelot, " therefore, stand aside."

" I pray you, my lord, retire ; it is more than my head is worth to let you pass."

" Ay, or attempt to bar my way," returned Launcelot. " Churl, stand back !"

The next instant Sir Launcelot threw aside the arras, and entered the queen's chamber.

With scorn playing upon her lips, the queen rose from her couch.

" For shame, Sir Launcelot !" she exclaimed. "What brings you here ?"

Launcelot smiled, caught her hand and pressed it to his lips.

" Sweet lady," he said " I trust I have not outworn my welcome. If so, I will depart."

"Stay," said the Queen, "stay, Sir Launcelot."

" Sir Launcelot, you are to blame thus to hold you behind my lord," she said. " You know as well as I that all your courage cannot protect you against the tongue of slander. Our early love is known to all the court, save to Arthur. Our every look is watched by the envious and malignant, who are eager to put a foul construction on the most innocent conduct. I know I have been indiscreet in suffering you to linger about me—in listening to your professions of attachment : but this must end."

"Madame, I allow your wit," said Launcelot. "You were not always so wise, nor so cold. A malison upon calumniators ! Not the boldest of knights dare breathe a whisper to your wrong ; but I perceive the king has all your heart, and you grow weary of my service."

"Arthur the good, the noble !" sighed Guinevere. "I call the saints to witness that my lord commands my highest esteem—I cannot give my love. The heart can never be directed by the will—at least mine cannot. The king is too pure—too high above me—I feel myself his unequal ; while for you, dearest Launcelot, let me be silent, rather than speak my shame."

Launcelot drew her to his bosom. She remained silent for a moment. Then she wrested herself away.

"Oh, leave me, I beseech you," she said. "It touches near your honour, mine yet nearer still, that we should part, lord Launcelot. Is it not time ? Why have I stayed from the jousts ? Only that I might disprove the scandal that I follow you wheresoever you go, to feast or tourney. To silence these reports I linger here, a voluntary captive in this castle, chilled by the mournful looks of my poor maidens, deprived of long-expected enjoyment on my account. Then you mar all by intruding upon my solitude.

"My queen and mistress," said Launcelot, "I accept this rebuke in all humility, and will cease to trouble by my unwelcome presence."

"Well, if you love me, go to these jousts."

"And yet, madam, I know not upon what pretext I may do so," returned Launcelot, "seeing I told the king that I still suffered from my wound, and could scarce keep the saddle."

"Listen, then," said the queen. "Go as though you sought but glory. Disguise yourself, and let men wonder who the strange knight may be that does such deeds of arms as yet were never achieved except by lord Launcelot."

"It is well thought," said Sir Launcelot.

"Then let the thought find action," said the queen; "for my sake, Launcelot."

"I fly!" cried Launcelot. "It joys me well, this strategy! I will take a blank shield, and set myself against King Arthur and all his fellowship!"

"You must do as you list," said Queen Guinevere; "but if you take my counsel you will not be against your sovereign and your friends, who may take the trick in bad part. Be prudent, I entreat you; and so farewell, dear Launcelot."

"Queen of my heart, farewell!" returned the knight, and kissing her hand, he quitted the chamber, and remounted took the road for Camelot.

CHAPTER XXXIX.

Sir Launcelot's ride to Astolat—His meeting with the fair Elaine—His introduction to her brothers, Sir Torre and Lavaine—His reception at the castle of Astolat—His conversation with Sir Bernard—He borrows Sir Torre's shield.

It was early morning when Sir Launcelot pursued his way to Camelot. Spurring his horse, he galloped down the hill. In the centre of the plain below lay the little town of Astolat (now Guilford) with its quaintly-gabled houses, and thither the errant knight directed his course.

He passed along the banks of a brook for a while, when his ear caught the music of a female voice. Peering through the trees, he beheld a young girl sitting upon the bank of the brook. She was singing to herself from very joy of heart.

"Ah, sweet maid!" sighed Sir Launcelot. "How sweeter far than the boastful romaunts of our troubadours, that breathe of illicit loves, are these thy simple wood-notes! Would thou mightest ever be kept free from the defiling contact of this false world."

The lovely girl stood gazing upon his gallant form with timidity and fascination.

"Good-morning, fair maid," said Launcelot.

"Ave Maria! and to you, Sir Knight," returned the maiden.

"What is your will?"

"I seek the nearest path to Astolat."

"I will show you the way," replied the maid.

"I thank you, fair maid," replied Sir Launcelot. "And let me ask you to let me know by what name I shall thank you for your kindness."

"My name is Elaine, and I am the daughter of the lord of Astolat!" replied the maiden. "I have two good brothers—Sir Torre and Sir Lavaine. Our mother is in heaven."

While they were speaking, the sound of a bugle rang upon the air.

"What means that blast?"

"It is my brother Torre, who sounds his horn to call me home," replied the maiden. "He and my brother, Lavaine, are out a-hawking. See, Sir Knight, they come!"

Presently two youths approached the spot. They were dressed in green doublets, and each carried a small hawk, and over their shoulders each had slung several herons and mallards which their hawks had killed.

Elaine sprang forward to meet her brothers. When they had come up with Launcelot, they saluted him with respect.

"Sir Knight, we bid you welcome to Astolat," said Torre. "Whence come you?"

"Nay, brother, you have scant courtesy," said Lavaine. Then addressing Launcelot, he added; "Fair sir, by your equipments, it is not hard to guess you are a knight of worship."

"I am one of Arthur's knights," said Launcelot; "and if I do not presume too much, I would beseech that you would lend me a blank shield, for I go to joust at Camelot for the diamond."

"By my faith, you are provided," answered Lavaine. "You bear a right good shield, with a noble device thereon."

"Yes; 'tis that I would conceal," replied Launcelot. "Were I to ride into the field with my own shield, I should at once be known. I wish to go thither in disguise, and would have a shield that does not bear mine own arms."

"Mine is at your service, Sir knight," replied Sir Torre. "My brother here, though younger than myself, unhorsed me this morning, when we did tilt for sport. Heaven knows, the shield will not do you much honour, but such as it is, 'tis yours right willingly."

"Fair youth, I gladly accept your offer," returned Launcelot, "and thank you heartily."

"Come then, Sir Knight," returned the lad, "let us ride to the castle : my father will be proud to give you welcome."

With this he raised his sister behind him on the croup of the saddle, and the party turned towards the castle of Astolat.

Upon reaching the gate Sir Torre blew the horn that hung there. Presently the draw-bridge was lowered, and they entered the court-yard.

Apprised of the arrival of his noble guest, Sir Bernard of Astolat, came forth to meet Sir Launcelot and conducted him into the great hall with all hospitality; and ordering the dinner to be served, placed the knight-errant at his right hand, on the dais.

Meanwhile, Elaine had filled the loving-cup, and presented it to the strange knight, who pledged her in a heavy draught, with full gallantry.

The board was spread, and the knight's family and retainers thronged into the hall, each taking his allotted place above or below the salt, while the minstrels, commenced their strain of harmony.

During the evening Sir Bernard and the knight held converse together.

"Whence comest thou, my guest?" enquired the lord of Astolat. "Known as are the knights of Arthur's court, to me they are unknown, but I should take thee to be one of them."

"Known am I, and of Arthur's court," replied Launcelot, "and known by my shield; but since I go to joust at Camelot as one unknown, ask me not at present for my name.

Hereafter ye shall know me, but if you have a blank shield, or one with any device save mine, I pray you lend it me."

"That will I gladly do," said the lord of Astolat. " Here is Torre's. Hurt was my son, Sir Torre, in his first tilt, and so, in faith, his shield is blank enough, and his you shall have."

CHAPTER XL.

Sir Bernard and Sir Launcelot converse in the garden— Sir Bernard's faithful Huon—Sir Launcelot tells of King Arthur's battles—Lavaine wishes to go as squire with Sir Launcelot—Elaine's love for Sir Launcelot.

AFTER the banquet, Sir Launcelot, accompanied by Sir Bernard, with Sir Torre and Sir Lavaine walked in the gardens of the castle. They discoursed of court and camp, of Arthur's mighty wars against the heathen, and of the noble deeds of the Knights of the Round Table.

Old Sir Bernard was delighted; his face lit up with smiles of animation, and the slumbering fires of his gray eyes glowed from under his bent brow.

"Trust me, Sir Knight," he said; "although you find me poor and unknown beyond this narrow bounds of this, my poor estate, the time has been when I, too, and couched my lance at royal tournament; but that was long ago, in Uther's days, before the Saxons stormed my tower, pillaged my store of wealth, and left my walls, as you now see them, half dismantled. All honour to our valiant Pendragon, great Arthur who hath rid the land of those marauders, and hath established peace."

" It is a noble prince !" rejoined Sir Torre.

"I and my brother saw him yesterday, as at the head of all his chivalry, he entered Astolat.'

"Ah, brother! was not that a gallant sight?" rejoined young Lavaine.

"Yes, in my time I have seen service," returned old Sir Bernard. "I have fought in many a desperate battle against the heathen hosts. But let us cheer our talk with a cup of wine. Ho, Huon, there!" he shouted to an old man who was in the garden.

The man approached.

"Go, Huon," said the knight, "go bid my daughter Elaine bring some wine."

He bowed, and moved slowly away to do his master's bidding. Sir Launcelot marvelled at his lack of speech.

"Ay, poor Huon!" sighed Sir Bernard. "The heathen caught and reft him of his tongue, ten years ago, because he gave me warning of their design to attack my house and murder me and mine. I, with my wife, my sons, and my little daughter, fled from bonds or death. We hid us in the woods, in a boatman's hut. It was winter time, and my sweet wife—Heaven's peace be with her!—being but sickly, perished from cold and hardship. Those were bitter times; but thanks to Arthur's prowess, they are changed; and though reduced almost to penury, I spend my days in peace among my children; and for myself I am content, yet grieve sometimes that I lack means to give my lads such advantages as become their birth and breeding."

"Doubtless, great lord," said Lavaine, with enthusiasm, "you have fought in Arthur' glorious wars; pray tell us of them."

"I have been," said Sir Launcelot, "with Arthur in the fight which raged by the mouth of the Glem; and in four battles on the shore of Duglas; then in the war that thundered within the gloomy forest of Calidon; afterwards by the Castle Gurnion, where the noble king bore Our Lady's head, carved of one emerald centred in a sun of silver rays, upon his cuirass. And at Caer Leon have I stood by my lord, when the strong neighing of the wild, white horse made every gilded parapet shake; and up in Agned Cathregonion, and down on the sandy shores of Trath Treviot, have I beheld the heathens fall in slaughtered heaps. Then on Badon's mount I saw the king charge at the head of all his Round Table and overthrow the Pagan host, and afterwards stand, and cry to me in sonorous voice, "They are broken!" For though our king seems so mild in peace, in war he is a lion, and no man's courage can match his."

Thus did Sir Launcelot arrest the attention of his hearers, until the fair Elaine came forth with a flagon and cups; setting them upon the table, she poured out the wine, and presented a cup to Sir Launcelot.

The courtly knight kissed the cup ere he drank, and smiled upon the maiden, who cast down her dove-like eyes beneath his eagle glance, blushing and trembling.

"If there be aught that I can do to serve your brave sons, you may rely upon my zealous will to do it," replied Sir Launcelot. "The king is ever gracious, and where he sees true promises, readily bestows his favours."

"Oh, my lord," said Lavaine, "may I request that I may ride with you as your esquire to Camelot, that I may break a lance in the great jousts, when I will do my best to win?"

"Your request is granted," said he. "So you will grace me with your fellowship as my guide across these barren wastes whereon I lost myself, and then you shall win this diamond—if you can."

"And if I do, I will give it to my sweet sister, Elaine la Blanche," replied Lavaine.

"A priceless diamond for our sister," said Sir Torre. "Nay, such gauds be for queens and dames of high degree, and not for simple maids like our Elaine."

Then spake the knight: "If what is beautiful be for the beautiful, there is surely none who has a better claim to wear the diamond, once worn by the king, and won anew by valour, than is Elaine la Blanche, the lily of Astolat."

The girl lifted her eyes, and gazed with admiration on the speaker's countenance, then turned her face away.

"I marvelled much when, yesterday, I stood to see the entry of the knights into our town of Astolat, that Sir Launcelot was not among them," said Lavaine. "But then an archer I encountered told me that the valiant knight had stayed behind, disabled by a wound he got from one Sir Mador de la Porte. It was in the queen's quarrel."

"Speak not of Sir Launcelot of the Lake," said Sir Bernard. "If report belie him not, he loves the queen, is a dishonour to the Round Table."

"Does common rumour speak thus of him," asked the stranger knight.

"Ay, and I fear there is some germ of truth," replied Sir Bernard. "It is said that Sir Launcelot remains in the great city that he may be near the queen."

"He is villainously slandered!" replied the knight. "And that will I prove upon all comers to-morrow; but I have myself been wounded, and my ride has wearied me. I will retire by your good leave, and refresh myself with sleep."

"Do so, my lord," returned Sir Bernard, "come, I will show you to your chamber."

CHAPTER XLI.

Sir Launcelot and Lavaine leave the Castle of Astolat—Sir Launcelot discloses his name to Lavaine—How Sir Launcelot dwells at the house of a rich burgess at Camelot—King Arthur sees him walking in the garden.

THAT night Elaine recalled every gesture of the stranger knight. To her he appeared a being of more than mortal mould, for the girl was enamoured 'with that love which was her doom.' She woke with the first peep of dawn, and rising from her couch, dressed herself, and descended to bid adieu to her brother Lavaine.

She heard the knight call to Lavaine, and bid him mount, for that it was time they had got on their way. "Where is the shield, good lad?" he asked.

"I will bring it to you," replied Lavaine.

Elaine saw Sir Launcelot smoothing the steed's shoulder. With timid step Elaine approached him; he was not a little surprised at finding how lovely she was.

"Good-morrow, lady," said Sir Launcelot.

Sir Bernard then bade his guest farewell,
527   Q

accompanied by Lavaine, who looked very gal
lant in a fine suit of armour. He brought with
him the shield that belonged to his brother Torre

"Farewell, Sir Knight, may victory crown
your arms!" said the old baron. "And you
my boy, Lavaine, attend this noble lord as be
comes his worship. But ere you depart, Si
Knight, I beseech you tell me your name?"

"As for that," said Sir Launcelot, "yo
must hold me excused, if Heaven give me grac
to speed well at the jousts, I shall come agai
and inform you."

He then handed his shield to Lavaine. Blush
ing deeply, Elaine approached the knigh
"Fair sir," she said, "I have a boon to ask."

"'Tis granted ere 'tis asked," said the knigh

"Will you wear my favour at this tourney?

"Fair lady," said Sir Launcelot, "if I do tha
I shall do more for your love than for any othe
damsel's."

Then he bethought him he would ride to th
jousts disguised; and he consented to wear h
token, that none of his kindred might know hir

"Fair damsel, I will wear it on my helmet,
he said. "Fetch it out to me."

"It is a scarlet sleeve, broidered with pearls,
she answered, and forthwith brought it, an
bound it on his helmet as her token.

"Never yet have I done this for any maide
living," he said.

The knight then shook hands with old S
Bernard, and again addressing Elaine, he sai
"Do me this favour, sweet maiden, to have m
shield in keeping till I come."

"I accept the charge with pleasure," repli
Elaine. "Be sure that I will guard it well."

Lavaine kissed his sister; Sir Launcelot kissed his hand to her; and the adventurers moved away. As they rode on their way, Sir Launcelot exclaimed, "Since thou art to bear me company, fair youth, methinks it but fair to let you know with whom you ride, but you must promise not to divulge it."

"Doubt me not, my lord," replied Lavaine.

"Then you ride with Launcelot of the Lake."

The boy gazed with admiration and exclaimed, "Sir Launcelot! What honour is mine! And you, my lord, unknown to all your friends, will eclipse conception by your feats of arms, that all shall wonder who the unknown knight may be! It is a noble jest."

So they came to Camelot. Now it happened that as Sir Launcelot walked in the garden, the king espied him from the neighbouring battlement, and knew him.

"It is well," said Arthur to his knights; "in yonder garden beside the castle I have seen a knight who will play his part at the jousts; he will do marvellous deeds of arms."

"Who is that?" asked the knights.

"Ye shall not know from me," replied Arthur, "at least, not at this time."

Early on that morn King Arthur and all his knights departed. And so when the king was ridden, Sir Launcelot and Sir Lavaine made themselves ready for the lists, and each of them had a white shield, and the red sleeve hung from Sir Launcelot's helm.

Lavaine assisted his companion in buckling on his armour, and then, amidst the sounding of the trumpets, they dressed their unblazoned shields, and mounting their horses, rode to the lists

CHAPTER XLII.

The lists at Camelot—The tournament—Sir Launcelot
and Lavaine tilt against King Arthur's knights—Sir
Launcelot after defeating many knights is wounded by
Sir Bors—Sir Launcelot leaves the field and is followed
by Lavaine.

EARLY Sir Launcelot and his companion reached Camelot. The enclosure was an oblong
square; the openings for the entry of the combatants were at the northern and southern ex-
tremities of the lists, accessible by gates, wide
enough to admit two horsemen riding abreast.
At each of these portals were stationed two heralds attended by six trumpeters, as many pur-
suivants, and a strong body of men-at-arms for
ascertaining the quality of the knights about to
engage in the jousts.

The galleries were richly hung with tapestry
and densely thronged with a company of kings,
knights, and ladies, with squires, pages, and
yeomen, in attendance upon them. In the centre
of the eastern side of the lists was a gallery,
richly decorated and graced by a throne emblazoned with the royal arms. It was occupied
by King Arthur, surrounded by a throng of his
chief barons. On his right hand sat Sir Gawain; for King Arthur knowing that Launcelot would be there, would not let Sir Gawain go
from his side, for never had Sir Gawain the
better when Sir Launcelot was in the field.

At the flourish of trumpets, the gates at each
end of the tilting-ground were thrown open,
and the two opposing companies of knights
rode in. On King Arthur's side were the
Kings of Scotland, and Ireland; on the other

part the King of North Wales, the King of Northumberland, the King of Northgales, and the King with the hundred knights, Sir Galahalt, and other princes.

When all was ready Arthur raised his warder and amidst the flourish of trumpets all the knights spurred on their horses and rushed to the encounter. They met with a thunderous shock, and then was heard the clashing of shields and the shivering of lances ; and while the King of Scotland smote down the King of Northumberland, Sir Galahalt unhorsed the King of Ireland ; and Sir Pelamoides, encountered with Sir Galahalt in such a shock, that both of them rolled in the dust. Then their squires ran, and helping their lords to rise, set them on horseback again and supplied them with fresh lances. So there began a strong assail on both parties : but the king's party had the advantage. When Sir Launcelot saw this he turned to Lavaine.

" See yonder," said he, " is a company of good knights, and they hold themselves together as boars that are chased by dogs."

" That is truth," returned Lavaine.

" Now," said Sir Launcelot, briskly, " if you will help me you shall see yonder fellowship which chased these men of one side, that they shall go as far backward as they went forward."

" Spare them not," replied Lavaine.

Then Sir Launcelot and Lavaine dashed in, and Sir Launcelot smote down Sir Brandiles, Sir Sagramore, Sir Dodinas, Sir Kaye, and Sir Griflet, all with one spear. Meanwhile, Lavaine, unhorsed Sir Lucas, the butler, and Sir Bedi-

vere.   Then Sir Launcelot got another spear,
and smote down Sir Agravaine, Sir Gaheris, Sir
Mordred, and Sir Meliot de Logris.

Neither was Lavaine idle, for he hurled down
a champion, named Ozana le Cœur Hardi. Then
Sir Launcelot drew his sword, and hewed down
Sir Safire, Sir Epinogris, and Sir Galeron.

"Ah, mercy!" cried Sir Gawain, "what
knight is that I see yonder that doth such
wondrous deeds?"

"I wot well who he is," said King Arthur,
"but will not name him till the joust is over."

"My liege," returned Sir Gawain, "I would
say it were no other than Sir Launcelot, by the
riding, and by the buffets that I see him deal.
Yet methinks, it cannot be he, because he beareth the red sleeve on his helmet, and I know yet
that he never bare a lady's token at any jousting."

"Let him be," said Arthur, "for he will be
better known and do more ere he depart."

Then the party that were against King Arthur were well comforted and they held them
together, which beforehand had been sorely rebuked.

Sir Bors, Sir Ector de Maris, and Sir Lionel
called unto them the knights of their blood with
nine knights of Sir Launcelot's kin. All these
thrust in mightily, for they were all noble warriors. And they thought to rebuke the valiant
Sir Launcelot and the stripling Lavaine, for
they knew them not.   So they charged, and
overthrew many knights of North Wales and
Northumberland.

And when Sir Launcelot saw how ill it fared

with the party he had espoused, he got him a third spear, and encountered them all at once, and three of them were hurled from their saddles. At last, Sir Bors smote Sir Launcelot through his shield into the side, and the spear broke, leaving the point in the wound.

When Lavaine saw his friend upon the ground, he ran to the King of Scotland, and secured his charger, which he brought to Launcelot, and, maugre them all he made him mount upon that horse ; then, despite his wound, he made a last charge, and carried all before him ; but the blood flowing fast from his side, he was fain to ride out of the press, scarcely able to keep the saddle.

"By St. George !" said Sir Gawain to King Arthur, "I marvel more and more who he can be, this knight with the red sleeve."

"Let it rest," replied the king. "I tell you he will be known ere he depart. But the knights grow furious, and it is time to put an end to the contest. '

So saying, he flung down his warder, and then the trumpets sounded the retreat, and the heralds proclaimed that the prize of the day, was awarded to the knight with the white shield, that bore the red sleeve.

Then came the kings and nobles of the party for which Sir Launcelot had fought, and Sir Galahalt thus addressed him :

"Fair knight, the saints guard thee ! for much have you done this day : therefore we pray you that you will come with us, that you may receive the prize you have so nobly deserved."

"My fair lords," answered Sir Launcelot,

" wit ye well if I have deserved thanks I have sore bought it : I am wounded unto death; therefore, as I am sore hurt let me depart whither it pleaseth me. I care not for the prize nor honour—I pant for air, and would rather enjoy a few hours' rest than wear a crown over all this broad kingdom."

Then galloping forth from the lists, he betook himself to the neighbouring wood. Lavaine pursued and overtook him just as he had reached a little dell in the green depths of the copse.

Just as he reached him, he reeled in the saddle, and slipping from his horse sank on the ground. In an instant Lavaine dismounted, and running to the wounded knight, raised him to his arms.

" Oh, gentle Lavaine," groaned Sir Launcelot, "help me, that this truncheon were out of my side ! for it sticketh so sore that it almost slayeth me.

" Oh mine own lord !" sobbed Lavaine, " I would fain help you ; but it dreads me as I draw out the spear that you shall be in peril of death."

Then Lavaine, shuddering in sympathy for the pain he was inflicting, drew the spear.

Sir Launcelot bit his lip to quell a shriek, his brow sweated with the torture, then the blood gushed from the wound and he fell into a swoon.

" Alas !" exclaimed Lavaine. " How shall I help him now."

He ran to a spring that flowed close by, and filling his bascinet, he returned to Sir Launcelot, and threw water upon his brow. But he lay nigh half an hour as he had been dead; at last he feebly raised himself and said :

"Help me to horse, Lavaine; for within these two miles, lives a gentle hermit—Whilhom—a knight of worship and a lord of great possession."

"I have heard of him," said Lavaine. "Sir Bawdewine is it not?"

"The same," rejoined Launcelot. "He is a noble surgeon. Help me to reach his cell. I may trust his loyalty."

Then with difficulty Lavaine raised Sir Launcelot, and helped him to remount, and led him through the wood. At length they reached the hermitage. Then Lavaine beat in the door with the end of his spear, crying:

"Let me in for the sake of St. Michael and the holy angels!"

CHAPTER XLIII.

The Hermit discovers the wounded knight to be Sir Launcelot—Lavaine goes to communicate tidings to his sister—King Arthur sends Sir Gawain with the diamond to search for Sir Launcelot—Sir Gawain goes to Astolat and sees Elaine with Sir Launcelot's shield.

When the hermit beheld Sir Launcelot bleeding, he said, "What knight are ye."

"Father," replied Sir Launcelot, "I am a knight adventurous that laboureth to gain worship, and am hurt."

Then the hermit saw by a wound on his cheek that he was Sir Launcelot, and said, "Alas, mine own lord, why hide your name from me, for I know you to be the noblest knight of all the world."

"Sir," replied Sir Launcelot, "Since you know me, help me, for I would be out of pain, either to death or to life."

Then the hermit staunched the blood and made him drink good wine, so that Sir Launcelot was much revived.

Lavaine leaving Sir Launcelot to the care of the hermit, went on his way to Astolat, and as he entered the chamber of Elaine, he laid his hand on her shoulder.

"Lavaine, dear brother!" she exclaimed. "Returned safe, Heaven be praised!"

"Sweet sister, not only did I come off unhurt but victorious," replied Lavaine. "I have won my spurs, and my heart's wish is accomplished; I am to be admitted into the fellowship of knighthood."

"But he—the stranger knight?" faltered Elaine, "how did he fare?"

"Dear sister, he is wounded," returned Lavaine. "But what of that? I would shed my heart's best blood so I might be a knight of such worship as Sir Launcelot."

"Sir Launcelot!" returned Elaine. "Was our knight that noblest of men?"

"He is no other, sister dear."

"And he is wounded?" gasped Elaine.

"Ay, grievously," answered Lavaine. "I left him in the care of Sir Bawdewine.

"Elaine, be comforted," returned her brother, "Sir Launcelot is in good hands, and if the power of man can aid him, he will recover; he sends you back the token and trusts you will approve him to be a worthy champion, and to have done his devoir as a true knight should."

"And did he send me this kind message?" replied the artless girl. "The noble knight! —the gracious prince! But tell me, Lavaine, how he got his wound."

Her brother recounted all that had happened at the tournament, and Elaine listened with interest.

"I must return to the hermit's cell," said he, "for Sir Launcelot requires my services, and intends to send me on an errand to the Joyous Gard, a castle belonging to him."

Meanwhile King Arthur, as soon as Launcelot had fled, called together a council of his knights of the Round Table to discuss the question of the disposal of the diamond won by the fugitive knight. Then King Arthur, addressing Sir Galahalt, asked him where was the knight that bare the red sleeve.

"Bring him before me," said the king, "that he may have the prize, as it is right."

Then spoke Sir Galahalt. "The haut knight is hurt, and is never likely to see you or ourselves again."

"Alas!" said King Arthur, "Is he so grievously hurt? Know ye not his name?"

"We neither know his name, nor whence he came, nor whither he is gone. replied Galahalt.

"This is bad tidings," said the king. "I would not for my realm that the noble knight were slain."

"Does my lord Arthur know him?" asked Galahalt.

"As for that," said Arthur, "whether I know him or not, pray Heaven I hear good tidings of him."

"By my head!" said Sir Gawain, "if it be so, and the good knight is so injured, it is great damage and pity to all this land, for never did nobler knight handle a spear or sword. And if he may be found I will find him, for wounded as he is, he cannot be far away."

"Seek him," said King Arthur; "and when you find him, bring him hither with all speed, unless he cannot bestir himself, then we will come to him."

"Heaven forfend that I should fail in my purpose," replied Sir Gawain; "I will find him if I may."

"It is well said, Gawain," returned the king, "therefore ride forth and find the knight; take the diamond and give it with all grace, and return and let us know how he fares."

"I go, Sir Arthur," replied Sir Gawain; "nor will I come again till I have found him."

So the knight rode forth from Camelot and sought in vain for Sir Launcelot.

At length he reached Astolat, and came to the gate of the castle of Sir Bernard. The good master of the place, had just returned from hunting, and when he saw Sir Gawain, and asked him whence he came.

"From Camelot," replied the knight. "I seek the wondrous knight who tourneyed in the jousts this morning, and won the prize; he was one of the best knights I ever saw, but he retired from the lists sore wounded, after he smote down forty valiant good knights of the Round Table."

"Sir, we are happily met," answered Sir Bernard, "for that knight was here—my guest before the jousts; my daughter has his shield in keeping for him."

"His shield—what is the device?"

"Three lions rampant, crowned Or!"

"The arms of Launcelot," cried Sir Gawain. " I knew it must be he. No other knight is his equal."

Sir Bernard invited him to enter the castle. Sir Gawain asked to see the shield which Sir Launcelot had left in the charge of Elaine.

" The foolish girl, she hath it in her chamber," returned the old baron; " and guards it like some precious relic. Here, Leofric," he continued, turning to a page, " conduct this lord to my daughter's bower."

The page stepping lightly in before, led Sir Gawain to the chamber of Elaine. The Lily of Astolat rose as the knight entered and advanced towards him with anxious countenance.

"What news, my lord, from Camelot ?" she asked.

"Lady, the prize was won by one of the best knights that ever set spear in rest," answered Gawain. " He bore a red sleeve on his helmet, and he smote down forty valiant knights of the Round Table."

"And do you know the name of the great champion ?" asked Elaine.

" Madam, 'tis thought to be Sir Launcelot," replied Sir Gawain. " But, if it please you, let me have sight of that shield."

Elaine disclosed the shield with its device : three blue lions rampant crowned with gold.

"Right was the king !" exclaimed Sir Gawain. "It is Launcelot."

"I knew it," returned Elaine. "For I dreamed my knight the greatest knight of all !"

"You love him, fair Elaine ?" sighed the knight. " Thrice happy Launcelot!"

" I know not," replied Elaine, " My brothers have been my only companions since my
childhood, yet I feel that I could never love if
I love not him."

"Nay, but you love him ; the truth is fatal,"
answered Gawain.   " But if you knew him as
others know him, your affection would soon
grow cold.   His heart is given to another."

" Be it so," replied Elaine.   " I know his
worth and my unworthiness.   Farewell, my
lord."   She extended her hand and made as if
she would leave the room.

" Oh, stay a little while, dearest lady," returned Gawain.   " He is not true to you, but
false to her he loves.   Would I had worn your
sleeve, and won for you the prize, for were it
so my life should be devoted to give you proofs
of knightly love and constancy."

" No more of this, my lord," she said.

" My quest is ended ;" he said.   " I leave
you with the diamond your fickle knight has
won ; I leave the heart by your true lover lost.
Farewell ! but we shall meet at court, and there
trust you will learn more of him and more of
me, and fairly judge between us both."

With this he left the room, and rode back to
the court ; and told the king what the king already knew, that the knight was Sir Launcelot.
But Arthur was angry because Sir Gawain had
left the diamond in Elaine's charge, for he had
little faith in Launcelot's honourable intentions,
and was displeased that the chief knight of the
Round Table should have sought to deceive
him by a shallow artifice.

Then the news was buzzed about the court

that Sir Launcelot had fallen in love with the maid of Astolat, and the report reached Queen Guinevere, who paced her chamber half mad with jealous passion.

CHAPTER XLIV.

Elaine entreats her father to permit her to go to attend on Sir Launcelot—Her arrival at the hermitage—Elaine attends Sir Launcelot in his sickness—The return to Astolat—Sir Bor's visit to Sir Launcelot.

THE fair maid of Astolat pined away in her lonely tower, heart sick and vainly awaiting the return of her brother Lavaine, with news of Sir Launcelot, until unable longer to endure the torture of suspense, she sought her father.

"My dearest father," she said, "there is, I know no limit to your indulgence of your loving child. Grant me my wish, I long to see my brother Lavaine."

"And soon now will you see him, child," answered the old baron. "We know he is well, and we must soon hear news from him, and Sir Launcelot."

"Then you know, dear father, that Sir Gawain, brought hither the diamond won by the greatest of the knights; it vexes me that it should remain in our tower, seeing we have no right to keep it ; and I cannot rest for thinking how my champion lies wounded in the hermitage, I behold him in my dreams as a gaunt skeleton. I think out of gratitude I should attend him in his sickness. Let me do so, my father—I pray you let me go hence."

"Ay, the diamond," answered Sir Bernard. "I grieve that this knight should languish uncared for ; besides, it is but right the diamond should be placed in his hands who won it. Sweet, you shall go ; but bide not long from me. This mighty prince is not for such as you."

Then Elaine called to her brother, Sir Torre, and requested him to get the horses saddled, and with Huon accompany her on her journey. After a time they came to the hermitage, where Launcelot was lodged, and found Lavaine at the door. "Lavaine!" cried the maid of Astolat, "how fares my lord, Sir Launcelot ?" Lavaine looked on them with surprise, and inquired the cause of their presence.

"I bring the diamond-prize won by Sir Launcelot. But answer me ; how fares it with my lord ?"

"He is sore sick, Elaine," replied her brother. "I fear it will be long ere he will once more take the lead in real or mimic battle. But come in ; my lord will be pleased to see you."

Then Lavaine knocked at the door. The old hermit welcomed them, and ushered them into the cell, where they found Sir Launcelot. As she entered, he rose to meet her ; but he sank heavily in a chair.

Elaine uttered a sharp cry of anguish, and then throwing herself upon her knees clasped his hand.

"My lord," she said, "I bring you the prize —the diamond sent by the king."

Sir Launcelot faintly pressed her hand.

"My prize, sweet maid," he answered. "Ah the prize I crave is the renewal of my strength but your presence seems to re-inspire me with that hope." Elaine blushed and hung her head

Launcelot raised her face, and kissed her as he would kiss a child. Then he seemed to sleep.

Elaine returned home ; but next morning, rising early sought him again. And so day by day she attended him.

In his mad moods he was at times uncourteous, but Elaine bore with him. Sometimes he would call on Guinevere, and call her his false love ; then he would curse himself for treason to his king. Elaine would listen to him, while every word pierced her heart. Yet she controlled herself with an air of cheerfulness.

As Launcelot recovered, his brother-like affections for the maid of Astolat grew stronger, and he would bless her by the name of sister, regret her parting step, and watch for her coming. He would have given his life for her, but he could not love her, for his heart was Guinevere's.

Elaine saw all this, and often she would murmur : "Vain, in vain ! It cannot be. He will not love me ! How then must I die ?"

One day Launcelot called Lavaine to his side.

"Listen, my friend," he said ; "I know not whether I shall recover from this sickness, and I would be at peace with the knight who gave me this wound."

"You know him then ?" answered Lavaine.

"Yes,'twas good Sir Bors ; he knew me not, and was not to blame," returned Sir Launcelot. "But seek him out ; and pray him that he will come to me, that we may exchange forgiveness, lest I die."

"I will go, my lord."

"Gramercy, Lavaine, let not the king know of this."

527 R

"My lord, I will not," said Lavaine; "and be sure if I meet Sir Bors, that I will bring him to the hermitage."

"Do so, I pray you," answered Launcelot.

So Lavaine rode to Camelot, where he found him and told him his errand.

"Now, fair knight," said Sir Bors, "I require that you will at once bring me to Sir Launcelot."

"Sir," said the youth, "take your horse and within this hour you shall see him."

And so they came unto the hermitage where Sir Launcelot was; and when Sir Bors saw Sir Launcelot, haggard and pale, he could not speak but wept for a long while.

"Fair cousin," said Sir Launcelot, "you are right heartily welcome; and, believe me, the fault was not yours but mine, and I alone deserve the consequence. I came disguised, and thought to overmatch one and all; my pride has met with a rebuke. Therefore, cousin, let this matter pass, and come what may, hold yourself blameless."

"Be hopeful yet, Sir Launcelot," said Sir Bors. "You are in good hands; Bradewaine is the best of physicians, and will restore you to health."

"We will hope the best," said Launcelot, "but tell me, what news from court? How fares Guinevere?"

"The queen is wroth with you," said Sir Bors, "because you wore the red sleeve at the jousts."

"She hath no cause for anger," returned Sir Launcelot. "I could not refuse the request of the daughter of Sir Bernard of Astolat. I did but wear the token in mere courtesy."

"And so I told the queen," replied Sir Bors. "But there is no reasoning with a jealous woman. Tell me, who is the maiden that glided from your chamber. Is she the maid of Astolat, with whose name the court is busy?"

"A malison upon the court!" growled Sir Launcelot. "She is far above the tinselled crew of parasites. The queen! the court! a pack of sycophants—I have no patience! Ah! that my wound were whole! And yet, I speak it in all modesty and sorrow—I fear the poor maiden loveth me, and I cannot thrust her from me."

"And wherefore should you so?" replied Sir Bors. "She is passing fair."

"'Tis truth beyond denying."

"Then marry the girl whom you have proved to be so worthy of your love."

"It may not be," said Launcelot. "My heart is dead, and I can love no lady."

"But one who shall be nameless," said his kinsman. "Yet, I would to heaven I could see you wrested from a passion that dishonours you; but I may not counsel you."

"I prythee, cease," said Launcelot, holding up his hand. "To myself my sorrow."

"By the rood! I pity this sweet maid of Astolat!" said Sir Bors. "There are no pangs so bitter as those of unrequited love."

And so he turned the conversation on other matters, until the hermit gave Sir Bors a hint that it was time to leave the wounded man.

Sir Launcelot wrung his kinsman by the hand.

"I pray you, cousin, he said, "when next you meet the queen, say that as soon as I am able to bestir myself I will return to court."

In a month, Sir Launcelot was so far recovered as to be able to ride on horseback, and he returned to Astolat.

CHAPTER XLV.

Elaine's confession of her love—Sir Launcelot's departure from Astolat—Elaine's despair—Sir Launcelot's return to court—The Queen's displeasure—Elaine's sickness—The father's remonstrance—Elaine's dying injunction.

SIR BERNARD entertained Sir Launcelot at the Castle until he had recovered his strength. He pressed Elaine to accept some gift from him, in token of his gratitude; but all were refused.

"Speak, sweet Elaine. I take great shame that I should leave you without some gauge of my gratitude," he said. "Delay no longer; speak your wish, since I must go to-day."

"Going? To-day? And we shall never see you more!" said Elaine, trembling. "Ah! my lord, would I dare speak my wish!"

"Speak, sweetest sister. Why do you tremble so?" said Launcelot, gently.

"I needs must tremble at my own boldness—I needs must blush at what I dare not confess. Yet where fore shame? True love is honour! Ah, Sir Launcelot, I love you, and I cannot bear the thought of this our parting!"

"Oh, love me not, sweet Elaine!" said Launcelot. "I am unworthy of your affection. All that is mine would I give—wealth, my life, my sword; but my heart is gone from me—I cannot give you that."

"My lord, I know you cannot love me," said Elaine; "I'm resigned to that. Yet what harm that I might still be with you to follow you through all the world."

"The world! Alas! Elaine, is heartless—lives on cruel slander. Ill should I requite your brother and your father for their kindness did I expose your innocence to the world's misconstructions."

"Yet to see you never more, to feel myself alone!" sobbed Elaine. "Enough, my lord, I speak madly. When sense returns I shall curse myself for shame, to think of what has passed my lips. Oh! ignore it. Think of me as your foolish sister—as your loving friend. For me, my pain will not last long; death is an angel that is oftentimes moved by the prayers of the unhappy. Farewell, my lord! forgive me." So saying, she, with faltering step, moved away.

"We part not thus, Elaine!" cried Launcelot. He hastened to follow her, but she fell in swoon.

"Sir Launcelot," said Sir Bernard, "my foolish girl is stricken with sickness," his voice faltered. "She loves you, sir; the heart will own no mastery. Now, I pray, you, by some discourteous act, convince her that she loves in vain; so that maiden pride may triumph over her weakness."

"She loves me," sighed Launcelot. "Woe the while. Her best cure would be to know my unworthiness. Yet what I may I will do."

He then turned to his page, and said, "Go, and ask for that shield I left with Elaine."

The page entered the chamber of Elaine, and delivered his message.

The maid of Astolat took the shield down from the wall, and gave it to the boy, who took it to Launcelot.

"Farewell, Sir Bernard," said he, "and many thanks for your hospitable welcome. Blest in my memory be the hours I spent at Astolat; and sir, what influence I have at court shall be pushed for young Lavaine's advancement. When I am gone, your daughter's pure affection will find some worthier object; and for me, I shall regard my gentle nurse with more than brotherly love."

So saying, and, springing on his steed, made the animal curvet upon the stones of the courtyard. Elaine hearing the sound, and knowing that she so hopelessly loved, and with the tact of love, she was aware he knew she was looking at him, and yet he glanced not up, nor bade farewell, but rode away. Meanwhile, Elaine, seating herself, gazed on the wall where the shield had hung, then she pressed her hand to her brow.

"He is gone," she murmured—"he is gone, and he loves me not!"

Sir Launcelot returned to London. King Arthur received him kindly, as also did the knights of the Round Table ever excepting Sir Agravaine and Sir Mordred. But the Queen avoided him, when she met him she treated him with coolness, which he resented, by assuming a corresponding demeanour.

Elaine pined away in her tower; the old Baron, her father, watched her, as day by day she grew weaker.

"Father, I am not much amazed," said La-vaine. "For I, since first I saw Sir Launcelot, could never depart from, nor will I ever, so I might follow him."

Her father and her brothers fostered her with tenderest solicitude, but she grew worse and worse, until her case became hopeless.

One morning they sat watching her as she slept, and listening to her broken utterances, for she was restless.

"She wakes," said Sir Bernard. Elaine gazed at them with a wan smile.

"Father and brothers, I have been dream-ing," she said. "Methought I was a child again, and that my brothers rowed me in a boat on the river. Now there was a certain head-land that they would not pass; and then I cried for wilfulness, for my desire was to sail up that shining river to the palace of the King; this my brothers would not allow me to do. By-and-by, methought, I was alone upon that river, and to myself I said: 'Now I shall have my wish,' and then I awoke; let me but pass that head-land, let me go to the fair city of the great Pen-dragon; there let me enter in the court, where none shall mock me, not even the Queen herself."

"Peace, my dear child," said her father. "You are distrait; this cruel fever makes you light-headed. How can you go so far, being so sick? And wherefore should you seek Sir Launcelot, who scorns us all?"

"Oh, there is naught can shake my faith in him—and in my faith I die, and so die hap-py!" "Sweet daughter, courage!" replied Sir Bernard. "The fever will pass."

"Dear father, would it might!" she answered. "'Tis hard to leave so fair a world, and you and my read brothers so kind to me, by me so well-beloved; but since it is Heaven's will I should be so, I pray you send for my confessor, and let him shrive me of my sins before I die."

"As you will, my child," sobbed her father; and then, pierced to the heart's core with anguish, he left her to the care of her maidens.

The holy man was sent for, and adminstered the last sacred rites; but ever poor Elaine spoke of Sir Launcelot. Her confessor implored her to turn her mind from such thoughts.

"Why should I leave such thoughts?" she answered. "Am I not a woman? and while the breath is in my body I may complain, for my belief is I do no offence. Enough I love an earthly man, I take Heaven to my record, I never loved any but Sir Launcelot, nor ever shall!"

Then she called her father and brothers, and thus be sought them : "Dear father, ere I die, write me a letter as I shall indite it."

Her wish was granted; and when the letter was written, as she had devised, she said :

"As soon as my soul has parted from my body let this letter be put into my right hand, and my hand bound fast with the letter until I be cold; and then let me be laid upon a bier, with all the richest clothes I have about me, and deck the bed on which I die as though it was a queen's; then place it on a barge, and let me float down the river to King Arthur's court. Let none go with me but he who must steer the barge—your trusty henchman, dumb Huon. Thus, father, I beseech you, let all be done."

Her father gave her the promise: whereupon she grew more cheerful, and her relatives began to entertain some faint hope of her recovery, but on the tenth day she expired.

CHAPTER XLVI.

The interview of Sir Launcelot and the Queen—The Queen's anger and jealousy—The corpse of Elaine arrives in the barge—Elaine's letter to Sir Launcelot—The Queen and Sir Launcelot's regret for Elaine.

WHEN the sun rose next day the two brothers bore her to the barge. Her maidens had attired her in festal costume. The barge was covered with black samite, and upon the deck sat the old servitor, Huon, the mute. The brothers set a lily in the hand of their dead sister, and hung the case she had made for Launcelot's shield above her. Then, kissing her brow, and murmuring, "Farewell, sweet sister—for evermore farewell!" they parted, with bitter tears.

Then the dumb servitor steered the barge up the river, his eyes resting upon the face of his dead mistress, the letter in her right hand, and her golden hair streaming upon the embroidered coverlet. And so, the vessel swept on.

Meanwhile, Sir Launcelot, aggrieved by the queen's coldness, sought an interview with her, to bid her an eternal farewell. His more immediate object, however, was to present her with the diamonds which he had won at the nine yearly tournaments. The queen received him with chilling hauteur; but he perceived, by the flush upon her cheek, that she had much ado to restrain her feelings.

Sir Launcelot kissed the queen's hand.

"My lady," he said, "accept these jewels that I have won for you alone, and thereby make me happy. Madam, I have heard that there have been false rumours of me spread at court; but I am bold to hope that you do not believe them."

The queen took the gems and laid them down.

"My liege and lady," said Launcelot, "I entreat you to tell me if I have been so unhappy as to have incurred your undeserved displeasure."

"I will deal frankly with you, my lord Launcelot," returned Guinevere. "Some rumours I have heard that did not please me. I have suffered you to profess for me the devotion of a knight."

"And, dear lady, no more wordy professions can express my unalterable constancy."

"It may be so, my lord," said the queen, "and whether it be so or not, you have a right to do as you will. I have no claim on you further than pertains to me as Arthur's wife, and queen of this realm; but, I beseech you, take back these gems, for they are not for me, but for the lady of your heart—the maid, Elaine of Astolat."

"Madam, you wrong me much," said Sir Launcelot, gravely; "and even more do you wrong her, the good and gentle maid to whom I am so deeply indebted for her kindness when I lay so ill of my wound. With brotherly affection and due gratitude do I esteem the maid; but, for my love, it has but one object under heaven, as well you know."

"And yet men say that Elaine is sick with love for you," said the queen. "You wore her red sleeve in your helmet as a token: you have chosen her brother, Lavaine, as your companion. Take the diamonds, and give them to the lady for whom you have won them on the day when you approved yourself her champion. 'Tis better—wiser so, my lord. Farewell!" and she swept from the room.

"Have I deserved this?" muttered Launcelot, half mad with vexation. "And this is my reward for all I have done and suffered. Heartless Guinevere! would that your suspicions were more just—my love less fervent!"

As he mused thus, he stared out of the window upon the Thames which ran below, when

> Slowly pass'd the barge
> Where upon the lily maid of Astolat
> Lay smiling like a star in the blackest night.

The astonished Launcelot hurried to the bank. The barge glided to the palace doorway, and the oarsman disembarked. A throng of nobles gathered round him; but so strange was the look of his haggard face, that they were appalled.

"He is enchanted!" said Sir Galahalt. "He cannot speak, and she sleeps! Is it the fairy queen? What are they?"

Arthur approached, surrounded by his knights. Then the dumb man rose, and made signs that he was tongueless. He then pointed first to the damsel, and then to the palace, as though requesting that she might be carried in. At the king's command, Sir Galahalt and Sir Percival reverently bore her into the hall; then Sir Launcelot gazed on her, and the queen wept for pity. But King Arthur, seeing the letter, stooped, took it, broke the seal, and read as follows:—

"Most noble knight, Sir Launcelot du Lac.

"I, the maid of Astolat, come—for you left me without bidding me farewell—hither to take my last farewell. I loved you, and my true love has been my death. Therefore, to our Lady Guinevere and all other ladies, I make moan that they may pray for my soul. And thou, too, Sir Launcelot, pray thou for my soul, as thou art a knight peerless."

As the king read these words, the knights and ladies wept, and gazed with sorrow upon the face of the victim of an unrequited passion.

Then Sir Launcelot addressed them all:

"My sovereign liege, Arthur, and all you who now hear me, know that I am right heavy for the death of this fair damsel," he said; "for she was good and true, and loved me beyond measure. Yet to love makes not to love again. I swear, that I never gave her cause for such love. My friends at Astolat will bear testimony of what I avow. Her father even asked me to put some slight upon her that should convince her of the hopelessness of her attachment. I left her abruptly, and spake no parting word."

Then said the queen, "You might have shown her some gentleness, that would have saved her from death."

Sir Launcelot raised his head, their eyes met, and hers fell instantly. "Madam," he said, "she would none other way be answered, but that she would be my wife, or else follow me through the world. I told her that her love would change in favour of some other; and, madam, I cannot be constrained to love, for love must arise of the heart, and not of constraint."

"'Tis true," returned King Arthur. "Love will never be bound, for when he is bound he looseth himself. But Sir Launcelot, it will be to your worship, as well as to mine, that this maid be buried worshipfully."

"Sir," replied Launcelot, "that shall be done as I can best devise."

Then they left the body upon a bier, but Launcelot lingered alone by the side of the corpse. Guinevere softly crept to the side of Launcelot. Hand in hand the pair gazed upon the girl's placid face.

"Launcelot," sighed the queen, "in the presence of this touching sight, I ask you to forgive me for my womanish jealousy."

"Madam, all is forgiven," he answered.

"The innocent Elaine!" sighed the queen. "Would that I might have died for her!"

Next day the maid of Astolat was buried with pomp, Sir Launcelot appearing as chief mourner.

CHAPTER XLVII.

Visit to Sir Launcelot of the strange gentlewoman—He accompanies her to the abbey where he finds Sir Bors and Sir Lionel—Sir Launcelot knights Galahad—Returns to Camelot with Sir Bors and Sir Lionel—The marble and the sword floating on the river—Sir Galahad sits in the seat 'Perilous'—Sir Galahad draws the sword from the marble.

AT the vigil of Pentecost, when all the fellowship of the Round Table were at Camelot, and the tables were set for the feast, a fair gentlewoman came before the king and saluted him, and asked where Sir Launcelot was.

When Sir Launcelot was pointed out to her by the king, she approached him and said, "Sir Launcelot, I salute you on King Pelles' behalf, and require you to go into a forest close by."

"Well," said he, "I will gladly go with you."

So Sir Launcelot bade his squire bring his arms. Then the queen came to Sir Launcelot, and said, "Will you leave us at this high feast?"

"Madam," replied the gentlewoman, "he shall return to you to-morrow by dinner-time."

So Sir Launcelot departed with the gentlewoman, and rode into a forest, where was an abbey of nuns, and they alighted from their horses, and entered the abbey ; and there came forth a fair fellowship about Sir Launcelot. Then they led him to the abbess' chamber and unarmed him, and he saw lying upon a bed Sir Bors and Sir Lionel, who arose at his approach, and welcomed him with much joy.

"Sir," said Sir Bors to Sir Launcelot, "what adventure hath brought thee hither, for to-morrow we expected to have found thee at Camelot."

"A gentlewoman brought me hither, but I know not the cause," replied Sir Launcelot.

In the meantime there came twelve nuns, bringing with them Galahad, who was so well made, that none could find his match.

"Sir," said the ladies, "we bring you this child, and pray you to make him a knight, for of a more worthy man's hand may he not receive the order of knighthood."

Then said Sir Launcelot, "Cometh this desire from himself ?" and all present said "Yea."

"Then shall he," said Sir Launcelot, "receive the high order of knighthood on the morrow." And on the morrow he made him a knight, and said, "God make you a good man, for beauty faileth you not."

"Now, fair sir," said Launcelot, "will you come with me to the Court of King Arthur ?"

"Nay," said Sir Galahad, "I may not go with you at this time."

Then Sir Launcelot took Sir Bors and Sir Lionel to Camelot. And when the king and his barons returned from service, they saw all the seats of the Round Table written on in letters of gold, where each knight should sit, and when they came to the seat 'perilous,' they found thereon letters of gold that said, "Four hundred winters and fifty-four accomplished after the passion of our Lord Jesus Christ ought this seat to be filled."

Then they all said, "This is a marvellous thing;" and Sir Launcelot counted the time of the birth of our Lord, and said, "It seemeth to me that the time is now arrived that this seat should be filled, for this is the feast of Pentecost after the four hundred and four and fifty years; and I would that none of these letters be seen this day till he come that ought to achieve the adventure."

Then took they a cloth of silk to cover these letters in the seat 'perilous.'

As they stood talking, in came a squire, who said to the king, "Sir, I bring you good tidings."

"What be they?" said the king.

"Sir, there is in the river a great stone of red marble which I see floating upon the water, and there is also a sword."

Then the king and his knights went to the river, and found a stone of red marble floating on the water, and therein was stuck a sword, in the pommel of which were precious stones wrought with subtle devices and letters of gold.

Then the barons read the letters, which said,

"Never shall man take me hence, but only he by whose side I ought to hang, and he shall be the best knight of the world."

When the king saw these words, he said to Sir Launcelot, "Sir, this sword ought to be yours, for you are the best knight in the world."

"Certainly, it is not my sword, and I have not the hardihood to attempt to take it; for whosoever assayeth to take the sword, and faileth, he shall receive a wound by that sword, and I would that ye should know that this same day will the adventures of the Sancgreal, which is called the holy vessel, begin."

"Now, fair nephew," said the king to Sir Gawain, "assay ye to take the sword."

Gawain grasped the pommel of the sword, but could not stir it.

"My lord, Sir Gawain," exclaimed Sir Launcelot, "that sword shall touch you so sure that ye shall repent that ye ever put your hand upon it for the best castle in this realm!"

When the king heard this, he said unto Sir Percival that he should assay it for his love.

Sir Percival therewith set his hand on the sword, and drew strongly, but could not move it.

"Now may we dine," said the king, "for a marvellous sight have ye all seen." So they went into the court, and all the seats were full save the seat 'perilous.'

And there came in an old man, and with him he brought a young knight, in red arms, with a scabbard hung by his side; the old man said to King Arthur, "Sir, I bring a young knight, of the kindred of Joseph of Arimathæa, whereby the marvels of this court shall be fully accomplished."

"Sir," said the king, "ye are right welcome, and the young knight als ·."

Then the old man said to the young knight, "Sir, follow me;" and he led him to the seat 'perilous,' and the old man lifted up the cloth and found this inscription, 'This is the seat of Galahad.'

"Sir, this place is yours," said the old knight And Sir Galahad sat down in the seat, and with that the old man departed.

Then the knights of the Round Table marvelled that Sir Galahad durst sit in the seat 'perilous,' and said, "This is he by whom the Sancgreal shall be achieved;" and Sir Launcelot knew him to be his son, born of dame Elein.

When this adventure came to the queen's ear, she marvelled who this knight was that durst sit in the seat ' perilous.'

Then came King Arthur unto Sir Galahad, and said, "Sir, ye are welcome, for ye shall move many good knights to the quest of the Sancgreal, and ye shall achieve what no other knight could bring to an end." And he took Sir Galahad from the palace to show him the miracle of the stone. And the queen with many ladies, came to see the stone where it floated upon the water.

And the king said to Sir Galahad, "Sir, here is as great a marvel as ever I saw, and good knights have assayed to draw the sword, and failed."

"Sir," said Sir Galahad, "this adventure is not theirs but mine. And for the surety of this sword, I brought none with me, for by my side hangeth this scabbard." And he laid his hand on the sword, drew it and put it in the sheath.

"Sir," said the king, "a shield God shall send you."

"Now have I," said Sir Galahad, "that sword that sometimes was the knight's Balin le Savage with this sword he slew his brother Balan."

Thereupon the king and all espied a lady on a white palfrey, riding towards them. And she enquired for Sir Launcelot. When she saw him she said, "Until this day ye were the best knight in the world, but there is now a better than ye, and it is proved by the adventure of the sword."

CHAPTER XLVIII.

The feats of Galahad at the jousting—Sir Gawain reports the words of Merlin to King Arthur—Arthur advises his knights of the quest of the Sancgreal—The miracle of the Sancgreal—The vows of the knights—The grief of the Queen and her maidens—Sir Launcelot takes leave of the Queen—The knights arrive at night at Castle Vagon —The adventure of the white shield.

"Now," said King Arthur, "I know that from this day the quest of the Sancgreal shall begin, and all ye of the Round Table will be scattered, so that nevermore shall I see ye again together, therefore let me have a tournament amongst ye for the last time, that after your death men may speak of it."

To this they acceded all, and prepared for jousting; and the queen and her gentlewomen sat in the tower to see it.

Then Sir Galahad put on a coat of armour, but shield would he take none, and grasping a spear, he drove it into the middle of the press, and so marvellously did he joust that all men were full of wonder, for in short space he over-

came all save Sir Launcelot and Sir Percival.
Whereat the king and all the knights went
back to the palace at even-song, and sat down
to supper, every knight in his own seat. And
suddenly there burst a peal of thunder. In the
midst of this blast entered a sunbeam, and from
the 'perilous' seat its rays fell greater than
ever was daylight. And the knights beheld
each other fairer than ever were seen before,
and no man could speak a word.

Then came Sir Gawain, and said to the king,
"But five days since, I heard the voice of Merlin
speaking to me from the mountain. I besought
him to come forth, but he replied he never more
might do so, for that none could free him, save
the damsel of the lake, who had enclosed him
there by his own spells which he had taught
her. "But go thou Sir Gawain to King Arthur, and tell him to prepare his knights and
all his Round Table to seek the Sancgreal, for
the time is come when it shall be achieved. And
there shall be three white bulls that shall
achieve it, and the two shall be maidens and the
third shall be chaste. And that one of the three
shall pass his father as much as the lion passeth
the leopard. And by my craft I have ordained
the seat that no other man shall sit in except he
shall surpass in prowess all other knights in the
world." When Sir Gawain had thus spoken,
the king mused of the Holy Greal. Then he
addressed his knights, 'Lords and fair knights,
have ye no fear. To-day we have seen him
who may sit in the 'perilous' seat, and shall
achieve the Sancgreal, that holy vessel wherefrom at the Supper of our Lord, before his

death, He drank wine with His disciples hath been ever since it held the holiest treasure of the world, and wheresoever it hath rested peace and prosperity have attended it. But since the stroke which Balin gave King Pelles, none have seen it ; for Heaven hath hid it none know where, and it is left to this noble order of the Round Table to find it."

Then the Sancgreal was borne aloft, through the hall, covered with white samite, to conceal it from sight. And the hall was filled with incense, and every knight was fed with the food he best loved. And when the holy vessel had been borne through the hall, it disappeared ; and King Arthur yielded thanks to God.

Then Sir Gawain exclaimed, " Now have we all been fed by miracle with whatsoever food we desired ; therefore I make a vow that I will labour twelve months and a day in the quest of the Sancgreal, nor will I come again unto this court until mine eyes have witnessed it."

Knight after knight to vowed make the same quest, till the greater part of the knights had thus sworn. Then King Arthur said, " Sir Gawain, much I fear my true fellowship shall never meet together again, surely never Christian King had such worthy knights of the Round Table."

On the morrow the knights rose early, and when they were armed, they went to service at the minster. Then the king counted all who had made vow to take the adventure of the quest, and found them one hundred and fifty knights of the Round Table. And so they rode away from the court.

Then the queen went alone to her chamber, but Sir Launcelot followed to bid her farewell.

When he entered her chamber, she cried out, "Oh, Sir Launcelot, thou has grieved me thus to leave the king!"

"Madam," said Sir Launcelot, " be not displeased, for I shall return as soon as I can with honour."

Then Sir Launcelot joined the rest, and came that night to Castle Vagon. And the lord of the castle made them good cheer. On the morrow they all departed. Now Sir Galahad went forth without shield, and on the evening of the fourth day he came to an abbey of white monks, and he was led to a chamber to unarm. Shortly he was joined by King Bagdemagus and Sir Uwen. And when they saw Sir Galahad they welcomed him. "Sirs," said Sir Galaad, " what adventure brought you hither?"

"Sir," said they, "it was told us that within this place there is a shield which none may bear without receiving sore mischance, or be killed within three days, or else maimed forever."

"To-morrow," said King Bagdemagus, "I shall assay this adventure, and if I fail, do thou, Sir Galahad, take it up."

"I will, willingly," replied Sir Galahad; "for, as ye see, I have no shield."

On the morrow King Bagdemagus asked where the shield was kept, and a monk showed him where the shield hung behind the altar.

"Sir," said the monk, " this shield should hang from no knight's neck, unless he be the worthiest in the world. I warn ye, therefore, knights, consider well before ye touch it."

"I know that I am not the best knight in the world," said King Bagdemagus, "yet will

I make the trial, and if it please thee, Sir Galahad, abide here until thou hearest how I speed."

Then taking with him a squire, who might return with tidings to Sir Galahad, the king rode forth and before he had gone two miles he came to a hermitage, from whence rode forth a knight against him. In the shock, King Bagdemagus brake his spear upon the knight's shield, but was hurled to the ground wounded.

Then the knight took the white shield from the king, and said, " Knight, this shield ought never to have been borne but by him who hath no living peer."

Then to the squire the knight said, " Bear this shield unto Sir Galahad, and greet him well from me." Then the squire went to his master, and found him wounded nigh to death, and he bore him back to the abbey, and attended to his wounds.

CHAPTER XLIX.

Sir Galahad beareth the shield sent to him by the white knight—The history of the shield—Sir Galahad knights Melias de Lile—Sir Galahad defeats the seven knights of Maiden's Castle, and restores the castle to the maiden—Sir Galahad jousts with Sir Launcelot and Sir Percival, who are in disguise.

THEN the squire went to Sir Galahad and said, "The knight who overcame King Bagdemagus sendeth you greeting, and bade that ye should bear this shield, through which great adventures shall be achieved."

" Now blessed be God and fortune," said Sir Galahad. And by the hermitage he met the white knight, and each saluted the other.

" Sir," said Sir Galahad, "this shield I bear hath surely a marvellous history."

"Thou sayest rightly," said the knight.
"That shield was made in the days of Joseph
of Arimathæa, the knight who took our Lord
from the cross. He departed from Jerusalem
with a party of his kindred, and went to Sarras,
where King Evelake dwelt, who warred with
one Tolleme la Feintes, a Saracen, who was
cousin to King Evelake. On a certain occasion
the two met to do battle. Then Joseph went
to King Evelake, and told him he should be
slain unless he believed in the new law. And
when, by the teaching of Joseph, King Evelake
became a Christian, this shield was made for
him in our Lord's name, and through its aid
King Tolleme was defeated; for when King
Evelake met him in battle, he hid the shield
under a veil, and suddenly uncovering it, he
displayed to his enemies the figure of a bleeding
man nailed to a cross, and at the sight they fled.
After that many miracles were worked by the
shield of the cross, and both Joseph and King
Evelake came to Britain. In this land they
found a great felon, Paynim, who put Joseph
into prison. So by chance tidings came to a
great man, Mondrames, and he assembled all
his people, and disinherited this Paynim, and
released Joseph from prison; and by the preaching of Joseph, the people were made Christians.

"And when Joseph lay on his death-bed, King
Evelake begged of him some token ere he died.

"Whereupon Joseph called for this shield,
saying, 'This cross shall ever show as bright
as now, and the last of my lineage shall go forth
and achieve many marvellous deeds.'"

When the white knight had thus spoken, he

vanished away, and Sir Galahad returned to the abbey. Next morn a squire came to Sir Galahad, and wished to be made a knight. He told Sir Galahad that his name was Melias de Lile, and he was a son of the King of Denmark.

"Now, sir," said Sir Galahad, "since ye come of kings and queens, now look that knighthood be well set in you, for you ought to be a mirror to all chivalry;" and he made him a knight.

And Melias desired to join Sir Galahad in quest of adventures, and Sir Galahad consented; and armour were brought for Melias, and he rode forth with Sir Galahad.

Now they came to the meeting of two roads, and on the cross were letters written thus:— "All ye knights who seek adventures see here two ways. The one on the right defendeth thee from danger, but the one on the left thou shalt not there lightly win prowess, for thou shalt in this way be soon assayed.'

"Sir," said Melias, "suffer me to take the way on the left, for there I shall prove my strength."

"It were better," said Sir Galahad, "that ye rode not that way; for I deem that I should better escape in that way than ye."

"Nay, my lord, I pray you let me have that adventure." "Take it, in God's name," said Sir Galahad.

On a certain day, Sir Galahad entered a ruined chapel, and kneeled before the altar, and prayed for counsel. And he heard a voice say, "Depart unto the maiden's castle, and redress the wrongs there committed."

After hearing these words, he mounted his horse, and saw a strong castle; and meeting an old churl he asked the name of the castle.

"That is the maiden's castle," replied he.

"It is a cursed place," said Sir Galahad, "and all mischief dwelleth therein."

"Therefore, sir knight, I counsel thee to turn."

"For that same reason I will ride on," quoth Sir Galahad. Then he went forward, and presently he was met by seven damsels who cried out, "Sir knight, thou ridest in great peril, for thou hast two waters to pass over."

"Why should I not pass over them?" said he.

Anon he met a squire, who said, "Sir knight, the masters of this castle bid thee approach not nearer till thou showest thy business here."

"I come here to destroy their wicked customs," replied Sir Galahad.

"If that be thy purpose thou wilt have much to do," said the squire.

"Go thou forward with my message," returned Sir Galahad.

In a few minutes, seven knights rode forth furiously from the castle, and bore down upon Sir Galahad, who smote the foremost to the earth and brake his neck, and warded the spears of the others so that they were shivered to pieces. Sir Galahad then set upon them so fiercely that they fled up to the castle gate, where he slew them.

Then came out a venerable man in priest's vestments, and delivered up to him the keys of the castle. And as soon as Sir Galahad had unlocked the gates he was met by a multitude of people, who cried out, "Sir knight, long have we waited for thy deliverance, for the seven felons thou hast slain have long enslaved the people round about, and killed all knights who passed this way."

"Where is the maiden?" asked Sir Galahad.

"She lingereth below in a dungeon," said they.

Then Sir Galahad released her, and restored to her her inheritance, and departed.

As he rode, he met two knights, in disguise, who proffered him to joust. These were Sir Launcelot, his father, and Sir Percival, but he knew them not, and they knew not him. So he and Sir Launcelot encountered first, and Sir Galahad smote down his father; then he fought with Sir Percival, and clave his helm, and felled him from his horse. Then Sir Galahad saw a pious woman come forth from an hermitage, who cried out, "God be with thee, the best knight in the world; had yonder knights known thee as well as I do, they would not have encountered with thee." When Sir Galahad heard this, he rode off at a quick pace.

When Sir Launcelot had recovered from his fall, he went forward, and came to a stone cross hard by a chapel, and within the chapel he saw an altar, whereon there stood a candlestick of silver, bearing six great lights. And when Sir Launcelot saw the light, he tried to get within the chapel, but could not; so being weary, he ungirded his sword, and laid himself down to sleep before the cross. And as he lay he saw pass by two white palfreys, bearing a litter wherein a sick knight lay, and he heard the sick man say, "Oh, sweet Lord, when shall this sorrow leave me, and the holy vessel pass by me, through which I shall be blessed. Then Sir Launcelot saw the candlestick with the six tapers come before the cross, but he could see no one who bore it. Then came also a table of silver, and thereon the holy vessel of the Sanc-greal. And when the sick man saw that he sat up, and lifting both his hands said, " Fair Lord, sweet Lord, who art here within this holy vessel, have mercy on me, that I may be whole;" and creeping on his hands and knees, he kissed the vessel. And then he leaped up and cried, "Lord God, I thank thee, for I am made whole. Then the Holy Greal departed with the table and the silver candlestick into the chapel, so that Sir Launcelot saw it no more.

As he marvelled, he heard a voice say, "Sir Launcelot, go thou hence from this holy place." Then he bethought him of his sins, and said, "My sins have brought me into dishonour; for when I sought earthly honour I achieved them ever; but now I take upon me holy things, my guilt doth hinder me; therefore had I no power to speak when the holy blood appeared before me." With that he departed on foot, for his horse had strayed away.

CHAPTER L.

Sir Percival attacked by twenty men-at-arms—He is rescued by Sir Galahad—Sir Bors fights for the lady of a castle, and restores to her her possessions—Sir Galahad jousts against many knights and overthrows them—He sorely wounds Sir Gawain—Sir Percival and Sir Bors welcomes Sir Galahad to the ship—Sir Galahad draws the miraculous sword from the scabbard.

SIR PERCIVAL rode till he came to a valley, where he met twenty men-at-arms bearing a dead knight. They inquired of Sir Percival whence he came, and on his telling them from King Arthur's court, they set upon him. After slaying several, Sir Percival would have been overcome, had not Sir Galahad come that way, and seeing Sir Percival sore beset, he rushed on the foremost man and struck him down; the rest turned and fled, pursued by Sir Galahad.

As Sir Percival proceeded after Sir Galahad, a knight on a black steed passed by. And they encountered together, and Sir Percival's horse was smote in the chest, and fell dead. Then cried Sir Percival, "Turn, false knight, and fight me on foot;" but he would not, and rode fast away. Then Sir Percival lay down and slept till midnight. At noon next day he came where he saw a ship sailing before a strong wind towards him. And when it came to shore, he found it covered with white samite, on the deck there stood an old man, dressed in priest's robes, who asked him from whence he came.

"I am a knight of King Arthur's court, and follow the quest of the Sancgreal," replied he.

"Fear nothing," said the old man, "for I am come from a strange country to comfort thee."

Then was Sir Percival rejoiced, and entered the ship, which sailed from the shore. When Sir Bors rode forth from Camelot to seek the Sancgreal, he met with a holy man who saluted him. And they rode to his hermitage together, and anon they went into the chapel, and Sir Bors was confessed. And they afterwards ate bread and drank water together. "Now," said the hermit, "I pray thee eat no other food till thou sit at the table where the Sancgreal shall be, and it were wise that ye should wear sackcloth next your skin for penance.

Sir Bors did as he was counselled, and rode away. And as he was passing an old dry tree, he saw many little birds round one great one, nigh dead with hunger. Then did the big bird smite himself in the breast with his own bill, and bled until he died among the little ones, and they recovered life in drinking up his blood. When Sir Bors saw this he knew it was a token, and rode on in deep thought. And at eventide he came to a tower, and prayed for admission, and the lady of the castle gladly asented.

After supper came a squire, and said, "Madam, bethink to provide a champion for to-morrow for the tourney, or else shall thy sister have thy castle."

The lady of the castle told Sir Bors that she and her sister were daughters of King Anianse, who left them all his lands; and her sister was the wife of a knight, named Sir Pridan le Noir, who had taken all the lands save the one tower in which she dwelt. "And now," said she, "this also will he take, unless I find a champion by to-morrow."

"Be comforted in that," said Sir Bors, "to-morrow I will fight for thee." On the morrow the lady prayed him to eat ere he commenced the fight, but he refused to break his fast until the tournament ended. And the heralds cried that whichever should win, his lady should have the other's lands. Then the two knights came together with such force that both their spears were shivered, and their shields and hauberks pierced through, and they both were sorely wounded. At last Sir Pridan grew faint, and Sir Bors rent off his helm. Then Sir Pridan cried for mercy, and said, "For God's sake, slay me not, and I will never war against thy lady more." Then all those who held their lands of the lady did homage to her and swore fealty. And Sir Bors departed; and met him two knights, bearing Sir Lionel, bound on a horse with thorns, so that the blood flowed from the wounds on his body; but he uttered no groan. As soon as Sir Bors saw this he put his spear in rest to rescue his brother; but he heard a woman's voice cry, " St. Mary, succour thy maid !" and he saw a damsel dragged by a felon knight into a thicket. Then was Sir Bors sore troubled, and knew not what to do. For he thought within himself, " If I let my brother be he will be murdered, but if I help not the maid she is shamed for ever, and my vow compelleth me to set her free; wherefore must I help her, and trust my brother unto God." So riding to the knight who held the damsel, he smote him through both shield and shoulder. Then the maid thanked Sir Bors and besought him to come to her father who was a great lord.

" Truly," said he, " I may not for I have a great adventure yet to do." And he departed to find his brother. And after he had discovered his brother, there came a voice, as it were from a cloud, and said, " Sir Bors, leave thy brother, and ride towards the sea, for there Sir Percival abideth thee."

Then he departed, and on the strand he found a ship, in the midst of it stood an armed knight whom he knew to be Sir Percival. Then they rejoiced over each other and said, " We lack nothing now but Sir Galahad."

When Sir Galahad had rescued Sir Percival from the twenty knights, he came to a castle where a tournament was being held ; and the knights of the castle were put to the worse ; which when he saw, he rode to help them, and smote down their adversaries. Now Sir Gawain happened to be among the stranger knights, and when he saw the white shield with the red cross, he knew it was Sir Galahad, and proffered to joust with him. So in a fierce shock their spears were broken ; then drew they their swords, and Sir Galahad smote Sir Gawain so on the helm clove it through, and carved the horse's neck and shoulder, and Sir Gawain fell to the earth. Sir Galahad then beat back all that warred against the castle, and rode off.

That night he rested at a hermitage, and he was roused by a knocking at the door. So he arose, found a damsel there, who said, " Sir Galahad, mount your horse, and follow me, for I will show you within three days the most marvellous adventure that ever knight saw."

So Sir Galahad did as she desired, and they rode towards the sea, and arrived at a castle inclosed by a stream, and they entered into the castle and had good cheer, for the lady of the castle was the damsel's mistress. Before day the damsel called Sir Galahad, and bade him arm himself, and when he was prepared to depart, he and the damsel rode off together.

And at length they came to the sea-side, and lo ! a ship, wherein were Sir Percival and Sir Bors, abode by the shore, and when they saw him they cried, " Welcome, Sir Galahad, we have awaited for thee long."

And the damsel went into the ship, and addressing Sir Percival said, " Know ye not who I am ?" and he answered he did not know her.

"I am thy sister, the daughter of King Pellinore, and am sent to help thee and these knights to achieve the quest ye follow."

Sir Percival rejoiced at the meeting. After they had been to sea some time a whirlwind arose so that the ship could not live. Then they saw another ship near to them and went towards it; and on the ship was written, "Thou who shalt enter me, beware that thou be in steadfast belief; for I am Faith, and if thou doubtest I cannot help thee." Then were they all adread, but they entered. On the ship they saw a bed, whereon lay a crown of silk, and at the foot lay a sword half drawn from the scabbard. The pommel of the sword was of precious stones of divers colours, and the scales of the haft were of bones. The one was a bone of a serpent and its virtue saveth all men who hold it from weariness, and the other was the bone of a fish of the floods of Euphrates, named Ertanax, and its virtue causeth whoever holdeth it to forget all other things, save the thing he seeth before him.

"I will handle that sword," said Sir Percival, and set his hand on it, but could not grasp it. Then Sir Bors set his hand upon it, and failed also. Upon which Sir Galahad came, and seeing these words written, red as blood, "None shall draw me forth save the hardiest of all men; but he that draweth me shall never be wounded to death," feared to try.

"Ye may try safely," said the damsel, "for the drawing of this sword is forbid to all but you. For this was the sword of David, King of Israel; and Solomon, his son, made for it this scabbard, and laid it on this bed until thou shouldst take it up." Then they prayed Sir Galahad to take the sword, and he drew it forth.

" Now reck I not though I die, for I have made thee noblest knight of all the world," said the damsel.

Then the ship sailed and brought them to land near the castle of Carteloise, and they saw a multitude of knights come forth, who bade them yield or die, and ran at Sir Percival, Sir Bors, and Sir Galahad, who smote them to the earth, and entered the castle. And a priest came to meet them; and Sir Galahad said, "In sooth, good father, I repent me of this slaughter; but we were first assailed, or else it had not been."

" Repent ye not," said the priest, " for among the knights slain are all the felon sons of a good knight, Earl Hornox, whom they have confined in a dungeon."

Then Sir Galahad prayed the priest to bring him to the earl, who, when he saw Sir Galahad, cried out, "Long have I waited for thy coming, and now hold me in thy arms that I may die in peace." And therewith Sir Galahad took him in his arms, and he died.

CHAPTER LI.

The vision of the three knights at the hermitage—Sir Launcelot's vision—The meeting of Sir Launcelot and Sir Galahad—The separation—Sir Launcelot's adventures—Sir Galahad restores sight to King Evelake—The visions of Sir Galahad, Sir Bors, and Sir Percival—Sir Galahad's death.

THEN departed the three knights, until they came with them, into a forest. And they saw before them a white hart, led by four lions, and they marvelled at the sight; they followed until they came to a hermitage and chapel, whereinto the lions and hart entered. Then a priest offered mass, and they saw the hart changed into a man; and the four lions also became a man, eagle, a lion, and an ox. And these figures vanished. Then the knights fell upon their knees, and begged the priest to tell them what these things meant.

"What saw ye, sirs," said the priest, "for I saw nothing." Then they told him what they had seen.

"Oh, lords!" said he, "now know I well ye be the knights who shall achieve the Sancgreal, for unto them alone such mysteries are revealed. The hart, ye saw, is One above all men, without blemish, and the four lions with Him are the four Evangelists."

When they heard that, they thanked the priest and departed, and performed many adventures. After Sir Launcelot had left the hermit, he wandered a while and laid himself down and slept. And a vision came to him and said, "Launcelot, take thine armour, and enter the first ship thou shalt find." He obeyed the vision, and entered a ship without sails or oars, and looking round he saw a bed, and thereon a damsel lying dead, who was Sir Percival's sister. And he saw in her hand a paper, which he took, and therein read her story. On a certain night he went on shore, and heard a horse coming towards him, from which a knight alighted, and went into the ship; who, casting his eyes on Sir Launcelot, said, "Fair sir, ye be welcome to my eyes; for I am thy son Galahad, and long have I sought for thee."

With that he asked his blessing. And Sir Launcelot kissed him with great joy. Then they dwelt in the ship, and served God with all their powers, and visited many islands. And upon a time they came to the edge of a forest, and they saw a knight leading a white horse. Then the knight saluted Sir Galahad, and said, " Ye have been long enough with your father ; now ride this horse until ye achieve the Holy Quest."

Then went Sir Galahad to his father, and said, " Father, I am now about to depart, and I know not when I shall see thee again."

And as he took the horse a voice said, " Ye shall meet no more in this life."

" Now, my son," said Launcelot, " since it is ordained we meet no more, I pray the High Father of Heaven to preserve both you and me."

Then they bade each other farewell; and Sir Galahad entered the forest, and Sir Launcelot returned to the ship, and the wind drove him more than a month through the sea, and ever prayed Sir Launcelot that he might see the Sancgreal.

And on a certain night he came before a castle, whose gate was guarded by two lions. And Sir Launcelot heard a voice saying, " Leave thy ship now, and go within the castle, and thou shalt see a part of thy desire."

Then he went towards the gate ; and approaching the lions, he drew his sword, when he was struck on the arm, and his sword fell from his grasp, then he heard a voice say, " Oh, man of poor belief, wherefore trusteth thou thy arms before thy Maker's power." Then he picked up the sword, and made a cross on his forehead, and passed the lions without hurt.

And going in he found a chamber with the door shut, which in vain he tried to open. And listening he heard a voice within, which sang so sweetly, that it seemed no earthly thing, ' Joy and honour be to the Father in Heaven.' Then he kneeled at the door, for he knew the Sancgreal was there within. And the door was opened and so great a splendour shone forth as if the torches of the world had been alight together. But when Sir Launcelot would have entered in, a voice forbade him. And he stood on the threshold and he saw a table of silver and the holy vessel covered with red samite, and many angels round about holding burning candles, and a cross of the ornaments of the altar. Then a priest offered mass, and when he took the holy vessel up, it was too heavy for him to bear. On seeing which Sir Launcelot cried, " Oh, Father, take it not for sin that I go to help the priest who hath much need thereof." So he approached the table, and a breath of fire smote him to the ground, and he was taken up and laid outside the chapel door, where he lay in a swoon all the night. Then Launcelot knew that he had seen as much as his eyes may behold of the Sancgreal, and he returned to his own country.

When Sir Galahad had parted from Sir Launcelot he rode many days until he came to the monastery where the blind king, Evelake lay.

On the morrow Sir Galahad desired to see the king, and he was brought into his presence, and Sir Galahad embraced him, and the king said " Fair Lord Jesus, suffer me to come to Thee ;" and he died. And Sir Galahad after that met Sir Percival and Sir Bors. When they had each told their adventures, they rode to the castle of Corbonek; and there King Pelles gave them a hearty welcome. As soon as they was come into the castle, a voice cried. " Let them who ought not now to sit at the table of the Lord arise and depart hence."

Then all save those three knights departed. Other knights came in—three of whom had come from Gaul, three from Ireland, and three from Denmark.

Then came forth the likeness of a bishop, and four angels stood round about him, and a table of silver was before them, whereon was set the vessel of the Sancgreal. Then came other angels, two bearing burning candles, and the third a towel, the fourth a spear from which fell blood, the drops of which fell into a box he held in his hand. Anon the bishop took the wafer up to consecrate it; and at the lifting up they saw a figure of a child, who smote itself into the middle of the wafer and vanished, so that all saw the flesh made bread. Whereat the bishop went to Galahad and kissed him, and bade him kiss his fellows and say, "Now, servants of the Lord, prepare for food such as none ever yet were fed with since the world began." The knights were filled with a great dread.

Then came from the vessel the vision of a man bleeding, at which they fell on their faces and were dumb. And he brought the holy Grealeund, spoke words of comfort, and when they drank thereof, the taste was sweeter than tongue can tell or heart desire.

Then a voice said, "Galahad, son, with this

blood which drippeth from the spear anoint thou the maimed king and heal him; and when thou hast so done, depart with thy brethren in a ship that ye shall find, and go to the city of Sarras, and bear with thee the holy vessel, for it shall no more be seen in Logris."

Then Sir Gahalad walked to the bloody spear, and anointing his hands with the blood, went to King Pelles and touched his wound, and he arose from his bed as whole as man ever was.

Then Sir Galahad, Sir Bors, and Sir Percival departed as they had been commanded.

And Galahad prayed that he might now pass to God, and a voice said to him, " Galahad, thy prayer is heard, and when thou asketh the death of thy body thou shalt have it, and find the life of thy soul." And while they prayed and slept, the ship sailed on, and when they awoke they saw the city of Sarras before them.   Then the three knights took up the holy table and the Sancgreal, and went into the city.   When they had abode in the city twelvemonths, Sir Galahad prayed before the Sancgreal, and a bishop with a company of angels came around him, and the bishop said, to Galahad, " Come forth, good servant of the lord, for the time hath come thou desireth so long."   Then Sir Galahad prayed, " Now, blessed Lord ! would I no longer live if it might please thee."   Then the bishop gave him the sacrament, and when he had received it with unspeakable gladness, he asked the bishop who he was.

"I am Joseph of Arimathæa," said he, "whom our Lord hath sent to bear thee fellowship."

Therewith Sir Galahad went to Sir Bors and

Sir Percival and kissed them, and then began to pray. And his soul departed, and a multitude of angels bare him to heaven. Then came a band from heaven and took the vessel and the spear, and bare them out of sight. Since then the Sancgreal was never seen by man.

After this had come to pass, Sir Percival betook himself to a hermitage, and so passed out of the world. And Sir Bors, returned to King Arthur, at Camelot.

CHAPTER LII.

The Queen is displeased with Sir Launcelot—He is banished from the court, and retires to a hermitage—Sir Pinal seeks to destroy Sir Gawain by poisoning the apples at the feast—Sir Patrice partakes of them and dies—The Queen accused of poisoning the apples—Launcelot in disguise fights on her behalf—The Queen's innocence made known by the Lady of the Lake.

AFTER the quest of the Sancgreal was fulfilled, and all the knights left alive were come to the court, there was joy, and glad were the king and queen of the return of Launcelot and Sir Bors.

And Sir Launcelot withdrew from the company of Queen Guinevere, to eschew slander and noise ; wherefore the queen waxed wroth with him, for she counted him as her own knight. On a certain day she called him to her chamber, and said to him, " Sir Launcelot, I see and feel daily that thy loyalty for me doth slack, for thou hast no joy to be in my presence.'

" Ah, madam," said Sir Launcelot, " in this ye must hold me excused for divers causes. One is, I thank God that I saw in that my quest as much as ever saw sinful man, and if I had not my privy thoughts to return to your love again, I should have seen as great mysteries as ever saw my son Galahad, Percival, or Sir Bors, and therefore, madam, it may not be forgotten the high service in which I did my labour. Also, madam, wit ye well that there be many men about this court, who speak of our love and would fain discover us, as Sir Agravaine and Sir Mordred, and, madam, I dread them more for your sake, than for any fear I have of them myself."

The queen said, " Launcelot, now I well understand thee for a false, knight, and therefore shall I never love thee more, and never thou more come into my sight, and I discharge thee from the court, and return not to it on pain of losing thy head."

Then Sir Launcelot departed, and called Sir Bors, Sir Ector, and Sir Lionel, and told them how the queen had dealt with him.

" Fair sir," said Sir Bors, "remember how ye are called the noblest knight in the world, wherefore go not, for women are hasty and do what they sore repent of afterwards : therefore by mine advice ye shall ride to the hermitage be sides Windsor, and abide until I shall send thee better tidings."

To this he consented, and departed for the hermitage. As soon as it came to the queen's ears that he was gone, she was sorry. And on a certain day she made a great feast, to show that she had as great joy in other knights as in Sir Launcelot. And at the feast were Sir Gawain and Sir Agravaine, Sir Gaheris and Sir Gareth, with Sir Bors, and Sir Blamor de Ganis, Sir Bleoberis, Sir Ector de Maris, Sir Lionel, Sir Palomides, Sir Mador, Sir Safere, Sir Persant,

Sir Brandilus, Sir Patrice, a knight of Ireland; Sir Astomore and Sir Pinel le Savage, cousin to Sir Lamorack de Galis, the good knight that Gawain slew by treason. Now Sir Pinel hated Sir Gawain; and Sir Gawain had a great love for all kinds of fruit, especially apples, which when Sir Pinel knew, he poisoned certain apples that were on the table with the intention to slay him.

But as they ate and made merry, Sir Patrice took of the poisoned apples, and when he had eaten he fell dead. At this every knight became enraged, and as the queen had made the feast, suspicion fell upon her.

"My lady," said Sir Gawain, "I know well this fruit was for me, and I have been nigh slain, and I fear me ye will be ashamed."

"This shall not be so ended," said Sir Mador de la Porte, "for here have I lost a noble knight of my blood, and therefore upon this shame will I be revenged to the uttermost; and openly he impeached the queen of the death of his cousin, Sir Patrice."

"Fair lords," said King Arthur, "ye trouble me sorely. I may not do battle for my wife although I deem this deed is none of hers, but I suppose she will not lack a champion, some good knight would surely put his body in jeopardy to save her."

But all present said they could not hold the queen excused or be her champion.

"Alas!" said the queen, "I made this dinner for no evil, so God help me in my need."

"My lord, I require you to give me a day when I may have justice," said Sir Mador.

"Well," replied the king, "fifteen days hence ye shall be armed in the meadow beside Westminster, and if there be a knight to fight with thee God speed the right, and if not, then must my queen be burnt."

When the king and queen were alone together, he questioned her as how the case befell.

"I know not," replied she.

"Where is Sir Launcelot," said King Arthur, "for he would do battle for thee."

"My lord, I cannot tell ye, but all his kinsmen deem he is not in this realm," she said.

"These be sad tidings," said the king, "but I counsel ye to find Sir Bors, and pray him for Sir Launcelot's sake to do this battle for ye." So the queen sent for Sir Bors, and besought his help.

"Madam, it may not be," said Sir Bors, "for I was at that same dinner, and the other knights would have me in suspicion if I was to do so. Now do ye miss Sir Launcelot, for he would not have failed you in right or in wrong, as ye have often proved."

"Alas, Sir Bors," replied the queen, "I put me wholly at thy mercy; I will amend, as ye counsel me." And in came King Arthur and prayed him to help her for the love of Sir Launcelot.

"My lord," said he, "ye require of me the greatest thing that any man may grant. If I do battle for the queen I shall make many of my fellowship of the Round Table wroth against me; but for Sir Launcelot's sake, and for your sake, I will be the queen's champion, unless there should come a better knight than I am to do battle for her, and this I will promise you by my faith."

Then was the king and queen glad, and thanked him heartily. Sir Bors rode to the hermitage, and told Sir Launcelot of his adventure.

"Ah!" said Sir Launcelot, "this is come as I would have it, and I pray you make ready for the battle, but on that day tarry until I come, for Mador is a hot knight when he is chafed, and the more ye delay the hastier will he be to do battle."

"Leave me to deal with him," said Sir Bors.

Then was it noised abroad that Sir Bors should do battle for the queen, whereat many knights were displeased. Then Sir Bors answered them, "Wit ye well, lords, it were shamed to us all to see the queen of the world shamed openly, considering her lord and our lord is the man of most worship in the world."

"As for our noble Arthur we love and honour his name as ye do; but as for Queen Guinevere, we love her not, because she is a destroyer of good knights," said the knights.

"Fair lords," replied Sir Bors, "ye say not as ye should say, for never hath she been the destroyer of any good knight, but at all times has been a maintainer of good knights, and always hath she been the most bounteous lady of her gifts and good grace that ever I heard of, therefore it were shame to us all that we suffered her to be slain; and I will not suffer it, for I dare say so much that the queen is not guilty of Sir Patrice's death, for she owed him nor none of the twenty-four knights any ill will, but nevertheless there was treason among us."

Then some said, "Sir Bors, we may well believe your words." When the eve of the battle arrived, Sir Bors told the king he would make good his promise, and the king doubted him not, for he considered him one of his best knights. On the morn, the king and queen, and the knights drew to a meadow beside Westminster where the battle was to take place, and there the queen was put into the constable's ward, and a fire made about an iron stake.

Then came forth Sir Mador, and took his oath before the king that the queen did this treason unto his cousin, and he would prove it with his body. On which Sir Bors de Ganis said, "That as for Queen Guinevere, she is in the right, and that I will make good with my hands, and that she is not guilty of this treason, but this much I have promised my lord, King Arthur, and my lady, the queen, that I shall do battle for her in this case to the uttermost, unless there come a better knight than I, and discharge me of my promise."

Then Sir Bors took his horse and came to the end of the list, when a knight, well armed, bearing strange arms, came out of a wood, and rode up and begged him to withdraw, as the battle was his.

Then the king called to the strange knight, and asked him if he would fight for the queen; to which the knight replied, " Therefore came I hither, for it is dishonour, knights, to you all to see and know this noble queen thus to be rebuked and shamed."

Then said Sir Mador unto the king, " Let me know with whom I have to do," and rode to the lists end and couched his spear. Then they rushed together, and Sir Mador's spear brake all to pieces, but the strange knight's spear held, and bare Sir Mador's horse and all backwards to the earth. But suddenly Sir Mador drew his sword, and bade the other knight alight, and do battle with him on foot. The strange knight then drew his sword; and so they came to the battle, and gave each other many fierce strokes. Thus they fought, until the strange knight smote Sir Mador to the earth, and stepped forward to put off his helm, when Sir Mador smote the knight in the thigh. When the knight felt himself wounded, he let Sir Mador rise upon his feet, and then gave him such a buffet upon the helm that he fell to the earth. Then Sir Mador prayed the knight for his life.

"I will not grant thee thy life," said the knight, "unless thou release the queen for ever, and no mention be made on Sir Patrice's tomb that queen Guinevere was privy to the treason."

"All this shall be done," said Sir Mador.

Then the king and queen thanked the knight, and prayed him to take a cup of wine. When he put his helm off to drink, all saw that it was Sir Launcelot. But when the queen beheld him she was joyful that he had done her such great goodness. Then the knights of his blood gathered round him, and there was great joy.

Sir Mador and Sir Launcelot were soon healed of their wounds; and not long after Nimue, lady of the lake, came to the court, and told them all there by her enchantment how Sir Pinel and not the queen was guilty of Sir Patrice's death. Whereat the queen was held excused, and Sir Pinel fled to a far country.

CHAPTER LIII.

Sir Agravaine and Sir Mordred's hate towards Sir Laun-
celot—They spy him to the Queen's chamber—Sir
Launcelot attacks and slays Sir Agravaine and the
twelve knights who guard the door—Sir Gawain seeks
Sir Launcelot to avenge the death of his three brothers
—King Arthur and his knights besiege the castle of La
Joyous Grade.

AFTER a time there was jousting at the court,
whereat Sir Launcelot won the prize. And
two of the knights he overthrew were Sir Agravaine, and Sir Mordred. Becauseof this victory Sir Agravaine and Sir Mordred had hate
against Queen Guinevere and Sir Launcelot,
and constantly watched them. And Sir Agravaine spoke before many of the knights of Sir
Launcelot and the queen. Then spake Sir Gawain and said, "Brother, Sir Agravaine, I pray
you speak not so before me, for I will not be of
your counsel. And Sir Gaheris and Sir Gareth
said, " We will not be knowing of your deeds."
"Then will I," said Sir Mordred. "I well believe it," said Sir Gawain; "for I know what
will befall of it." "Whatever may befall of it
I will disclose it to the king," said Sir Mordred.

So on a certain night the queen sent for Sir
Launcelot, to her chamber, and Sir Agravaine
and Sir Mordred having espied him there, called
twelve other knights and told them how Sir
Launcelot was in the queen's chamber, and
that King Arthur was dishonoured.

Then they came to the queen's chamber, and
cried, "Traitor! now thou art taken."

"We are betrayed," said Sir Launcelot.

Then Sir Mordred called out, "Traitor, come
out of the queen's chamber, for thou shalt not
escape."

"This shameful noise I may not suffer; better were twenty deaths than this outcry," said Sir Launcelot. Then taking the queen in his arms, he kissed her and said, "Christian queen, I beseech you, as I never failed you in right or in wrong, that ye will pray for my soul if I be here slain, for well am I assured that Sir Bors, and all my kin, will not fail to rescue you from the fire ; therefore comfort yourself whatever may become of me."

Weeping, the queen said, "Would God that they should slay me, so that thou should escape."

"That will never be," said he, and he unbarred the door so that only one could enter at a time. Then first rushed in Sir Chalaunce, a strong knight, and lifted his sword to smite Sir Launcelot, who struck Sir Chalaunce and felled him dead. Then Sir Launcelot stripped off his his armour and put it upon himself:

"Ye will not take me," replied Sir Launcelot, "therefore depart, and to-morrow will I meet ye before the king."

"No such grace shall ye have, but we will slay thee or take thee as we list," they answered.

"Then save yourselves," he thundered, and unbarring the door, he leaped at them. At the first blow he slew Sir Agravaine, and with twelve buffets he slew the twelve knights, and none escaped excepting the wily Sir Mordred, and he, sore wounded, fled for his life.

Then returned Sir Launcelot to the queen, and said, "Now, will I depart, and if ye be in any danger I pray you come to me."

"Here will I stay, for I am queen," she answered. "Yet I trust to thee for rescue."

"I will well," said Sir Launcelot; "for have ye no doubt while I am living I shall rescue you." Then he kissed her, and each gave the other a ring, and so he departed, and told Sir Bors and all his kindred what had happened.

"We will be with thee in this quarrel," replied they all.

And in a short space of time it was ordained that the queen had caused the death of the thirteen knights, and she was condemned to be burnt.

But when Sir Gawain heard thereof, he said, "My lord, I counsel thee stay the judgment of the queen a season, for it may be that Sir Launcelot was in her chamber for no evil, peradventure she had sent to thank him, and did it secretly that she might avoid slander."

But King Arthur, answered him, "Alas! what can I do. I may not help her, for they have judged her by the laws as any other woman. I pray you make you ready in your best armour, with your brethren, Sir Gaheris and Sir Gareth, to bring my queen to the fire, there to receive her death."

"Nay," replied Sir Gawain, "that will I never do. For, wit ye well, I will never be in that place where so noble a queen as is my dame Guinevere shall take a shameful end, for my heart will never suffer me to see her die, and it shall never be said that I was, of your counsel, the cause of her death."

Then said his brother to the king, "Ye may command us to be there, but since it is against our will, we will do no battle against her."

The morrow Queen Guinevere was led forth

to die by fire; a mighty crowd was there of knights and nobles. She was shriven by a priest, and the men came to bind her to the stake, and light the fire, when Sir Launcelot and twenty knights, who had concealed themselves in a wood, rushed into the midst of the throng to her rescue. And certain of King Arthur's knights sallied forth to meet them, and there was great fighting. Sir Launcelot struck fiercely among the press, and smote down knights on every side, so that the queen was set free. Then Sir Launcelot caused the queen to be placed behind him on the horse, and Sir Launcelot rode off to the castle of La Joyous Garde. Now it happened that in the fighting, Sir Launcelot had slain Sir Gaheris and Sir Gareth, for he saw not that they were unarmed. When King Arthur heard of the battle, he sorrowed for the knights, and was wroth with Sir Launcelot and the queen.

But when Sir Gawain heard of his brothers' death, he was very sorrowful, for he thought Sir Launcelot had killed them for malice, and he went to the king, and said, "O, King Arthur, my brothers, Sir Gaheris and Sir Gareth are slain by Sir Launcelot, and I swear that I will not fail until one of us hath slain the other; and now, unless ye make haste to war with him that we may be avenged, I will go after him."

Then the king sent to call his knights together, and went to besiege the castle of La Joyous Garde, which Sir Launcelot and his knights defended; but he would not suffer any to attack the king's army, for he was loath to fight against the king. After fifteen weeks had passed, and

King Arthur's army toiled in vain against the castle, it chanced Sir Launcelot espied King Arthur and Sir Gawain beside the walls.

"Come forth, Sir Launcelot," cried the king, "and let us two meet in the midst of the field."

"God forbid that I should encounter with thee my lord," said Sir Launcelot.

Then cried Sir Gawain, "Shame on thee, false knight, to slay my brothers, Sir Gaheris and Sir Gareth, who loved thee so well; for that treachery be sure I am thine enemy for life."

Then exclaimed Sir Launcelot with wroth, "I see that there can now be no more peace between us, or I would fain give back the queen."

Then the king would have listened to Sir Launcelot, for he grieved more for the damage to the realm, than for his own wrong, but Sir Gawain persuaded him against it, and cried out against Sir Launcelot. When Sir Bors and some other knights heard Sir Gawain's fierce words they prayed Sir Launcelot to allow them to be avenged upon him, for they were weary of waiting so long to no end ; to which at last Sir Launcelot consented, and on the morrow the two armies met, and there was a great battle. And Sir Gawain besought his knights to set chiefly upon Sir Launcelot, but Sir Launcelot commanded his knights to deal lightly with King Arthur and Sir Gawain. After the two armies had jousted fiercely, King Arthur came against Launcelot, but Launcelot would not strike him. At which Sir Bors rode up against the king and struck him down, but Sir Launcelot cried, "Touch him not on pain of thy head :" and going to King Arthur he said, "My lord, I pray thee forbear this strife, for it can bring to neither of us any honour." And when King Arthur looked on him, tears came into his eyes, and he said within himself, "Alas! that ever this war begun."

But on the following day Sir Gawain again led forth his army, and Sir Bors commanded on Sir Launcelot's side. And these two commanders together struck so that both fell to the ground wounded. At length the fame of this war was noised through all Christendom. And Sir Launcelot sent a message to the king, that it was never in his thoughts to withhold the queen from him, but since she was condemned to death, he deemed it but just to rescue her, and that in nine days he would bring the queen and deliver her into King Arthur's keeping.

CHAPTER LIV.

Sir Launcelot delivers Queen Guinevere to King Arthur— The hatred of Sir Gawain towards Sir Launcelot—Sir Launcelot leaves the court for his own land, and divides his lands between his knights—The war between Sir Launcelot and King Arthur—The jousting of Sir Gawain and Sir Launcelot—Sir Mordred left regent of the realm of Britain—His usurpation—Queen Guinevere seeks an asylum in a nunnery—Sir Gawain's death—The wars between King Arthur and Mordred—King Arthur's vision.

WITHIN the appointed time, Sir Launcelot rode from the castle with Queen Guinevere, and a hundred knights for company, each carrying an olive branch in sign of peace. Sir Launcelot approached the king and said, "My lord, I have brought hither the queen, as right requireth. I pray you take her to your heart, and forget the past. For myself, I ask nothing, and for my sins I shall have sore punishment, yet I would to heaven I might have thy grace."

But ere the king could reply, Sir Gawain cried aloud, " Let the king do as it pleaseth him, but Sir Launcelot, thou and I shall never be accorded while we live, for thou slewest my brethren traitorously and unarmed."

" I did it in ignorance, for I loved them well," said Sir Launcelot," but to make war with me, were of no avail, for I must needs fight with thee if thou assailest, and I may slay thee also, which I were loath to do."

" Forgive thee will I never," said Sir Gawaine. " And if the king accord with thee, he shall lose my service ; for thou art false to the king and to me."

Then the knights who stood round tried to reconcile Sir Gawain and Sir Launcelot, but Sir Gawain would not hear them.

Then said Sir Launcelot to the queen, " Madam, now must I depart from you for ever, and since it is so, I beseech you to pray for me and say me well ; and if ye ever be defamed by any false tongues, send me word, and as I have been ever thy true knight so will I be again, and if any knight's hands may deliver you by battle I shall deliver you." He stood up, and openly spake thus, " Now, let us see who dare say the queen is not true unto my lord King Arthur ;" and straightway he brought the queen to the king, kissed King Arthur's hand and departed on his way. And there was none in the court, save Sir Gawain, but wept to see him go. And Sir Launcelot journeyed with all his knights to the castle of La Joyous Garde which for his sorrow's sake he named Dolorous Garde.

When they arrived in France, he there divided all his lands among them equally, he sharing but as the rest.

From that time forth peace would have been between King Arthur and Sir Launcelot but for Sir Gawain, who persuaded him that Sir Launcelot was raising armies against him, which in time caused him to make ready a great host, to the number of threescore thousand, and all things were made ready for the ships to pass over the sea, and so they shipped at Cardiff.

On his departure, the king made his son, Mordred, chief ruler of all England, and placed Queen Guinevere under his charge, and then sailed to invade Sir Launcelot's lands, and there he wasted through the vengeance of Sir Gawain all that they passed.

Sir Launcelot would make no war upon the king, but sent a message to gain peace on any terms King Arthur may choose ; but the herald from Sir Launcelot was met by Sir Gawain ere he reached the king, and sent back with a taunting reply ; on receiving which, Sir Launcelot called his knights together, and fortified the castle of Benwicke, which was besieged by the army of great King Arthur.

Every day Sir Gawain rode up to the walls, and cried out foully to Sir Launcelot, till at last Launcelot answered him that he would meet him and put his boasting to the proof.

Then Sir Launcelot bade his horse to be sadled and his arms brought to the gate of the tower. Then Sir Launcelot said to King Arthur, " My lord Arthur, wit ye well I am heavy for your sake, I have for half a year, suffered you and Sir Gawain to do what ye would do, and now I may defend myself, insomuch as Sir Gawain hath appealed me of treason."

Then said Sir Gawain, "Sir Launcelot, if thou darest do battle, leave thy babbling, and come off and ease our hearts."

Then they came together as it had been thunder, and their horses fell, and both their lances broke. Then drew they their swords, and set upon each other fiercely. At length Sir Launcelot gave Sir Gawain such a buffet on the helmet that he fell down on his side, and Sir Launcelot withdrew from him.

"Why dost thou withdraw?" said Sir Gawain. "Now turn again, and slay me, for if thou leave me thus I shall do battle with thee some other day."

"I shall endure you, by God's grace; but wit thou well, I will never smite a fallen knight."

At that they bore Sir Gawain, wounded, to his tent, and King Arthur withdrew his men.

After a time Sir Gawain was healed of his wound, and he again taunted Sir Launcelot before the walls, until Sir Launcelot met him, and defeated him again but spared his life.

Now came there tidings to King Arthur which caused him to return. No sooner was Sir Mordred set up in his regency, than he forged letters, as though they came from beyond the sea, that the king had fallen in battle with Sir Launcelot.

Whereupon he proclaimed himself king, and had been crowned at Canterbury, where he held a coronation feast for fifteen days. Then

he had gone to Winchester, where Queen Guinevere abode, and had commanded her to be
his wife ; whereto, for fear, she feigned to give
consent, but the next day she fled in haste to
London, and took shelter in the tower, which
she fortified and provided with victuals, and
defended herself against Sir Mordred, and in
answer to his threats said that she would rather
slay herself than be his queen.

When King Arthur heard all this, he was
passing wroth, and sailed with all speed to
England. And when Mordred heard thereof,
he marched with all his host to meet the king at
Dover.

Then fled Queen Guinevere to the nunnery of
Almesbury, where she clothed herself in sackcloth, and spent her time in praying for the
king, and in good deeds, and fasting ; and in
that nunnery she evermore lived, sorely re-
penting of her sins, and the ruin she had
brought upon the realm.

And when Sir Launcelot heard thereof, he
put his knightly armour off, and went a pil-
grimage for many years, and then he afterwards
led a hermit's life until his death.

And so as Sir Mordred was at Dover with
his host, there came King Arthur with a great
navy of ships, galleys, and carracks : and there
they fought a fierce and bloody battle, and
many noble knights fell on both sides. But the
king's side had the victory, and Sir Mordred's
knights were driven back with fearful wounds.
But Sir Gawain was smitten in the wound Sir
Launcelot had given him, and wounded unto
death.

And when the battle was done, King Arthur began to bury his people who were slain, and then was Sir Gawain borne to the king's tent, and King Arthur sorrowed over him as he had been his own son, and took him in his arms, and said, " Alas, Sir Gawain, my sister's son, in you and Sir Launcelot I had my greatest earthly joy, and now is all gone from me !"

Then Sir Gawain made answer with a feeble voice, " Mine uncle, King Arthur, wit you well my death is come, and all through mine own hastiness and wilfulness, for I am smitten in the wound Sir Launcelot gave me. Alas ! that I should have been the cause of all this war ; for but for me, thou hadst now been at peace with Launcelot, and then had Mordred never done this treason. I pray you, therefore, my dear lord, be now agreed with Launcelot, and tell him, that although he gave me my death wound, it was through mine own seeking, wherefore I beseech him to come back to England, and here to visit my tomb and to pray for my soul."

And then Sir Gawain prayed the king to cherish Sir Launcelot above all other knights ; and when he thus had spoken Sir Gawain yielded up the ghost, and King Arthur grievously mourned for him.

Then was it told the king that Sir Mordred had pitched his camps upon Barham Downs. And upon the morn the king rode hither, and fought again a bloody battle, and overthrew Sir Mordred utterly, who fled with his party to Canterbury. Howbeit, he yet raised another army, and retreated ever before the king, adding to his numbers hordes of Saxons as he went, till at the farthest west in Lyonesse, he once more made a stand.

Then much people drew near unto King Arthur, and Sir Mordred was driven westward towards Salisbury, and there was it fixed that King Arthur and Sir Mordred should meet on the Monday after Trinity, upon a plain beside Salisbury. Then Sir Mordred raised much people about London—for they of Kent, Sussex, Essex, and Southfolk, and of Northfolk held with Sir Mordred.

Now it came to pass that upon Trinity Sunday night, King Arthur dreamed a wonderful dream, and saw Sir Gawain in his dream, who warned him not to fight with Sir Mordred on the morrow, or he would be surely slain, and prayed him to delay until Sir Launcelot and his father's knights should come to aid him.

So when King Arthur awoke, he told his lords and knights of his vision, and all agreed to wait the coming of Sir Launcelot.

Then a herald was sent with a message of truce to Sir Mordred.

Then the king commanded Sir Lucan and Sir Bedivere to take two bishops with them, and make a treaty with Sir Mordred for one month, and told them to spare not, but proffer him lands and goods as much as he should require. So they departed, and came to Sir Mordred, and at last he consented, on condition that he was to have Cornwall and Kent for King Arthur's days, and afterwards, at his death, to have all England.

It was then arranged that King Arthur with fourteen men, and Sir Mordred with fourteen men, should meet each other between their hosts.

Then King Arthur said to his knights, "Beware, lest Sir Mordred deceive us, for I in nowise trust him, and if a sword be drawn, be ready to encounter." In likewise Sir Mordred warned his host that, "If ye see any sword drawn, look that ye come on fiercely, and slay all that ever before you standeth, for in no wise will I trust to this treaty, for I know well my father will be avenged upon me."

And so they met, and were accorded together, and wine was fetched, and they drank. And as they were thus assembled, an adder crept from beneath an heath bush, and stung one of the king's knights on the leg. And when he felt the pain, he looked down and saw the adder, and forthwith, without thought of evil, he drew his sword to slay the reptile.

As soon as Sir Mordred saw the sword drawn, he forth with commanded all his army to assail the king's.

CHAPTER LV.

The war between King Arthur and Sir Mordred—Sir Mordred is slain and King Arthur wounded—King Arthur's charge to Sir Bédivere to throw Excalibur into the lake —Sir Bedivere twice conceals the sword—The sword is thrown into the lake and is caught by an arm from the water—The passing of Arthur.

Now as soon as the orders were given by Sir Mordred for the assault, both armies rushed to battle, and fought passing fiercely. And when the king saw all hopes past of staying the fight, he raged like a lion into the thickest of the press, and slew on the right and on the left till his horse went fetlock deep in blood, and many a noble knight was slain. And when the king saw his renowned knights lie dead on every side, so that there remained but two besides him, Sir Lucan and Sir Bedivere, and they, sorely wounded, he was passing sorrowful, and exclaimed "Now am I come to mine end; but, lo! that traitor, Mordred, liveth yet, and I may not die till I have slain him. Now give me my spear, Sir Lucan."

"Lord, let him be," replied Sir Lucan; "for if ye pass through this unhappy day, ye shall be right well avenged of him; remember well your dream, my lord, and what the spirit of Sir Gawain did forewarn ye. For blessed be God ye have won on the field, for here we be three alive, but with Sir Mordred there is not one left alive; and if we leave off now, the day of destiny is passed."

"Betide me life, betide me death," said the king, "for I see him yonder alone; he shall never escape my hands, for I shall never see him at better vantage."

"God speed you well," said Sir Bedivere.

Then the king got his spear in both his hands, and ran towards Sir Mordred, crying, "Traitor, now is thy death-day come."

And when Sir Mordred heard him thus speak, he drew his sword, and prepared to meet him. Then King Arthur smote Sir Mordred through the body. And when Sir Mordred felt he had his death-wound, he thrust himself with all his might up to the end of King Arthur's spear, and smote his father Arthur, on the head, so that it cut through the helm and brain-pan; and therewith Sir Mordred fell dead to the earth, and King Arthur sank down in a swoon.

Then Sir Lucan and Sir Bedivere bore him away to a little chapel upon the sea shore, and then Sir Lucan sank down with the bleeding of his wounds, and fell dead.

There lay King Arthur long in a swoon, and when he came to himself, he found Sir Lucan lying dead beside him, and Sir Bedivere over the body of his brother.

Then spake Arthur to Sir Bedivere, " Weeping will not avail, else would I grieve for evermore. Alas, this day the goodliest fellowship of the Round Table, and of famous knights whereof the world holds record, is dissolved, and all my realm I have so loved is wasted for ever, and I perish with my people. Yet Merlin swore that I should rule again, but be it as it may, I am so deeply smitten that I feel my last breath departing from my body! therefore, take thou my sword, Excalibur—which I have prized so dearly, and which rose from out of the lake to meet my hand—and fling it far into the middle mere; watch what befalls it, and bring me word."

To which Sir Bedivere replied, " It is not well to leave thee here alone, sore wounded as thou art; yet thy behest I will perform, watch what I see, and shortly bring thee word." But as he went he looked upon the sword, the hilt whereof was inlaid with precious stones, exceeding rich; and stepping down by zig-zag paths came to the shining level of the lake. Then taking in his hand the brand, he gazed so long that his eyes were dazzled with the brightness of the gems, and he said within himself, " If I throw this sword into the lake what good should come of it?" So he hid Excalibur among the water-flags, and strode back to the wounded king.

At his approach King Arthur, rising slowly, said to Sir Bedivere, "Hast thou performed my mission, and what didst thou see and hear?"

"I heard," replied Sir Bedivere, "the waters ripple among reeds, and dash among the crags"

"Thou hast untruly spoken," said the king, "and betrayed thy nature and thy name in not rendering a true account. It is a shameful thing for men to lie, therefore now I charge thee go again, and do the thing I bade thee."

Then went Sir Bedivere the second time, and paced beside the mere fixed in deep thought. And when he looked again upon the beautiful wrought hilt of the noble sword, he cried aloud, "If I cast this precious brand away it will be lost for ever from the earth; were it well then to obey, if the king demand an act unprofitable. The king is sick, and knoweth not what he desires. What record of his noble deeds but empty breath will be left to future ages if this sword be lost? But were it kept, it may be shown at some joust of arms, as "King Arthur's sword, Excalibur, wrought by nine years' toil within the bosom of the deep, by the lonely maiden of the Lake." And as he thought it sin and shame to throw away a thing so noble, he hid it yet again, and went back to the king.

Then spoke King Arthur, breathing heavily, "What didst thou see and hear?"

To which Sir Bedivere replied, "Lord, I saw nothing but the ebbing and flowing of the water."

Then King Arthur with much wrath, exclaimed, "Oh, thou traitor and untrue, twice hast thou deceived me, for sure sign had followed; either hand, or voice, or motion of the mere. Woe is me, I see thee what thou art, and thou the latest left of all my knights, would betray me for the precious hilt. Yet, as a man may fail in duty twice, and yet the third time prosper, I will trust thee once again, and if ye spare to fling Excalibur, I will arise and slay thee; for thy tarrying hath put me in sore peril of my life, and I fear my wound hath taken cold."

Then Sir Bedivere with all speed ran to the margin of the lake, and picking up the sword, threw it far into the water; and as the great brand whirled in an arch, and ere it dipped the surface, an arm arose, "clothed in white samite, mystic, wonderful," and caught it by the hilt, and brandishing it three times, descended beneath the water.

So Sir Bedivere came again unto the king, and told him what he had seen.

Then answered King Arthur, with gasping breath, "My end draws near, it's time that I were gone; help me from hence, for I dread me I have tarried over long. Make broad thy shoulders to receive my weight, and bare me to the margin of the lake, ere I shall die."

Then Sir Bedivere took the king upon his back, and bare him to the water's edge. And by the shore they saw a dusky barge. "Dark as a funeral scarf from stem to stern," and on the deck was the stately forms of three fair queens, dressed in black, with crowns of gold upon their heads, who wept and wailed at the sight of King Arthur.

"Place me in the barge," murmured the king; and as he was placed there, the three queens put forth their arms to receive him, with weeping. And the tallest and fairest of the three laid his head upon her lap, and unlaced the shattered casque, and chafing his hands, called him by his name.

"So like a shatter'd column lay the king;
Not like the noble Arthur who, with spear in rest,
From spur to plume a star of tournament,
Shot through the lists at Camelot, and charged
Before the eyes of ladies and of kings."

Then the barge put from the land. And when Sir Bedivere saw it departing, he cried out, "Alas, my lord, King Arthur, what shall become of me now ye have gone from me?"

"Comfort yourself, and be strong," said the king, "for I may no more help you. I go to the Vale of Avilion to heal me of my grievous wounds, and if thou hear never more of me, pray for my soul, for "More things are wrought by prayer than this world dreams of."

Then the three queens knelt down around the king, and wept and wailed, and the barge sailed on. And as soon as Sir Bedivere lost sight of it, he went forth into a forest, and dwelt in an hermitage.

Some men yet, in many parts of England, say that King Arthur is not dead, and that he shall come again and win the Holy Cross; and it is averred that it is written on his tomb—

> "Hic jacet Arthurus,
> Rex quondam, rex futurus."

THE END.

MILNER & COMPANY, PUBLISHERS, HALIFAX.

A CATALOGUE OF CHEAP BOOKS,

PUBLISHED BY

MILNER & CO.,

16, *PATERNOSTER ROW, LONDON,*

AND HALIFAX, YORKSHIRE.

THE NEW, NOVELIST'S LIBRARY,
FOOLSCAP 8vo. CLOTH.
ILLUMINATED SIDE LETTERINGS,
☞ PRICE 1s. 6d. EACH.

All for Love. By Miss Eliza A. Dupuy
Anna Lee, The Maiden, Wife, and Mother
Bridal Eve. (The).   By Mrs. Southworth
Bride's Fate. A Sequel to the ' Changed Brides'
Cancelled Will. By Miss Eliza A. Dupuy
Cast Adrift. By T. S. Arthur
Changed Brides. By Mrs. Southworth
Curse of Clifton, (The). By Mrs. Southworth
Deserted Wife, (The).   By Mrs. Southworth
Destiny ; or, The Chieftain's Daughter
Edwin and Lucy. Translated from the French
Exploits of King Arthur. Edited by J. H. Clark
Fair Play ; or the Test of the Lone Island. By Mrs
        Southworth
Farmer of Inglewood Forest, (The). By E. Helm
Fatal Marriage, (The). By Mrs. Southworth
Fatherless Fanny, or ; the Memoirs of a Little Men-
        dicant
Five Nights of St. Albans. By Wm. Mudford
Fortune Seeker. By Mrs. Southworth

1

Heiress of Bruges, (The). A Tale of the Year Sixteen Hundred

How He Won Her. A Sequel to 'Fair Play'

Inheritance, (The). By the Author of 'Marriage' and 'Destiny'

Jacob Faithful. By Captain Marryat

Justin Harley. A Romance of Old Virginia. By John Esten Cooke

Lamplighter, (The). By Miss Cummins

'Lena Rivers. By Mary J. Holmes

Lost Heiress, (The). By Mrs. Southworth

Mabel Lee. By Christian Reid

Mabel Vaughan. By Miss Cummins

Manfrone; or, The One-handed Monk. By Mrs. Radcliffe

Marian Grey. By Mary J. Holmes

Marriage; or, She Might have been a Duchess

Maxwell: or the Unwelcome Guest. By Theodore Hook

Missing Bride, (The). By Mrs. Southworth

Old Helmet, (The). By Elizabeth Wetherel

Old Manor House, (The). By Mrs. Charlotte Smith

Pamela; or, Virtue Rewarded. By S. Richardson

Peter Simple. By Captain Marryat

Queechy. By the Author of 'Wide, Wide World'

Queen's Badge, The. A Tale of the Sixteenth Century

Ruby Gray's Strategy. By Mrs. Ann S. Stephens

Righted at Last. A Story of New England Life

Striking the Flag. By Christian Reid

Tylney Hall; or, the Squire's Revenge. By Thomas Hood

Uncle Tom's Cabin. By Mrs. H. B. Stowe

West Lawn. By the Author of 'Lena Rivers

Who Shall be Victor. A Sequel to 'Cancelled Will'

Why Did He Marry Her. By Eliza A. Dupuy

Wide, Wide World. By Elizabeth Wetherell

* *Many of the above Books are done up in Illuminated Paper Covers, ONE SHILLING EACH.*

NOTE THE PRICE

OF THE

NEW EDITIONS

OF

HOULDSWORTH'S
CHEETHAM'S
PSALMODY,

WITH AN APPENDIX.

BY

J. V. ROBERTS, Mus. Bac., Ch. Ch., Oxon.

Organist at Halifax Parish Church.

	s.	d.
Quarto Edition, Paper Covers	6	9
Best Cloth, Red Edges	9	0
Half Morocco, Full Gilt Back, Gilt Edges	13	0
Royal 8vo., Best Cloth, Red Edges......	5	0
Royal 8vo., Paper Covers	4	6
Crown 8vo. Best Cloth, Red Edges	3	6

3

POETICAL SERIES.

Foolscap 8vo. In Coloured Cloth.

Burn' Complete Works. 8 Steel Plates. Full Gilt Back & Edges 3s. 6d. Plain Edges 2s. 9d.

Byron's Poetical Works. 8 Steel Plates. Full Gilt Back & Edges 3s. 6d. Plain Edges 2s. 9d.

Byron's Don Juan. Front. and Vignette. Royal 32mo. 1s.

Cowper's Poetical Works. 8 Steel Plates. Gilt Edges 3s. 6d. Plain Edges 2s. 9d.

Dryden's Poetical Works. 8 Steel Plates. Gilt Edges 3s. 6d. Plain Edges 2s. 9d.

Gems of Poetry for those we Love. 9 Plates. Gilt Back & Edges 3s. 6d. Plain Edges 2s. 9d.

Longfellow's Poetical Works. Full Gilt Back, Side, & Edges. 9 Steel Plates. Gilt Edges 3s. 6d. Plain Edges 2s. 9d.

Milton's Poetical Works. Full Gilt Back, Side, & Edges. 8 Steel Plates 3s. 6d. Plain Edges 2s. 9d.

Moore's Poetical Works. 8 Steel Plates. Gilt Edges 3s. 6d. Plain Edges 2s. 9d.

Poetical Keepsake, (The). 8 Steel Plates. Gilt Edges 3s. 6d. Plain Edges 2s. 9d.

Scott's (Sir Walter) Poetical Works. 9 Illustrations. Gilt Edges 3s. 6d. Plain Edges 2s. 9d.

Shelley's Poetical Works. 8 Steel Plates. Gilt Edges 3s. 6d. Plain Edges 2s. 9d.

Wordsworth's Poetical Works. 8 Steel Plates. Gilt Edges 3s. 6d. Plain Edges 2s. 9d.

MISCELLANEOUS.

ALL IN COLOURED CLOTH, UNLESS OTHERWISE DESCRIBED.

Anna Lee ; or, The Maiden, The Wife, and The Mother. By T. S. Arthur. With Nine Full Page Engravings. Fcp. 8vo. Gilt Edges—3s. 6d. Plain Edges—2s. 0d.

Arabian Nights' Entertainments. Crown 8vo. 8 Steel Plates—2s. 6d. Gilt Edges—3s. 6d.

Arabian Nights' Entertainments. Fr. and Vig. Royal 32mo.—1s. 6d. Gilt Edges—1s. 9d.

Artemus Ward—His Book. Paper Covers—4d.

Ball Room Manual. Paper Covers—2d. and 4d. Cloth. Gilt Edges—6d.

Basket of Flowers, and other Tales. By Christopher Von Schmidt. Eight Steel Plates. Gilt Back and Edges. Fcp. 8vo. Gilt Edges—3s. 6d. Plain Edges—2s. 9d. Limp Cloth 1s.

Beaumont's Cow Doctor. Fr. 18mo.—6d.

Beautiful Thoughts—1000 choice Extracts. Demy 18mo. Gilt Edges—2s. Plain Edges—1s. 6d.

Bibles Echoes. A Daily Text Book. Frontispiece. Demy 48mo. Red Edges—6d. Leather, Gilt Edges—9d.

Bogatzky's Golden Treasury. Fcp. 8vo. New Edition. Frontispiece. Full Gilt Back, and Edges—3s. 6d. Plain Edges—2s.

Boy's Own Conjuring Book. Front. and nearly 200 other Engravings. Fcp. 8vo. Gilt Back and Edges—3s. 6d. Plain Edges—2s.

Brewer's Guide, (The). Containing the whole art of Brewing, with Numerous Recipes for Preparing Liquors for Sale, &c. Royal 32mo. —6d.

Buchan's Domestic Medicine. Fcp. 8vo. Coloured Plate. Roxburgh Binding—2s. 9d. Plain Edges—2s. 6d.

Buchan's Domestic Medicine. Imp. 32mo.—2s.

Buffon's Natural History. 323 Engravings. Fcp. 8vo. Gilt Edges—3s. 6d. Plain Edges—2s.

Buffon's Natural History. 200 Engravings. Royal 32mo.—1s. 6d. Gilt Edges—1s. 9d.

Bunyan's Pilgrim's Progress. Three Parts, complete. Mason's Notes. Eight Steel Plates and 100 small Woodcuts. Fcp. 8vo. Gilt Back, Sides, and Edges—3s. 6d. Plain Edges—2s.

Bunyan's Pilgrim's Progress, complete. Three Parts. Mason's Notes. One Hundred Cuts. Royal 32mo. Gilt Edges—1s. 9d. Plain Edges—1s. 6d.

Bunyan's Pilgrim's Progress. Two Parts. Fcp. 8vo.—1s. 6d.

Cennick's Village Discourses. Fcp. 8vo. Cloth —2s.

Children of the Abbey. Front. & Vig. Crown 8vo. Plain 2s. 9d. Gilt Edges—3s. 6d.

Christian Preacher's Pocket Companion. Demy 18mo. 1s. 6d.

Christian's Morning Treasury, (The). A Daily Text Book. Front. Demy 48mo. Red Edges 6d. Leather, Gilt Edges 9d.

Christian's Evening Treasury, (The). A Daily Text Book. Front. Demy 48mo. Red Edges 6d. Leather, Gilt Edges 9d.

Clater's Every Man his Own Farrier. Fcp. 8vo. —1s. 9d.

Clater's Every Man his Own Cattle Doctor. Fcp. 8vo.—1s. 6d.

Clater's Farrier and Cattle Doctor, Combined. Fcp. 8vo.—2s. 6d.

Cobbett's English Grammar. Royal 32mo.—6d.

Cooke's Universal Letter Writer. Front. & Vig. Royal 32mo.—9d. Gilt Edges—1s.

Cope's Natural History. 425 Engravings. Medium 8vo.—5s.

Cope's (Dr.) Outlines of Sermons. Fcp. 8vo. Front.—3s.

Crumbs of Comfort. A Daily Text Book. Front. Demy 48mo. Red Edges—9d. Leather, Gilt Edges—9d.

Culpeper's complete Herbal. Numerous Coloured Plates. Fcp. 8vo.—4s. Plain—3s.

Culpeper's complete Herbal. Royal 32mo. Numerous Cuts—1s. 6d.

Culpeper's complete Herbal. Coloured Plates. Royal 32mo.—3s. 6d.

Cyclopædia of Songs and Recitations. Royal 32mo.—1s. 6d

Cyclopædia of Wit and Wisdom. Royal 32mo. —1s. 3d.

Daily Bread. A Daily Text Book. Front. Demy 48mo. Red Edges—6d. Leather, Gilt Edges —9d.

Daily Food. A Daily Text Book. Front. Demy 48mo. Red Edges—6d. Leather, Gilt Edges —9d.

Daily Manna. A Daily Text Book. Front. Demy 48mo. Red Edges—6d. Leather, Gilt Edges 9d.

Domestic Cookery. By Mrs. Rundell. Plates. Fcp. 8vo. Coloured Cloth—2s. 6d. Plain Cloth—1s. 6d.

Dr. King's Domestic Medicines. Fcp. 8vo—1s.

Edgeworth's (Miss) Stories for Children. Fcp. 8vo. Nine Engravings. Gilt Back and Edges 3s. 6d. Plain Edges 2s. 9d.

Edgeworth's (Miss) Popular Tales. Fcp. 8vo.

Nine Engravings. Gilt Edges—3s. 6d. Plain Edges—2s. 9d.

English Domestic Cookery. Fcp. 8vo. Limp Cloth—1s.

Finney's Lectures on Revivals. Royal 32mo.—1s. 6d.

Finney"s Lectures on Revivals. Fcp. 8vo. Portrait—1s. 9d.

Finney's Skeletons of Sermons. Fcp. 8vo. Front.—1s. 9d.

Finney's Lectures to Professing Christians. Portrait. Fcp. 8vo.—1s. 9d.

Fleetwood's Life of Our Lord and Saviour Jesus Christ. Imp. 32mo. Gilt Edges—2s. 3d.

Foxe's Book of Martyrs. 18 Engravings. Gilt Edges—3s. 6d. Plain Edges—2s.

Ferguson's History of the Roman Republic. Front. & Vig. Imp. 32mo. Gilt Edges—2s. 6d. Plain Edges—2s.

Goldsmith's History of England. Crown 8vo. Red Edges—2s. 6d.

Grapes of Eschol. A Daily Text Book. Front. Demy 48mo. Red Edges—6d. Leather, Gilt Edges—9d.

Hieroglyphical Bible. Nearly 200 cuts. Gilt Edges—1s. Paper Covers 6d.

History of England (The) from the Roman Period to the Present Time. By T. S. Birkby. Ninety Engravings. Fcp. 8vo—1s.

Hoppus's Practical Wood, Iron, &c., Measurer. Leather—1s. 6d. Cloth—1s. 3d.

Imperial-Royal Dream Book, Fortune-Teller, and Book of Fate Combined. Fcp. 8vo. Plain. Cloth—1s. 6d.

Imperial-Royal Dream Book. Fcp. 8vo. Limp Cloth—1s.

Imperial-Royal Fortune Teller and Book of Fate. Fcp. 8vo. Limp Cloth—1s.

Information for Everybody. By Dr. Chase. Fcp. 8vo. Limp Cloth—1s.

Joyce's Scientific Dialogues. Fcp. 8vo.—1s. 6d.

Joyce's Scientific Dialogues. Front. & Vig. 200 cuts. Royal 32mo.—1s. 6d.

Johnson's Dictionary. 18mo. Red Edges—1s.

Johnson's Dictionary. Royal 32mo. Red Edges 6d.

Josephus, (The Works of Flavius.) Front. Medium 8vo.—5s.

Lamplighter (The). By Miss Cummins. Full Gilt Back, Side, & Edges. 9 Engravings. Fcp. 8vo. —3s. 6d. Plain Edges, Lettered—2s. 9d.

Lempriere's Classical Dictionary. A new and complete edition, with the accents placed. Demy 8vo.—5s.

'Lena Rivers. A tale of American Life. By Mrs. M. J. Holmes. Full Gilt Back, Sides, & Edges. Nine Engravings. Fcp. 8vo.—3s. 6d. Plain Edges, Lettered—2s. 9d.

Mangnall's Historical & Miscellaneous Questions. Revised and corrected by E. H. Riches, L.L.D., F.R.A.S. Crown 8vo. Red Edges— 2s. 9d.

Manual of Croquet. Front. Royal 32mo. Paper Covers—3d. Limp Cloth, Gilt Edges—6d.

Markham's (Mrs.) History of England. With continuation to the present time, by E. H. Riches, L.L.D., F.R.A.S. Upwards of 100 Engravings. Crown 8vo.—2s. 9d.

Mr. Merryman's Broad Grins. Fcp. 8vo. Limp Cloth—1s.

Murray's English Grammar. Royal 32mo.—6d.

Mysteries of a Convent, Maria Monk, and Six Months in a Convent. Fcp. 8vo. Cloth, Boards—1s. 6d.

Mysteries of a Convent and Maria Monk. Fcp. 8vo. Limp Cloth—1s.

Pearls of Great Price. Crown 8vo. Beautiful new Edition. Handsome Steel Frontispiece and Vignette. Full Gilt Back and Edges—4s.

Pearls of Sacred Poetry. Demy 18mo.—1s.

Penny Table Book

Penny Books (Mrs. Sherwood's) 10d. per Packet of 12.

Penny Books (Mrs. Mitford's) 10d. per Packet of 12.

Precious Promises. A Daily Text Book. Front. Demy 48mo. Red Edges—6d. Leather, Gilt Edges—9d.

Precepts and Examples. A Daily Text Book. Front. Demy 48mo. Red Edges—6d. Leather, Gilt Edges—9d.

Queechy. By the Author of 'Wide, Wide World.' Full Gilt Back, Sides, and Edges. 9 Engravings. Fcp. 8vo.—3s. 6d. Plain Edges—2s. 9d.

Ready Reckoner. Royal 32mo. Red Edges—1s.

Ready Reckoner. Red Edges. Demy 32mo.—6d.

Reciter (The General). With Engravings. Fcp. 8vo. Limp Cloth. Part I—1s. Part II.—1s.

Reciter (The General). Numerous Engravings. Fcp. 8vo.—2s.

Robertson's History of the Reign of Charles V. Front. and Vig. Imperial 32mo.—2s.

Robinson Crusoe. 12 Illustrations. Fcp. 8vo. Gilt Back & Edges. Centre Block, &c.—3s. 6d.

Robinson Crusoe. Fcp. 8vo. 12 Illustrations—2s.

Sacred Garland (The). Crown 8vo. Beautiful new Edition. Handsome Steel Front. and Vig. Gilt Edges—4s.

Sacred Garland (The). Fcp. 8vo. Front. Gilt Edges—3s.

Sacred Garland (The). 1st. Series. Front. and
Vig. Royal 32mo. Gilt Edges 1s. 6d. Second
Series. Gilt Edges 1s. 6d.

Scottish Chiefs (The) By Miss Porter. Fcp. 8vo.
Eight Steel Plates. Full Gilt Back, Side, and
Edges—3s. 6d. Plain Edges—2s. 9d.

Seven Champions of Christendom. 8 Steel Plates.
Gilt Back Side, & Edges. Fcp. 8vo. 3s. 6d.
Plain Edges—2s. 9d.

Shakespeare's Complete Works. With Preface by
Dr. Johnson; Life of Author, and a Glossary.
Portrait. Demy 8vo.—5s.

Shakespeare's Poems. Demy 48mo.—6d.

Sherwood's (Mrs.) Juvenile Tales. 7 Plates.
Fcp. 8vo.—2s.

Skinner's Aids to Preaching & Hearing. Fcp.
8vo.—1s. 6d.

Smith's Bread from Heaven. Fcp. 8vo. Front.
Full Gilt Back and Edges—3s. 6d.

Smith's Early and Latter Rain. Fcp. 8vo. Front.
Full Gilt Back and Edges—3s. 6d. Plain
Edges—2s.

Smith's Daily Remembrancer—Morning. Front.
and Vig. Fcp. 8vo. Gilt Back, Edges, and
Centre Block—4s.

Smith's Daily Remembrancer—Evening. Fcp.
8vo. Front. and Vig. Full Gilt, &c.—4s.

Swiss Family Robinson. 24 Engravings. Fcp.
8vo. Gilt Back and Edges—3s. 6d. Plain
Edges—2s. 9d.

Tales and Stories of Ireland. By Carleton, Lover,
and Mrs. Hall. Demy 12mo. Cloth, Plain
Edges—1s. 9d.

Temperance Melodist. Paper Covers 4d. Cloth 6d.

The Book You Want.—How to cure Everything.
How to do Everything.—Receipts for Everything. Fcp. 8vo. Front. 2s,

The Rock Christ. A Daily Text Book. Front. Demy 48mo. Red Edges—6d. Leather, Gilt Edges—9d.

The New Temperance Reciter. Paper Covers 4d. Cloth 6d.

The New Band-of-Hope Reciter. Paper Covers 4d. Cloth 6d.

Tiler's Natural History of Beasts, &c. 100 Cuts. Royal 32mo.—1s. 6d.

Tregortha's Bank of Faith. Front. Royal 32mo. —1s. 6d.

Uncle Tom's Cabin. By Mrs. H. B. Stowe. Full Gilt Back, Side, and Edges. 9 Engravings. Fcp. 8vo. Gilt Edges 3s. 6d. Plain Edges— 2s. 9d.

Walker's Pronouncing Dictionary with Key, and upwards of 10,000 additional Words & Phrases in daily use, recently introduced into the English Language. By Francis R. Sowerby. Demy 8vo. New & Superior Edition. Portrait 4s. 6d.

Walkingame's Arithmetic—1s.

Key to Walkingame's Arithmetic—1s.

Watts' Scripture History. Fcp. 8vo. Front.—2s.

Wesley's Primitive Physic and General Receipt Book. Royal 32mo.—10d.

Wide, Wide World (The). By E. Wetherel. Full Gilt Back, Side, and Edges. 8 Engravings. Fcp. 8vo.—3s. 6d. Plain Edges—2s. 9d.

Wide World & All the Year Round Dream Book & Fortune Teller. Fcp. 8vo. Cloth. Boards —1s. 6d.

Wide World and All the Year Round Dream Book. Fcp. 8vo. Limp Cloth—1s.

Wide World and All the Year Round Fortune Teller. Fcp. 8vo. Limp Cloth—1s.

Wide World Letter Writer. Fcp. 8vo. Cloth. Boards—1s. 6d

THE WIDE, WIDE WORLD LIBRARY.
DEMY 18*MO.*

Bound in the Best Cloth. Plain Edges—1s. 3d.
Each—Various Coloured Cloth, Gilt Edges
—1s. 6d. Each. Frontispiece and Vig-
nette in each Book.

Abominations of Modern Society
Æsop's Fables
All For Love; or, the Outlaw's Bride
Anecdotes of Napoleon Bonaparte
Anna Lee, The Maiden, The Wife, and The Mother
Annals of the Poor (Richmond's)
Anson's Voyage Round the World
Arabian Night's Entertainments
Around the Tea-Table
Aunt Dinah's Pledge
Basket of Flowers (The)
Baxter's Saint's Rest
Beautiful Thoughts
Believer's Daily Remembrancer; or Morning Visit
Believer's Daily Remembrancer; or Evening Visit
Bogatzky's Golden Treasury—Morning
Bogatzky's Golden Treasury—Evening
Boy's Own Conjuring Book (The)
Bridal Eve (The)
Bride's Fate (The)
Brown's Concordance to the Holy Scriptures
Buchan'sDomesticMedicine
Buffon's Natural History
Bunyan's Pilgrim's Progress
Burn's Poetical Works
Cancelled Will (The)
Cast Adrift
Changed Brides (The)
Children of the Abbey
Clarissa Harlowe
Cook's Voyages Round the World
Cottage on the Cliff (The)
Cowper's Poetical Works
Crumbs Swept Up
Culpeper's British Herbal
Curse of Clifton (Tue)
Daily Comforter
Death-Bed Triumphs
Deserted Wife The)
Destiny, or the Chieftain's Daughter
Dialogues of Devils
Divorced Wife (The)
Doddridge's Rise and Progress
Domestic Cookery
Don Quixote de la Mancha (Adventures of)
Doubly False
Down in a Saloon
Dr. King's Domestic Medicine
Dr. Willoughby & his Wife
Edwin and Lucy
Etiquette and Dictionary of Love
Eva Stanley
Evenings at Home

Exploits of King Arthur
Fair Play
Farmer of Inglewood Forest
Fashion and Famine
Fatal Marriage (The)
Fatherless Fanny
Fern Leaves
Fisher's Daughter (The)
Five Nights of St. Albans (The)
Fortune Seeker (The)
Foxe's Book of Martyrs
Gates Ajar (The)
Gulliver's Travels
Heiress of Bruges (The)
Heiress (The)
Hervey's Meditations and Contemplations
History of England (The)
History of the Franco-Prussian War
History of the Russian War
Homestead on the Hill-Side
How He Won Her
Hugh Worthington
Information for Everybody
Inheritance (The)
Jacob Faithful
Justin Harley
Katharine Allen
Lamplighter (The)
Lena Rivers
Life and Ballads of Robin Hood
Life of Mrs. Fletcher
Life of Napoleon Bonaparte
Life of Washington
Life of Wellington
Lizzy Glenn, & other Stories
Longfellow's Poetical Works
Lost Heiress (The)
Love in a Cottage, & Mary Moreton
Love in high Life, & The Lost Bride

Mabel Clifton   [Reid
Mabel Lee. By Christian
Mabel's Mistake
Mabel Vaughan
Manfrone; or, The One-handed Monk
Marian Grey; or, The Heiress of Redstone Hall
Married in Haste
Marriage; or, She might have been a Duchess
Mary Derwent
Mary Howard; or, the English Orphans
Maxwell; or, the Unwelcome Guest
Melbourne House
Milton's Poetical Works
Minnie Hermon, the Landlord's Daughter
Missing Bride, (The)
Moore's Lalla Rookh and Irish Melodies
Mungo Park's Travels
Mysteries of a Convent and Maria Monk
Mysteries of Paris   [World
News from the Invisible
Nick of the Woods
Nina; or, Darkness and Daylight
Old Distillery (The)
Old Helmet (The)
Old Manor House, (The).
Out of the Fire
Pamela; or Virtue Rewarded
Pearls of Sacred Poetry
Peter Simple
Planter's Daughter (The)
Pope's Homer's Iliad
Queechy
Queen's Badge (The)
Rejected Wife (The)
Rest; or, The Hills of the Shatemuc

Robinson Crusos
Romance of the Forest
Rosa Lee
Rose Clark
Rose Mather
Ruby Gray's Strategy
Ruth Hall
Sacred Garland—1st Series
Sandford & Merton (History of)
Scottish Chiefs (The)
Shipwrecks & Disasters at Sea   [Stafford
Silent Struggles; or, Barbara
Soldier's Orphans (The)
St. Clair of the Isles
Striking the Flag. By Christian Reid
Sunday School Reciter(The)
Susan Gray and Lucy Clare
Swiss Family Robinson
Sybil Campbell; or, the Queen of the Isles

Tales of the Wild & the Wonderful
Temperance Reciter (The)
Temperance Tales
Tempted Wife (The)
Ten Nights in a Bar-Room
Three Sisters, & Lucy Sandford
Two Years before the Mast
Tylney Hall
Uncle Tom's Cabin
Upward Path (The)
Wandering Jew (The)
Wars of England (The)
West Lawn
White Slave (The)
Who shall be Victor?
Why did He Marry Her?
Wide, Wide World (The)
Wife's Secret (The)
Wife's Victory (The)
Young Man's Companion
Young Woman's Companion

JUVENILE SERIES—1s. EACH.

Demy 18mo. Various Coloured Cloth. Embossed in Ink and Gold, with an attractive Coloured Picture upon the Sides.

Angel and Child
Annie Benson; or, the Spoiled Frock
Babes in the Basket
Basket of Flowers
Birthday Present
Boys will be Boys
Blind Farmer (The)
Christmas Eve
Children of Hanson Lodge,
Children of England's Own Book
Dick Whittington (Life of)
Eliza Clifford; or, the Pious Orphan
Fanny and her Dog Neptune
Garden of Weeds & Flowers

Holiday Stories   [Affection
Home Restored: or Filial
Just Right; or A Little Wrong
Juvenile Keepsake (The)
Juvenile Tales
Kiss for a Blow (A)
Little Bertha's Secret
Little Girl's Keepsake
Little Henry & his Bearer
Little Woodman & his dog Cæsar
Mary Raymond
Pretty Little Poems for Pretty Little People
Pretty Little Stories for Pretty Little People

Raven's Feather   [Family
Rose Villa; or the Happy
Seymour Manor
Shepherd of Salisbury Plain
Tales about Animals
Tales about Birds

Tales from the Bible
Tales of my Father
Thoughtless Little Fanny
Uncle Paul's Stories
100 New Pretty Tales
100 Pretty Tales

ROYAL 32mo.—COLOURED CLOTH—GILT EDGES—1s. 4d. EACH.

Embellished with Frontispiece or Frontispiece and Vignette.

Smith(Life of theRev.James
Smith's the Book You will
. Like   [You
Smith's Book that will Suit
Smith's Book that You Want
Smith's Bread from Heaven
Smith's The Church as it
  Ought to be, and Refresh-
  ing Dew Drops
Smith's Early & Latter Rain
Smith's Food for Hungry
  Souls   [of Life
Smith's Fruit from the Tree
Smith's Glad Tidings
Smith's Gleams of Grace
Smith's God is Love
Smith's Good News for All
Smith's Good Seed for the
  Lord's Field   [News
Smith's Have you heard the

Smith's Light for Dark Days
Smith's Love of Christ &c
Smith's Manna in the Wil-
  derness
Smith's Messenger of Mercy
Smith's More of Christ
Smith'sPearlsfromtheOcean
Smith's Believer's Daily Re-
  membrancer — Pastor's
  Morning Visit
Smith's Believer's Daily
  Remembrancer —Pastor's
  Evening Visit   [of Ages
Smith's Rills from the Rock
Smith's Sabbath Reading
Smith's Sacred Poetry
Smith's Silver and Gold
Smith's Sunny Subjects
Smith's Voice of Mercy
Smith's Way of Salvation &c

NEW SPELLING BOOKS, Fcp. 8vo. CLOTH. 6d. EACH.

Carpenter's Scholar's Spel-
  ling Assistant
Dr. Markham's Spelling &
  Reading English
Guy's New British Spelling
  Book

Fenning's   New   London
  Spelling Book
Mavor'sEnglishspellingBook
The Elementary Spelling
  Book. By Dr. Webster
Vyse'suniversalSpellingBook

UNIFORM WITH THE SPELLINGS.

Æsop's Fables. With100 En-
  gravings   [lustrated
Buffon's Natural History. Il-
Markham'shistoryofEngland
Parley's 1st School Reader

Parley's 2nd School Reader
Peter Parley's Spelling and
  Reading Book
Walkingame's Arithmetic
Watt's Scripture History

ROYAL 32mo.—GILT EDGES.—1s. EACH.

Illustrated either with Frontispiece, Frontis-piece and Vignette, or Illuminated Title.

POETICAL GIFT BOOKS.

Bridal Gift (The)
Evergreen (The
First Love and other Poems
Forget-me-not (The) [Love
Gems of Petry for Those we
Gems of Sacred Poetry
Heart's Ease (The)
Heber's Poems [Affections
Heman's (Mrs., Songs of the
Hours of Thought [Poems
I Love but Thee and other
Language and Poetry of
   Flowers   [Songs, &c
Moore's Irish Melodies,
Moore's Lalla Rookh
More's (Mrs. H.) Miscel-
   laneous Poems
My Poetic Companion
Orange Blossoms; or,
   Breathings of Love
Poetic Gift of Friendship
Poetry of Love (The)
Sacred Harp (The) [Poetry
Sacred Harp of American
Thomson's Seasons, &c
Wedding Gift (The)
Young's Night Thoughts

———

MRS. SHERWOOD'S JUVENILE TALES.

Boys Will be Boys
Caroline Mordaunt [Tales
Christmas Carol, and other
Joys & Sorrows of Childhood
Juvenile Tales
Maid of Judah)The)

Susan Gray
Swiss Cottage & other Tales
Two Knights (The)

———

MISCELLANEOUS.

Æsop's Fables, with Appli-
   cations   [tyrs
Anecdotes of Christian Mar-
Anecdotes—Religious, Mo-
   ral, &c   [History
Aunt Emma's Stories from
Basket of Flowers   [Men
Beecher's Lectures to Young
Better Land, The   [&c
Bloomfield's Farmer's Boy,
Book for the Lord's Day
Book of Family Worship
Bunyan's Come and Wel-
   come to Jesus Christ
Bunyan's Law and Grace
   Unfolded
Byron's Don Juan
Children's Friend, Berquin's
Christian Pattern, and
   Christian Perfection
Clarke's Scripture Promises
Country Minister's Wife, The
Daily Food
Dictionary of Love, A
Doctor Syntax, in Search
   of the Picturesque
Fawcett's Christ Precious
Flashes of Wit & Sparks of
   Humour
Gems by the Way-side
Gems of Piety
Gems of Thought   [Happy
Great Secret; or, How to be

Heart and Hand
I'll Tell Thee all I know
Juvenile Friends, The [ford's
Juvenile Tales, Mrs. Mit-
Kiss for a Blow
Law of Kindness
Life of Colonel Gardiner
Life of Joseph and Death of
  Abel   [Folly
Lilliebright; or, Wisdom &
Love Gift for all Seasons
Mamma's Pictures from the
  Bible   [Knowledge
Mason's Treatise on Self-
May Flower   [Rogers
Memoirs of Mrs. Hester Ann
Memoirs of Mrs. Newell
Ovid's Art of Love
Paul and Virginia, Eliza-
  beth, &c   [forced
Pike's Early Religion En-
Pike's Persuasives to Early
  Piety   [ance
Pike's Motives for Persever-
Pike's True Happiness [Poor
Richmond's Annals of the

Sabbath Musings, by R.
  Bond
Smith's The Church as it
  Ought to be
Smith's The Love of Christ
Smith's Railway & Steam-
  boat Companion
Smith's Way of Salvation
Sunday School Reciter—1st
  Series   [Series
Sunday School Reciter—2d
Ten Nights in a Bar-Room
Todd's Angel of the Iceberg
Todd's Great Cities
Todd's Lectures to Children
Todd's Simple Sketches
Todd's Student's Manual
Todd's Sunday School
  Teacher
Todd's Truth made Simple
Vicar of Wakefield, Gold-
  smith's
Wilson (Bishop) on the
  Lord's Supper, and Sacra
  Privata
200 Pretty Little Tales

ROYAL 32mo.—GILT BACK, SIDES, AND EDGES.—COLOURED CLOTH—10d. EACH.

Illustrated either with Frontispiece, Frontispiece and Vignette, or Illuminated Title.

MISCELLANEOUS.

All the Year Round Dream
  Book   [Teller
All the Year Round Fortune
Angel and Child
Annie Benson; or, The
  Spoiled Frock
Art of Dancing, The
Babes in the Basket [tures of
Baron Munchausen, Adven-
Beautiful Gate, The
Blind Farmer & his Children

Book of Riddles, &c., The
Bunyan's Barren Fig-Tree
Bunyan's Grace Abounding
Bunyan's Heart's Ease in
  Heart Trouble [Saved, &c
Bunyan's Jerusalem Sinner
Bunyan's Solomon's Temple
  Spiritualized, &c
Bunyan's Word to Come
Children of England's own
  Book, The
Christian's Pattern
Cottagers of Glenburnie

Death of Abel. In Five Books
Economy of Human Life.
Eliza Clifford; or, the Pious
  Orphan   [Siberia
Elizabeth; or, the Exiles of
Etiquette for Ladies and
  Gentlemen, &c
Etiquette of Love, Court-
  ship, and Marriage
Etiquette; or, the Perfect
  Lady and Gentleman
Fanny and her Dog Nep-
  tune, &c   [Restored
Filial Affection; or, Home
First Glass of Wine, The
Garden of Weeds & Flowers
Garland of Flowers
Gates Ajar
Goldsmith's Poetical Works
Guide to Health & Long Life
Happy Winter; or, the Chil-
  dren of Hanson Lodge
Hermit of the Beach, The
Hole in the Pocket, The
Holiday Stories
Household Poems
Hoyle's Games
Imperial Dream Book
Imperial Fortune Teller
Jack & Ann, &c., History of
Joan of Arc. A poem
Just Right; or, a Little Wrong
Juvenile Keepsake, The
Juvenile Tales
Kiss for a Blow, A   [Plates
Language of Flowers. Col.
Life of Dick Whittington
Life of Joseph
Little Bertha's Secret
Little Town Lady, &c
Love in a Cottage
Lover's Offering
Lucy Sandford
Maria Monk
Mary Moreton
Mary Raymond
Mason's Select Remains

Mead's Almost Christian
Memoirs of Joan of Arc
Moore's Irish Melodies
Mysteries of a Convent
Nelson's Journal
Nursery Rhymes   [Youth
Pastor's Stories, Sketches for
Paul and Virginia
Poems for all the Year Round
Poetic Gift of Friendship
Poor-house Sam
Pretty Little Poems for Pret-
  ty Little People
Pretty Little Stories for
  Pretty Little People
Raven's Feather, & Mick &
  Nick, The   [Family
Rose Villa; or, the Happy
Royal Dream Book
Royal Fortune-Teller
Seymour Manor; or, Lucy &
  Sophia   [The
Shepherd of Salisbury Plain,
Six Months in a Convent
Sweet Mary; or, the Bride
  made ready for her Lord.
Tales about Animals
Tales about Birds, &c.
Tales from the Bible
Tales of my Father
Thoughtless Little Fanny
Three Experiments of Liv-
  ing, &c   [Fatal Dream
Three Sisters, The and the
Todd's Lectures to Children
  —1st Series [—2nd Series
Todd's Lectures to Children
Tom White, the Postboy
Two Half-Crowns, The
Two Shoemakers, The
Uncle Paul's Stories
Wesley's Life of Fletcher
Wesley's Christian Perfection
Wide World Fortune Teller
Wide World Dream Book
Wreath of Friendship
Young Lady's Letter Writer

MRS. SHERWOOD'S JUVENILE TALES.

Boys will beBoys[Governess
Caroline Mordaunt; or, the
How to please & otherTales
Christmas Carol, and other
  Tales   [hood
Joys and Sorrows of Child-
Little Girl's Keepsake, The
Little Henry and his Bearer
Little Lady, &c., The
Little Woodman and his
  Dog Cæsar [Good Nurse
Lucy and her Dhaye and the
Lucy Clare, History of
Maid of Judah, The   [The
Pope and the Emperor, &c.,
Sergeant Dale, and the Or-
  phan Mary, &c
Susan Gray
Swiss Cottage, &c
Tom, the Sailor, &c
Two Knights, The

MISS EDGEWORTH'S JUVENILE STORIES.

Basket Woman, and other
  Stories   [Stories
Birth-Day Present, & other
False Key, and other Stories
Forgive and Forget, & other
  Stories   [Stories
Lazy Lawrence, and other
Orphans, The, and other
  Stories   [Stories
Simple Susan, and other

MISS EDGEWORTH'S POPULAR TALES.

Contrast, The
Grateful Negro, The, &c
Lame Jervas, &c [Unlucky
Lottery, The, and Muradthe
Out of Debt Out of Danger
To-morrow   [Gloves
Will, The, and the Limerick

BY THE AUTHOR OF THE "BASKET OF FLOWERS."

Basket of Flowers [Tales
Christmas Eve, and other
Easter Eggs and other Tales
EustacethechristianWarrior
Garland of Hops, The, etc
Genevieve, and other Tales
Godfrey, the Little Hermit
Good Fridolin, The, etc
Henry of Eichenfels, &c
Lewis, the Little Emigrant
Pet Lamb, The, etc
Rose of Tannebourg
Timothy and Philemon, etc
Two Brothers, The, etc
100 New Pretty Little Tales
100 Pretty Little Tales

ARTHUR'S JUVENILE LIBRARY, &c.

Broken Merchant, The, &c
Cedardale; thePeacemakers
Debtor and Creditor
Drunkard's Wife, The, &c
Haven't-time & Don't-be-in-
  a-Hurry
Keeping up Appearances
Last Penny, The, &c
Lost Children, The, &c
Lovers and Husbands
Maggy's Baby, &c
Married and Single
Our Little Henry, &c
Pierre, the Organ Boy, etc
Poor Woodcutter, etc
Retiring from Business
Riches have Wings
Rising in the World
Sweethearts and Wives
True Riches; or, Wealth
  without Wings [Gift, etc
Uncle Ben's New Year's
Who are Happiest? &c
Who is Greatest? &c
Wounded Boy The, &c

THE COTTAGE LIBRARY.
MORAL AND RELIGIOUS SERIES.
ROYAL 32mo.—COLOURED CLOTH—LET-
TERED—ONE SHILLING EACH.

☞ *The following Works are well printed,
neatly and durably bound, Illustrated
either with Frontispiece, Frontispiece &
Vignette, or Illuminated Title ; being the
Cheapest Books ever offered to the Public.*

A Book that will Suit You.
By Nicholson   [Society
Abominations of Modern
Anecdotes of Christian
Martyrs
Anecdotes, Religious, Mo-
ral, and Entertaining
Angel and Child (The) &c
A Wreath around the Cross
Aunt Dinah's Pledge
Basket of Flowers, &c
Baxter's Saints' Rest
Beams of Silver from the
Star of Bethelem
Beautiful Gate (The) &c
Beecher's Lectures to Young
Men
Better Land (The)[Morning
Bogatzky's Golden Treasury
Bogatzky's Golden Treasury
Evening
Books for the Lord's Day A
Bromley's Life of Christ
Brown's Concordance
Bunyan's Pilgrim's Pro-
gress, 3 Parts. With Cuts
Bunyan's Choice Works—
First Series [2nd Series
Bunyan's Choice Works—
Bunyan's Choice Works—
Third Series [4th Series
Bunyan's Choice Works—

Bunyan's Holy War [Saved
Bunyan's Jerusalem Sinner
Christ's Famous Titles
Christian's Pattern, and
Christian Perfection
Christian's Every Day Book
Christ Precious
Clarke's Scripture Promises
Cottager's Key to the Holy
Scriptures
Crumbs Swept Up
Daily Comforter
Daily Food
Death-bed Triumphs
Divine Garland (The). By
Rev. W. Walters [Men
Dodd's Discourses to Young
Doddridge's Rise &Progress
Down in a Saloon, &c
Dr. Willoughby & his Wine
Eustace, the Christian War-
rior, &c Six Plates
Finney'sRevivalsofReligion
Foxe's Book of Martyrs
Franklin's Works
Gates Ajar
Gems of Sacred Poetry
Gems of Thought
Glory through Faith—Life
of Henrich Stilling
Heaven, the Abode of the
Sainted Dead

Heavenly Home (The)
Heavenly Recognition
Heber's Poems
Hervey's Meditations
History of the Inquisition
Kiss for a Blow [A]
Life of Colonel Gardiner
Life of Joseph and Death of Abel
Life of John Nelson
Life of the Rev. J. Fletcher
Life and Labours of, the Rev. T. Charles
Life of the Rev. J. Wesley
Life of Mrs. Fletcher [Dhaye
Little Henry & Lucy & her
Looking unto Jesus
Macgowan's Dialogues of Devils   [Bible, &c.
Mamma's Pictures from the
Medhurst's The Rev. T. W Light in the Dark Valley
Medhurst's The Rev. T. W Stream's from Lebanon
Melbourne House. By E. Wetherel   [Adam Clarke.
Memoirs of the Life of Dr.
Memoirs of Mrs. Rogers
Memoirs of Mrs. Newell
Messages of Mercy   [Series
Missionary Anecdotes—1st
Missionary Anecdotes—2nd Series   [Works
More's (Mrs. H.) Poetical
Mothers of the Wise and Good
Olney Hymns
Old Distillery (The)
Out of the Fire
Paley's View of the Evidences of Christianity
Paley's Natural Theology
Pope, Blair, Gray, Dodd, &c.
Power of Prayer (The)
Religious Courtship   [Poor
Richmond's Annals of the
Sabbath Musings, by Bond
Sacred Garland—1st Series

Sacred Garland—2nd Series
Sacred Harp (The)
Scripture Truths Illustrated
Sacred Harp of American Poetry   [phecies
Simpson's Key to the Pro-
Simpson's Plea for Religion
Smith's (Life of the Rev. J. of Cheltenham)
Smith's Book that You Want
Smith's Bread from Heaven
Smith's Early & Latter Rain
Smith's Good Seed for the Lord's Field
Smith's Light for Dark Days
Smith's Manna in the Wild-erness   [of Ages
Smith's Rills from the Rock
Smith's Sunny Subjects for all Seasons   [of Life
Smith's Fruit from the Tree
Smith's Book you will Like
Smith's Pearls from the Ocean
Smith's Food for Hungry Souls
Smith's Good News for All
Smith's Gleams of Grace
Smith's Believer's Daily Remembrancer—Pastor's Morning Visit
Smith's Believer's Daily Remembrancer—Pastor's Evening Visit   [You
Smith's Book that will suit
Smith's Sabbath Reading
Smith's Glad Tidings of Good Things   [News
Smith's Have you heard the
Smith's God is Love
Smith's Voice of Mercy
Smith's Messenger of Mercy
Smith's Way of Salvation
Smith's Sacred Poetry
Smith's Love of Christ, &c
Smith's The Church as it Ought to be, and Refresh-ing Dew-Drops

Smith's More of Christ
Smith's Silver and Gold
Stepping Heavenward
Sturm's Reflections on the Works of God
Sunday School Reciter— First and Second Series
Susan Gray and Lucy Clare
Sweet Mary, &c
The Book of Family Worship
Todd's Angel of the Iceberg
Todd's Lectures to Children

Todd's Student's Manual
Todd's Sunday School Teacher, &c
Tregortha's Bank of Faith
True Riches, and Riches have Wings [Mind
Watts' Improvement of the
Watts' Logic
Watts' Scripture History
Watts' World to Come
Wilson on the Lord's Supper
Young Christian, The

THE COTTAGE LIBRARY.
INSTRUCTIVE & ENTERTAINING SERIES.
ROYAL 32mo.—COLOURED CLOTH—LETTERED—ONE SHILLING EACH.

Frontispiece, or Frontispiece and Vignette.

All for Love
Anna Lee; or, the Maiden, Wife, and Mother
Annie Benson; or, the Spoiled Frock, &c
Æsop's Fables
American Receipt Book
Anecdotes of Napoleon
Anecdotes of Lord Nelson
Anson's Voyages round the World [ments
Arabian Nights' Entertain-
Artemus Ward, and Major Jack Downing
Bampfylde Moore Carew, Adventures of
Babes in the Basket, &c
Berquin's Children's Friend
Birth-day Present, &c
Bloomfield's Poetical Works
Boys' Own Conjuring Book
Breathings of Love
Bridal Eve, The
Bridal Gift, The

Bride's Fate, The
British Songster, The
Bruce's Travels in Abyssinia
Buchan's Domestic Medicine
Blind Farmer and Hamlain
Buffon's Natural History
Burns' Poetical Works
Butler's Hudibras
Byron's Childe Harold
Byron't Select Works
Byron's Choice Works
Byron's Don Juan
Cabin Boy's Story
Cancelled Will, The
Cast Adrift
Changed Brides, The
Chapone, Gregory, Pennington, and Dodsley
Children of the Abbey
Christmas Eve, &c
Clarissa Harlowe
Clater's Every Man his own Cattle Doctor [Farrier
Clater's Every Man his own

Cobbett's and Murray's English Grammars
Cooke's Letter Writer
Cook's Voyages   [Minstrel
Comic Album and Comic
Coleridge's Poetical and Dramatic Works
Cooper's Sea Lions
Cooper's Deerslayer
Cooper's Spy   [cans
Cooper's Last of the Mohi-
Cooper's Pilot
Comic Orations
Cottage Gardener. Cuts
Cottagers of Glenburnie, &c
Country Minister's Wife
Cowper's Poetical Works
Culpeper's British Herbal
Culpeper's Every Man his own Doctor
Curse of Clifton, The
David Price, Adventures of
Daring Deeds of Capt. Canot
Death in the Pot
Debtor and Creditor, &c
Destiny, by the Author of Marriage   [Book
Diprose's National Song
Divorced Wife, The, &c
Doctor Syntax   [speare
Dodd's Beauties of Shak-
Dodd's Beauties of History
Domestic Cookery. Cuts
Don Quixote de la Mancha, Adventures of
Doubly False
Dryden's Poetical Works
Dryden's Virgil
Eliza Clifford & Rose Villa
Etiquette; or, the Perfect Gentleman   [Lady
Etiquette; or, the Perfect
Etiquette for Ladies and Gentlemen   [Love
Etiquette and Dictionary of
Eva Stanley. A Novel
Evenings at Home

Exploits of King Arthur, &c
Fair Play
False Key, &c., The
Farmer of Inglewood Forest
Fashion and Famine
Fatal Marriage, The
Fatherless Fanny
Fern Leaves
First Love, & other Poems
Fisher's Daughter, The
Five Nights of St. Albans
Flowers, their Morals, Emblems, and Language
Flowers of Knowledge [Prose
Forget-me-not, in Poetry &
Forgive and Forget, &c
Fortune Seeker, The
Gems by the Way-Side [love
Gems of Poetry for those we
Godfrey, the Little Hermit
Goldsmith's Poetical Works and Vicar of Wakefield
Good Time Coming
Grateful Negro, The, &c
Great Secret, The, &c
Guide to Health and Economy of Human Life
Gulliver's Travels
Heart's Ease, The
Heiress of Bruges, The
Henry, Earl of Moreland
History of the Russian War
History of England. Cuts
History of the Franco-Prussian War
Homestead on the Hill-Side
Holiday Stories, &c
How He Won Her. A Sequel to Fair Play
How to Please, &c
Hugh Worthington
Hungarian Brothers, The
I love but Thee, &c
I'll tell Thee all I know, &c
Inheritance, The
Italian, The   [thers, &c
Jack and His Eleven Bro-

Jacob Faithful. By Capt. Marryat [hood, &c

Joys and Sorrows of Child-

Justin Harley. A Romance

Just Right, and Poor-house Sam [nile Tales

Juvenile Keepsake & Juve-

Katharine Allen; or, the Gold Brick

Keat's Poetical Works

Kirke White's Remains

Lamplighter, The [Flowers

Language and Poetry of 'Lena Rivers

Life of Joan of Arc, and Poem by Southey

Life of Lord Nelson

Life of Baron Trenck

Life of Washington [Hood

Life and Exploits of Robin

Life of Field Marshal the Duke of Wellington

Life of Napoleon Bonaparte

Life of Oliver Cromwell

Little Bertha's Secret, &c

Little Girl's Keepsake, &c

Little Woodman, The, &c

Lives of Pirates and Sea Robbers [Robbers

Lives of Highwaymen and

Lizzy Glen and other Stories

Longfellow's Poetical Works

Longfellow's Song of Hia-watha, & other Poems

Lost Heiress, The [Contrast

Lottery Ticket, The, & The

Love in High Life, and The Lost Bride, etc [Moreton

Love in a Cottage & Mary

Lovers and Husbands

Lover's Offering, & Poetic Gift of Friendship

Mabel Clifton—A Novel

Mabel Lee

Mabel's Mistake

Mabel Vaughan [Experience

Man-of-war Life—A Boy's

Manfrone; or, The One-Handed Monk

Man Demon, The

Marian Grey

Marriage; or, She might have been a Duchess

Married in Haste

Mary Derwent

Mary Howard [come Guest

Maxwell; or, The Unwel-

Memoirs of a Cavalier

Milton's Poetical Works

Minnie Hermon, the Land-lord's Daughter

Missing Bride, The

Moore's Choice Works

Moore's Lalla Rookh and Irish Melodies. 9 Plates

Mungo Park's Travels

Mysteries of New York, 1st Series [Series

Mysteries of New York, 2d

Mysteries of a Convent and Maria Monk

Mysteries of Udolpho

Mysteries of Paris [World

News from the Invisible

New Shilling, The

Nick of the Woods [light

Nina; or, Darkness & Day-

Nothing but Money

O'Halloran; or, The In-surgent Chief

Old English Baron, and Castle of Otranto

Old Helmet

Old Manor House, (The).

Out of Debt Out of Danger

Pamela, or, Virtue Rewarded

Pauland Virginia, Elizabeth and Rasselas [Marryat

Peter Simple. By Captain

Planter's Daughter, The

Pleasing Instructor, New

Poe's Tales of Mystery and Imagination

Poems for all the Year Round

Poems & Tales, Mrs. Hemans
Poetical Keepsake, The
Poetry of Love, The
Pope's Poetical Works
Pope's Homer's Odyssey
Pope's Homer's Iliad
Popular Song Book
Pretty Little Poems for
    Pretty Little People
Queechy, by E. Wetherel
Queen's Badge, The
Queen of the Isles, The
Reciter for the Million
Rest; or, The Hills of the
    Shatemuc
Righted at Last ●
Robinson Crusoe
Rob of the Bowl   [tures of
Roderick Random, Adven-
Romance of the Forest
Rosa Lee
Rose Mather
Rose Clark. &c
Royal & Imperial Fortune-
    Teller   [Book
Royal & Imperial Dream-
Ruby Gray's Strategy
Ruth Hall, &c   [tory of
Sandford & Merton, His-
Scottish Chiefs, The [Lake
Scott's, Sir W., Lady of the
Scott's, Sir W., Lord of the
    Isles   [Last Minstrel
Scott's, Sir W., Lay of the
Scott's, Sir W., Marmion
Scott's, Sir W., Rokeby
Seven Champions of Christ-
    endom, History of
Shady Side, The
Shelley's Queen Mab, &c
Shelley's Choice Works
Shelley's Select Works
Sherwood's, Mrs., Parting
    Gift   [Sea
Shipwrecks and Disasters at
Sidney De Grey

Silver Star
Simple Susan, &c
Songs of the Affections
Sprig of Shillelah
St. Clair of the Isles
Stephen's Travels in Egypt
Striking the Flag.   By
    Christian Reid   [Lands
Sunny Memories of Foreign
Swiss Family Robinson
Tales of Battles by Sea and
    Land   [and Fishes
Tales about Animals, Birds
Tales and Stories of Ireland
Tales for Rich and Poor
Tales of Home Life
Tales of Fairy Land
Thaddeus of Warsaw
The Garland of Hops
The Biglow Papers, and the
    Nasby Papers
The Heiress
The Cottage on the Cliff
The Deep, Deep Sea.   A
    Sailor's Voyage   [Prose
The Evergreen, in Poetry &
The May Flower
The Soldier's Orphans
The Rejected Wife   [Book
The New Joe Miller's Jest
The Wandering Jew   [dar
The Modern Newgate Calen-
The Wife's Secret
Temperance and Band of
    Hope Reciters
Temperance Tales
Tempest and Sunshine
Ten Nights in a Bar-Room
Thompson's Poetical Works
Tiler's Natural History
Tiler's Natural History, 2d
    Series
Tom White, the Postboy &c
Two Half-Crowns, The, &c
Two Shoemakers, The, &c
Two Years before the Mast

Twice-Told Tales
Tylney Hall. By Tom Hood
Uncle Tom's Cabin
Uncle Paul's Stories, etc
Vara, the Child of Adoption
Wars of England. Six Cuts
War Path, The
Waverley, by Sir W Scott
Wesley's Primitive Physic
West Lawn
White Slave, The
Who Shall be Victor
Why did He Marry Her ?
Wide, Wide World, The
Wide, Wide World Reciter
Wide World Letter Writer
Wide World Dream Book

Wide World Fortune Teller
Wife's Victory, The, etc
Wilson's Wonderful Characters
Wit of the World
Wonders of Nature and Art
Wordsworth's Select Poems
Wordsworth's Excursions, White Doe of Rylston, etc
Young Man's Book of Amusement
Young Man's best Companion
Young Man's Own book
Young Woman's best Companion
Young's Poetical Works
200 Pretty Tales

DEMY 32mo.—MISCELLANEOUS—GILT EDGES—COLOURED CLOTH—6d. EACH.

A Full Christ for Empty Sinners
A Kiss for a Blow
Babes in the Basket
Basket of Flowers
Baxter's Now or Never
Baxter's Call to the Unconverted
Brook's Apples of Gold [Son
Chesterfield's Advice to his
Christian's Journal
Dairyman's Daughter, The
Fawcett's Advice to Youth
Fenelon's Pious Thoughts
Heart and Hand
History of Jesus, The
History of Jack and his 11 Brothers [Sisters
History of Ann & her 11

Hill's Deep Things of God
Hill's It is Well
Hussey's Glory of Christ
Janeway's Token for Children
Law of Kindness
Little Henry and his Bearer
Mason's Crumbs [Wisdom
Pure Gold from the Mines of
Rowe's Devout Exercises
Sabbath Talks about Jesus
Sabbath Talks with Little Children on the Psalms
Sacred Poetry
Scott's Force of Truth [Glory
Smith's Guide to God and
Susan Gray
Young Cottager, The
Young Lady's Letter Writer

DEMY 32mo.—ABBOTT'S WORKS—GILT EDGES—COLOURED CLOTH—8d. EACH.

Caleb in the Country
Caleb in Town
Child at Home
China and the English
Corner Stone

Every Day Duty
Fireside Religion
Hoary Head
Little Philosopher
Mc Donner
Mother at Home

Path of Peace
School Boy
Teacher
Way of Salvation
Way to do Good
Young Christian

Demy 32mo. Limp Cloth. Gilt Edges. 6d. Each.

Ball-Room Manual
Etiquette of Love
Etiquette of Courtship
Etiquette of Marriage
Etiquette for Gentlemen
Etiquette for Ladies
Elixir of Beauty
Forget-me-not and Blue-Bell

Golden Wedding Ring
Hand-book to the Flower Garden
Language of Flowers
Language of Love
New Toast Master The
Rose and Lily
Snowdrop and Daisy

THE JUVENILE SERIES.

Royal 32mo.—Limp Cloth.—Frontispiece, or Frontispiece and Vignette.—6d. Each.

All the Year Round Dream Book　[Teller
All the Year Round Fortune
Alleine's Precious Promises
Almost Christian, The
Angel and Child
Annie Benson; or, the Spoiled Frock
Art of Dancing, The
Artemus Ward. His Book
Babes in the Basket
Baron Munchausen, Surprising Adventures of
Beautiful Gate, The
Blind Farmer, The
Book of Riddles, etc., The
Bridal Gift, The　[Book
Children of England's Own
Children of Hanson Lodge,
Comic Album
Comic Minstrel　[Writer
Cook's Universal Letter
Cottagers of Glenburnie
Death of Abel
Diadem, The
Dick Whittington, Life of
Economy of Human Life
Eliza Clifford; or the Pious Orphan　[Siberia
Elizabeth; or, the Exiles of

Etiquette for Ladies & Gentlemen, etc.
Etiquette of Love, Courtship, and Marriage
Etiquette; or, the Perfect Lady & Gentleman
Evergreen, The　[tune, etc.
Fanny and her Dog Neptune
Filial Affection; or Home Restored
First Glass of Wine, The
Garden of Weeds & Flowers
Gates Ajar
General Receipt Book
Goldsmith's Poetical Works
Guide to Health & Long Life
Heart and Hand
Heart's Ease, The
Hermit of the Beach, The
Hole in the Pocket, The
Holiday Stories
Hours of Thought
Household Poems
Hoyle's Games
Imperial Dream Book
Imperial Fortune Teller
Jack and Ann, History of
Joan of Arc. A Poem
Just Right; or, A Little Wrong
Juvenile Keepsake

Juvenile Tales
Kiss for a Blow, A
Language of Flowers [Israel
Life of Joseph, the Son of
Little Bertha's Secret [Poems
Little Town Lady, & other
Love in a Cottage
Lover's Offering
Lucy Sandford
Major Jack Downing
Manual of Croquet
Maria Monk
Mary Moreton
Mary Raymond
Memoirs of Joan of Arc
Modern Reciter
Moore's Lalla Rookh
Moore's Irish Melodies
My Poetic Companion
Mysteries of a Convent
Nelson's Journal
New Domestic Cookery
New London Letter Writer
Nursery Rhymes
Pastor's Stories
Paul and Virginia
Perfect Lady and Gentleman
Poems for all the Year Round
Poetic Gift of Friendship
Poor-house Sam
Pretty Little Poems for Pretty
   Little People [Little People
Pretty Little Stories for Pretty
Raven's Feather, &c [Family
Rose Villa; or, The Happy
Royal Dream Book
Royal Fortune Teller
Semi Quaver   [Sophia
Seymour Manor; or, Lucy &
Shepherd of Salisbury Plain
Six Months in a Convent
Smith's Refreshing dewdrops
Sweet Mary; or, the Bride
   made ready for her Lord
Tales about Animals
Tales about Birds & Fishes

Tales from the Bible
Tales of my Father
Thoughtless Little Fanny
Three Experiments of Living
Three Sisters, The
Todd's Lectures to Children
   —First Series [2nd Series
Todd's Lectures to Children
Tom White, the Postboy
Two Half-Crowns, The
Two Shoemakers, The
Uncle Paul's Stories
Wedding Gift, The
Wesley's Primitive Physic
Wit and Wisdom
Wide World Dream Book
Wide World Fortune Teller
Wreath of Friendship, The
Young Lady's Letter Writer

———

BY THE AUTHOR OF "THE
   BASKET OF FLOWERS."
Basket of Flowers
Christian Warrior, The
Christmas Eve, &c
Easter Eggs
Garland of Hops, The
Genevieve, and other Tales
Good Fridolin, The
Henry of Eichenfels, etc,
Little Emigrant, The
Little Hermit, The
Pet Lamb, and other Tales
Rose of Tannebourg
Timothy and Philemon
Two Brothers, The
100 New Pretty Little Tales
100 Pretty Little Tales

———

T. S. ARTHUR'S WORKS.
Broken Merchant, The [kers
Cedardale; or, the Peacema-
Drunkard's Wife, The
Debtor & Creditor [a-Hurry
Haven't-time & Don't-be-in-
Keeping up Appearances

Last Penny, The
Lost Children, The
Lovers and Husbands
Maggie's Baby
Married and Single
Our Little Harry
Pierre, the Organ-Boy, etc
Poor Woodcutter, The
Retiring from Business
Riches have Wings
Rising in the World
Sweethearts and Wives
Ten Nights in a Bar-Room
True Riches, etc.
Uncle Ben's New Year'sGift
Who are Happiest?
Who is Greatest?
Wounded Boy, The

BY MRS. SHERWOOD.
Boys will be Boys
Caroline Mordaunt
Christmas Carol
How to Please   [hood
Joys and Sorrows of Child-
Little Girl's Keepsake, The
Little Henry and his Bearer
Little Lady, The, &c
Little Woodman, The, and
    his Dog Cæsar

Lucy and her Dhaye
Lucy Clare
Maid of Judah, The
Pope and the Emperor, Th
Sergeant Dale, his Daughter
    and Orphan Mary
Susan Gray
Swiss Cottage, The
Tom, the Sailor Boy, &c
Two Knights, The

EDGEWORTH'S JUVENILE
STORIES.
Basket Woman, The
Birth-day Present, The
False Key, The
Forgive and Forget
Lazy Lawrence
Orphans, The
Simple Susan

EDGEWORTH'S POPULAR
TALES.
Contrast, The
Grateful Negro, The
Lame Jarvas   [Unlucky
Lottery, The & Murad th
Out of Debt Out of Danger
To-morrow   [Glove]
Will, The, & the Limerick

THE JUVENILE LIBRARY.
Royal 32mo.—Paper Covers—Sixpence Each.

MRS. SHERWOOD'S TALES.
Boys will be Boys
Caroline Mordaunt
Christmas Carol, etc,
How to Please, etc.   [hood
Joys and Sorrows of Child-
Little Henry & his Bearer
Little Girl's Keepsake, The
Lucy Clare
Maid of Judah, The
Sergeant Dale, his Daugh-
    ter, and the Orphan Mary

Susan Gray   [Tales
Swiss Cottage, and   other
The Little Woodman, etc.
The Little Lady
The Pope and the Emperor
Tom, the Sailor Boy
Two Knights, The

MISCELLANEOUS.
A Kiss for a Blow
Angel and Child
Annie Benson

Baron Munchausen Adventures of
Babes in the Basket
Book of Riddles, The, etc.
Cottagers of Glenburnie
Death of Abel
Elizabeth ; or the Exiles of Siberia
Filial Affection ; or Home Restored
Garland of Flowers
Garden of Weeds & Flowers
Grandpapa's Tales about Animals
Grandpapa's Tales about Birds and Fishes
Grandpapa's Tales about the Bible
Heart and Hand
History of Jack & his Eleven Brothers, & Ann & her Eleven Sisters
Hieroglyphical Bible
Holiday Stories
Just Right ; or a Little Wrong
Juvenile Keepsake
Juvenile Tales for Boys and Girls
Life of Joseph
Life of Dick Whittington
Little Bertha's Secret
Mary Raymond
Nursery Rhymes
Pastor's Stories
Paul and Virginia
Poetic Gift of Friendship
Poor-house Sam
Pretty Little Poems for Pretty Little People
Pretty Llittle Stories for Pretty Little People
Rose Villa ; or, the Happy Family [& Sophia
Seymour Manor ; or Lucy
The Beautiful Gate

The Shepherd of Salisbury Plain
The Two Shoemakers
The Raven's Feather
The Little Town Lady, etc
Todd's Lectures to Children—First and Second Series
Thoughtless Little Fanny
Tom White, the Postboy
Wreath of Friendship

———

UNIFORM WITH THE ABOVE.
Alleine's Precious Promises
Comic Album
Comic Minstrel
Cooke's Letter Writer
Economy of Human Life
Eliza Clifford
Etiquette of Love, Courtship, and Marriage
Etiquette for Ladies & Gentlemen
Experiments of Living
General Receipt Book
Goldsmith's Poetical Works
Household Poems
Hoyle's Games
Imperial Dream Book
Imperial Fortune Teller
Language of Flowers
Lover's Offering
Maria Monk
Modern Reciter
Moore's Irish Melodies
Moore's Lalla Rookh
My Poetic Companion
Mysteries of a Convent
Royal Fortune Teller
Royal Dream Book
Seaside and Fireside
Seaforth's Letter Writer
Semi Quaver
Six Months in a Convent
Smith's Dew-Drops
Sweet Mary ; the Bride, &c

Tales of my Father
The Children of Hanson Lodge
The Perfect Lady and Gentleman
The Art of Dancing
The Two Half-Crowns
Voices of the Night
Wesley's Primitive Physic
Wit and Wisdom
Young Lady's Letter Writer

MISS EDGEWORTH'S STORIES
Forgive and Forget, &c
Lazy Lawrence, &c
Simple Susan, &c
The Basket Woman, &c
The Birth-day Present, &c
The False Key, &c
The Orphans, &c

MISS EDGEWORTH'S TALES.
Contrast, The, &c
Grateful Negro, The, &c
Lame Jervas, &c
Lottery, The, &c
Out of Debt Out of Danger,
To-morrow
Will, The, &c

BY THE AUTHOR OF "THE BASKET OF FLOWERS."
Basket of Flowers
Christmas Eve, &c
Easter Eggs, &c
Eustace, the Christian Warrior
Genevieve, &c
Godfrey, the Little Hermit. &c

Henry of Eichenfels, &c
Lewis, the Little Emigrant
Rose of Tannebourg
The Good Fridolin and the Wicked Thierry, &c
The Garland of Hops, &c
The Pet Lamb, &c
The Two Brothers, &c
Timothy and Philemon, &c
100 Pretty Little Tales
100 New Pretty Little Tales

ARTHUR'S WORKS.
Who is Greatest? etc
Who are Happiest? etc
The Poor Woodcutter, etc
Maggy's Baby, etc
Haven't-time and Don't-be-in-a-Hurry, etc
Cedardale; or, the Peacemakers
Uncle Ben's New Year's Gift, etc
The Wounded Boy, etc
The Lost Children, etc
Our Little Harry, etc
The Last Penny, etc
Pierre, the Organ-boy
Debtor and Creditor
Lovers and Husbands
Sweethearts and Wives
Married and Single
Riches have Wings
True Riches
Broken Merchant, The, etc
Drunkard's Wife, The, etc
Ten Nights in a Bar-Room
Rising in the World
Retiring from Business
Keeping up Appearances